UPROOTED

sands press
Brockville, Ontario

UPROOTED

A NOVEL BY

PETER PARKIN

sands press

sands press

A Division of 3244601 Canada Inc.
300 Central Avenue West
Brockville, Ontario
K6V 5V2

Toll Free 1-800-563-0911 or 613-345-2687
http://www.sandspress.com

ISBN 978-1-988281-89-6

Edited by Laurie Carter
Layout Design by Sandeep Likhar

Author Agent: Sparks Literary Consultants
Author Website: www.peterparkin.com

Publisher's Note

This book is a work of fiction. References to real people, events, establishments, organizations, or locales, are intended only to provide as a sense of authenticity, and are used fictitiously. All other characters, and all incidents and dialogue, are drawn from the authors' imaginations and are not to be construed as real.

For information on bulk purchases of this book or any book published by Sands Press, please call 1-800-563-0911.

1st Printing September 2020

To book an author for your live event, please call: 1-800-563-0911

Submissions

Sands Press is a literary publisher interested in new and established authors wishing to develop and market their product. For more information please visit our website at www.sandspress.com.

Acknowledgements

In 2018, more than 42,000 children were reported missing in Canada. For more than thirty years, the Missing Children Society of Canada has worked tirelessly to protect children and serve families. Due to the subject matter of 'Uprooted,' a donation out of author's royalties will be made to this wonderful organization.

The author acknowledges the wonderful help and encouragement provided during the writing of this novel, by his focus group members -- Paul, Jason, and Sindy. Sincere thanks for providing valuable input, chapter by chapter.

Chapter 1

He was only vaguely aware of his chin bouncing down onto his upper chest—and back up again with its usual flourish. After a few rounds of this he knew he'd suffer the next day with the predictable ache in his neck. Fitting punishment for not just going to bed in the first place. He never learned, and his wife had given up trying to get him to change.

It seemed to get worse the older Ken got; naps came easier—even during exciting shows on TV or extra innings in a baseball game. It didn't seem to matter what intriguing thing he was watching. The chin would inevitably drop. And eventually, usually around three in the morning, he would forlornly drag himself upstairs to bed, cursing with each step. By that time Cathy was asleep. Their sex life was taking a hit the longer that Ken was allowing this terrible habit to persist.

Every single day he vowed to change. Promised himself no more wine during dinner, but that was a tough promise to keep. And wine only added fuel to the hypnotic combination of a leather recliner and a TV screen.

But tonight was different. He was awakened instead by a wet nose nestling into his neck and the sound of fearful whimpering. Their German shepherd, Max, clearly wanted Ken to wake up, and wake up fast.

He wrapped his arms around the massive canine and scratched between his ears. A caress that always calmed him down. Max knew he wasn't allowed up on the furniture, but something had caused him to break that rule tonight.

"What are you doing, boy? You're not supposed to be up here." Ken didn't have the heart to push him to the floor, because his whimpering was non-stop. And there was usually only one thing that caused him to whimper. Thunderstorms.

Ken opened his eyes and gazed through the family room sliding glass doors. Yep, sure enough. Flashes of light were streaking across the dark sky and there was the distant rumble of thunder. But not too distant. The storm was close indeed. And Max was stressed.

"Okay, Max. Wanna go upstairs?"

The dog's tail went into instant wag-mode. Max jumped off his lap and headed for the staircase. Ken was amazed at how many words his dog actually knew.

Ken followed close behind as Max darted up the stairs as fast as he could go. He clearly wanted the comfort and safety of their bedroom, and on nights like this, Ken and Cathy usually let him sleep in the bed with them. Luckily, Max knew it was only on these special occasions when he was scared shitless. He never took advantage of the luxury, which would have been a problem if he did. He was a large dog and took up a lot of room. Worse than that, though, he was a shedder.

Ken stripped off his clothes and crawled into bed—shuffled himself over towards Cathy and kissed her bare back. She stirred and moaned softly, either pleased at the gesture or enjoying some kind of erotic dream. Ken made a mental note to have dirty sex with her first thing in the morning. He knew she loved morning sex. He wasn't a fan of that himself but he felt he owed her since the nighttime sex had virtually disappeared.

Max jumped up onto the king-sized bed and politely stretched out at the foot. He seemed to know instinctively that they didn't want his face pressed into theirs. Or, maybe it was the other way around—he didn't like their faces pressed into his.

Ken's eyes adjusted to the dark, and he took a few seconds to admire his pretty wife. Smoothed his fingers through her long brown hair and pulled it back away from her face. Then he leaned across her back and kissed her cheek. Another satisfied moan. He hoped she remembered these lovely gestures in the morning and refrained from lecturing him again for falling asleep on the recliner.

He rested his head back onto the pillow. Before closing his eyes, he watched the lightning streaks dance across the dark walls. They were non-stop now, and the thunder was rolling louder. Max had stopped whimpering. Being in the bedroom always gave him comfort. Ken was amazed at how such a tough dog was really just a wimp when it came to storms.

He closed his eyes and thought back, way back, as he usually did when he first started to fall asleep. Always the same images, usually smothered during his waking hours. But for some reason he always ventured back to those cherished memories when he fell asleep. He'd never talked to Cathy about it, but he wondered if she did the same thing.

Somehow those old memories gave him some semblance of comfort when he closed his eyes. The blonde locks bouncing as she ran, and sweeping the child up into his arms when he got home from work. Her tiny lips kissing his cheek, telling him how much she'd missed him. Pulling him over to the fridge, showing him the drawings that she'd done at school during the day, now immortalized by frames of fridge magnets. Begging him to take her out for a bike ride. She was so proud of her little pink bike with the white handle bars. The smile on her face, the dance in her step, and usually a lollipop in her hand.

Tears snuck out through Ken's closed eyelids, and he wiped

them away with his finger.

Emily was frozen forever in his mind at a tender eight years of age. Frozen images for him to retrieve whenever he closed his eyes. Perhaps over the years he'd deluded himself into thinking that in a near-sleep state there was a connection. A cosmic connection of some sort.

Suddenly there was a loud crash. Cathy lurched up in bed and screamed, "What was that!"

The wind had gusted without warning, blowing through the open side window and knocking the table lamp off the nightstand. But that wasn't the source of the crashing sound—it was something else.

Ken ran over to the window and picked up the table lamp. Then looked outside onto the backyard deck, which was right outside their window. The barbecue had been tossed onto its side, and the patio table and chairs had been blown against the railing. The sun umbrella was nowhere in sight. Ken remembered that he'd forgotten to close it, so it could be sailing over the neighborhood by now.

He cranked the window closed, and pulled on a pair of jeans and a T-shirt. "It's okay, Cathy, just a big storm. Came up all of a sudden. Some stuff blown around outside."

Max jumped off the bed. He could tell that Ken was going to wander around, and must have felt more comfortable being with him than with Cathy.

"Ken, stay here, please. Don't go out there."

"Don't worry. I'm just going to take a quick peek to make sure the roof is intact."

The wind was howling now, and they gasped in unison as the house made worrisome creaking noises.

"Don't! It sounds like it might be a tornado!"

"We don't get tornados here. Not to worry."

Ken opened the door to the bedroom and motioned to Max.

"C'mon boy." Max took one last look at Ken, then crawled under the bed. He'd changed his mind.

Ken laughed. "Big suck. Okay, Cath, be back in a few minutes."

He ran out into the hallway and hit the light switch. Nothing. He yelled back to Cathy, "The power's out hon. Just stay there in bed. I'll grab a flashlight."

He meandered into the dining room and felt his way to the corner cabinet. Pulled out a powerful flashlight and clicked the button. Now he could see. Walked back to the kitchen and carefully opened the door that led out to the back deck. The wind was still howling and he had to hold tight to the door to make sure it didn't blow off its hinges. Got down on his hands and knees and closed the door behind him. Crawled over to the edge of the deck and shone the flashlight up towards the roof. Seemed okay. Then he turned the flashlight towards the backyard area.

Ken gasped. All three of his trees were uprooted, and one seemed to be split down the middle. Luckily they hadn't fallen towards the house.

He crawled back to the door and carefully opened it. But he could tell now that the storm had subsided as quickly as it had started. The lightning was less frequent and the thunder was more distant. And the powerful winds seemed to have completely dissipated.

Back in the bedroom, he slipped into bed again and crept up close to Cathy, who had the comforter pulled up tight to her chin.

"I'm afraid to ask."

"Our trees are history. But the roof and everything else seem okay."

Cathy started to cry. "Oh, I loved those trees, Ken."

"We'll plant new ones. But right now, I have to run down to Aaron's house to make sure it's okay."

"Now?"

"Yes, I won't be long. You know I promised to look after his house while he and Sherry were down in Mexico. They only moved into that place a year ago. It was their dream home."

"But what can you do this late at night?"

"If the windows are blown out, I can board them up to prevent any more damage. Stuff like that. But I can't just ignore this. They trusted me. And he's my best friend."

"He's my friend too, Ken. We've all known each other since high school. Don't make it sound like I don't care."

Ken leaned over and kissed Cathy's lips. "I know you care. Sorry if I said that wrong."

"Okay, well, be careful. And don't be long."

Max had crawled out from under the bed and seemed more energetic now that the storm had stopped.

Ken picked up his flashlight and switched it on. "C'mon boy. You can protect me."

Together they ran down the darkened street, leaping over downed trees and light standards along the way. It looked like a war zone. Several of Ken's neighbors were out on the street with flashlights, their faces reflecting the shock that Ken felt.

They tried to stop him to chat, but he waved them off. Aaron's house was a couple of blocks away, just around the corner. It was an old character home with massive trees. Ken worried that one of them might have fallen onto the house.

There it was—in all its majesty. A colonial style home with a large front verandah. Right away he noticed two trees had been split by lightning on the front lawn, and one of them had fallen onto the overhang of the verandah. He shone the flashlight up to the roof; remarkably, it seemed to be intact. All of the front windows were also okay.

Ken and Max headed through the side gate and into the backyard. An old poplar tree had been completely uprooted. Pulled from the ground by unseen hands—the extensive skeleton of roots exposed, leaving a deep chasm in the ground.

Ken shone the flashlight into the abyss, which was a good ten feet wide and at least six feet deep. Max didn't hesitate. He dove headlong into the hole and started sniffing around.

Then he started to whimper as his nose took him from one end of the chasm to the other. He looked up at Ken and barked. Then again. He was trying to tell his master something.

Ken focused the flashlight into the bottom of the opening. There was something there. And Max was trying to tell him that.

He got down on his ass and slid along the slope of the abyss until he reached the bottom. He focused his flashlight down onto the area that Max was sniffing.

Something slightly shiny, despite being partially covered in earth. He got down on his hands and knees and brushed away the dirt.

Ken's stomach heaved. Burning acid rushed into his throat. He gasped. Max crawled to his side and nestled his wet nose into his neck. The dog seemed to know, even though there was no way he could know. He just wasn't old enough.

It was a little pink bicycle with white handlebars.

Chapter 2

Cathy sat hunched over the kitchen table, head resting in her hands. She gazed up at her husband and spoke softly, a plea in her voice. "I need to see it."

Ken sighed. "We can do that if you want. Together."

"Do Aaron and Sherry know?"

Ken nodded. "Yes. I talked to them about an hour ago. They're catching the first flight back from Puerto Vallarta—should be home tomorrow."

Cathy looked out the window at the carnage in their backyard. Trees uprooted, barbecue still lying on its side. It was midday; the sun was bright, and the sky was blue. Hard to imagine that the fiercest storm to hit Calgary in half a century or so was only a few hours into the history books.

She started to cry, and struggled to find the right words. "Ken … it's like ripping a bandage off a wound. I'd accepted that Emily was gone and that we'd … never … see her again. I even put all of her things in storage—to help us move on. Now this."

Ken walked behind her and started massaging her shoulders. Spoke in a whisper. "It's okay. I'm with you and we'll get through this."

Cathy shook her head. "I need to see that bike before they find … something else."

"We can walk over there now if you want. The police already have the lot taped off, but they'll let us in—they promised me they would."

"They're digging out the yard, the whole yard?"

Ken nodded.

She could feel the tears rolling down her cheeks in a torrent now. Reached for a tissue and dabbed at her eyes. "They might find her."

Her husband went silent and his hands stopped massaging her shoulders. She gently pushed back her chair and stood. Cathy cradled Ken's face in her hands and stared into his soul.

"I don't know if I'm ready for that. It's been fifteen years, but I don't think I'm ready. "

Ken lowered his eyes. "I'm not either."

She walked to the kitchen window and stared out at the large oak tree that was now lying helplessly on its side. The oak tree that was once adorned with a swing hanging from a particularly sturdy branch. Suddenly in her mind the tree was upright again, looking majestic just as it should, during a time in Cathy's life that was itself majestic.

Emily was swinging to her heart's content, blonde ponytail bouncing around in the wind, pretending she was swinging on a star. She loved that old song, and always giggled at the line that mentioned bringing moonbeams home in a jar.

Cathy glanced at her watch, and then banged on the window glass, pointing to her watch in a gesture that said, "Time for school." Emily laughed and jumped off the swing. Scampered up the deck stairs and into the kitchen.

"Can I ride my bike to school today, Mommy? Please, pretty please?"

Cathy hugged her little girl and tugged on her ponytail. "Of course you can. In fact, it's so late now that you'll have to. Just be careful, watch out for cars."

Emily squealed with delight. "I love riding to school. It makes going there fun!"

"Well, get going, then. And when your dad gets home from work tonight,

we're going out for pizza and a movie. What do you think of that?"

Emily jumped up and down with delight. "I'm so excited! What are we going to see?"

"How about that new Shrek movie? It's just come out."

"Oh, I loved the first one. The second one should be even better! Yes, yes!"

Cathy smacked her gently on the bum. "So, get riding then, so we can get this day started."

Emily hugged her mother around the waist. "I love you, Mommy. You're the best mommy in the world. And Dad's the best daddy, too."

Cathy watched her precious eight-year-old daughter leave through the front door, scampering out to the driveway where her pink bicycle awaited.

The image of Emily pedaling down to the sidewalk and turning in the direction of her school was an image that would stay with Cathy forever. Because it was the last image she would ever have of her darling little girl.

Less than an hour after she left the house, the principal had phoned and asked if Emily was home sick. An hour later, after scouring the entire neighborhood and adjacent streets, Cathy was on the phone with the police. They were hopeful.

Ken had rushed home from work and begun his own search. And continued that same search, the same streets, every day for a week. He knocked on hundreds of doors, something the police had also been doing.

Emily Clarkson had disappeared into thin air.

Ken and Cathy Clarkson had also disappeared that day. Out of the realm, into themselves, their souls hiding in a place with a darkness beyond anyone's concept of how black blackness could be.

She turned away from the window and faced her husband.

"I want to go now. Before they find her."

*****

The lead detective met them on the street. He introduced himself, but Ken wasn't paying attention. The officer lifted the yellow tape allowing them to pass into the restricted area, and then glanced at his clipboard.

"Just a couple of things I want to say before we go into the backyard. I know this is disturbing for both of you, and I can't possibly convey how sad I am for you."

Ken interrupted. "I didn't catch your name."

"Oh, I'm Inspector Bill Rogers. I'm with the … homicide division."

Ken nodded. "Were you involved in the original investigation fifteen years ago?"

The detective shook his head. "No, that was the missing persons division."

Cathy protested. "Emily is still a missing person."

"Yes, Ms. Clarkson, she is. But once physical evidence is found, we take all precautions, just in case."

Cathy repeated. "She's a missing person."

"Yes, well, let me see here." The detective looked down at his clipboard. "This house is owned by your friends, Aaron and Sherry Dixon?"

Ken shuffled his feet and turned his head to look back at the crowd of curious onlookers out on the street.

"Yes, they moved in about a year ago. I talked to them this morning—they're flying back from Mexico tonight."

"We'll talk to them once they return. Now, as for the backyard, please follow only where I lead. Don't touch anything or disturb any of the ground. I think you probably understand how crucial that is. I can tell you now that we've already taken five sets of fingerprints off the bike. Believe it or not, even though covered in dirt for all these years, prints are still possible.

"We'll be running them through our database. One of the print sets was a child's so we'll assume that's Emily. And we'll need to take fingerprints from both of you, because more than likely two of those other sets are yours. So, that will enable us to eliminate three of the five sets. The remaining two may be from the perpetrators."

Cathy folded her arms across her chest. "You'll keep us informed?"

"Yes, of course. Now, follow me, please."

He led them down the pathway, through the side gate, and into the backyard.

Ken gasped. It was a hive of activity. A few dozen workers with shovels were carefully digging and pushing dirt back.

Others wore plastic gloves and were on their hands and knees sifting through the dirt that had been carefully pushed back by the diggers.

The uprooted poplar tree had already been chain-sawed into small sections and moved over to a corner of the yard. Half of the area had already been dug up, down to at least four feet deep.

The bicycle was still in the exact same spot. Now, completely cleared of dirt, there was just the hint of the shine that it used to have.

Ken noticed that even though it was in the same spot where he had found it, the bike was propped up now on some kind of bracket anchored in the surrounding dirt. Underneath the bike was a chasm that the diggers had created. It almost looked like a cave and it went down fairly deep.

He pointed at it. "What's the purpose of that?"

The detective looked away as he answered. "Sometimes, with physical evidence like this, the … body … is found directly underneath. We wanted to make sure."

Ken noticed that Cathy had started trembling. He wrapped his arm around her shoulders. "Do you want to go home, hon?"

She shook her head. "No, I want to look at her bike for a few more minutes. That's all I want to do."

Bill gestured with his hand in a waving motion.

"You'll see that we're well underway in digging up the whole yard. So far, we've found no other evidence. Just the bike."

Cathy looked at him. "That's a good thing, isn't it?"

The detective swallowed hard.

"It could be, Ms. Clarkson. But … it has been fifteen years. I need to be honest with you. After this much time, usually nothing is good news. All this might mean is that she's not here."

Ken turned around and looked back at the old colonial house.

"Inspector, we haven't talked about this at all, but it's an obvious question to me. Who owned this house back when our daughter disappeared?"

Bill glanced down at his clipboard.

"Let me see—it was vacant at that time. In fact, it had been vacant for a couple of years. The owner was foreclosed on by a private equity firm; no longer in business from what our records show. No information on them now, anyway.

"And the former owner died before your daughter disappeared. The house was heavily mortgaged, so the foreclosure was against the estate. That's all we have for now."

Ken scratched his chin. "So, it was the perfect place to bury something—or do anything else that someone might have wanted to do."

Bill nodded forlornly.

Cathy glared at Ken. "What do you mean by that?"

Ken turned his gaze back down to the pretty pink bicycle resting in its own special grave.

"I didn't mean anything, Cathy. Emily's bicycle is the one telling the story here, not me."

Chapter 3

It was a spacious office, nicely finished off with little touches that came from the suggestions of others. Jeff knew he wasn't good at that sort of thing, so he deferred. As far as he was concerned, it was just an office. It didn't need too much spice. He'd envisioned in his mind sort of a "Manland."

But once it was finished, he realized how short-sighted he'd been. It was now a comfortable place to hang out, and since he spent a lot of time here, he was thankful that he'd taken the advice he'd been given. It wasn't exactly Manland because of all of the womanly touches that had been installed, but he was surprised how okay he was with that.

His home, in the trendy Beaches neighborhood of Toronto, now had an additional twelve hundred square feet to roam around in—down in his basement, an area that he'd always avoided before. He'd seen it as just a storage space and always kind of musty. But his contractor had transformed it into a little piece of heaven.

Jeff Kavanaugh was starting his morning on a happy note. One of his cases had wrapped up yesterday and he was anxious to dig his nose into a few of the other pending cases he had piled up on his desk.

But he was going to miss working with the client who had just paid him his nice fat fee. A young woman who'd hired him to track down her biological father. It took several months, but Jeff had found him. The poor guy hadn't even known that he had a daughter. That little fact had been kept from him by the mother. A one-night stand followed by a couple of uninspired dates. He stopped seeing her, but when the woman realized she was pregnant she kept that to herself. Even though she knew where he lived, where he worked, and they'd even communicated with each other over the phone once every so often.

Eventually he moved away, and started up a business in Spain. Jeff's client's mother had already died, so the trail was cold. But through some brilliant detective work, and some darn good luck, Jeff had tracked him down. DNA tests eventually confirmed what Jeff had already been confident of. Happy daughter, happy father—and happy Jeff—with a big payday.

He enjoyed detective work when it involved making people happy. Not all cases were like that, though. Divorces were the worst, and the slimiest, but unfortunately, they made up about forty percent of the revenues for Nicholson Investigations Inc.

Jeff decided it was time for another coffee. Headed upstairs to the kitchen where a full pot awaited him. Poured himself a cup, and then for some reason aimed his eyes in the direction of the front door and the staircase banister to his second floor.

A disturbing memory flashed through his overactive brain.

All he had to fight with was his toothbrush.

Jeff ran in his stocking feet to the top of the stairs and looked down through the front windows. The shadows were still out there, and the metal scraping sound was getting more frantic. Whoever they were, they were getting frustrated with the lock on his front door.

Deciding he had no time for the stairs, Jeff hoisted himself up onto the smooth mahogany banister railing. He put one foot on each side and then slid on his bum all the way down to the main floor. A smooth landing at the bottom—but then he heard a resounding click as the deadbolt slid inward. Jeff's chest began squeezing the breath out of him.

He leaped over to the side of the door opposite to where it would open. And waited.

One dark figure entered cautiously. He had a penlight in his hand and began swooping the beam around in a gentle arc. Then he whispered something to the figure behind him—to Jeff it sounded Russian. The first man moved forward and the second man began to enter. Once he was clear of the door, the second one quietly closed the door behind him. The first intruder moved slowly down the hall toward the kitchen and Jeff could see something in his hand that was reflecting the streetlights beaming in through the living room window. It was a knife, and a large one. They intended overkill.

The second intruder had a knife out now, too, and he moved forward in a crouch, jungle ambush style.

Jeff decided not to wait. He wouldn't bother to ask why they were in his house. He already knew why.

He lunged from his spot against the wall and jammed the end of his toothbrush into the soft base of the second man's skull. The vulnerable area between the skull and the neck sometimes referred to as "no man's land." Instant paralysis if not death. The spine's Achilles heel.

The man immediately stiffened and quivered, his body yanking itself upright at the thrust. An involuntary movement that lasted no more than a second. Then he began his collapse to the floor. Jeff's hand was still on the bristle end of the toothbrush, with most of the length of the instrument having disappeared through the base of the man's skull.

Jeff shook his head to clear the memory, spilling some of his coffee in the process. Took one last look at his mahogany banister and then escaped back down to the refuge of his basement office. Sat down at his desk and started scrolling through the day's news headlines.

Then turned away and glanced up at the framed photo mounted

on the wall. A photo of the loveliest woman he had ever met in his life. Short dark hair, eyes as black as night, but paradoxically as warm as a summer breeze. Her pretty face flashing a smile that would melt an igloo. And the tattooed image of a beautiful green and red parrot on the inside of her right forearm. Gaia Templeton had been the love of his life.

He smiled as he looked at the photo. But suddenly that damn mahogany banister shoved another memory into his brain.

Gaia poured some more wine. "I think I'm ready to hear about those commanded suicides that Brandon was doing."

Jeff frowned. "Are you sure?"

"Tell me. I want to know."

Jeff took a long sip of his Chianti. "Okay, in a nutshell, with the illegal insider trading that was going on, Brandon protected himself by putting executives under very deep hypnosis. He used his own radical techniques—very dangerous. In his mind, he needed to plant some kind of protection for himself in the subconscious of these innocent victims. If things got dicey and risky, he could command them to carry out an act that he'd already predetermined, planted, and suggested in their minds."

Gaia leaned her elbows on the table and rested her chin on her tiny fists. Jeff could see she was intrigued. "My God, how did he do this?"

"Well, he used a phrase—he picked one that was obscure and would never normally be heard in normal day-to-day life. So as to prevent accidental premature suicide. He'd tell them that if they ever heard that phrase again, they would have to kill themselves."

"What was that phrase?"

"It was, Thou shalt go forth."

Gaia let out a long breath. "Wow. That is obscure."

"Yes, and it had to be."

She shivered and folded her arms across her chest. "It's chilling, Jeff. Absolutely chilling."

"Yes, it is."

"I think I've heard enough. And I'm feeling kind of cold right now. Do you mind terribly if I leave you with the dishes? I feel like I need a nice hot bath. I'll take my wine with me and maybe you could join me in a few minutes?" She smiled coyly at him.

Jeff smiled. "I like the sound of that. You go ahead—and yes, I'll wait an appropriately respectful amount of time and then I'll come up and slide in with you."

Gaia came around the table and planted a big kiss on his lips. "I do love you, you know. And I'm so grateful that you've kind of forgiven me for what I did. I don't think I could have gone on if you hadn't."

Jeff hugged her. "I had no choice but to forgive you. I love you, too."

Gaia smiled and headed up the stairs. Jeff could see that she was taking the steps slowly; holding tight to the banister with one hand, glass of Chianti in the other.

He cleared the table, then poured himself another glass of wine.

Suddenly he lurched back against the kitchen counter, almost as if he'd been shoved. He held on tight to the edge, afraid he was going to topple over. His eyes became blurry and he saw the number 1 dancing in his field of vision. Then he saw Gaia's smiling face mouthing the word, "Goodbye."

She had a halo of yellow surrounding her head, rays of light pulsating upward.

And held a razor blade in her right hand.

Jeff staggered forward into the living room and almost fell over the coffee table. He felt drunk, but he knew that he wasn't. Lurched toward the stairs and fought with all his might against the strange gravity that seemed to be trying to pull his body down to the floor. He had to get upstairs!

Jeff screamed, "Gaia! No!"

As he grabbed onto the banister, the same one that he had surfed down on his ass just seven months before, he agonized over what he'd said to Gaia just before she suddenly decided to take a bath: "Thou shalt go forth."

Jeff shook his head once again to clear the images. Ran his hands through his thick brown hair, now lathered in sweat. Swept a shirtsleeve across his forehead, and took a long sip of the coffee which had now gone cold on him.

Then he sighed and rested his feet up on the desk.

Suddenly the sound of a soft voice trying hard to sound stern. "Hey, your feet don't belong up there, buster."

Jeff turned and smiled at his beautiful wife standing in the doorway.

She sashayed over and plopped herself down in his lap. Then gently touched his forehead.

"You're sweating. Feels like you have a fever. You feeling okay, hon?"

Jeff kissed her on the lips. "I'm fine." He pointed to the wall. "Was just looking at that sultry photo of you before you came in. Always does things to me, Gaia."

Chapter 4

She giggled in that special way that only Gaia could. Jeff eased his feet off the desk and started bouncing her up and down on his lap.

"Is that a hint? Wanna fool around?"

"What? Right here in the office?"

She gently bit his earlobe. "Why not? At least it's more private than the executive digs you used to have at Price, Spencer and Williams."

"No doubt. We couldn't even imagine doing it there. And your special fan was watching you all the time, anyway."

Gaia slid off his lap. "Now you've ruined my mood. I try not to think of that creep."

"Ancient history. That was two years ago now."

"Not so ancient, Jeff. Fresh in my mind. I still get the chills when I remember being in that dingy vault of his. And then when the ventilation system failed I thought I'd suffocate to death. Until you broke in." Gaia flashed Jeff a warm smile. "My knight in shining armor."

Jeff nodded. "Yeah, those images are fresh in my mind, too. I remember the ache in my gut while searching for you. Thought I was going to lose my mind."

She rubbed his shoulder. "Thank God you have the mind that

you have. Your spooky psychic skills saved my life."

He shook his head. "Not just me. Couldn't have done it without Aunt Louise. Her skills are sharper than mine. Helped me make sense of everything."

Gaia rolled up the right sleeve of her sweatshirt, and pointed to the tattoo on her forearm. "Let's not forget my little Bingo. He gave you a nice hint as to who had me."

Jeff laughed. "He almost got me killed, too! The first thing that parrot did was blurt out Frank Palladino's name. Which sent me rushing off to a Mafioso's coffee shop foolishly thinking I could beat the truth out of him."

Gaia smiled. "I love Frank. Like a father to me."

"It was a tangled web. He could have commanded from his thugs something pretty nasty, but instead he calmed me down and filled in some of the blanks that I didn't know about. Later, when I went back to your house, Bingo blurted out Brandon's name. Then I knew. I knew where you were. All the pieces fit together."

"I forgot to tell you. Frank phoned the other day. Wants us to have dinner with him and his wife sometime this summer. A barbecue, he said."

"Hey, Gaia, anytime Frank Palladino wants us over for dinner, we'd better go. In his field of work, they make offers that you can't refuse!"

She laughed. "Not our Frank. At least, not to us. He's a big teddy bear. You're forgetting how he let me out of my loan. I'm sure he doesn't do that for just anyone."

"I'm just joking. He does adore you. He says you remind him of his daughter, the one who died. I think with you, he's trying to make up for lost time, and fill that void in his heart."

"I think you're right. Behind that tough-guy exterior, Frank's a very sweet man. A big heart, and surprisingly gentle. More than I could ever say for Brandon Horcroft."

Jeff shook his head, as he remembered his former boss. "He was evil personified, Gaia. But he's out of our lives now."

Gaia sat down in a plush chair across from Jeff's desk. Then she whispered. "We killed him, Jeff. You, me and Dan."

He winced at her comment. "Well, we locked him in his own vault."

"No, we killed him. We just didn't stick around to watch him die—that's the only difference between us and garden-variety killers. And I hope that as he lingered there, dying slowly, he spent the rest of his miserable life remembering all that he did."

"A man like that doesn't get redemption. I'm sure he had no regrets at all for the deaths he caused. Or for holding you captive as his personal slave. He felt he was entitled. That's who Brandon Horcroft was."

Gaia shivered and folded her arms across her chest. "Don't ever drive me through that Forest Hill section of Toronto. I never want to see that house on Briar Hill Avenue again. I think I'd have a nervous breakdown."

"We'll never go there, don't worry."

Jeff felt a pang of guilt knowing that there were a couple of things he hadn't told Gaia. That house on Briar Hill was sold shortly after their ordeal—Gaia didn't know that. And he had to assume that by the time it was sold, Brandon was already dead, his body still in the vault hidden behind the bookcase. A macabre surprise for the new owners if they ever discovered there was a vault and then figured out how to get into it.

He'd driven by the house a few months after they'd locked Brandon in, and was puzzled to see the Sold sign. Sold by whom? The owner was dead, locked in his own vault. How could it have been sold?

But even worse than that, the house was now gone. He'd driven by the address again out of curiosity just last week. Now just an empty lot. The house had been demolished, and all the debris had been hauled away. Which meant that the vault too had been hauled away. With Brandon still inside?

These were things he hadn't told Gaia. He'd told his partner, Dan Nicholson, but both of them had decided to keep Gaia in the dark. Her episode of captivity by the obsessed and twisted Brandon Horcroft was still fresh in her mind.

And here she was reliving it again today, like she did every so often.

Jeff felt guilty for not telling her what he knew. Didn't like keeping secrets from her. Yet, he really didn't know very much at all to even tell her about. But if she knew that the house was no longer there, it might be a stress point that she would have a tough time dealing with. He'd convinced himself that not telling her was for her own good.

"Penny for your thoughts?"

Jeff smiled at her. "Oh, nothing, sweetie. I tend to drift off into daydreams once in a while."

"Daydreams? You call those daydreams? No, Jeff, they're visions and whenever you get them I pay close attention. You saved my life twice with those visions." She shivered again. "You stopped me from slitting my wrist because of a vision you had."

Jeff walked over and sat on the arm of Gaia's chair.

"That was one scary night. And as I rushed up the stairs to get to you, all I could think about was how stupid I'd been. I'd carelessly mentioned that hypnotic phrase to you, and I should have known that Brandon would have hypnotized you while he had you. That's what he did to everyone in his life that he exerted control over. He programmed them to kill themselves. And stupid me, there I was telling you about that and saying that phrase."

"But you got to me in time. And then, deprogrammed me. Is that what you psychologists call it?"

"Something like that. There's an official term for it."

"What is it?"

"Reversing what you went through is called 'systematic reindoctrination.'"

Gaia chuckled. "Sorry I asked."

Jeff grimaced. "The main thing is that you're okay now. We have nothing more to worry about on that hypnotic brainwashing he put you through."

She flashed him one of her patented coy smiles. "My hero."

He rubbed her shoulders and laughed. "Much more than that. I'm your husband now, too. I had to marry you just to keep you safe and sound!"

"And our partner seems kind of protective too. I'm such a lucky girl to have two strong men looking out for me."

Jeff glanced at his watch. "Speaking of Dan, he's coming over for dinner in a few hours. We need to tidy up. What are you cooking?"

Gaia shook her head. "Nothing at all, my dear. I was surprised to learn that our Dan Nicholson, former tough guy RCMP inspector, loves curry. So, I'm going to order in an Indian meal for us."

Jeff winced. "I'm not a fan, as you know. But for Dan, I'll suffer through that curry crap."

She looked up at him and patted his hand. "Good boy. Dan seems happy with how our partnership is going, so the least I can do is feed him curry once in a while."

Jeff got up and walked over to his desk. Tapped his finger on the mouse, lighting up his computer screen. Entered his password, and glanced back at Gaia.

"Yeah, our revenues are impressive. And with Dan's connections from his days with the Mounties, we've attracted a lot of clients we wouldn't have had without him. So, a lot of reasons to be happy."

Suddenly the sound of a loud raucous shriek from upstairs.

Gaia jumped to her feet. "Sounds like Bingo wants out of his cage. I'll go let him out, and leave you to your investigation stuff."

"Okay. A few boring cases in the queue, but I think I'll just read some news for a bit. Then I'll do my manly duty and vacuum the house. Can't have Dan discovering what a lousy housekeeper you are."

Gaia started up the stairs. "Don't forget to scrub the toilets too, darling. I'm not too good at that either."

Jeff laughed and sat down in front of his computer. Maybe if he read the news long enough she'd forget about the toilets.

He clicked on MSN News and started scrolling. Plenty of headlines about conflicts in the Middle East and the trade war between the United States, China, and virtually every other country on the planet. He skipped over those tedious stories and clicked on Canadian News.

Some weather warnings out for the East Coast and the usual electioneering that seemed to be constantly in the news. It seemed like there was always an election somewhere, and if there wasn't, the campaigning went on as if there was. Politicians never made time for actual governing anymore—once elected, they just began positioning for the next election.

Something made his eyes stop and stare at the headline for a story out of Calgary, Alberta. Apparently about a cold case—cold for fifteen years. A missing girl.

Jeff opened the story and began to read. An eight-year-old girl named Emily Clarkson who had gone missing while riding her bike to school. Presumed dead, but a body was never found. It was like she'd disappeared into thin air.

But a recent violent storm had uprooted a tree in the backyard of a house around the corner from where she'd lived. And the uprooting had ripped a massive chasm in the ground—exposing what was apparently Emily's bicycle, buried near the tree.

Jeff opened up the photos attached to the article.

Suddenly an invisible force lurched him back in his chair. The photo of a little pink bicycle with white handlebars lunged into his brain.

He caught his breath, closed his eyes, and leaned his head back for a few seconds. Then, reluctantly, directed his gaze down once again to the heartbreaking photo of the missing child's bike.

In a swirling haze, it came to life. On the sidewalk now, as shiny as if it was brand new. No longer smeared in dirt.

Its wheels were turning. At first, all by themselves.

Gradually, a ghostly figure began to take shape on top of the bike. A little girl, with her blonde hair in a ponytail. She was pedalling happily along and singing a song about moonbeams in a jar. Her ponytail swung from side to side as she rode.

The vision now moved in front of the bike, and Jeff could see her face clearly. She smiled at him, and mouthed the words, "Would you like to swing on a star?"

Her face was radiant, and her eyes were as blue as a robin's egg.

The view switched to the rear again, and she was putting distance now between herself and Jeff's vision. Pedalling faster, in a hurry to be somewhere.

The girl and the bike became blurrier the further she pedalled down the street. No matter how hard he focused, Jeff couldn't catch up.

Suddenly there was a van. A dark blue van. Jeff squinted to see the license plate, but it seemed to be obscured. It stopped alongside the curb. The blurred image of a man got out and walked around to the sidewalk side of the van. Waved at the girl and motioned with his hand for her to come over. He opened the side sliding door, and Jeff could just barely see that there were no rear seats. Just an empty cabin.

The girl waved and stopped. Then she dismounted and walked her bike over to the van. Chatted for a few seconds with the man.

He playfully pulled on her ponytail, then bent over and lifted up her bike by the crossbars. Carefully placed it through the side opening of the van, and slid the door shut.

Opened the front passenger door and the girl happily hopped inside.

Then, just as suddenly as it had appeared, the van was gone.

Jeff didn't see it drive off.

It just vanished into thin air.

Chapter 5

Jeff grumbled his way through the meal, all the while Dan and Gaia taking pleasure in teasing him incessantly about his unsophisticated palate.

Dan stuffed a forkful of tandoori chicken in his mouth. He continued his nagging. "Yum. Jeff, I just don't get why you don't like this food. You can't live on hamburgers alone, you know."

Jeff took a bite of some kind of puffy flat bread and then waved it in the air. "I like this stuff, whatever you call it. And as for eating habits, Dan, I don't think you're supposed to talk with your mouth full. That chicken is practically falling back out onto your plate."

"Touché. That's naan bread you're eating, by the way. Yeah, it is good, isn't it? They make it sometimes with yogurt."

Jeff put the bread down. "Well, I did like it until you said that."

Gaia chuckled listening to the two of them. She picked up a platter and held it close to Jeff. "Let me serve you some of this butter chicken. I think you'd like this dish."

"I don't like the look of it."

"It tastes better than it looks. Okay, how about some saffron rice and rogan josh, then?"

"I'll take some rice. But that other stuff—rogan who?"

"Rogan josh. It's lamb, made with red chilies and cream."

Jeff winced. "Okay, I'll give that a try. Just to shut you guys up."

Dan and Gaia laughed. They both knew he was deliberately being stubborn about the food—just to give them a hard time.

He cut into the red lamb and stirred it around in the rice. "Next time we have dinner together, I'm choosing the menu, guys. Deal?"

Gaia squeezed his hand. "Yes, dear, we'll leave it to you. I'm bracing myself now for cheeseburgers and fries!"

They ate in silence for a few minutes. Then Dan pulled a sheet of paper out of his shirt pocket, unfolded it, and placed it on the table in front of him. He grimaced as he looked at it, then folded it back up and stuffed it back into his pocket.

Jeff noticed the sudden serious look on his face. That sheet of paper had meaning.

"What was that?"

"I'll leave it for now. Will share it with you guys later. Let's talk about the business first. We seem to be doing pretty well, particularly you guys out here in our branch office in the Beaches."

Gaia laughed. "Hey, we're not the branch office. Your house in Lawrence Park is the branch; we're the head office here."

Dan grinned at her. "Gaia, I would just ask you to remember that the company is named after me—Nicholson Investigations."

"Yeah, and we wanted to talk to you about that. With all the revenue we're generating, we think the name needs to be expanded to something like, "Nicholson, Kavanaugh, and Kavanaugh.""

"Too cumbersome. Okay, we'll just agree that my house is the branch office then."

Jeff sighed. "Well, glad we got that settled. Now, what was that sheet of paper?"

"You're the psychic here. I shouldn't even have to answer that."

"I'm also a psychologist, and I can tell by body language when someone is disturbed."

"I promise I'll tell you guys about it while we're having our after-dinner liqueurs."

"Okay. In the meantime, I should tell you that we just collected a big fee from one of my clients. Fifty thousand plus expenses. A few months of work, but it all paid off nicely. My client is happy. Found her long-lost father. I could use a few more clients like that. Getting sick of all the divorce work."

Dan clapped his hands. "That's great news, guys! And satisfying work too. Yes, that divorce stuff is depressing, but it does pay a lot of the bills for us."

Gaia went over to the bar cabinet and brought back bottles of Remy Martin Cognac and Baileys Irish Cream. Then she laid out three liqueur glasses.

Dan rapped his knuckles on the table. "Our second financial year is coming to a close. Knock on wood, but it looks like our revenues will close out at over half a million. Not bad at all. It can only get better from here on as our reputations become more and more recognized."

Jeff got up and went into the kitchen. Came back with his laptop. As he logged on, he said, "I'd like us to do some 'pro bono' work. We can afford it now, and sometimes it's just the right thing to do."

Dan looked over at Gaia. "Do you know what he's talking about?"

She nodded. "He shared this with me before you came over."

Jeff slid his laptop over to Dan. "Here, read this article."

Dan scrolled through it slowly, sighing heavily as he read it. Then he clicked on the photos. Pushed the computer back to Jeff, then rubbed a tear away from his right eye.

"Those poor parents. Fifteen long years, and now this. It just opens it all back up for them, doesn't it? It would have actually been better for them if they'd found her body in that yard."

Jeff could see that Gaia's eyes had teared up as well. She poured each of them shots of cognac, and took a small sip from her glass. She gasped from the burning liquid, then looked up at Dan. "Jeff and I aren't parents yet, but you and Caroline are. When you read stories like this, it must hit close to home."

"Yep, we've been married eighteen years now—anniversary next week. And Wade and Marilyn are twelve and ten. Still at that vulnerable age where they could be taken. We try our best to make them street-smart, but you can only do so much.

"Kids have to have some freedom, and we don't want to scare them too much to the point where they live their lives in fear. But they're also used to living with some degree of fear, with my career in the RCMP.

"There were a lot of scary moments, but the worst for them was during the ordeal the three of us went through with Brandon Horcroft. When I was pushed onto the subway tracks, it was all over the news before I even had the chance to tell them about it. My photo splashed all over the internet, kids at school asking them about it. It left them pretty jittery."

Jeff cracked his knuckles, and opened his mouth to speak. Then he paused and poured himself a second snifter of cognac.

Dan sucked his glass back and poured another as well.

"I know that look, Jeff. You were about to say something."

Jeff took a deep breath. "These things are always difficult for me. I'm psychic, but I was raised to deny it. I'm better able to accept it now after what we went through at Price, Spencer and Williams.

"That office massacre was the nightmare of my life. But it taught me to pay attention to the visions I get from time to time. I can't control when they come and go, but I don't run away from them anymore. As you know, I've used them in some of our investigations, and so far I'm batting a thousand."

Dan reached over and squeezed Jeff's shoulder. "I know, and our little firm has benefitted from your skills. I don't think our revenues would be even half of what they are if it wasn't for you."

"Thanks for that. For some reason, my aunt and I were given

these talents, if that's the right word for them. I'm not quite able to refer to them as 'gifts,' yet, but I'm getting there. But if they are truly gifts, I feel as if I should once in a while be using them to help someone without being paid for that help. People who might not be able to afford us otherwise."

Dan pointed at the computer. "Are those the people you want to help?"

Jeff nodded.

"What help can you give? After fifteen years, that girl is surely dead. All you'd be doing for them is confirming that, or helping them find the body. I don't know if that would be satisfying for you or for them."

Jeff looked down at the table. "I had a vision when I read that article. No symbols of death. I saw the girl, riding her bike. She had blonde hair in a ponytail, and the bike was pink with white handlebars. A man stopped his van, put her bike in the back, and drove off with her. She seemed to know him."

"Geez. That's spooky. Did you get a good look at the guy?"

Jeff shook his head. "No, that's the strange part. For a portion of the vision, Emily was very clear, but then became blurry. The man was never clear—just an image. A dark blue van, but I couldn't focus in on a license plate. It seemed as if it was covered up or something."

Gaia jumped in. "Jeff wants to offer his services to the Clarksons, Dan. Wants to see if he can give them some closure."

"The story says they live in Calgary. Won't be easy, or cheap, to help."

Jeff folded his arms across his chest. "No, it won't be easy. As for expenses, I'll pay those out of my own pocket, not the firm's. I just wanted your okay to spend some of my time on this."

"Of course you have my okay. And the expenses can come out of the firm. Don't worry about that. I support you. But it seems like a hopeless pursuit. She's dead."

Jeff shook his head. "That's the kicker, Dan. I don't think she is dead. It's hard to describe what feelings I get from visions. Some of them spell obvious death or danger. They're very symbolic in what they show me. I think she's alive, that's the feeling I get. At one point in the vision I was staring directly into her face—like, mere inches from mine. She was singing a song, that old 'swinging on a star' song. She smiled at me, and asked, *Would you like to swing on a star?* My psychic reaction to that was instantaneous. She was asking me to come find her."

Dan shivered and folded his arms together. "God, that gives me goosebumps."

"So, you're okay with this?"

"Yes, I'm totally okay with it. And don't hesitate to involve me if I can be of any help."

Jeff sighed. "Okay, thanks. I'll get in touch with the Clarksons. Hey, they might even just tell me to get lost. But something's driving me to offer them help. I have to at least do that."

"I understand. Go for it, Jeff. As a father, I hope you're right. I hope she's alive. But if she is, that might present an entirely different set of stresses for the Clarksons. We all know what I mean by that. Why was she taken? What was she used for? I shudder to think about it."

Gaia covered her eyes with her hands. Jeff could tell she was crying. He got up from the table, went around behind her and squeezed her tightly. "It's okay, hon. I know this hits close to home for you."

Through sobs, she managed a few words. "You both know … my history. I did it voluntarily, to … pay off crushing debts. I finally got out. But for girls who are forced into it, there's usually … no way … out. And … if she was used that way … back to when she was a little girl, I don't know … how much of her soul would be left to save."

Jeff kissed her on the cheek, and reached for the bottle of cognac. "I think we all need a top-up, and a change of subject. Dan, it's your turn. Pull that sheet of paper back out of your pocket and tell us a story."

Dan nodded. He unfolded the paper and laid it on the table.

"This is a typed letter I received in the mail last week. Sent to my home. I'll read it to you, then we can talk about it. "Warning you in advance—you're not going to like this."

Chapter 6

Dan poured himself another glass of cognac. Then sucked it back.

"I may have to sleep on your couch tonight, guys."

Gaia smiled at him. "It wouldn't be the first time, Dan. You know you're always welcome. But I want you to use the guest room this time."

"Okay, deal. So, here goes with this letter. As I said, it was sent to my house. No handwriting, all in type. My sources tell me it came off a Canon MF4700 Series. A lot of them have been sold in Canada. So, we wouldn't have much luck trying to track the owner down. As well, I've had the letter and the envelope dusted for prints. Aside from mine, there are none."

Jeff leaned his elbows on the table. "So far, this sounds serious and I haven't even read the letter yet. And you're no longer with the RCMP—how can you still get those things done?"

Dan cocked his head to the side. "Well, you know how things are done, Jeff. Contacts you nurture in your career never really leave you. They're usually willing to help as long as it's under the table. And I slip them some cash once in a while. They're not technically supposed to help me, but they trust that it will remain discrete.

"And of course, I'll always have access to them, full access, if I stumble across anything that might involve the commission of a crime."

"I understand. Okay, share the letter with us."

"I'll read it out loud first, then you guys can look it over yourselves."

Dear Inspector Nicholson:

I Know What You Did Last Summer. Okay, correction—it was two summers ago, but I thought I'd add some dramatic flair here by quoting the title of a famous horror movie. Did you see that movie, Dan? It was a goody.

Quite the secret you and your two friends have been keeping. Naughty, naughty. Bad Mountie. Of course, I know you're not a Mountie any longer, but I wanted to address you as "Inspector" out of pure unadulterated respect.

The three of you were clearly confident that there were no witnesses to what you did. You've gone on with your lives as if nothing happened.

Well, Dan, something did happen, and there are consequences in life, as you're fully aware. You dealt with consequences your entire career, and made sure that dastardly deeds always resulted in someone paying a price.

It's time for you and your friends to pay a price. I haven't decided what that price should be yet, but give me some time to think on it. I'll come up with something and get back to you.

Sleep well.

Sincerely yours,

Reper Cussion, *Esq.*

Dan looked up, and grimaced. "That's the extent of it. Nothing else was in the envelope. And it sounds like he, or she, intends to write to me again."

Jeff, who'd been holding his breath throughout the reading, let it out loudly. Gaia brought her hands up to her mouth and held them there, eyes flicking back and forth between Dan and Jeff.

There was silence in the room for a very long minute. Finally, Jeff broke the spell.

He whispered, but didn't know why. "There was a witness? How is that possible?"

Dan shook his head. "Your guess is as good as mine. This is a puzzler."

"Quite the comedian, too. That name he used—let's assume it's a man for now. Reper Cussion—very funny. He intends repercussions and wants us to know that. But does that mean money … or something else?"

"I wondered about that as well. The separation of the word repercussion into a first and last name was a cute touch. As well, he concluded with the title "esquire" after his name. This is what makes me tend to agree with you, Jeff, that it's a man who wrote this letter. The title esquire was used in the British gentry, as a designation for a commoner just below knight status. It's also used in the United States as well, though. Lawyers will sign off letters and documents with *Esq*."

Gaia spoke for the first time since the letter was read. "That's true—at Price we dealt with American lawyers a lot. I saw that many times, but the designation is also used by women lawyers down there, not just men."

"You're right, Gaia. So, it could be a woman trying to make us think she's a man."

Jeff reached out his hand. "Let me see that letter, Dan."

Dan slid it across the table. Gaia stood behind her husband and read over his shoulder.

Jeff ran his finger down the page as he read, and stopped on the name. "Not only was he creative in the name he chose, but there's significance to it as well. A play on words. He wants us to know that there will be repercussions, but separating the word into a first and last name is also significant. The first name, Reper, brings up images of the Grim Reaper. I think he wanted us to get that little hint of danger."

He could sense Gaia shivering behind him. Jeff turned and wrapped his arm around her slender waist.

Dan nodded in agreement. "You're right. He's playing little mind games here."

Gaia spoke softly. "I don't think a woman wrote this. It's too sarcastic, too biting. Women don't generally write like that—they might talk like that in conversation, but their writings are more deliberate, gentler, and even emotional. There's no emotion in this letter—it's just cold and biting."

"Well, he clearly knows there are three of us, although he didn't mention your names. He knows I was a Mountie, but that's easily discovered by anyone.

"He also started off quoting the title of a movie. I did see that movie, and it was pretty gruesome; typical slasher-fare. But it involved mental torture of the victims. They knew someone was privy to their secret and it was driving them crazy with fear."

Jeff put his finger to his lips gesturing for silence, and held the letter up in front of him, staring at it hard.

After a couple of minutes he sighed. "Sorry, guys, I'm not picking anything up from this. But if you don't mind, Dan, I'd like to keep it for a while. Get my Aunt Louise to have a look, run her fingers over it. Her psychic skills are stronger than mine, so she might sense something that I can't."

"No problem. Keep it. I have a copy."

Gaia nervously drummed her fingers on the table. Then took the letter out of Jeff's hands and studied it herself.

In a voice that was just above a whisper, she said, "This writer is remarkably articulate. The construction of the letter is businesslike. The paragraphs, the punctuation, the way each paragraph leads to the next to make an impact. This person has business experience, and I would guess he performed at a high level. There's real confidence in this letter."

Jeff rubbed her back. "Bang on, cutie. A great observation."

Dan poured himself another glass, this time with Baileys.

"And arrogance goes along with that confidence you observed, Gaia. Signing off with *Esq.* shows that side of him.

"If we're to take this writer at face value, as to what he's showing us—it's a man who's articulate, confident, arrogant, probably highly educated, sarcastic, and someone who's functioned in the business or legal worlds.

"He gives himself away by showing us these qualities in the letter. And he was astute enough to wear gloves when he touched the paper and envelope."

Jeff raised his finger in the air. "Hey, what about DNA tests on the stamp and envelope?"

Dan shook his head. "Nope. Both of them had adhesives."

Gaia got up and walked into the kitchen. Jeff could hear the running of the tap and glancing back, he could see that she was splashing water on her face.

Newly refreshed, she came back into the dining room and sat down. "Okay, guys, let's think about the possibilities of who this man might be. Is it a neighbor, maybe? It has to be someone who saw us first hand at Brandon's house. It can't be someone who Brandon told, because Brandon's dead."

Dan scratched his forehead. "It could have been a neighbor, but those houses had a lot of distance between them. Or a gardener, or janitor, but neither of those would fit the profile of the writer we've just described."

Jeff leaned back in his chair and crossed his legs. "When I broke into Brandon's house to get Gaia, I didn't notice signs of an alarm system. But he could have had a discreet system, and perhaps we're on video? This writer could be someone from the alarm company?"

Dan shook his head. "No, if there was an alarm system, it would have registered to a central station at the time you came in through that side window, and again minutes later when I came in through the front window. There would have been a response while we were still there. Brandon's house was in Forest Hill. Response times in that expensive area are under five minutes."

"Good point. Yeah, you're right."

Gaia folded her arms across her chest and once again whispered. "What if there was someone else in that house? The place was a mansion. Jeff, you and Dan only saw the main floor, and only certain rooms. What if someone was hiding while all the chaos was going on? There were so many rooms on that main floor. And I was kept in the vault, but Brandon would let me out in the evenings when he came home. I saw the dining room, the kitchen, the living rooms … and … his master bedroom." She started to cry. "Sorry … Jeff."

Jeff reached over and gently wiped her tears away. "It's okay, hon. I know what you went through. You had little choice in the matter. You had to survive. I'm so sorry you have to relive all of this again."

Through sobs, she continued. "But I never saw the other bedrooms. Is it possible … someone else … was living there with him? Or, some other captive like me who was kept … elsewhere in the house?"

Dan looked away. Jeff could tell he was uncomfortable watching how upset Gaia was. With his eyes gazing off into space, he said, "It's possible, Gaia. The man was demented. And you're right, it was a mansion. After we locked the pervert in his vault, we got out of there fast. We didn't check out the entire house or the basement. That's my fault. As a police officer, I should have known better."

Jeff protested. "But if it was someone else held captive, it would have been a woman. We've already decided that the writer is probably a man. If it was a roommate or something like that, it was probably a man. But this letter doesn't sound like it was written by someone content to be just a roommate or tenant. This letter was written by someone authoritative, and probably successful in his own right."

Dan nodded. "All true. However, we do still need to keep open minds on this. A woman could be skilled enough to write in a way that we would think she's a man. And someone uneducated could be in cahoots with someone who is educated—could have enlisted that person to write the letter on behalf of him or her."

Gaia sighed and wiped away the remaining tears from her cheek.

"This is terrible. I was hoping we could put this whole Brandon Horcroft thing behind us, but here he is haunting us from the grave. Well, in his case, from the vault.

"I never thought I'd suggest this, but maybe we should go back to his house and scout around. Break in again like you guys had to do to save me.

"It's vacant now, so should be an easy thing to do. We might find signs of someone else who was living there at the time. Maybe some clues as to an identity. It's been two years. Anyone else who was living there would be long gone by now."

Jeff and Dan exchanged grimaces. Dan nodded slowly in silent agreement.

Jeff reached out and took Gaia's hand in his. He looked deep into her beautiful black eyes, still misted in tears. "There's something I have to tell you. The house is gone. Demolished. It's just an empty lot now."

Gaia stammered, "How … do you … know this?"

Jeff lowered his eyes. "I never told you. I drove by his house six months after Dan and I rescued you. There was a Sold sign on the property. And I drove by again a few days ago—the house has been torn down. Gone. Empty lot."

Abruptly, she pulled her hand away. "Why didn't you tell me these things?"

Jeff leaned towards her. "I wanted to protect you. You suffered serious PTSD for months after your captivity. You know that. And that bastard had even hypnotized you to kill yourself if you ever heard that phrase again. I helped you through it all, and reversed the hypnotic suggestions he'd given you. As a psychologist, I could recognize and understand what you were going through. I didn't want to open up old wounds."

Gaia glared over at Dan. "Did you know about this?"

"Not right away. But yes, I knew. We both agreed that it was best not to alarm you."

Gaia's black eyes flared fire. She turned her attention back to Jeff.

"You're my husband, for God's sake. With me you should never be a psychologist. You don't own my mind. And the three of us are partners. I'm not some gentle little flower that you need to water and nurture."

She jumped to her feet in anger and stomped towards the mahogany staircase—that staircase that held nothing but bad memories for both of them.

She turned her head to the side and shouted defiantly, "Jeff, I'm going upstairs to take a bath! Check your psychic vision screen in a few minutes to see if I have a razor blade in my hand!"

Chapter 7

Rachel pulled on the long chord and raised the heavy blinds on her bedroom window. Squinted her eyes as she looked outside. Another sunny day, but what else was new?

Barefoot, she walked into her ensuite bathroom and began her morning routine. Washed her face, brushed her teeth, and tied her blonde hair up into a ponytail.

He insisted she always wear her hair in a ponytail. Got angry if it wasn't, and she didn't like it when he got angry.

Rachel gazed at her face in the mirror. Some dark circles under her eyes. Well, no wonder. Even though she'd lived in this godforsaken place for what seemed like an eternity now, she was never able to fall asleep when the sun was still shining. And at this time of the year, it seemed like it was always shining. For a scant five hours a day, it wasn't, but even then you could still see its glow from just slightly below the horizon. It never really got dark in the summer.

And in the winter, it was dark for about eighteen hours a day, so at that time of the year she found it hard to stay awake.

It was a constant battle, and Rachel knew that there were areas in the country that enjoyed better balance. But she knew that only from television, the internet, and newspapers. And from her recollections of the lessons she'd been taught by her private tutors.

Those lessons seemed so long ago now. She knew she'd learned enough to achieve a high school diploma, but she wasn't quite sure what she had really learned and whether it was the truth. Isolation, she figured, does that to a person. Nothing to compare to, no friends to talk to, no stimulus other than what her immediate circle provided to her.

Rachel stared at herself in the mirror again, deeper this time. Her blue eyes were still blue, and she knew she had a pretty face. Her benchmark for that opinion of herself was, again, only television, the computer, and newspapers. And the few magazines that were permitted in the house.

She applied some makeup under her eyes to hide the black circles—today, those seemed to be the only flaws she had—and if she hid those properly she wouldn't hear about it. On other days there were other flaws—like her monthly menstrual period, which was never a happy day when it started. Because she knew she'd be cursed with it for at least four days, and he never liked that. He acted like she was deliberately robbing him of pleasure. Didn't seem to care that it was a natural thing.

She pulled on some jeans and a light T-shirt, and walked out into the cavernous living room. It was huge; in fact, the entire house was huge compared to most. She knew this from television and some of the home décor magazines she was allowed to purchase when they were out together. Also, the houses of friends and family that they visited.

Everyone always commented on their house—no, more than just commented—they literally gushed. Described by most as a mansion. Rachel didn't know whether that was the proper word or not, but it was big. She knew, because she had to clean it. It had to be spotless. If it wasn't, there'd be hell to pay. And she didn't like the kind of hell he created.

Rachel made her way into the kitchen and started thinking about what she'd make for dinner. Even though that meal was about ten hours away, she always needed to plan in advance.

She was a gourmet chef. And she had a gourmet kitchen to give proper justice to her talents. Home schooling had included intensive courses in the culinary arts. Rachel had taken to it like a fish to water. Cooking came naturally to her, and out of all the courses she'd been tutored in, culinary was her favorite. In the kitchen she always came alive, shone like the midnight sun, and it was probably the only real talent she had.

Well, that wasn't true. She was a good singer too, but he never cared about that. So, she'd sing to herself when he wasn't around—which was often.

But cooking for him and others always guaranteed she'd receive compliments. And she'd discovered long ago how important that was to her. Compliments made her feel good, as if she had some purpose in life. Hearing others gush about the delectable meals she could whip up with very little effort gave her a warm feeling inside.

She just wished she could go shopping on her own. To take her time browsing the aisles, choosing her ingredients, smelling the fresh produce. But she was only allowed to shop with him. And it wasn't very often he wanted to do that. Shopping bored him to death. And she couldn't drive—was never allowed to get a license. Maybe he'd change his mind one day. She hoped so, because their garage had four cars to choose from.

So, Rachel had to be content with shopping through online catalogues from local stores, and they would deliver her selections to her. She had an account with virtually every major store, and the delivery service was first class. She couldn't complain. Even though their house was on a large ten-acre parcel, a few miles outside the city, delivery drivers loved coming out to the isolated area where they lived.

It was lucrative for them—and Rachel suspected that a couple of the regular drivers also just wanted to get a look at her. She didn't know why she knew that—because she hadn't had much social practice at that sort of thing—instinct just told her that they wanted to fuck her. But she doubted any of them would dare even suggest such a thing. Because if she tattled to him, there would be hell to pay. While these drivers probably wanted to fuck her, they sure didn't want to fuck with him. They seemed content to look at Rachel as just forbidden fruit, eye candy.

And Rachel was learning to enjoy it. Gave her some practice at flirting. She knew what men liked, knew what they wanted to see—had learned that from him alone.

When deliveries were scheduled, she made sure to squeeze into her tight little shorts—the ones that left most of her shapely ass hanging out. Topped off with a skimpy halter top—and in her usual bare feet—the image was complete. She enjoyed watching the men's faces turn red, listening to them stammer with nervousness, and seeing the noticeable bulges in the crotches of their jeans. It always gave her a rush.

And while they never made a move on her, she wondered if she'd ever get the courage one day to make a move on one of them. She did have a favorite. Rachel wondered if his passion for her would overcome his fear of *him*. She smiled to herself. Maybe one day.

She'd had sex for as long as she could remember. And that was the problem—she couldn't remember back very far. It was as if parts of her life had been erased from her memory. She didn't know why that was. But one thing was certain—she'd always had sex, and she didn't know how that was possible. Because, at one time, she must have been very young.

The sex had always been with him, though. She'd never ventured outside that boundary, and neither had she had much opportunity to. Except for the delivery men, of course.

She knew she was good at it, because he always moaned and

groaned and blew his load far too early. It didn't matter to him if she enjoyed it—it only mattered that she performed to his liking. For her own pleasure, he'd taken her out one time to buy some sex toys. Spared no expense—let her choose the best of the best.

Rachel glanced around the kitchen and decided in an instant that it would be rack of lamb tonight. She'd start preparing it soon. For now, she'd just catch up on some news.

Started singing to herself as she made her way into the study. A little song by Doris Day. "Que Sera Sera." She loved that song—the tune was catchy and the lyrics seemed to symbolize what her life was—or perhaps what it should have been?

She continued singing as she sat down at the desk and fired up her computer. Absent-mindedly, she opened the lid of a jewellery case she kept on the desk. Ran her fingers through the expensive items that gleamed from within the case. All diamond pieces. And of course they would be—that's what he did for a living. He owned a diamond mine.

Every night when he came home from either his office in the city or from the mine a few hundred miles to the north, he expected her to be dressed up for dinner and wearing some of the diamond pieces from this very case. She had to rotate her choices around a bit, so he didn't become bored at seeing the same old things. Luckily, there were plenty to choose from.

Today he was up north all day, and would be flying back in his private plane. Whenever he flew he was extra hungry—and extra horny. Something about the wild blue yonder fired him up, made him feel powerful. She always braced herself for more active evenings after he'd spent a few hours playing pilot.

Rachel turned her attention to the computer and started scrolling through the news. All stories about places she'd never been to, and events she had little first-hand knowledge of. She loved baseball, even though she'd never been to a game in her life. Had developed a following for the Toronto Blue Jays, because, well, it was Canada's only team. She knew she was a Canadian, but had only seen the country through the narrow prism of where she lived. She wondered if she'd ever get to visit Toronto—it looked like such a lovely city. And if she did, would she be able to see a baseball game? A nice dream.

She checked the schedule as to when the Jays would be playing next. She'd try to catch it on television. Looked over the scores—they'd lost their last three games, but Rachel knew they'd snap out of their slump.

The news out of the Middle East wasn't good. Had never been there either, but she'd researched it so much over the years she felt as if she had been. One of the gifts that Rachel possessed was a vivid imagination. She could conjure herself into places and situations, inserting herself into the scenes. Walking, talking, and laughing with the locals. And running for her life from the bombs. Her imagination was colorful, and it was good entertainment for her. She figured that this part of her mind must have developed from spending so much of her life alone.

Sometimes she had images pop into her head without even commanding them. She wondered where they came from. A mask over her nose and mouth and being told to breathe in. Feeling groggy, hearing deep voices repeating the same phrases over and over again. At times, bright lights shining in her eyes for what seemed like forever—and those same deep voices repeating words over and over again. Occasionally, she'd envision someone in a white coat jamming a needle into her arm. She didn't know why her imagination would invent such a thing, because she hated needles.

Rachel turned her attention back to the news. Clicked on Canadian News, and then scrolled along city by city. She enjoyed reading about what life was like in the major cities, because the city she lived close to wasn't that major. In fact, it was pretty tiny from what she compared with in the news.

She clicked on a story about a discovery that was made in the city of Calgary. She knew Calgary was a big city and knew where it was—but could only imagine what it would be like to live there. She wondered if they had houses bigger than the one she lived in.

It was a story about an eight-year-old girl who had gone missing fifteen years ago. A recent storm had caused a tree to uproot in the backyard of a home, exposing what was presumed to be the young girl's bicycle.

Rachel clicked to open one of the photos. It was the face of a pretty blonde girl by the name of Emily Clarkson—beautiful blue eyes, hair in a ponytail. She stared at the photo for the longest time. Could feel her heart begin to race, and a rush of warmth to her cheeks. Something about the photo tugged at her heartstrings. In an instant, her eyes misted over. Rubbed her knuckles over her eyelids and cleared her vision.

Such a sad story, and such a pretty little girl.

Rachel clicked again to open up the second photo. She gasped and took a few seconds to catch her breath.

Lying in the excavated dirt was a little pink bicycle with white handlebars. She stared at the photo, transfixed. Her vivid imagination allowed her to picture the little ponytailed girl riding along the sidewalk, a smile on her face, proud as punch.

In fact, Rachel went a bit further and forced herself into the scene. She became the girl named Emily and could actually feel the pedals under her feet, felt the wind blowing against her face, sensed her ponytail bouncing from side to side as she rode.

Tears started flowing down her cheeks as she continued to stare through misted eyes at the photo of the bicycle.

And much to her surprise, Rachel started singing a song that she couldn't recall ever singing before.

"Would you like to swing on a star, carry moonbeams home in a jar …"

Chapter 8

Jeff swept his keys off the dining room cabinet and headed for the kitchen. Gaia was sitting at the table; resting her chin on one hand and staring at the computer screen, while mouse-scrolling with the other.

She'd given him the silent treatment for two days now.

Jeff pulled up a chair beside her and gently slid his fingers across the back of her slender neck.

She smiled slightly. He sensed an opening.

"Gaia, it makes me sad when you shut me out. Will you please at least look at me?"

She turned her head towards him and stared into his eyes, unblinking.

"I know you're angry with me, and that you needed some time the last couple of days. But we need to talk. I screwed up. I'm sorry. I should have told you those things but I was afraid to. I wanted to protect you, which was stupid of me. With the ordeal you went through with Brandon, I should have given you more credit than that. Please—talk to me?"

Gaia lowered her eyes and then spoke softly. "I know you meant well. I'm sorry, too. Shouldn't have clammed up the way I did. That was childish."

She leaned forward and wrapped both arms around his neck.

"Thank you for trying to protect me." Then she kissed him lightly on the lips.

Jeff returned the kiss. "Glad to have you back. I thought I'd lost you."

"You'll never lose me." She grimaced. "But I guess we should talk about what it means about Brandon's house being demolished. That vault would have been hauled away, probably intact. Where would it be? A landfill somewhere?"

Jeff shook his head. "I don't know. But maybe we should just leave it alone. It's been two years. Would probably be impossible to locate it now. And if it was opened and they found Brandon's body inside, we would have read about it in the news. Hopefully the damn vault ended up in a scrapyard and got flattened into a single sheet of steel."

Gaia shuddered. Then shook her head and glanced down at the keys in his hand.

"You're taking the Vette out? Where are you going?"

"Gonna drive up to Port Perry to pay a visit to Aunt Louise. Wanna come along?"

"No. I know what you're going up there for, and it's best if you and Louise chat privately together. I'll go with you when it's just a social visit. Does she know you're coming?"

"Yeah, I phoned her yesterday. Okay, next time. We'll go for a swim in Scugog while we're there. And maybe some water-skiing? Whaddaya think?"

Gaia smiled. "That would be nice. Has she had her boat in the water yet this summer?"

"Only to launch it and test it out. It sits in a slip at the marina. So, it's waiting for us."

She ran her fingers through his hair. "Do you wish you hadn't sold your cottage?"

Jeff shook his head. "No. I loved Moon Lake, but the ordeal

with Brandon sucked that part of my life out of me. I don't know why, but it just did. I just didn't enjoy it anymore, and hardly ever went up there. Maybe someday you and I can buy another cottage, one that will be truly ours, together."

"I'd like that."

Jeff stood. "I'll be home for dinner. Maybe we can go out somewhere and celebrate the fact that you're talking to me again?"

Gaia laughed. "Deal."

"So, what have you planned for today?"

Gaia glanced back at her computer screen. "Well, I've managed to track down Ken and Cathy Clarkson in Calgary. Got their address, phone number, the whole kit and caboodle."

"Really? That's great!" He grinned. "Hey, you're far more productive when you're not talking to me!"

She faked a swing at him. "The two of them own a camping and outdoors equipment store. Not large, looks like a small boutique kind of operation. And in the winter their store rents out skis, bindings, and boots."

"Well, now I can get in touch with them."

"I'll do that myself while you're up in Port Perry. See if they'd like our help, and what might be a convenient time for us to fly out there."

Jeff gave her the thumbs-up. "Might be best for now to just say we're a detective agency, and not say anything about my psychic vision. Might spook them—or give them false hope."

Gaia nodded. "I was thinking the same thing. Some people aren't open-minded about that sort of thing. But can I say we'll do it pro bono?"

"Absolutely."

He leaned down and laid a gentle kiss on the top of her head. "See you for dinner, hon."

*****

Jeff steered his vintage 1970 black Corvette Stingray down the long maple-lined driveway leading to Louise's Victorian home. He visited her at least once a month, usually just to hang out. She was fifty-seven now, but looked around forty. Retired for seven years and widowed for six. There was no other man in her life and probably never would be. Her marriage had just been one of those once-in-a-lifetime love affairs that couldn't be repeated or surpassed. Jeff hoped that he and Gaia were in that category too.

Louise had worked for the Toronto Police Service for thirty years and retired at the rank of deputy chief. Her specialty had been homicide.

She was in her usual spot whenever he arrived, rocking away on the massive covered porch. In fact, Jeff couldn't remember the last time he'd actually been inside her house. They always just hung out on the porch. Usually she had a pitcher of lemonade ready for them to share, but he noticed that today there was a cooler on the floor beside her.

Louise jumped up and greeted him with a big hug. He kissed her on the cheek and pointed down at the cooler. "So, what's in there?"

"Well, it's so hot today, and I know this is a business call, so I figured some nice cold beers would be in order."

Jeff sat down in one of the Adirondack chairs and opened his laptop. "Still using the same Wi-Fi, Louise?"

"Yep, your machine should remember it."

Jeff turned on his computer and waited patiently for it to go through its paces. He looked up. "How have you been?"

"I'm doing just fine. Was hoping you'd bring Gaia up with you today."

"She decided to stay home, knowing I'd be busy with you on this other stuff. And she only started talking to me again this morning after two days of cold comfort."

Louise cocked her head. "Why? What happened?"

"Well, it's my fault. Dan and I told her about Brandon's house being sold and how it's now been demolished. She got a bit stressed out over that."

"I thought you weren't going to tell her?"

"Yeah, well, keeping her in the dark was clearly a mistake. Dan got an anonymous letter from someone, kind of threatening. One thing led to another, and we had to admit to her what we knew about Brandon's house. She didn't take it well."

"I see. Poor Gaia. Having to relive that horror in her mind all over again. And I'm sure she's wondering how that house could have sold, and who arranged to have it demolished."

"Yeah. We have a bit of investigating to do now, especially in light of this letter."

"What does the letter say?"

Jeff reached into the side pocket of his computer case, pulled out a sheet of paper and passed it over to Louise. "Here, take a look at it and see if you pick up anything."

She ran her finger down the middle of the page and finished reading the letter in about three seconds. Louise was a speed-reader; just one of her many talents.

Louise held the paper tightly in her hands and raised it up to eye level. Then closed her eyes for a couple of minutes. Jeff knew enough not to say one word, in fact he even held his breath. The slightest noise could break the spell.

Suddenly, she shuddered. Put the letter down on the table, stood up, and started pacing along the length of the verandah.

Softly, she began speaking. "The letter itself is indeed threatening. A clever person wrote that letter, very devious. And supremely confident. I'm sure you three were also startled by the sarcasm and arrogance.

"But here's where it gets interesting. It's most definitely a man, but I can't see his face. I can only see him from behind. He's walking down a highway. There are two lanes close together, but he's not walking in one lane—he's walking in both. One foot in one lane, one in the other. He's quite tall, I sense well over six feet, although there's nothing in my vision that would give me a point of reference to be able to say that definitely. I just sense it.

"Looking at him from behind, I can tell he has light colored hair—could be blonde or gray, can't tell which. What is prominent is that he's well dressed, wearing an expensive tailored suit—could be cashmere from the sheen of it.

"And while I can only see the rear of his shoes, his pants in my vision seem to want to show me his shoes. The pants are tailored high enough that I can tell the shoes are shiny and expensive, probably Italian. I don't know why that's significant, and it probably isn't—it's just trying to show me this guy is some kind of dude."

Louise paused to take a breath.

"Now, what's really stunning here is that he's walking along the highway, one foot in each lane as I mentioned. But he comes to a dead end in the left lane—there's some kind of wall that's been erected across just that lane. He moves his left foot over to the right lane and continues walking along with both feet in that lane. There's a view that shows the road continuing unhindered farther than my vision could see. It seemed endless."

It was Jeff's turn to shudder now. "Geez, Louise. I don't know what to make of all that."

She sat down. "I know. It's cryptic, and in some ways perhaps symbolic of something. I wish I could be more specific with you. But that's it. That's all I can conjure up."

"Did you sense that anyone is in danger?"

"No, I didn't. That scene of the road was actually kind of peaceful."

"Did you sense that any of us know this man?"

Louise shook her head. "No, I didn't get that. But that doesn't mean you don't. Sometimes additional visions are needed to clarify further. And then, just as often, there's nothing else to see."

Jeff sighed. "Thanks for this. It gives us something to ponder, see if we can make some sense out of it. At least you've confirmed it's a man, which we also thought. And a successful man, which we guessed as well just from the letter itself. So, you've confirmed we're on the right track. That highway stuff though is indeed spooky. There is some symbolism there. He had two paths that he was taking—one got blocked, and he moved over and concentrated on the other path. Make sense?"

Louise nodded. "That's the way I read it. But here's a question you probably don't want to consider. And I'll clarify first that I don't see this at all. I'm just asking. Do you think there's a possibility that Brandon Horcroft could still be alive?"

Jeff gulped. "You're right, I don't even want to ponder such a thing. Let's move on to the other reason I wanted to see you today."

Jeff made a couple of clicks on his laptop, then passed it over to Louise.

"Read this article, and look at the two photos."

She quickly scanned the article, then stared at the photos for the longest time. Wiped a tear from her eye and passed the computer back to Jeff.

"So sad. Must be terrible for the parents after all this time."

Jeff folded his arms across his chest, bracing himself. "Anything?"

She shook her head. "No, I'm picking up nothing at all. Sorry, Jeff."

"Okay. Thought it was worth a try. I did pick up something. I saw the bike pedalling down the sidewalk, first with no one riding it. Then, gradually the little girl took shape on the bike, kind of ghostly. She was singing a song. Then my vision switched to being right in front of her while she was riding. Her blonde hair in a ponytail, bright blue eyes—she was looking right at me. Then, she mouthed the words, "Would you like to swing on a star?" I was left with the feeling that she wanted me to come look for her.

"The vision switched back to behind her. I saw a man motion to her. He'd parked a van by the side of the road. She went over to him—seemed like she knew him. I couldn't see a license plate. He played with her ponytail and then put her bike into the van. She willingly got into the passenger seat and the van drove off. That was it.

"I've been overwhelmed by this. We're going to offer our investigative services to the parents, free of charge. That's how strongly I feel. It's consumed me. I think little Emily is alive."

Louise gazed into his eyes for a few seconds. Then, she leaned forward and spoke in a whisper. "If Emily is alive, she won't be so little anymore. Have you ever had feelings like this before from just an article or photos?"

Jeff shook his head. "No, never. Sure, I've had visions sometimes during our investigations that have helped us track down missing people, but only after getting well into the investigations."

"And those would be from cases that people approached your agency to investigate? In other words, the initiative didn't come from you?"

"Correct. Only after we were hired, my skills sometimes helped us get to a conclusion."

"Have you ever offered pro bono work before, based on visions or feelings you've had?"

Jeff leaned back in his chair and crossed his legs. "No. Was never compelled like this before."

Louise continued in a whisper. "Jeff, you have a connection to this. Somehow, there's some kind of connection between you and that couple in Calgary—or Emily herself. That's why the vision was so powerful, so compelling. There's something that you don't know."

He closed his laptop and shoved it back in the case, along with the letter.

"That's impossible, Louise. I don't know that family, and I've only been to Calgary a couple of times in my life. I don't know them, period."

Louise reached out and stroked his cheek. "Keep an open mind on this, dear nephew. There's only one reason why you would have had a vision like that for complete strangers, since it's never happened to you before. There's a connection—maybe not a direct one, but there is a connection. Trust me. Be alert—and be careful."

Chapter 9

Ken reached out for Cathy's hand, and they walked side by side into The Ranche Restaurant, one of Calgary's more elite establishments. They normally couldn't afford to eat at a restaurant like The Ranche, but their friends Aaron and Sherry Dixon had invited them out for a relaxing dinner as a sort of consolation for the discovery of Emily's bike in their backyard.

The friendly maitre d' took their names, then escorted them to an intimate table in a far corner of the restaurant where their friends were already seated.

They exchanged hugs and a few tears, then sat in silence for a few minutes while they each nervously looked at their menus.

Ken broke the silence. "How was Mexico?"

Aaron laughed. "Would have been better if we didn't have to leave halfway through our holiday."

Sherry stared at him, a look of disbelief on her face. "You didn't mean that, did you?"

Aaron fidgeted nervously. "Well, maybe I said it wrong, dear, but it's always puzzling to me that things like this always happen when people are on vacation."

Cathy raised her glass of wine and made a mock toast, sarcasm in her voice. "Here's to dead girls' bicycles being dug up only when people aren't on vacation."

Aaron held onto his glass and didn't raise it. "Cathy, I get the message. I was being insensitive, and I'm sorry. I can't tell you how sad Sherry and I were on the entire flight back from Mexico. That's all we talked about."

The waitress came by and they each ordered their meals. Ken decided it was time to talk about the elephant in the room.

"Thanks for inviting Cathy and I out for dinner. You didn't have to do that. We could have just met at our house, or yours."

Aaron shook his head. "Our place is a mess. The entire yard has been dug up, and there's construction equipment everywhere. And Sherry and I didn't want to come to your house—we thought you'd welcome an escape out after the shock."

Ken nodded. "Yeah, I think that was a good call. We saw your yard when it was half dug up—I can't imagine how bad it looks now."

Sherry shook her head. "It's horrible. A nightmare. Mainly from knowing that Emily's bike was found there."

Aaron jumped in. "And all the gawkers—my gosh, we're the curiosity of the neighborhood now. And I don't even want to calculate what it will cost to get our backyard back to normal again. And no doubt, the house has probably also lost value, too, because of this newfound notoriety."

Ken tried hard to sound like he cared. He didn't, but his high school friend had always been self-centered, so faking empathy usually relaxed the man. "What will your mortgage company have to say about this? The de-valuation may affect your renewal."

Aaron scoffed. "Mortgage? What's that?" He laughed. "We've been mortgage-free for years now—can't even count how many."

Ken was stunned. His old buddy was a goddamned high school teacher and football coach. And their house was worth at least a couple of million. Sherry was a day care counsellor.

Cathy beat him to the punch. Never one to hide how she felt.

"Mortgage-free? How is that possible?"

Sherry glared at her. "Possible? Who are you to ask that? We've been smart with our money, and it's none of your business whether or not we have a mortgage." She turned her head towards Aaron. "Sometimes, in your need to brag, you share too much shit."

Ken sat back in his chair and crossed his legs. "Guys, we just discovered our daughter's bicycle in your backyard. Maybe we could chat about that for a second or two? I thought that's what this dinner was supposed to be for."

Aaron poured himself a glass of wine. "Yes, you're right, Ken. We've been buds for a long time, and I can't imagine the shock you two experienced seeing Emily's bike again."

"Not just seeing it again, Ken. It was buried—in your backyard."

Sherry's face turned red, and Ken watched as her temper flared in her nostrils once again. "It wasn't our backyard when Em disappeared. I don't know what you're insinuating."

Cathy grabbed her wine glass, stood up, and tossed the contents into Sherry's face. "What the hell is wrong with you? You two have never been parents, and are our oldest friends. But all I've heard so far is how your vacation was interrupted and that you're mortgage-free on a multi-million dollar house! We've been without our daughter for fifteen years, and her bicycle was found in your backyard. Do you ever give a shit about anyone other than yourselves?"

With that, Cathy turned on her heel and headed for the ladies room.

An uncomfortable silence enveloped the table while Sherry used a napkin to wipe the wine away from her face, being extra careful not to smear her mascara.

Aaron finally spoke. "This hasn't gone well, Ken. I think Sherry and I were both just at a loss to know what to say. And we said all the wrong things. I'm sorry."

Ken leaned forward in his chair. "When Cathy comes back from the washroom, we're going to leave. We can try to do this again some other time when everyone's calmed down a bit. But right now, all I want from you is whatever history you know about the house."

Aaron grimaced. "Well, not much to tell. As you know, we considered it our dream house when we bought it a year ago. And we bought it from a private equity firm. They'd foreclosed on the house years before, in fact, before Emily disappeared. And then, with the real estate market being in the doldrums for so long, they just rented it out until we came along. Until we bought it, there were just renters in there. It was kind of a mess when we bought it—as you know, we pumped a lot of money into it to bring it up to date."

Ken nodded. "Okay, thanks. That's a dead end, then."

Aaron reached across the table and squeezed his shoulder. "I wish I could be of more help to you, Ken, old buddy. It sounds like the house was actually vacant when Em's bike was buried there. Impossible to trace now."

Ken nodded and rubbed his eyes.

"I think you and Cathy may have to just accept the fact that Emily's gone. You'll never get on with your lives unless you do that. This bike thing has opened up old wounds for you, and it's not healthy."

Aaron hadn't noticed that Cathy had returned to the table, standing off to the side.

She lunged forward and jammed her index finger into his chest. "No, I'll tell you what's not healthy for us! Hanging out with people like you!"

Ken jumped to his feet, wrapped his arms around Cathy, and began escorting her towards the exit. Before leaving the restaurant, he glanced back for one final look at their friends. Wanted to give Aaron a soothing thumbs up or something like that.

But he couldn't see his friend's face. Sherry was on his lap, and it appeared as if their lips were locked.

*****

Morning coffee was always a pleasant time for Ken and Cathy. They would usually gaze out into the backyard, watching the birds flitting about, and revelling in the almost non-stop sunshine that Calgary seemed to be proud to bestow on its residents.

But not today. The storm had turned their backyard into a disaster zone with all of the uprooted trees. It would take some time to get contractors out to remove the pathetic skeletons of what were once majestic timber. And poor Max didn't know what to do—the trees he usually raised his right leg up against were now lying on the ground.

Cathy stared into her coffee cup and then whispered, "I'm so sorry, Ken. I don't know what got into me. I totally overreacted last night."

He rubbed her shoulder. "Hey, you're a mom. You're entitled. They were insensitive as hell, but I think they just didn't know what to say or how to say it. They don't have kids. No concept of how a parent would feel or how hurtful it would be to lose a child. I don't want to make excuses for them, but I think that's all it was."

She looked up. "He's always been a prick. Even back in high school. I don't know how you and I were ever friends with him."

Ken chuckled. "Well, it's simple if you think about how shallow things were in high school. Aaron and I were stars on the football team, and you were a cheerleader. That's all it took back then to become friends, pathetic as that sounds."

Cathy shook her head. "Sherry is a piece of work, though. I forget where he found that tramp, but she's made him even more of an asshole than he was back in school."

Ken nodded. "He picked her up in a bar, not long after graduation. They've been inseparable ever since."

Cathy took a sip of her coffee. Then looked up at Ken with fire in her eyes. "I don't want to sound resentful, but how the hell can those two own a two-million-dollar house mortgage-free? That doesn't make any sense at all. They have ordinary jobs, for God's sake. We own our own business, and we're not mortgage-free."

Ken leaned over and kissed her on the lips. "Sometimes when people get upset about one thing they get upset about everything. Human nature. It's none of our business, Cath. Maybe they had an inheritance or something."

Suddenly the tension was broken by the ringing of the landline.

Ken reached over to the side-stand and picked up the phone.

"Hello?"

"Hi. Is this Ken Clarkson?"

"Yep, that's me. Can I help you?"

"Mr. Clarkson, forgive me for being forward, but my name is Gaia Kavanaugh. I'm a partner in a detective agency in Toronto. Our company name is Nicholson Investigations Inc. Feel free to google us—you'll see that we're a very successful firm."

"Okay, what does this have to do with me?"

"I know this must be a sad time for you and your wife. So, forgive me, please. But I think it's important that we meet. We read in the news about the discovery of your daughter's bicycle and how she's been missing for fifteen years. We'd like to help, if we can."

Ken was finding it hard to swallow. His throat felt like sandpaper. "In … what way … do you think you could … help us?"

"There's always the chance that your daughter could still be alive. In fact, when remains aren't found, the statistics are 50/50. We'd like to help you get closure—all the while hoping that the closure would be a happy outcome rather than a sad one."

"What if it's a sad outcome?"

There was a pause at the other end of the line. Then the lady spoke again, softer this time. "Right now, you and your wife are in limbo. You have no idea what happened and where Emily is. We've discovered that even sad outcomes give survivors comfort. An ending, which is better than never-ending grief."

Ken swallowed hard and looked over at Cathy. He could tell that she was grasping some essence of what the conversation was about. With a curious expression, she nodded.

"What will this cost us, Miss Kavanaugh? We're not wealthy people."

"It will cost you absolutely nothing, Mr. Clarkson. We don't do pro bono work very often, but when we do, it's because we care about the case and how we feel about the situation."

Ken took a deep breath. "I'll do some research on your firm. If you don't hear back from me within the hour, book your flights out here."

Chapter 10

Jeff and Gaia had just finished dinner. She'd whipped up a nice pasta—good old basic spaghetti and meatballs—accompanied by a platter of garlic bread. And the bonus being a nice bottle of Masi to wash it all down.

Jeff cleared away the dishes and stuffed them into the dishwasher—only to watch Gaia re-stuff them the way they should be stuffed.

She shook her head in feigned disgust as she knelt in front of the machine. "You're just never going to learn, are you?"

He rubbed her back. "No, probably not. I'm just a guy. But hey, while you're down there on your knees maybe you could make yourself useful?"

Gaia laughed and jumped to her feet. Grabbed the dishtowel and flicked it at him. "You're right; you are just a guy!"

Jeff managed to duck out of the way before the towel made a connection with his chin. She was a darn good flicker; Jeff had found that out the hard way many times.

They grabbed their glasses of wine and went into the living room.

Jeff sat down in his favorite recliner, and Gaia curled up on the couch.

"So, we're off to Calgary."

"Yes, I booked the flights for this Friday—we leave around noon. And I phoned the Clarksons back and they're okay with our timing. They did some research on us, too, and were happy with what they read."

Jeff beamed with pride. "Well, I would have expected nothing less."

"They're very happy we're coming. And appreciative—they can't believe we're going to do this for free."

He laughed. "Neither can our partner."

Gaia shifted out of her curled position and drained her glass of wine. "That's a real strange visit you had with Louise."

"Yeah, it was strange. That tall well-dressed guy walking along a highway into some kind of roadblock, then shifting over to the one lane. Weird symbolism. And then to tell me that she thought I had some kind of a connection to the Clarksons or the missing girl. I don't get that, been puzzling over it."

"From another case we had, maybe?"

Jeff shook his head. "No, I went through all of our old cases this morning—can't find any connection at all. And most of our work has been done right here in Toronto, not out west. So, I'm at a loss to understand her comment."

"Has Louise ever been wrong before, that you know of?"

He paused. "No—that's what makes her comment worth remembering."

Gaia went into the kitchen and came back with the bottle of Masi. She filled their glasses and sat down again. "Jeff, what do you think we're up against with this Emily case?"

Jeff winced. "We've handled quite a few missing person cases, and so has Dan. But all adults and teenagers. For the adults, it was usually a dementia thing, and for the teenagers it was almost always a runaway thing. Or, a wild drunken adventure without telling mom and dad.

"We've never investigated a missing child this young, and we've never handled a kidnapping before. Dan's okay with us getting this thing started, but I have to get him involved eventually to help us out. Being former RCMP, he has the experience and network of contacts that can take the case to the next stage."

Gaia nodded. "You're right. But we don't know this was a kidnapping."

"No, we don't."

"It could be a murder."

"Yep, it could. But I'm putting faith in that vision I had. I sense that Emily's still alive, and for now I think we need to pursue that angle unless I experience a sudden change in that intuition."

Gaia gazed off into the study. "I watched you researching in there this afternoon. Didn't want to disturb you. What did you find?"

Jeff sighed. "Geez, Gaia, it's all so damn depressing. This underworld of child trafficking is disturbing as hell. I had to pop antacids a couple of times while researching this.

"Each year, an average of 40,000 kids go missing in Canada alone—teenagers and youngsters. But about seventy percent of them are just runaways, and are usually found within days or weeks. Another big chunk of them are domestic kidnappings, where the kids are taken by one of the parents out of the country. Fairly easy to do because the parent has their identification, passport, etc., and sometimes a permission letter from the other parent. Then they just don't come back, and it's pretty hard to get them back if they whisk off to a country with no extradition treaty with Canada.

"So, that leaves about 5,000 children each year that are just gone—no trace. Some may be dead and buried somewhere, but who knows how many? The rest of them are presumed to be used in some kind of sex-trafficking or child porn rings. Until they're no longer—desirable."

Gaia shivered and wrapped her arms across her chest. "But

wouldn't they have left the country too?"

Jeff shook his head. "No, surprisingly. But maybe not so surprising. Trying to get a child out of the country when you're not the parent is pretty risky. So, it's assumed that most of them are still right here, but in different cities than where they lived with their parents.

"Apparently, sex trafficking is organized crime's fastest-growing business sector, and one of the largest criminal enterprises on the planet. According to the FBI, annual profits are now well in excess of 100 billion. The technology age has made it even more lucrative, with online ads that use secret code words that only pervs and pedophiles understand. And not to mention the underground pornographic movie scene. But just for sex alone, a victim can average a take of up to $350,000 a year, all of that of course going to the scum who run the stable. Kids under ten years of age can fetch from half a mill to a mill each year."

Gaia rested her forehead on her hands. "God, what a sick world. I saw some of it first-hand of course when I was an escort, but at least I wasn't being exploited. I took the risks of my own free will."

"Yeah, a different world entirely—but still a bad world. You got to see the raw underbelly of the type of people who seek out this stuff, except that the ones you met weren't necessarily into kids. That's the part that's most sickening.

"And the law doesn't seem to be a deterrent. Trafficking carries a sentence of four to six years depending on the age of the victim. It does allow for a life sentence if the offense is particularly egregious, or if the victims are very young—but no one has ever been convicted for a sentence of that length despite the law now being in place for over a decade. The longest sentence handed out was to a guy in B.C. who lured kids as young as fourteen—he got twenty-three years— but most of that sentence was for other charges that were unrelated.

"And get this—there are even instruction manuals online. One book I found contained the advice: 'You'll start to dress her, think for her, own her.' Unreal, huh? All this stuff hiding in plain sight.

"And they know where to find them. They stalk neighborhoods, schools, playgrounds. And for the teenagers, they hunt the shopping malls, amusement parks, bus depots. The average age that girls are first exploited, or taken, is thirteen. Bloody hell—thirteen years of age!

"Then, of course, there are the dangers of social media luring, and parents letting their kids explore that world with very little censorship. Even young pre-teens. Kids in foster care have also been exploited—easy targets because they're insecure and isolated. No one for them to turn to, and the ones who exploit them are the ones they depend upon for basic needs.

"The RCMP and FBI both report that, while exploiters are mainly men, there's a new trend with women and girls getting involved.

"The women are usually in partnership with the men, but the women are put out there as being more trusted and more sincere. Kids let their guards down more with women than men. And even some of the teenagers being exploited are used to attract other girls—they're given certain favors or not required to work as often if they can bring more kids into the stable. So it functions sometimes as kind of a pyramid scheme.

"And the sad part is, drugs are used to make these kids addicts. Then they're told they have to perform in order to pay off their drug debts. And even threats against their families if they don't perform. A vicious circle. And many of them suffer from a sort of Stockholm Syndrome. They believe they're in love, that they're loved in return— totally divorced from reality.

"That instruction book I mentioned—it discusses how to manipulate: 'Slow it down and become colder. She'll start to crave the intimacy and be willing to get back into your good graces. After you have broken her spirit, she'll have no sense of self-worth. Now, go put a price tag on the product you've manufactured.'

"The Toronto police saved a victim recently. They found her locked in a basement apartment. She was being forced to service men there and at hotels and in cars. They said her spirit was completely broken. And Gaia, she was only thirteen."

Gaia was crying now. She got up and came over to Jeff's chair. Sat on his lap and wrapped her arms around his neck. Her cheek nestled up against his, he could feel the wetness of her tears against his skin.

She pulled her head back and gazed into his eyes, sadness oozing out of her beautiful black orbs.

"Jeff, can we just cuddle in bed tonight? Nothing else? Would you mind terribly?"

Chapter 11

It was a miserable night in Toronto. A massive storm had rolled into Canada's largest metropolis after hovering for hours over Lake Ontario. Thunder, lightning, torrential rain, and tornado warnings out for areas north of the city.

Too miserable for him to venture out onto the balcony, so he stayed nicely sheltered inside, gazing out at the mayhem through the floor to ceiling glass doors.

His spacious suite in The Gainsboro Residences actually gave him two balconies—one facing south and the other north. Located on the twentieth floor, he occupied the penthouse. The condominium was three thousand square feet of pure luxury and had cost him eight million dollars a year ago—but with Toronto's rabid real estate market, it was already worth two million more.

He loved the area. Situated on the north side of Front Street, it was right in the center of the entertainment district. Everything was walkable—theaters, restaurants, pubs, shopping. The man felt privileged to be living there—no, that wasn't quite correct—he felt entitled to be living there.

The buzz of St. Lawrence Market was wonderful on Saturdays, and he was close to the Hockey Hall of Fame. He loved hockey, and had visited that museum more times than he could count. And if he desired a baseball game, hockey game, football game, or even basketball, those venues were all within reach. Much more convenient than where he used to live.

He went by the name of Trevor Kincaid. As good a name as any, he thought.

He had separate identification documents under that name—driver's license, passport, even an authentic-looking birth certificate. Anything was available for a price. Of course, he still had his other identification too, for his real name. Just in case he wanted to use it again.

Trevor examined the image reflecting back at him from the sliding glass doors. Still impressive, he thought. At six foot, three inches, he dominated most rooms he entered. An imposing physique and a presence most men could never even begin to mimic. Even with his advanced age of sixty-four, he was more desirable than men half his age.

Trevor's neatly trimmed gray beard rounded out his handsome face—the beard was a new addition, and Trevor quite liked it.

His bald head actually shone a bit in the reflection—that part he didn't like too much. He'd have to apply some more powder on it in the morning—just part of his early hours grooming routine. He missed his long thick silver hair, but he knew this new look was safer for him. He'd get used to it. And the women he'd met since he started shaving his head told him that they thought his baldness was sexy. And a sign of virility. He liked that, but didn't volunteer to them that he was bald by design. Didn't want to take the glow off the virility thing.

One thing that was still constant, though, were his piercing blue eyes. Not many blue-eyed gents had the azure glow that his did. Women found his eyes intoxicating—and so did Trevor. He enjoyed looking at himself.

He turned away from the window and glanced at his watch. His guest should be arriving any minute now. Another business meeting, another successful conclusion, he hoped. The client's name was Heath Woodrow, and he'd flown in from Halifax. This would be their third meeting and all of the due diligence had been done. Trevor had dug into his background and everything seemed legit. A multi-millionaire, fifty years old, confirmed bachelor, owned a seafood packing business in the Yarmouth area of Nova Scotia. Lived on a private estate along the province's south shore. He fit the bill. Seemed perfect.

Trevor went into his study, fired up his computer, and pulled a sheath of papers out of the top drawer of his desk. He placed then in a neat pile on top of his leather blotter and checked to make sure that the signature pages were in sequence.

His preparations were interrupted by the ring of the phone. Yanked it out of its cradle and gave the security guard permission to let his guest enter the building.

Before heading out to the foyer of his apartment, Trevor opened the bottom drawer of his desk and removed his 9mm Glock pistol. Checked to make sure it had a full magazine, then withdrew a silencer from the same drawer. Screwed it on to the barrel, and placed the pistol back in the drawer. One could never be too careful.

*****

Heath Woodrow sat upright in the chair, looking as if he had twelve inches of wood rammed up his ass. Trevor chuckled to himself as he watched him. Not surprised at all that losers like this guy had to come to him to get a life.

Woodrow was short and stubby, with pathetically white skin and even more pathetic red hair. Despite being a successful businessman on the East Coast, he didn't carry himself with the air of a successful executive. Not like Trevor, who knew his way around boardrooms—as well as bedrooms. He was dominant in most places.

Despite this being their third meeting, Trevor's opinion of the nerd had diminished from his first underwhelming encounter. Usually people got more impressive over time, but not this guy. He figured that perhaps the man was just intimidated by Trevor's presence, which happened to people quite regularly—or maybe intimidated by the subject matter of their meeting.

"Would you like another coffee, Heath?"

The nerd shook his head. "No, I've had enough, thanks."

"Well, are you ready to sign on the dotted line then?"

Heath fidgeted with his fingers. "I've tried to track you down, research you online. You don't exist."

Trevor leaned forward and rested his elbows on the desk.

"We've been through this before. I have another identity which I will never disclose to you. The name I use with you is the only name you will know me by. You're a successful man—surely you can understand that with the business we're discussing, that's the way it has to be."

"I'm just … a bit … uncomfortable with it."

Trevor gestured with his finger towards the door. "Fine, then. Leave."

Heath fidgeted again. "No, no, it's okay. I don't want to leave. I understand. Let's just get this done."

Trevor smiled and shuffled the papers on his desk. "Okay, we have this agreement that's been drafted up by my secretary. You will need to sign, and then I will sign. The agreement specifies that this is a management consulting contract. For the sum of money you entrust with me, I will provide coaching, psychological, and strategic services to your company for a period of ten years."

Heath winced. "Well, as we both discussed before, that agreement is just all bullshit."

Trevor chuckled. "Yes, it is all bullshit. Just for appearances— audit purposes. You would show the amount on your company's income statement as a legitimate business expense, written off against your company's income. Since the agreement is for ten years, you can amortize the amount over that period of time. A nice tax advantage for you."

"Pretty slick. Has this stood the test of time?"

Trevor nodded. "Yes. I've been providing these professional services for over twenty-five years now. In fact, you know that, because I gave you some references to call. I assume you checked with them?"

"Yes, I did. They were all very satisfied. Is this all you've been doing for all this time?"

"Don't think you can trap me into giving you information, Heath. I'm sharper than you are. I'll just say that, no, this is not all I've done. This has just been a lucrative sideline. And I told you that I'm a psychiatrist by education. That's a big part of the service I provide to clients like you, and of course I have a team who work with me across the country to help me provide those services."

"Okay, I'm in. Let me see the products you have available."

Trevor chuckled. "First we sign. Then you can see the merchandise."

"What if I don't like what I see?"

"I'm sure you will. But if not, we'll keep looking until we find what you like."

"I guess that's fair. And once I sign, when do you need payment?"

"I'll want to see a bank transfer into my account within five days. And the fee is non-negotiable. Ten million. That fee covers my services for ten years. Covers everything—any expenses I incur to maintain and manipulate your product during that time. And it includes a guarantee as well. If things don't work out, we'll dispose of the product and provide you with a replacement within that ten years. But regardless, my involvement with you will not extend beyond that initial ten years."

"I understand. Okay, where do I sign?"

Trevor passed the papers over to Heath and pounded his finger down on two spots on the last two sheets. "Here, and here. You've already read a draft of the agreement, so you can just sign it. I'll make sure a final copy is sent to you in Nova Scotia, once the money is in my account."

Heath signed, then Trevor noticed him tremble. "Can I see the products now?"

Trevor spun his computer around to face Heath. "I've got them displayed on this page. You can scroll down. All of these girls are under nine years of age, and they currently live in western and central Canada. It's important that we provide girls from sections of the country far away from where they'll be living with our clients. Not necessarily across the country, but at least a few hundred miles away. That's for your safety—less chance of them being recognized."

"Why no girls older than nine?"

"Good question. As a psychiatrist, I know that the likelihood of programming these kids to forget their previous lives—in fact, basically erase their previous lives—has a higher probability of success if the children are under ten years of age.

"Their brains are quite pliable when young, and already prone to forgetting images and memories from those early years. For example, even without manipulation, I'm guessing there's very little that you can remember vividly from your own childhood years. We increase the odds of success by providing hypnotherapy and other techniques for usually the first two years after your adoption papers are given to you."

"I understand. Makes sense. So, you'll be handling that programming for me without me having to hound you?"

"We're a full-service agency. And it's in our best interests to make sure that you're happy, and that your new daughter is settled into her new life with you."

"Do you enquire as to what I do with her?"

Trevor grimaced. "Listen, bud, this is a dirty business. And let me be blunt with you—you're a miserable little pedophile. I get that. You actually make me sick, but this is business and I can put that behind me.

"Fuck her all you want—she's yours. And we'll arrange legitimate-looking adoption papers; all that jazz. You'll be her official adoptive father.

"I only do a handful of these deals a year, because it would draw too much attention to have too many kids disappearing in a short span of time. And of course, we only deal with single wealthy men like you. Lonely fuckers like you who can't get it up for a woman, but prefer kids. You're our target market.

"And we only deal with men who have businesses that my fee can be billed to, for disguise purposes. As well, we only agree to sell to men who live on private estates, where a new arrival won't be easily noticed.

"And I've gone through this with you before, but you have to agree to keep her confined to your house for the first two years. No tutors, no nothing. None of your friends or family can see her. You basically have to become a hermit for a couple of years. My experience is that after two years of my brainwashing techniques, and you following through on the assignments I give you, she's yours in mind and body. There is little risk of her remembering anything after that two years."

"What do I do when I have to leave the house, for work, shopping, things like that?"

Trevor shrugged. "Your problem. You figure it out. You live in a big home. Lock her in a soundproofed room, or even a vault if you have one."

Heath leaned back in his chair and folded his arms across his chest.

"I don't appreciate those things you said about me."

Trevor laughed—an extended mocking belly laugh. "Suck it up, buttercup. I provide a service to perverts like you, and if I had any real morals I probably wouldn't do it. But to me it's just business—and money in my pocket.

"You actually make me sick, and just looking at you I can understand why a vulnerable little kid is the best you can do. You know what you are; I'm not disclosing any big revelation here. But people like you have helped make me a rich man, and for that I can overcome my disgust.

"And I'll repeat what I told you the first time we met. You cannot, under any circumstances, sell our product to a sex trafficking ring. She's yours and she has to stay with you. No sidelines. We're not in the sex trafficking business. We're in the *adoption* business. So, all that being said, shut the fuck up and look at the photos."

Heath swallowed hard and stared at the computer screen. He scrolled down and then came to a sudden stop. His voice went up an octave or two, as he tapped his finger on the screen. "That one."

Trevor swung the computer around with Heath's finger stubbornly stuck to the same spot on the screen. "Cute. Good choice, I guess. She lives in Winnipeg. We'll get on it right away."

Heath dropped his hands onto his lap. Trevor noticed a bulge in his crotch and resisted the urge to punch him in the face. The little pedophile's voice quivered as he asked, "How do you get these photos?"

"I have what are known as 'bird-dogs' across the country. I pay them to scout out candidates, take photos, and then carry out the extractions once people like you put in an order. After that, I let you know the expected delivery date."

"Extractions? You mean kidnappings, right?"

"Well, aren't you a bright little man? Of course, you fool. I'm trying to be gentle with my words."

Heath ignored the insult. "What if I'm not happy?"

"We'll do everything we need to do to provide the best prospect of success. I've already told you about our guarantee policy. What else do you expect?"

The bulge in Heath's pants had disappeared. He started fidgeting with his hands again. "Well, what if I have a dispute with you? What recourse do I have?"

Trevor sighed and opened the bottom drawer of his desk. He pulled out the silenced Glock and pointed it at Heath's forehead.

"If you want recourse, you can kill me. Or, more likely, I'll kill you first."

Chapter 12

He seemed to enjoy his dinner, but Rachel was never quite sure with him.

He wasn't one to give compliments out easily, so he usually needed to be prodded. "Daddy, how did you like it?

He nodded, and managed to mumble a full-mouth reply.

"It was good, really good. I love trout."

She smiled. "I'm glad. That's locally-caught trout. The stuffing was my own creation."

He wiped his lips with a napkin. "Delicious. What's for dessert?"

Rachel stood and started clearing the plates. "I didn't make anything for tonight. We have some ice cream in the freezer, though. Want me to get you a bowl?"

Her father frowned. "I don't feel like ice cream. Was in the mood for some cake."

"Sorry, no cake tonight." She took the dishes into the kitchen and came back with a pot of coffee. "Can I pour for you?"

"Sure. Still pissed off about the cake, though."

She poured full cups for each of them and sat down again. He leaned back in his chair and patted his full belly. "Probably no room for cake anyway."

Rachel studied him as she sipped her coffee. Almost as if she were looking at him for the first time, even though she'd been with him for fifteen years. Her father had a ruddy complexion and a head that she always thought was shaped like an oversized kettle. And ears that were a bit pointed like that character Spock in *Star Trek*. Not quite as bad, but they still reminded her of Spock.

He was about sixty years old now, but looked older. And he had a wide frame, with a protruding stomach that hung out in all directions. Sometimes he drooled when he talked—little lava flows of whitish saliva would drain out of the corners of his mouth. That always grossed her out, especially when they were having sex.

He had beady little eyes, framed by bushy eyebrows that he never bothered to trim. In fact, they almost connected in the middle, forming the grotesque illusion of one continuous line of hair.

She'd seen good-looking men in magazines and on TV, some older than her father. But he didn't come close to competing with those images. In fact, he didn't even come close to competing with the ugliest of the delivery men who came to her door each week.

His appearance made her want to puke.

"Dad, when are you going to get a woman in your life? Don't you think you'd like that?"

He stared at her in the kind of way he probably used in boardrooms. She was accustomed to this look.

"I don't need a woman in my life. I have you."

Rachel frowned. "That doesn't sound right. Aren't I a woman?"

"Now you are, yes. You're going on twenty-four now, so definitely all grown up. But I still see you as that little eight-year-old girl who came into my life when I adopted you. That image never leaves me."

She probed, because for some strange reason Rachel was in a probing frame of mind tonight. Reached behind her head and flipped her ponytail up in the air. "Is that why you make me wear my hair in a ponytail? To remind you?"

"I don't know. Why are you asking these questions? No point to them."

Rachel persisted. "There is a point. I'd like to wear my hair down. Don't you want me to be me?"

"Not really. I want you to be *for* me. There's a big difference."

"I'm your daughter. Even though you adopted me, I'm still your daughter. So, of course I'm for you. But I also want to be my own person. I was reading online today about how some adopted kids are tracking down their biological parents once they become adults. Isn't it time I learned where I came from?"

Her father grimaced. "You were told a long time ago that you were an orphan. Your parents died. You were in a foster home when I came into your life."

"Yes, I know all that. That's what you told me. I don't remember any of that foster home stuff though. But I'd like to learn who my parents were. Their history. I know nothing about them."

Without warning, he slammed his fist on the table. "That's enough! I do not give my permission!"

Rachel was startled by the sudden anger, but surprisingly, not as startled as she usually was. She'd noticed that a change had come over her in the last few days—a strange transformation. Ever since she'd read that article about the little girl and the bicycle. Seeing the photo of little Emily and her bike. It seemed to her that the face was vaguely familiar—but only vaguely. Aside from that, the story was just so sad. Even though Rachel was a grown woman now, she herself felt like a little lost girl.

A newfound strength rushed through her veins. She could feel her brain behaving in a strange way—suddenly she had lots of questions, and images started popping up in her mind. They always had from time to time—mainly the strange voices, bright lights, repetitive phrases. And of course, the occasional needle. But now other things were flashing across her vision. Memories, long smothered.

Rachel glared back at him. "Why did she leave?"

"Who?"

She hesitated for a second. Then it just came tumbling out. "Angie."

"Angie? That was so long ago. She was only here for three years—she left twelve years ago."

"We were sisters. Like twins. She also wore her hair in a ponytail."

"Yes. So what?"

"Why did she leave?"

"I'm sure I've told you about that before."

Rachel shook her head. "All you told me was that the adoption didn't work out. She was here for three years—she was like my sister—and then she left. You never told me why it didn't work out. I recall we were happy, the three of us. Or, at least I was happy. Happy because of her."

He scowled while staring into his coffee cup. "We may need to schedule a few more sessions for you. It's not healthy to be reliving memories from that long ago. I'm concerned."

Rachel stirred her coffee, idly clanking the spoon gently against the side of the cup. "I can remember thinking back then that soon I would be gone too. That I'd better be the best little girl I could be or I'd be sent away somewhere."

"You were a good little girl. And Angie went to a new family. I'm sure she's doing okay."

"What didn't you like about her that you had to give her up?"

He squeezed his big hands together and cracked his knuckles. "I'm not going to talk anymore about Angie. That's ancient history."

"Fine. I just wanted you to know how lonely that made me feel. I'm still lonely. We hardly ever go out except to visit a couple of your old aunts, and a few of your friends from work. You're gone a lot. I have no life. No friends of my own. Don't you think we should talk about me getting a life of my own now?"

"Rachel, you're starting to make me angry. You know what that means."

She pressed on, despite knowing full well what that meant. "Can I get my driver's license? We have four cars in the garage—you only use one. I could have my pick of the others."

He growled, "What the hell has gotten into you? We've been over this before. Driving around here is dangerous—lots of blue collar workers who drive drunk, moose and deer on the roads. It wouldn't be safe."

"You taught me to fly your plane. That's not all that safe either."

"Sure I did, because I thought you'd enjoy it. But I never allowed you to get your pilot's license. You may know how to fly, but legally you can't without me in the plane with you. Same as driving. You've watched me drive, you could probably just do it yourself. But you can't, because you don't have a license."

Rachel smirked at him. "I get it. On both counts, it's the freedom thing, isn't it? You just don't want me to have any freedom."

He jumped to his feet. "Okay, I've had enough for tonight." He undid his belt, and slipped it out of his pants. Then, sat down again.

"Assume the position, bad little girl."

She got up slowly, pulled down her jeans, and lay on her stomach across his lap. Within mere seconds she felt the first vicious impact across her buttocks.

*****

Rachel was lying face down on her bed, a cold wet washcloth resting across her bare bum. She knew her ass was beet red, but didn't want to look at it. Would just let the washcloth do its work, and a few minutes from now, replenish it with some fresh cold water. It usually only took a couple of days for her ass to feel better. He was careful never to bring it to the point where there would be blood or permanent marks, so she was glad for that at least.

Her head was swimming with images. Had never been so active before. She knew what it was—that article in the paper had opened up some old memories; some happy, some sad. Happy to have had Angie as a sister, then sad that she suddenly wasn't anymore. Those images had been buried for years—in fact, she'd practically forgotten all about Angie. Perhaps she'd blocked it out of her mind because it had been so sad, so tragic.

And while she had been asking questions of her father tonight, she knew that some of the answers were already there. Somewhere in her head.

She closed her eyes and concentrated. Thought back, replayed those images from twelve years ago over and over in her head. Allowed her brain to dig deeper.

Suddenly she lurched up onto her knees, gasping. Hands over her mouth.

My God, she left me a letter!

A letter, left under her pillow. Rachel had been at the doctor's that day, taken there by one of her father's aunts. When she got home, Angie was gone. Her dad told her a car had taken her away. But the next morning she discovered an envelope under her pillow.

Where did I put it? What did it say?

Rachel slid off the bed and began pacing her room, hands on her forehead, naked from the waist down. Frantic. Angie loved to write—was a very talented little writer.

Where did I put it?

Suddenly she remembered! Knelt down on the floor and reached underneath her dresser. Felt around with her fingers, and sure enough, there it was. Taped to the underside.

Rachel ripped off the tape and removed the envelope. Sat down on her bed, propped up the pillows, and opened it. Excited, she began to read once more the ancient letter from her sister. She had to dive deep into her brain to remind herself that it was written by a clever and precocious eleven-year-old.

Dearest Rachel,

By now you know I'm gone. I loved you. You were my best friend and like my sister. The only one I've ever known, but both of us wondered what we were before we met. Because we couldn't remember. Maybe we had brothers and sisters before each of our parents died. I don't know. I can't remember. And I know you never could either.

We had so much fun together. Picking flowers, riding on the swings. Playing hide and seek. Chasing the prairie dogs around the fields—they kept popping up in new spots. It was so much fun.

Some things weren't fun, though. But at least I always had you. I'm going to miss you.

But maybe we can plan to meet up again someday. I wished you were here today so I could have said goodbye to you. I think they planned your doctor's visit so it wouldn't be sad for us.

You'll be proud of me, though. I did some snooping. Two men arrived in a big car to take me away. We've seen one of them before—a tall man with thick white hair. We talked about him before. His eyes were even bluer than ours.

He visited with us many times after we were adopted. Always nice—I liked him. Never mean. But he would take us into a room and just talk to us in that deep voice, over and over again. Then turn those bright lights on us for the longest time, with recordings playing stuff. The same stuff. We didn't understand why. But he was always nice. Until he stuck those needles in our arms—I didn't like that. He said it was to stop diseases. I always wanted to just go to sleep afterwards.

I'm writing to you as if I'm talking to you. You were always so easy to talk to.

Anyway, when these two men met with dad, they sent me outside. But I crouched down underneath the open kitchen window and listened. They talked about money. Sounds like the white-haired man paid dad some money—I heard him say it was a fair refund. They talked for a while, and then I heard him say I would be going to live with my new father in some place called Saskatoon. I don't know if I spelled that right. And guess what, I even know what my new last name will be—'Hunt.' They're keeping my first name the same, though, which is nice. So, I'll be Angie Hunt. Sounds nice, eh? I think it sounds better than Angie Milton. You'll still be Rachel Milton, and now I'll be Angie Hunt. But we can still be sisters, can't we? Pretty please?

Maybe one day we can meet up again. I hope so. Wouldn't it be nice to swing on a star and collect some moonbeams in a jar together?

Love always,

Angie (Hunt, or Milton, or whatever)

Rachel wiped the sleeve of her sweatshirt across her face, steering away the tears that were streaming down her cheeks. Reading this letter again after all these years was just like reading it for the first time.

So, her adoptive father, Rod Milton, had received a nice refund for sending her sister off to live with someone else. *A refund? What was that all about?* The sole owner of Great White North Diamonds

Inc., was always the businessman first and foremost.

The tears wouldn't stop flowing. And while they did, Rachel questioned in her mind why she hadn't reread this letter before in the twelve years since Angie had been gone.

Yet she now had the answer to another question she'd been puzzling over since the day she read that article about Emily and saw those photos of her and the bike. She'd been wondering why she suddenly started singing that song about swinging on a star. A song she could never remember singing before.

Rachel had indeed sung it before. She and Angie had sung it together.

Chapter 13

They were greeted at the door by a massive German shepherd. Normally an intimidating breed, but this particular version seemed to be just darn friendly.

The owners stood behind him until he finished his ritual. Lifted his left paw, which Jeff was more than eager to shake. The dog then bent his head down and licked the back of Jeff's hand. He looked up at Gaia, inviting her to repeat the ritual. She did. They both laughed as the dog turned around and ran into the back part of the house.

"That's one very special Walmart greeter you have there!"

The man stepped forward and shook Jeff's outstretched hand. "He sure is. I promise I won't lick your hand, though!"

After they finished their introductions, Cathy invited them into the living room, where some snacks were already laid out. "I have coffee on in the kitchen, or, if you guys prefer, I can make a pot of tea."

"Coffee's fine for both of us," Gaia replied.

Jeff turned to her. "Hey, I wanted tea!"

"Since when?"

Jeff chuckled and rubbed her shoulder. "Just kidding, hon. I actually loved the way you ordered for me."

They all laughed. Cathy came back with a thermos of coffee and poured four cups.

"So, what's your dog's name? He's a beaut."

Ken wrapped his arm around Cathy's shoulder as they sat together on the couch across from Jeff and Gaia. Jeff could tell they were a close couple. Looked to be in their mid- to late-40s, and both seemed to be in great physical shape. It was typical of Calgarians to take advantage of the great outdoors, with the Rocky Mountains sitting on the city's doorstep. And he reminded himself that they owned a sporting goods shop, so it made sense that they looked athletic.

"Max is his name. And he's our pride and joy, and probably the one who really runs things in this house. A terrible watchdog, though. You saw how friendly he is—he'd probably lick a burglar to death."

"Driving through your neighborhood, I noticed that there's quite the unusual mix of new versus old. And some monster homes as well."

Cathy gushed, "It's a lovely neighborhood—we feel so lucky to live here. We probably couldn't even afford to buy our own house now. Prices in here have gone up so much in the last few years. Ours is a modest house, but there are some really old character homes here that have pulled values up for all of us."

Gaia chose a particularly interesting cookie out of the fancy dish sitting on the table. "How long have you guys lived here?"

Cathy looked up at the ceiling for a second as she thought. "You'll have to forgive me, but I measure everything now by how long we've been without Emily. She was eight when she disappeared and she's been gone fifteen years. So, we've been here about twenty-five years. It was our first home; we thought it was the perfect family home and at that time we were planning just that."

"Forgive me for asking—but did you have any other children after …?"

Ken shook his head. "No. I think you can understand why."

Jeff nodded, and looked down at the floor. "Yes, I certainly can. Gaia and I would like to have kids one day, but we only talk about the joys that would bring us—not the possibility of heartbreak. I feel for you."

Ken withdrew his arm from around his wife's shoulders and leaned forward on the couch. "We've never really recovered from this—everything in our lives was different from that moment forward. Emily was our treasure. Then, this storm had to come along and literally open up old wounds right from the ground itself."

Gaia reached into her purse and pulled out the article—she'd printed it off before flying out of Toronto. "When Jeff read this and studied the photos, he was determined that we reach out to you."

Ken nodded. "I'm glad you guys did. By the way, you're staying here with us tonight."

"No, we couldn't impose like that. A hotel is fine."

"Absolutely not. We have lots of room and it's no imposition at all. You're staying here, and that's final."

"Okay, that's kind of you. Thanks."

"You're the kind ones. Doing this investigation for us without charging us anything. I can't believe it. Why would you want to do that? What is it about our case?"

Jeff sighed. "I'm a psychologist. Used to be an executive with a headhunting firm in Toronto. That's how Gaia and I met. A couple of years ago we both left that firm and joined up with a former RCMP inspector. The three of us are partners in the detective agency. We've done a lot of missing person cases, but never for someone who went missing as young as Emily.

"And—and I don't want to spook you guys here—but I also have kind of a gift. Occasionally I get psychic visions or feelings. Not always, just sometimes. Runs in the family. My aunt, who was high up in the Toronto police service, is also psychic—actually much more powerful than me."

Jeff could tell he had their attention. Both Ken and Cathy were staring at him with their mouths open.

He continued. "Okay, that cat's out of the bag. Whether or not you believe in stuff like this, I wanted to be honest with you. And I don't want to get your hopes up, but I wouldn't have reached out to you if I hadn't had some feelings about Emily."

Cathy interrupted. "What feelings did you get?"

"I read the article, looked at the photos, and I saw her on her bike riding down the sidewalk. Your sidewalk. I noticed as we pulled up to your house that the scene was exactly as I saw it in my … vision. The same street, same boulevard, same houses.

"Now, I'm going to warn you, the next part may be disturbing to you. Do you want me to go on?"

They both nodded.

"Okay, here goes. I saw her riding her bike down your sidewalk. Some kind of blue panel van pulled over to the curb. A man got out. I can't describe him, and couldn't see a license plate. Emily kept riding, her blonde hair in a ponytail bouncing from side to side. He motioned her over. She stopped, got off her bike, and he played with her ponytail for a bit. They seemed to know each other. He then put her bike into the van through the side door—there were no seats other than in the front. Emily hopped into the passenger seat, and they drove off."

Cathy started sobbing. Ken wrapped his arm around her and hugged her tight.

He shook his head. "My gosh, that's vivid. And it makes her disappearance real, which hits home. Of course, we always suspected something like that, but right here, on our street?"

Jeff interjected. "I have to add that most of the time these visions can be more symbolic than anything else. Sometimes I don't know how to read them. Who knows, it could have been my own imagination working overtime without me controlling it.

Envisioning how she might have been taken. I really need to stress that."

Ken looked up from his trembling wife. "Jeff, I've never really been a big believer in this stuff, I have to be honest with you. But I'll keep an open mind."

"Good. But I have to ask you one more thing. At one point, my vision moved to the front of Emily, almost as if I was sitting on her handlebars staring back at her as she rode. I could see her beautiful blue eyes. She smiled and asked me a question: *"Would you like to swing on a star?"* Does that mean anything to you?"

Cathy stopped sobbing and looked up at Jeff. She put her hands to her mouth and gasped. Tried to say something, but no words came out.

Ken replied for her.

"That was Emily's favorite song. Sometimes it drove us crazy; she would sing it all the time. A kind of 'crazy' that I wish I had back now."

Jeff grimaced. "Well, Ken and Cathy, the feeling I got was that she was asking me to come find her. That's when I knew we had to get in touch with you."

Chapter 14

"Did you guys sleep well last night?"

Gaia rubbed Cathy's shoulder. "We did. That bed was so comfortable. And we had the extra bonus of Max snoring on the floor beside us!"

"Oh, I'm so sorry about that. He seems to like you guys—or, maybe just curious."

"I love dogs. And he's such a darling. I enjoyed having him there."

Ken and Jeff wandered into the kitchen and joined the ladies. Poured themselves some coffee and stood beside the large island.

Jeff allowed his eyes to wander around the cavernous room. "This is a beautiful house. I can see why you never moved from here."

Cathy smiled. "Thanks. But it pales in comparison to the house owned by our friends. You'll be meeting them this morning."

Ken looked at his watch. "Thanks for the reminder. We need to start walking over there in a few minutes."

Jeff looked at Cathy. "Are you going to join us?"

She shook her head. "Most definitely not. We had an altercation with them at a restaurant the other night. Their attitude was so insensitive, I lost my temper. And they made a point of bragging about how they're mortgage-free on their house. It's worth more than double ours, and we have a big mortgage still. I can't understand how they could be mortgage-free. Sounds petty and resentful, doesn't it?"

Gaia jumped in. "Did they not care that the bike was found in their backyard?"

"No, not at all. Seemed annoyed that they had to cut their vacation short, and how their backyard was dug up. I threw a glass of wine in her face."

Gaia giggled. "Well, I guess she knows how you feel!"

"Yep. So, no surprise I don't want to see them right now."

Jeff rested his elbows on the counter and fiddled with his cup. "Did they come into some money? They're about your age, aren't they?"

"I don't know. Both their parents are still alive, so they wouldn't have had an inheritance. And we didn't hear about any lottery winnings. I know it sounds silly for me to be so angry about it, but it wouldn't have bothered me if their attitude hadn't been so insensitive."

"You've known them a long time, I remember you saying."

Ken laughed. "Right back to high school days. Aaron and I were on the football team and Cathy was a cheerleader. That's how the three of us hooked up. As for Sherry, well, he picked her up in a bar after graduation and they've been together ever since."

Cathy seethed. "She's a tramp."

"Dear, that's not fair. She's just—different."

"I've seen her flirt with you, Ken. Right in front of me. And the way she dresses sometimes, it just makes me wonder."

Ken glanced at his watch again. "Okay, guys, let's get going."

✱✱✱✱✱

They were sitting on the front porch of the massive colonial-style home of Ken and Sherry Dixon. The tour was over—Jeff and

96

Gaia were amazed at how beautiful the interior of the old home was. And they'd taken some time to walk around in the backyard. The uprooted tree had been hauled away, and the ground had been filled in. Not much to see. Aaron pointed out the spot where the bike had been found. Jeff stood on the spot, hoping to pick up some kind of vision. But—nothing.

Aaron brought some beers out onto the porch for each of them. Sherry hadn't said very much so far. Sat with her arms folded across her chest, sending silent messages that she was annoyed by their intrusion. But Aaron seemed friendly enough.

He took a sip of his beer. "So, you guys are investigating this incident, are you?"

Jeff gazed out over the verandah railing. "Yes, we are. Not the discovery of the bike itself, but mainly this fifteen-year-old cold case."

"After all this time, there doesn't seem to be much to investigate. A sad story, for sure, but it's been so long now. What experience have you had with this sort of thing?"

Jeff ignored his question. "So, you're a high school teacher, Aaron?"

"Yep, I deal with selfish brats every day of my working life. Coach the football team, too."

Jeff turned his attention to Sherry. "And you're involved with day care centers?"

She couldn't hide the scowl on her face, or in her voice. "I'm an expert in day care management. I counsel centers on how to run their operations and how to supervise the children in their care."

"I see. Sounds like satisfying work."

She just nodded and looked away.

Jeff didn't let that put him off. "You guys have a lovely home. You've been here about a year now?"

Aaron guzzled the rest of his beer. "Yeah, just over a year. We'd had our eyes on this place for a long time. It had been vacant, then rented out, and finally went up for sale. We jumped on it once we could afford it."

"Where did you live before you bought this?"

"Across in the southeast section of Calgary. We always wanted to live in the southwest though, so once we had the chance to do it, we made the move. It was nice also to move close to our good friends Ken and Cathy."

"Who did you buy the house from?"

"It was a private equity firm. They foreclosed on it many years before, and then just rented it out."

"It was empty when Emily disappeared?"

"Apparently."

"What's the name of this private equity firm?"

Sherry suddenly jumped in. "You are nosy, aren't you?"

"I'm a detective."

"Yes, but a private one. We don't have to answer your questions."

"No, you don't. But it would be nice if you did."

Aaron turned to his wife. "Sherry, anything we can do to help our friends is what we should do."

Her expression turned instantly sour. Sherry got up and went back into the house.

Aaron grimaced. "I'm sorry. She's been stressed out ever since she had an argument with Cathy. Please forgive her."

"No problem. Ken told me they had an argument. Those things happen. So, if you don't mind, I'll ask again—what's the name of the private equity firm?"

Aaron shook his head. "I can't remember. And they're out of business now anyway."

Jeff was surprised that Aaron had volunteered that. It wasn't really relevant.

"You do have sale of property documents, don't you? It would show on those."

"I have them somewhere. Can't recall where right now."

Aaron jumped to his feet. "I'm gonna get another beer. You folks want any?"

They all shook their heads.

"Okay, be right back."

As soon as Aaron went inside, Jeff reached over and grabbed his empty beer bottle. Then, replaced it with his own. He handed Aaron's bottle to Gaia and whispered, "Shove this in your purse."

She did as he asked.

Aaron came back out with a fresh bottle and sat down.

Jeff continued. "Aaron, have you ever owned a panel van?"

He stared at Jeff, clearly taken aback by the question. "I've owned a lot of cars in my life. Can't recall a panel van, though." He jokingly flexed his muscles. "Do I look like a panel van kind of guy to you? I have two cars in my garage—one's a Lexus and the other's a Benz."

Jeff laughed. "No, I wouldn't peg you for a panel van." He stood up. "I think we've taken enough of your time today. Thanks." He looked over at Ken and then Gaia. "Do you guys have any more questions?"

They shook their heads.

Jeff reached out his hand to Aaron, and they shook. Suddenly he saw an aura over the man's head—black and red swirls radiating outwards.

*****

Cathy was preparing dinner. The four of them stood in the kitchen chatting.

While prepping the chicken, she finally popped the question. "So, what did you think of our friends?"

Jeff poured some Merlot into his glass, and paused for a few seconds before answering.

"If I were you, I'd avoid them for a while. I didn't get a good feeling. Best if you stayed away from them."

He reached into Gaia's purse, which was sitting on the counter, and pulled out the empty beer bottle, careful to hold it by the neck.

"Ken, do you have a large plastic baggy you can put this in?"

He nodded, reached into the cupboard and pulled one out of a box. Jeff carefully inserted the bottle into the bag.

"Take this to the detective you met and ask him to run prints on it. See if there's a match with either of the two sets of unidentified fingerprints that they found on the bike."

"Geez, Jeff—you don't really think—"

"I don't know, Ken. Just get the prints run and let me know what they find out. At this stage, don't tell the detective whose prints are on this bottle. My collection of the bottle isn't legal anyway, but at least it might confirm or deny.

"I'm also puzzled by Sherry's attitude—antagonistic. Aaron's responses were okay, but then he got defensive when I asked about the private equity firm and the van. My instinct tells me there's something odd going on there. I'll check on those two things myself, because he was clearly no help at all.

"I can also tell you that I got some bad vibes when I shook his hand. Vibes I've had before. An aura over his head that signaled danger, evil, or both."

Ken rubbed his forehead. "You're starting to spook me out here, Jeff."

"Sorry. I'm just being honest with you. And remember, all of this is geared towards finding your daughter. And that I have the strong feeling that she's still alive. She'd be twenty-three years old now, but she's still Emily."

Cathy suddenly threw her arms around Jeff and hugged him

tightly. "I love what you're doing for us." She turned her head and looked at Gaia. "This is one special man you have, Gaia."

Gaia smiled. "You have no idea. Someday I'll tell you all about it."

Ken pulled open the drawer of the kitchen desk and withdrew some photos. He handed them to Jeff. "These are some old photos of Emily."

Jeff took them and started fingering his way through.

He stopped at one. A photo of Emily on a swing in a playground.

He handed it to Gaia and asked her to describe the photo.

"Well, she's wearing a pink blouse, and blue pants. Hair in a ponytail."

"Nothing else?"

"Nope. That's all I see."

Jeff held the photo up for all to see. "No one else sees a diamond necklace?"

Silence. He could feel their eyes boring into him, but no one seemed to want to disturb the eerie silence with the obvious question.

Jeff handed the photos back to Ken. Then he turned to Cathy. "You're working so hard here, and the three of us are gabbing away. I need to do something useful. What can I do?"

She laughed. "Okay, I happen to think that you've been pretty useful so far, but if you want to help out with the prep, be my guest."

She pulled several multi-colored cutting knives out of the drawer and laid them out on the counter. "Take your pick—they all have different levels of sharpness. If you can cut up the cucumbers for the salad, that would be a big help."

Jeff chuckled. "Well, the slices may not be all that aesthetic, but I'll do my best."

His hand hovered over the knives until stopping on one. It was yellow with what looked like a particularly sharp blade.

He picked it up and was just getting ready to slice the cucumber when he lurched backwards. His eyes clouded over and he felt like he was going to faint. Out of the far corners of his ears he could hear Gaia crying out as he fell to the floor, the yellow knife still in his hand.

"Jeff! Jeff! What's wrong? Talk to me!"

He opened his eyes and gazed up at the three sets of concerned eyes peering down at him.

Jeff yelled out, not even half believing what he was saying. But he was finally learning to trust the feeling.

"Diamonds in the photo! A yellow cutting knife! Christ, they took Emily to goddamned Yellowknife! The Northwest Territories! Land of the diamond mines!"

Chapter 15

Bags packed and stacked in the foyer. Hugs all around.

"It was so nice of you guys to fly out here to meet with us. I'm at a loss for words."

Jeff jangled the keys to his rental car. "You and Cathy are good people. We're glad to be able to help out, although I think at this point I may have alarmed you more than helped."

Cathy shook her head. "Not at all. But before you head off to the airport, we should talk a bit about that vision you had last night. You've been quiet with us since then."

"I usually am after those things happen. When I was a kid my mom steered me away from these vision things. She discouraged me from paying any attention to them. The only one who encouraged me was my aunt. So, when I have them now I usually keep them to myself—just engrained in me, I guess, since was young. But last night, it felt kind of triumphant, so I blurted it out in front of you. Gaia's used to this, but you guys aren't. I'm sorry."

Ken reached out and squeezed Jeff's shoulder. "Don't be. We're glad you felt comfortable sharing what you saw. But is it really possible, do you think?"

Gaia pulled on her coat and frowned. "I could tell you a story of my own—maybe I will one day over a few glasses of wine. It seems that whenever there's plenty of money, and determination, anything's possible. Despite how reckless. Your daughter was taken in broad daylight. That alone is brazen, yet it happens again and again, all across this country."

Jeff grimaced. "What came out of my first vision when I read the article, was that Emily knew the man who took her. But last night's vision was weird. I saw diamonds around Emily's neck in that photo, yet none of you saw those diamonds. Then, out of all the multi-colored knives you put on the counter, Cathy, my hand immediately went for the yellow one. Once I picked it up, something shoved me backwards. That's happened to me before—a couple of years ago it happened with something to do with Gaia. It saved her life."

"Do you really think Emily's in Yellowknife?"

Jeff shook his head. "I don't want to give you false hope. Remember, I saw an image of her as a child in that photo, wearing a diamond necklace. I didn't see a grown woman. I still saw a child. And that yellow knife that I picked up right on the heels of seeing diamonds, shoved that sudden vision in my mind that they took her to Yellowknife. But that was then, this is now. None of these things I see are a guarantee that she's still in Yellowknife or—even still alive. But diamond mines are a direct link to the city of Yellowknife. That's a big part of the world up there."

They both nodded their understanding. Then Cathy shuddered and wrapped her arms across her chest. "This … is hard … to say. But I'll … say it anyway. Ken and I have hardly even talked about this over the years. Okay, here goes. When kids are taken, it's usually for … sex … and then those kids are … discarded. Killed. I'm right, aren't I?"

Gaia nodded. "Yes, Cathy. When it's not a family member who does the kidnapping, that's usually the story—the sad story."

Cathy continued. "So, that's why Ken and I never really talked about it that way. Too painful. But now, having met you guys, I feel more courage in facing reality. Particularly since Jeff had the feeling from his first vision that Emily was still alive."

Jeff started to say something, but Cathy held up her hand to stop him. "Let me finish my thoughts here, Jeff, while I've found this new courage. If I think about this too long, I'll start crying.

"So, what's puzzling to me is why Emily might still be alive. If she was taken for sex, they probably wouldn't have kept her afterwards."

Jeff grabbed hold of Cathy's hand and squeezed gently. "Forgive me for what I'm about to say, but you seem to be open to hearing the cruel facts right now. So, I'll be honest with you. She might have been taken for sex trafficking. Sent to a child sex brothel or even sent out of the country, although that's less likely. If she was sent to a brothel, she could have been … employed that way for years. And if she's still alive, she could still be in that business, but as an adult now. She would have been brainwashed and hypnotized long ago to forget her past, and possibly even turned into a drug addict."

Cathy looked down at the floor. "I understand. That would explain why she might still be alive. And would never have tried to contact us."

"Her memories are buried deep now, if they did their jobs properly. A young child's brain is much easier to work mind games with than an adult's. But while those memories may be suppressed, they're never gone. They're merely sent deep into the subconscious, and it's entirely possible they can be retrieved again. Sometimes, by the simplest thing."

Cathy smiled. "I forget that you're a psychologist. You're the least clinical person I've ever met."

Jeff laughed. "I'll take that as a compliment. Yep, my psychology training was useful back when I was an executive in the business world. And being a hypnotherapist as well, I used that skill to help coach executives into overcoming their fears and insecurities. It's powerful stuff—but because it's so powerful, it can also be abused if in the hands of the wrong people. Gaia and I found that out the hard way. To the point that it almost cost us our lives."

Ken jumped in. "Whenever you're ready, we'd love to hear your stories."

"Someday, we'll tell you. But trust me, you probably won't *love* them too much."

Cathy reached down and petted Max's head. He was sitting patiently beside them in the foyer, probably hoping the visitors would just leave so he could have his masters all to himself again.

"One thing I'm confused about, Jeff. If Emily was sold into sex trafficking, wouldn't Yellowknife be an odd place? That's a small remote city. Everybody probably knows everybody—it's hard to imagine a kiddy porn ring could operate up there and be kept secret. Wouldn't cities like Toronto or Vancouver be more likely choices for something like that?"

Jeff nodded, and scratched the back of his head. "That's a puzzle to me too. I agree with you—it's not the likeliest of choices. Which makes me sort of question my vision a bit. I'm actually sorry I blurted it out, because it doesn't make much sense, does it? I hope I haven't sent us down a rabbit hole."

Gaia glanced at her watch and then picked up her suitcase. "We have to get going, Jeff. Flight leaves in two hours."

"Okay, that's it for now, then." Jeff grabbed his duffle bag, scratched Max behind the ears, and opened the front door. "Ken, don't forget to get that beer bottle over to your detective friend. Let me know what he finds out. And we'll do some digging of our own back in Toronto on your old classmate—Aaron Dixon—and Sherry too."

"I will. What should I say when he asks me whose bottle it is and how I got it?"

"Just say that you're acting on a hunch. Nothing more."

"What if he refuses to check the prints?"

"Then tell him we'll get a lawyer and conduct our own independent print analysis of the bike and the bottle. It's okay to tell him that you're working with a private investigation firm. The police don't like people like us too much, but we usually force them to get their asses in gear.

"The thing about most police departments—cold cases—especially one as old as yours, don't get a lot of attention from them. They have so many current cases on their plates, it's understandable—but still sad. There are a lot of people walking around who should be behind bars, but because they weren't caught, they just keep doing what they do."

Chapter 16

It was a nice day for a drive, particularly down in the Beaches area of Toronto. He'd always loved this area of the city. Eclectic, eccentric, and upscale.

Trevor Kincaid loved upscale.

Of course, it wasn't as upscale as where he lived in The Gainsboro Residences on Front Street, and definitely not as upscale as where he used to live in Forest Hill. But it was still darn nice.

He'd driven along Queen St. East, weaving in and out of the streetcar tracks—a bloody nuisance—and turned south down Lee Avenue. He saw the old Edwardian-style house that he was looking for but kept on going to the end of the block until he reached the shores of Lake Ontario. Did a U-turn, and headed back up the street.

Across from 40 Lee Avenue, and just a few doors down, he pulled up and parked, being careful not to rub the tires of his silver Mercedes AMG S-63 coupe up against the curb. He hated curb burn.

His coupe wouldn't look out of place, even though he was parked on the wrong side of the street. There were lots of Mercedes, Audis, and BMWs on this street. A good mixture of high-end opulence. Even though most of the houses looked old and tired, he knew that didn't matter. They were each worth at least a couple of million.

He felt safe sitting there, idle. No one really cared or paid much attention to cars on the street. This was the big city. His windows were darkly tinted, so he could spy with impunity. And today was just a good day for spying. It was Wednesday, hump day—as good a day as any.

No activity outside, but he could see movement behind the upper floor windows. Couldn't tell who it was, or whether it was a man or a woman, but there was definitely someone moving around up there.

He knew who lived there. Had kept track of them over the last couple of years. He knew they'd gotten married, a thought which made his blood boil. Not that he'd ever wanted to marry Gaia, not at all. He'd just wanted to own her. More than any woman he'd ever met in his life.

And marriage hadn't worked out for him anyway back in the day. Well, financially it had, because he'd married into money. But being around her had been painful and boring. He finally ended it in the way only he was capable of doing. Masterfully hypnotized her and commanded her to kill herself. Worked like a charm. He got the estate, the life insurance, and all the sympathy that poured out for the sad widower.

Trevor chuckled to himself. He could outsmart anyone and always had.

And anyone who challenged his power always paid the price; usually the ultimate price. Even something as material as his $200,000 Mercedes with its 603 impatient horses was symbolic of who Trevor was. He was powerful and impatient. And no one got away with crossing him.

He smiled as he remembered the day two years ago when Jeff, Gaia, and that RCMP guy locked him in his own vault. They closed the heavy door, spun the lock, closed the bookcase, and left him to die. They knew that he'd already smashed the safety release catch with a hammer before he'd thrown Gaia in there. Gaia had been his personal slave for days. And she never knew there was another way out. So, in their minds, there was no way for him to escape either.

Left him there to rot.

Well, he didn't rot. There was another way out. An electronic release button that he'd had built into the vault as the ultimate back-up plan. Never thought he'd need it, but he always thought two steps ahead of everyone else. The button had been hidden in a corner, painted over to match the walls. One had to look very close to see the difference in texture.

They thought they were so smart. And for two years the three of them had thought they'd committed murder.

Wouldn't they be shocked to see him again? Brandon Horcroft resurrected as Trevor Kincaid. Risen from the land of the dead. Still with his millions. No longer associated with his old firm, because he really couldn't afford to show his face there again. But that headhunter work had become boring anyway.

Jeff, Gaia, and that Mountie might not even recognize Brandon now. His thick silver hair was gone; now he was as bald as a soccer ball. And his handsome face was partly obscured by a distinctive beard. It had to be distinctive—because even though he was now Trevor Kincaid, he was still Brandon Horcroft at heart. Everything Brandon did had been distinctive. The one thing they would indeed recognize if they got up close, were his azure eyes. No one's eyes compared to his. But they wouldn't get that close. Well, not all three of them. He fully intended to be up close and personal with Gaia again. Because—well—just because. He was Brandon Horcroft and entitled to have what he wanted.

And he still wanted Gaia. He wouldn't be denied. He was never able to get his mind off her when she'd worked for him at Price, Spencer and Williams, and he hadn't forgotten her since then. She'd rejected him every step of the way, which had only made him want her more. And then she hooked up with that media hero, Jeff

Kavanaugh. The guy whose career Brandon had literally created out of thin air. A guy who would have been a loser if it hadn't been for Brandon's brilliance.

Trevor had drifted off into a kind of daydream, but luckily he was still alert. His brain was like that—it could function on different levels at the same time.

He knew he was still alert, because he was fully aware of the front door of 40 Lee Avenue opening up and a vision of loveliness stepping out into the bright mid-day sunshine.

There she was—Gaia Templeton, now known as Gaia Kavanaugh. He caught his breath as the object of his obsession filled his vision. Trevor reached into his glove compartment and pulled out a pair of binoculars. Put them to his eyes and twisted the focus knob.

He gasped. That body that he was more than familiar with was as intoxicating as it had always been. She was dressed in short shorts and a tight-fitting T-shirt. A part of his brain was telling him that she was dressed this way today just for him—that she knew he was watching.

She walked down the front steps and picked up a watering can. Then, over to the outside tap and filled the can to the brim. She bent over the potted plants that were positioned across the patio and started watering. Trevor could feel his heartbeat racing as he focused the binoculars in on the edges of her shapely ass sticking out of the red shorts.

Then she stood and looked across the street, waving at a neighbor who'd called out. Trevor gasped again as his binoculars gave him a clear view of the tattoo of a green red-headed parrot on the inside of her forearm.

He put down the binoculars and awkwardly squeezed himself across the console over to the passenger seat. Then he pushed the power button and rolled down the tinted side window.

Trevor held up his phone and snapped several photos of the vision of loveliness standing in front of the house. He made sure also to get a good shot of the house itself, including the plaque displaying the number 40.

She was the kind of woman who could not be easily confused with anyone else. Gaia was one of a kind. No one else compared. The short jet-black hair, the cute pixy face, the midnight black eyes, and the body of a supermodel. As well, the tattoo of a stupid parrot that had bitten Trevor's hand so hard that it had drawn blood. If he got the chance, that parrot would die—just because.

At one time Gaia had been his executive assistant. After that she'd been his slave.

Soon, she would wish she had never tried to kill him.

Chapter 17

Rachel peered out the front window. Watched in eager anticipation as he got out of the van, slid open the side door, and pulled out a large plastic cooler.

He headed up the front walk and her heart fluttered. This was her favorite delivery man, by far. His name was Gerry.

Gerry was right out of central casting—the type of man she saw in the magazines that she read. Tall, dark and handsome, with an athletic build that told her he'd done a lot more in his life than deliver groceries. And maybe he still did.

She figured he was about her age.

Rachel had made sure to place her order with his store today—because she had the sudden urge to see him. She even dressed up a bit for him—a nice flowery summer dress. It was summer after all, and another hot one. She figured maybe he'd appreciate seeing her in something different than shorts and a halter top.

Gerry liked her, she could tell. Like all of the others, it was just the way he looked at her, and even how he glanced away nervously at times.

But unlike the others, he never leered or tried to act like a cool dude. Gerry was actually quite shy, and she liked that about him. She thought it was amazing that a guy as handsome as him would be shy. From movies she'd seen, she figured all men with his charms would be confident and forward. At least, that's the way they always seemed to be in the movies.

She opened the door before he had a chance to ring the doorbell.

He seemed a little shocked. "Well … hello, Rachel. I didn't expect …"

She smiled and waved him through the doorway. "I was just walking by the front window and saw you. You're a little bit early today."

Gerry carried the cooler through the house and into the kitchen. She followed close behind, her eyes locked onto his perfect stud butt the whole way.

He called back to her as he walked. "Yeah, sorry if I caught you at the wrong time. Are you on your way out? You're all dressed up today." He placed the cooler on top of the large island and opened the lid.

Rachel played with the fringe at the bottom of the dress. "Oh, this little thing? No, I'm not going out. I never go out. Just had the urge to put on a nice dress today."

"That is indeed a nice dress. Looks very pretty on you."

She giggled, then reached behind her head and removed the banana clip from her ponytail. Ran her fingers through her hair, and shook her head, allowing her thick blonde hair to fall down over her shoulders.

Gerry stared at her, his mouth hanging open in shock.

"Cat got your tongue, Gerry?"

He stammered, "Uh … no … I've never seen … Looks great."

She continued to run her fingers through her hair. "I usually don't wear it down, but once in a while I like to—when Daddy's not here."

"He tells you how to wear your hair?"

Rachel nodded. "He likes to remember me as a little girl. The ponytail reminds him of that."

"But you're a grown woman now."

"To him, I'm not."

Gerry shook his head, then turned his attention back to the cooler. "Let me unpack this stuff and put it in the fridge for you."

"That would be nice. Thank you." She opened the fridge door for him and took out two cold beers.

"Would you like one?"

He gazed around the kitchen and took a peek down the hall. "Is he here?"

"No, he went to his office in Yellowknife this morning. Meetings all day. Don't worry, you can have a beer with me."

"Okay." Gerry finished putting the groceries into the fridge, then joined Rachel over at the kitchen table.

They clinked bottles and toasted to the midnight sun.

"Have you always lived in Yellowknife, Gerry?"

"No, only for about two years. I played football for a while until I blew my knee out. It was kind of a shock. Was a star at university, and got drafted. It was always a dream of mine to play pro ball, at least for a little while. Didn't expect that 'little while' meant only one season."

"Oh, that's so sad. Your dream taken away. Who did you play for?"

"Calgary Stampeders. That's my home town—Calgary."

"I've never been there. In fact, I've never been anywhere. Why did you leave?"

"I dunno. Just felt I needed to get away after the injury. Figure out what I wanted to do with the rest of my life. I have my degree, but I kinda went into a depression when I learned I couldn't play ball anymore. But time to get back to reality, I guess. Can't deliver groceries forever."

Rachel took a long sip of her beer. "What's your degree in?"

"Economics."

"That sounds impressive. You should be able to land a good job with that."

Gerry shook his head. "Not here. Yellowknife's too small a city. Would have to go to Calgary or Edmonton—maybe even as far away as Toronto."

"Wouldn't the diamond mining companies up here want to hire someone like you?"

He shook his head. "No, it's a small world and very insular. Not much need for an economist in that industry. It's a simple business, one commodity—and that commodity either goes up in price, or down."

"So, how will you look for a new job?"

Gerry played with his beer bottle, twirling it around on the table. Rachel could tell he was getting more comfortable and less nervous the longer they talked.

"Well, I'll send out my resume to a bunch of companies by email; start out that way and see if I get some responses. Also, my dad runs a company in Calgary—he's offered to help out with his contacts, but I'd rather do it myself. Wouldn't feel right if I didn't do it on my own."

Rachel crossed her legs and noticed that for the briefest instant Gerry's eyes glanced down to catch the sudden bareness of her thigh.

She leaned forward. "If I bring my laptop in here, can you show me how to set up an email account?"

He looked at her in shock. "You don't have email?"

Rachel shook her head. "Was never allowed. But what he doesn't know won't hurt him."

"Geez. He does control you, doesn't he? Rod has the reputation of being a pretty tough guy, but you're his daughter for God's sake."

She corrected him. "His adopted daughter."

"I see. Well, I always wondered about that. There's no resemblance at all between the two of you. When were you adopted?"

"I was eight."

"What happened to your real parents?"

"They died."

"That's sad. How?"

Rachel paused for a few seconds. "Funny, I don't know that, and I've never even asked."

Gerry drained his beer and walked over to the fridge. "Do you mind if I crack open another?"

"No, help yourself. Bring me another one too."

He twisted the caps off the fresh bottles and handed one to Rachel.

"What were your parents like?"

Rachel shook her head. "I can't remember them at all."

"But you were eight when he adopted you. Strange you wouldn't have memories."

"Apparently I was in a foster home for a couple of years."

"Yeah, but still—that would have made you six when they died. You'd have some memories I would think, unless of course you blocked them out because it was so heartbreaking for you to lose them."

Rachel stared into his dark eyes.

The longer she talked to this man, the more she liked him. He was easy on the eyes, much easier to look at than her ugly father. But he was also really smart and charming—and seemed to have a warm heart.

"How old are you, Gerry?"

"Twenty-nine."

"Oh, you look much younger. I'm almost twenty-four; I thought you were more my age."

"Thanks. I think maybe living up here in the land of the midnight sun slows down the aging process."

She giggled. "Perhaps you're right. Then, maybe you should stay here after all, just to stay young."

He shook his head. "No, this is a redneck hellhole. Can't stay here. Time for me to move back to civilization and get on with my life."

"I understand. I'll just have to email you once in a while."

Gerry snapped his fingers. "I almost forgot. You want me to set you up on email. Go get your laptop and I'll do that for you."

Rachel ran off in her bare feet down the hall to the corner office. Came back with her laptop, fired it up, and entered her password.

It only took him a few minutes. "Okay, I've set you up on Gmail." He pointed to the screen. "And I've inserted a shortcut icon for you, right here. Just click on that and you're in. Your password is Groceryman29. Easy to remember, huh? All you have to do is think of me."

She was standing behind him and decided in that instant to wrap her arms around his chest. Then she leaned forward and kissed him on the cheek.

"You're so sweet. Let's send an email from me to you—test it out."

Rachel could feel him shudder as she trickled her fingers back and forth across his chest.

"Okay … we can do that. Actually, it's a good idea. My email address will then be the first one in your contact box."

She laughed. "You'll probably always be the *only* one in my contact box."

He shook his head. "I doubt that. You'll be in a whole new world now."

Gerry opened up her email account, entered the password, and then typed in his email address. "What would you like to say?"

She trickled her fingers down to the area of his belly button and began gently tickling him. He shuddered again.

"How about—'Hello there, handsome delivery man, football

player, economics genius.'"

He laughed. "Well, that will be the nicest email I'll have ever received."

He typed the message and then pointed his finger to the Send button. "All you have to do is click on that when you want to send a message." He moved the curser over and clicked.

"There. It's been sent." He turned his head and looked back at her while her fingers continued to play with his belly button. "I'll treasure that message forever."

Rachel could see it in his eyes. Even though she'd had no experience with this sort of thing, her long-suppressed womanly instincts kicked in. Their faces got closer and closer, just like in some of the movies she'd seen.

He licked his lips nervously, and she leaned forward and captured his tongue with hers. Then their lips locked.

It was like an explosion had gone off in Rachel's head. Her brain was swimming with desire, and she quickly slid her fingers down under his jeans until she reached his erect penis. Then pulled out, unsnapped his snap, and unzipped his zipper.

He spun his chair around and without a moment's hesitation she flung herself down and filled her mouth with his penis.

It was a new sensation for her. This one was young, hard, and bigger than she ever imagined in her wildest erotic dreams. Much different than the old tired penis she'd been sucking on for longer than she could remember.

Gently, Gerry pulled it out of her mouth and picked Rachel up under the arms. Eased her up onto the kitchen island and dropped his jeans to the floor.

She could see the passion and determination in his eyes, as he unzipped her dress and pulled it down past her shoulders. Rachel was braless today, purposefully, so it was no effort at all for him to plant his lips on her nipples.

He was breathing heavily as he reached under her dress, expertly sliding it up to her waist. She was commando down there as well—again, purposefully—so the next part was easy.

He pulled her gently to the edge of the island and entered her effortlessly.

Rachel was wetter down there than she'd ever remembered. Love-making with her father usually meant a wad of Vaseline. But with her handsome delivery man, there was no need for Vaseline.

She felt her face flush as he gyrated in and out—teasing her—entering, then pulling out, over and over again. Rachel finally just grabbed him by the shoulders and pulled him into her for good—wouldn't let him go.

He kissed her passionately on the lips as she felt the rush coming. It came in waves and she screamed out when the moment arrived. It seemed as if they both came at the same time, another new experience for Rachel.

And no grunting, groaning, or rude swearing.

Gerry was overcome with what she sensed was real passion. And while she always thought she'd had orgasms before with her father, she never really knew. Didn't know what they were supposed to be like.

Now she knew for sure—this was the first orgasm she'd ever had in her life.

They didn't hear him coming.

Her eyes had been closed tight as she savored the moment.

But they opened just in time to see the sunlight reflecting off of a metal computer case in the right hand of her father.

It was a baseball swing reminiscent of her beloved Blue Jays. The case made contact with Gerry's head—a sickening *clunk* sound, a sound Rachel knew she'd remember for the rest of her life.

Gerry's body hurled itself like a rag doll to the other side of the kitchen.

Her father turned to her and growled, "Cover yourself up, slut. And put that hair back into a ponytail."

Rachel quickly shifted her dress down to cover her crotch, and slid the upper half back up over her shoulders. Reached behind her for the banana clip, and once again her hair was back the way he liked it.

He nodded his approval, and turned his attention to the prone figure on the kitchen floor.

Gerry was dazed, but starting to come around. Her father's computer case was heavy and had dealt a vicious blow to the side of his head. Blood was oozing out of a spot above his right ear.

Rod leaned down and delivered a punch with his closed fist straight into Gerry's nose. Rachel heard the bones crack, and watched in horror as the blood began to pour.

Gerry pushed himself crab-like over to the edge of the kitchen, to a spot right before it connected with the hardwood floor of the dining room.

He held up his hand. "Stop this! I like your daughter very much. We weren't doing anything wrong."

Rod glared at him, fire in his eyes. "You were fucking her! That's my child!"

"She's a grown woman, for God's sake!"

"No, she's not! She's a child! You have no idea what you've done here!"

Rachel was crying now, hands in front of her mouth. There was something surreal about seeing the man she just made love with lying on the floor, blood pouring out of two wounds, her father standing over him threateningly.

"Stop it, Daddy! He's my friend!"

Rod whirled around and pointed his index finger at her. "You shut the fuck up! I'll deal with you later!"

He turned his attention back to the man on the floor. "I know all about men like you. And I know about you specifically, as I do for most people in this town."

Gerry stared up at him, and slid his forearm across his bleeding and broken nose. "I'm going to the police."

Rod laughed. "Really? They won't listen to a nobody like you. I own them. You do know who I am, don't you?"

"Yes, I do, Mr. Milton. But that doesn't matter. You've assaulted me, and I'll press charges."

Rod laughed again, louder this time. Rachel felt sick to her stomach watching his protruding belly shake like a bowl of jelly.

"I'll tell them you raped my daughter. Do you want a rape charge filed against you? Can you handle that shame?"

"I didn't rape her."

Rod turned his head and glared back at Rachel. "He did rape you, didn't he? You'll tell them that, won't you?"

Rachel was crying uncontrollably now. Seeing her lover helpless on the floor trying desperately to stand up to the most powerful man in town, left her with a feeling of hopelessness.

She nodded her head. "Yes, he raped me. I'll say that. Let him go. Please, Daddy. Don't hurt him again."

Rod laughed and glowered down at Gerry. "See? You have no power, little man. As I said, I know all about you. You're that football star who washed out. It was your right knee, if I recall."

With that, he executed one final baseball swing with the metal computer case—a vicious assault against the helpless man's right knee.

Chapter 18

The phone rang just as Trevor had taken a glass of Merlot out onto his south balcony.

It was a nice evening to sit outside, and the sun was just setting off to the west. From his penthouse apartment, he also had a view of a tiny portion of Lake Ontario, and there was something about the setting sun that made the lake resplendent enough to be able to forget for just a moment that it was polluted beyond repair.

He sighed and went back inside. The call must be important because it was coming in over his satellite phone. And probably from another satellite phone from one of his clients who knew that satellite was the only safe way they could talk.

"Kincaid here."

"Who?"

"Trevor Kincaid. Who are you?"

"I must have hit a wrong number. I'm looking for a Brandon Horcroft."

"That's me. Changed my name."

"Oh, okay, then, Brandon—or, Trevor. This is Rod Milton. We haven't talked in a few years, but I'm sure you remember me."

Trevor tapped a few keys on his laptop, and up popped Rod's profile.

"Yes, Rod from Yellowknife. How are things out there under

the midnight sun?"

"Fine. Well, not all fine. I'm glad you remember me."

"How can I help you, Rod? Is family life still treating you well?"

Trevor could detect some stress in the man's voice. And a distinctive deep breath just before he spoke again.

"Not really. Having some problems. She's growing up."

Trevor scrolled down on the profile.

"Yes, it's Rachel, isn't it?"

"That's correct."

"It looks like she'd be twenty-three years old now, Rod. Of course, she's grown up. What did you expect?"

"Well … I don't know. For years I was able to pretend, made her wear her hair the way she wore it when I got her, kept her isolated and reliant on me. Treated her as a little girl even when she'd blossomed into a woman. I'd never been a father before, so wasn't sure how it would all work out. Whether she'd change all that much. And she kept her childishness for years, so it seemed to be working. But something's triggered a change in her. I don't know what it was, but the changes are damn noticeable."

Trevor sighed. "Guys like you are incredible. You want little girls, and I give them to you. But for some reason you think they'll be frozen in time. My team and I are capable of hypnotizing them, brain-washing them, erasing their memories—but we don't have a magic wand that will keep them young forever."

"I understand that. I was probably not being very realistic."

"You're awash in nostalgia. You miss those little girl days, which is what men like you want. Now she's a big girl, and while you've been able to pretend and control her, she's spreading her wings. That's called normal development. You can't turn back the clock."

"Rachel has gone off the reservation—been tainted. No longer the purity that I want."

Trevor laughed. "I see. So, she's fucked around on you, huh?

Suck it up, buttercup."

Rod's voice suddenly turned angry. "Hey, I'm reaching out to you for help. I don't appreciate being belittled."

"Our ten-year contract ended five years ago, Rod. I'm no longer under any obligation to help you."

Trevor scrolled down further on Rod's profile.

"In fact, I see that I've been more than tolerant with you back in the day. I brought you two girls, exactly the same age. Eight years old when you got them. Both in ponytails—because that's what you chose from our catalogue. But after three years you decided that one of the girls—Angie, I see here—didn't cut it with you. I didn't know the reason back then and I never asked. I still don't want to know, because more than likely the reason you had would probably make me puke."

"I had a very good reason."

"And I really don't care. I gave you a full refund for Angie, and took her away from you just as you asked. Had to arrange new adoption papers, a change in her last name, and get her resettled in a new city. Looks like we placed her in Saskatoon. All that stuff I did for you involved extra risk to me and cost, but I still gave you a full refund anyway."

"I'm not asking for a refund on Rachel."

"So, what do you want from me, then?"

"Can you reprogram her again? Make her a little girl again?"

"Jesus Christ! Are you insane? No, I can't do that! Rachel is an adult now; I can't turn back the clock. I could hypnotize her into thinking certain things, or behaving certain ways, but she is still going to be a twenty-three-year-old woman. She'll never be a child again in her mind."

Rod persisted. "She's asking for certain freedoms now—wants a driver's license, wants to go out more. She even suggested I get a woman in my life. Also wants to know about her biological parents.

Started asking questions about Angie. Getting rebellious too—asked if she could stop wearing the ponytail."

Trevor let out a long breath. He'd been holding it while Rod was talking, and now, by releasing it slowly, it helped mask the disgust he was feeling.

"I've never been a parent, Rod, but it sounds like what you're going through is what most parents go through. Your situation is considerably different of course, and her rebellion has been long delayed. But what you're feeling now are the normal pangs parents go through when their kids become teens. It's been a long time since I practiced psychiatry, but I can recall plenty of patients who went through far more anxiety than you're going through."

Rod's voice had a calmer tone to it now. "I guess. But there are some freedoms I can't grant her. As far as she knows, her parents are dead. I can't tell her who they were because my version of it would be bullshit. I also told her she was in a foster home when she came to me. You and your team did a great job erasing her memories, because she doesn't recall a thing about being snatched off the street. But if she asks me the name of the foster home, I won't be able to tell her that either—because that's all bullshit too."

"You own one of the richest diamond mines on the continent. You're not a poor man, Rod. With your money, you could bribe people and create some backstories if it came to that. Feed her some more bullshit to keep her happy."

"I'm not too comfortable with that. Would involve more people, more lies."

"By now, you should be comfortable with lying."

"Fuck off. I paid you handsomely, and I don't need your editorials."

Trevor laughed, loud enough that Rod would hear the mocking tone.

"You are one piece of work. So, is this all you wanted from me tonight? Just to whine about the perils of aging?"

There was a long pause at the other end of the line. Then, "No, I want a new girl."

"Ah, ha—now we're getting to the point. And what do you want to do with Rachel? Do you want me to extract her?"

"No, no—in my own little way, I love her. She's family and has been for a long time. You may not understand that, but she is. I just think I can allow her role to change now. Let her have a few little freedoms. She could be a nanny for the new girl; keep the house clean, and cook meals as she does now. I just wouldn't be able to— be with her—the same way again. She's tainted now. If I had a new little girl in my life, I could more easily accept Rachel as she now is, I think."

"Okay, I get it. But if you change your mind, we do extractions—we would have to charge you extra."

"What—do you charge for that? And what do you do with them?"

"Five million for an extraction. As for what we do with them, you wouldn't need to know that."

"I see. Well, I don't think I want to go that route. What girls do you have available right now? I'd like someone in that eight-year-old range again, a pretty girl, hair in a ponytail or long enough that I can put it in a ponytail. Doesn't have to be blonde—I can always dye it."

Trevor's throat had gone dry listening to the pervert from the midnight sun. He took a sip of water and restrained himself from yelling at him.

"You do have a fetish for ponytails, don't you? As for length of hair, remember that hair does grow if you let it."

A sigh at the other end. "I'm getting weary of your sarcasm. Can we do business?"

"Yes, we can. The fee would be ten million, and that would give you another ten-year contract with me. Billed to your company, of course, as consultancy services."

"Ten million? I paid you that last time for two girls. This would just be one."

"Inflation, Rod. That was fifteen years ago. As well, there's more risk now than there was back then. Street cams, phone cameras, tablets, more active internet. And enhanced law enforcement focus on sex cults and trafficking. It's more high profile than before."

An indignant voice lashed back. "This isn't a sex cult or trafficking! Don't lump me in with them!"

Trevor was losing his patience. "If you're looking for some kind of redemption for who you are, go talk to a priest. And if you think the category that you're in is more respectable, you need therapy. You're a fucking pedophile. Get used to it. And this will be the third time you'll be a party to kidnapping. News flash—that's life in prison, bud. And for a guy like you, even a day in prison wouldn't be pleasant. You'd be at the very bottom of the social order and probably wouldn't live through your first week. At the very least, you'll end up being the sex toy for someone named Big Hal."

"I'm going to ignore that outburst. Do you have a line-up of photos you can email to me?"

Trevor chuckled to himself. Rod wanted to get on to the juicy part now. He could almost picture him with his dick in his hand just at the mere thought of looking at pictures.

"Yes, they'll be nice photos only, no kiddy porn. So, they'll be safe to send you by email. I won't include a message, and I don't want you to reply in a message. Just phone me back again on your satellite once you've made a decision and we'll conclude the transaction. I'll email the contract to you, and you can arrange for the money transfer. As before, my services will include adoption papers, and new identity documents. As well, two years of hypnotherapy and de-programming—done by me or my associates."

"Will the photos have names under them so I can easily identify my choice to you?"

"No, the photos I send you will be candid photos of the girls, snapped by our bird-dogs. Some of the photos might be from playgrounds, schoolyards, or neighborhood streets. It will simply be a catalogue of those photos, with numbers labelled on each of them. All you have to do is tell me the specific number you like, and we'll take it from there."

"Alright. Sounds like a plan. Email me and I'll get back to you quickly."

Trevor clicked off his satellite phone and poured himself a stiff scotch from a bottle sitting on his desk. His wine was still outside on the balcony, but he felt as if wine wouldn't do the trick now. He needed something stronger.

He sucked the liquid back and winced as it burned its way down his throat.

Got up and strode briskly to the nearest of his four bathrooms, stripping off his clothes along the way.

Brandon Horcroft, aka Trevor Kincaid, needed a shower badly. For some reason, at this very moment, he felt filthy.

Chapter 19

Jeff grabbed his briefcase and the Jeep Cherokee keys, and yelled out to Gaia. "Okay, I'm off, hon. See you tonight."

He heard her footsteps running to him from way back in the kitchen.

"Wait!"

She slid in her stocking feet along the hardwood floor until coming to a gentle stop against his chest.

"You just wanted to give me a kiss goodbye, didn't you?"

She laughed. "Well, yes—but mainly I wanted to check to see which car you were taking."

"The Jeep."

"No, no, you take the Vette. I'm going shopping today so I'll need the Jeep."

Jeff tossed the keys onto the top of the hall cabinet, opened a drawer and pulled out the keys to his sports car. "No problem. I just hate to park the Vette downtown—it always attracts attention."

"You're seeing Dan today?"

"Yep, he's finished his snooping around on those questions we had from our visit to Calgary."

"Do you know anything yet?"

"No, he didn't want to talk over the phone. I'll fill you in tonight."

Gaia kissed his cheek. "Good luck. See ya later. I'll buy some creative things at the grocery store—put my talents to work for a nice meal tonight."

*****

A black Chrysler 300 sedan was parked several doors down from the old Edwardian-style home in The Beaches. Two men were sitting in the front seat. One was smoking a cigarette while the other one fingered through some photos on his lap.

"Yep, we've got the right house. Matches the photo—and I can see the number on the front. This is 40 Lee Avenue. So, we weren't wasting our time yesterday."

His long-haired partner puffed hard on his cigarette. "So, now we wait, again. Another wasted day."

The bearded man sitting in the driver's seat waved his hand in the air. "Shit, open your damn window. I can't breathe."

Long-hair reached over to the driver's side and pushed the ignition button. "Can't open the window with the power off, fool." He then pushed down on his power window button. "There, so quit your whining. You guys who quit are the worst."

"Yep, I admit it. Never used to bother me when I smoked. Now, it's just terrible."

Long-hair tossed his butt out the window. "Okay, I'm done. You can relax. But if we have to wait too long, I'll be lighting up another. Pass me those photos, will ya?"

Beard handed them to him, then opened his own window and turned on the defroster fan to help clear the smoke.

"God, she's beautiful, isn't she? Did you ever find out who wants her?"

Beard shook his head. "No, and it's safer for us if we don't know. Just a paycheck for us—who cares."

Long-hair glared at him. "Don't be so casual. This is kidnapping, so we need to care."

"You know what I mean. For $20,000 I'll do almost anything—but I don't have to know why I'm doing it."

"Did you get the assignment through the usual channel?"

"Yeah, our friendly bar owner. I think he makes more money doing this kind of shit than he makes slinging beer at The Rude Rocker. But good for us, anyway. He has something else for us next week, too—not as big a payday as this one, but around $5,000. A break-in to some home in the west end."

"So, where are we taking this bitch?"

"I've got the address plugged into the satnav. Some storage unit in North York—I have the key. Won't take long to get there this time of day. Not much traffic."

Long-hair continued to stare at the photos. "This is an up-market move for us. We've never snatched anyone before."

Beard laughed. "Christ, how difficult can it be? She's just a little lady. We're big strong Neanderthals. If we pull this first one off, we'll be in demand for a few more. This is probably our biggest payoff yet."

Long-hair took off his sunglasses and rubbed his eyes. "Well, this is the second day we've stalked out this place. All we've seen so far is some guy coming and going in a Vette. No sign of her at all."

"She has to show eventually. Be patient. Light another smoke."

*****

Gaia pulled the Jeep out of the driveway, headed north on Lee Avenue, then turned west on Queen Street. It was a bright sunny day, and being early in the afternoon traffic was light.

Ever the organized shopper, she started planning the night's dinner. It would all depend on what she saw on the shelves, of course. But she was thinking that maybe roast leg of lamb would be nice; one of Jeff's favorites. She'd talk to the butcher, who by now she knew quite well. He always went out of his way to give her the best cuts of everything.

She could feel the smile on her face. Didn't have to look in the rear-view mirror to see it. She was happy today—and most days, for that matter. She was married to her very own hero, someone who had saved her life twice. And while the case they were working on right now was a disturbing one, she knew between her, Jeff, and Dan, they would have it solved.

And she trusted Jeff's intuition that Emily was still alive. Jeff was seldom wrong. And Dan was the ultimate pro. Not only a brilliant investigator, but as a former Mountie he had contacts that were priceless.

The only worry in the back of her mind was that letter Dan had received. He hadn't received a follow-up yet, and in weak moments she naively hoped that it was just a cruel prank. But she knew that was just wishful thinking. There would be more to that story. She'd racked her brain trying to figure out how someone could possibly know about their murder of Brandon Horcroft. And if that person had evidence, what did he, or she, intend to do with it?

She sighed and shook the disturbing thoughts out of her head. More important things to do today. Shopping, cooking, and then maybe some much-needed time in bed with Jeff after a couple of glasses of wine.

Her smile suddenly felt wider than ever as she started singing the lyrics to one of her favorite old tunes: "On days like these, when skies are blue and fields are green…"

Gaia pulled into the parking lot and parked in a spot along an empty row near the back. She hated being squeezed in between cars and didn't mind the extra minute it took to walk to the store entrance.

She was just about to open her door when a large black car pulled in beside her. Shook her head in annoyance.

With all the spots along this row, they had to choose that one!

She was tempted to back out and find another spot, but decided against it.

She forced a smile and nodded to the long-haired man in the passenger seat, indicating to him that he could exit first. He smiled and raised his hand, giving her a thumbs-up.

Gaia waited patiently while he got out and closed the door. At the same time, she noticed a bearded man getting out on the driver's side.

She sighed in frustration, grabbed her purse and got out of the Jeep. Clicked the fob to lock the doors, then stuffed it into her purse.

The two men had their trunk open and were fiddling with something. She walked past them and headed towards the store.

Suddenly her happy day took a wrong turn.

Grabbed from behind, an arm around her waist and a hand over her mouth. He was dragging her backwards.

The panic she felt accomplished three things. First—her heart was racing so fast that she thought she might faint. The second thing was the adrenaline rush, which she knew if she harnessed it, might work in her favor.

The third thing was the instant recollection of the training in martial arts that Dan had forced Gaia and Jeff to endure over the last two years. Intensive, painful, and conducted with total immersion for a couple of hours every single day.

As she was being dragged backwards, thoughts pulsed through her brain, not the least of which was self-recrimination for not being more alert. She should have been on her guard once these guys parked right next to her in an empty row. And she shouldn't have put her key fob back in her purse. No time to search for it now, but if it had still been in her hand she could have pushed the panic alarm.

The bearded man now appeared right in front of her, making a pushing motion in the air with his hand. "Hurry up, pull her back!"

"I'm trying, but she's heavier than I thought! And she keeps kicking! Grab her legs for me!"

Gaia knew that her chance would be gone if she allowed the guy in front to hold her legs.

Now or never.

She lashed out with her right arm, locked at the elbow, and crashed her flat palm into the nose of the bearded man in front. He screamed in pain, and fell backwards.

Gaia then planted her feet firmly on the pavement and brought both arms up over her head, clasping her hands behind the neck of the assailant behind her. She bent over as far as she could, pulling him with her. He was far heavier than she was, but the sudden motion and leverage made the move effortless.

Long-haired man flew over Gaia and landed on top of his partner who was still struggling on the ground with a grotesquely mashed-in nose.

She was free. Gaia ran, as fast as her legs would carry her. Focused her attention on the front of the store, and willed herself inside. Started yelling and screaming, even though right now there didn't seem to be anyone else in the parking lot.

She thought she was going to make it.

It wasn't far to go.

But suddenly it was. Airborne, thrust forward by a painful unseen force to the back of her head.

Gaia fell face down on the ground, and was only vaguely aware of being lifted into the air by two strong hands. Far too groggy and dazed to fight, she went limp.

Then she was tossed. Landed on a carpeted surface. She was vaguely aware that the sun was still shining. But along with her freedom, it too disappeared with the sickening sound of a heavy clunk.

Darkness enveloped her in waves. Spotty flashes of black at first, but as the seconds ticked away the waves lasted longer. A persistent dizziness that forced her to gag. Waves of nausea until she vomited.

Finally, Gaia Kavanaugh just closed her eyes and surrendered to the blackness.

Chapter 20

They met in the Venetian Room of the Royal York Hotel. A restaurant with the kind of classy refined décor one would expect in a hotel of that stature.

Dan ordered the poached salmon and Jeff contented himself with a Cobb salad.

"Just a salad? I'm surprised—you're usually a big eater."

Jeff rubbed his tummy.

"Too much meat lately, and I have the feeling that Gaia's going to cook me some more tonight. So, I'd better save room or she'll have a fit. In fact, she's out shopping right now."

Dan studied his younger friend. They'd had quite the history over the last three years. Considering how they'd met, he never could have guessed that they would become such close friends and eventually partners in business.

At one time Dan had Jeff under the threat of arrest for manslaughter, and used that charge to coerce him into being his "inside man" at Price, Spencer, and Williams.

Dan had been an Inspector with the RCMP's Organized Crime Division then, and was accustomed to using whatever and whomever to "get his man."

Jeff had been a brave and willing participant in Dan's attempt to bust wide open the insider trading and commanded suicides that

Brandon Horcroft had orchestrated at his headhunting firm.

The investigation finally culminated in Jeff obtaining photos of incriminating documents from Brandon's office vault. Documents that disclosed much more than even Dan had anticipated.

And in gallant fashion, Dan had brought down the hammer. Idealistic as always, he thought his superiors would have been ecstatic at what he'd uncovered in his investigation.

A monster would be brought to justice.

Alas, it wasn't to be.

Dan discovered that day the world was a far larger place than he ever knew. And more of a tangled web than even someone like him with a master's degree in criminology could have guessed.

He was ordered to drop the case, to leave Brandon Horcroft alone.

Apparently, even to the horror of his superiors at the RCMP, Brandon Horcroft was a CIA asset. An agent working on Canadian soil, but performing psychological tasks for the Agency around the world. A "mind-fucker," as one of his bosses had told him.

Dan and Jeff had already discovered from the documents Jeff recovered from the vault that the man had been making millions on the side by performing assignments for the CIA, and even the FBI. Nefarious hypnosis, and training in interrogation techniques.

But the insider trading and murders were different stories entirely, and Dan had counted on arrests and convictions on those crimes being slam-dunks.

The CIA and the top brass at the RCMP thought differently.

Out of professional courtesy, the RCMP was convinced by the CIA to simply bury it. No prosecution. The embarrassment to both countries would be severe, as well as taking several notches out of the national security umbrella.

Best to let sleeping dogs lie.

The RCMP demanded Dan's cooperation—and silence.

But they did extract a promise from the CIA to whisk Brandon out of Canada, and have him work from their headquarters in Langley, Virginia. He wouldn't be allowed back into the country, and his corrupt division at Price, Spencer and Williams would be dismantled.

Those were small and weak trade-offs as far as Dan was concerned. Justice would not be served in the least, and a monster would be allowed to roam free and continue his twisted and deadly deeds.

Dan couldn't live with his newfound cynicism. So, he resigned from the RCMP and joined up with Jeff and Gaia.

As for the CIA, well, they never did get to whisk their man Brandon back down to Virginia. Because, Brandon died before he could make the flight.

No doubt, the CIA were still puzzled to this day as to what had happened to him.

But maybe not.

Dan figured CIA agents probably disappeared all the time. Just another Wednesday.

He snapped out of his daydream at the tinkling sound of Jeff's fork against his wine glass.

"Hey, bud, you were off in space somewhere. You okay?"

Dan laughed.

"Yeah, I'm fine. I was watching you eat that wimpy salad, and started thinking back to how we met and all that's transpired since then. One of us is gonna have to write a book one day."

"Isn't that the truth? At one time I was your prisoner, threatened with five-to-ten years, and now I'm your partner. Life is strange sometimes, isn't it?"

Dan held up his wine glass and they toasted.

"You're more than my partner, Jeff, you're also my friend—both you and Gaia."

"Do you miss the RCMP, Dan?"

He shook his head. "No, not at all. Well—let me correct that. I miss the way it used to be. You and I got into something way over our pay grades, which exposed the corrupt underbelly. When politics gets in the way of justice, it leaves a bad taste.

"So, with what happened in the Horcroft case, I had no choice but to leave. I'd never believe in law enforcement the same way again, or put my heart and soul into an investigation like I used to be able to do.

"I feel better being on the outside, and between you and me, what we did to Brandon was what I call true justice. That's what that prick deserved and society is better off with him dead. I could never have admitted that before while I was on the force—not to anyone."

Jeff grimaced. "I know what you mean, I think. You're a criminologist and were one of only four hundred inspectors in the Mounties. Kind of like a sacred calling. And to have your bubble burst like that is a kick in the gut.

"It's similar for me in some ways—having a doctorate in psychology and then discovering how for some, that same reverent skill was being used and abused for profit, espionage, and murder, was hard to stomach."

Dan nodded slowly. "Yep, it's the same for both of us. I guess we're idealists, and I think that's a good thing. We best hold onto that."

"Is your family glad that you're off the force?"

"Caroline is thrilled. And Wade and Marilyn, luckily, are still pretty young, so they have some sense of the danger I faced in my job—but only a small sense. I think what they like most of all is that I'm home more now.

"All three do remember, though, that time I was pushed onto the subway tracks. I would have kept that from them, but it ended up being all over the news. That memory will stay with them, and me, forever.

"Despite the many gun episodes, I'd been involved in throughout my career, that incident was the closest I ever came to losing my life."

Dan motioned to the waiter, and he hurried over with the bill. Jeff drained the rest of his wine while his partner paid the tab.

"Okay, Dan, we've talked about everything today except what we were supposed to be talking about. Come clean, partner, what did you find out?"

Dan stood. "Come. Let's walk."

They crossed to the south side of Front Street, waited for the light to change at Yonge, and strolled past the Sony Centre for the Performing Arts.

Then east along Front Street for a bit until they came within sight of the Hockey Hall of Fame. Both stopped at the same time and gazed over at it in reverence.

Dan motioned towards a bench and they sat down.

"Okay, here goes. That Aaron Dixon guy is indeed a high school teacher—a rather respected one—and a successful football coach. His team has won two successive championships. Makes about $90,000 a year.

"His wife, Sherry, has a master's in early childhood education. A recognized expert in Western Canada, all four provinces. She helps day care centers get established, counsels them on tactics and techniques, and even works sometimes giving counseling and coaching to troubled children in day care centers and foster homes. She's self-employed and pulls in about $150,000 a year.

"Their house at 207 Hunter Lane is indeed mortgage free, and the estimated market value is around $2.2 million."

Jeff shook his head. "Doesn't make sense, does it?"

"No, it doesn't. And the bank accounts we were able to track down don't have a lot in them. So, we think there are others—

possibly offshore.

"And this will knock you for a loop. Brace yourself. The company that they bought their house from is a private equity firm called Trend Capital. That company did indeed foreclose on the home before Emily disappeared and remained as the registered owner for that entire fourteen years until Aaron and Sherry bought the house a year ago. After that purchase, Trend Capital folded its operations. It no longer exists."

Jeff interrupted. "So what? None of that tells me anything."

Dan smiled at his younger friend. "Control your impatience, bud. I'm not finished. The registered officers, and the *only* officers of Trend Capital, were Aaron and Sherry Dixon."

Jeff's eyes looked like they were on fire, and his mouth hung open for a good five seconds.

He found his voice. "They bought the house from themselves!"

"Yes."

"Which means they in effect owned the house at the time Emily disappeared! At the time the bike was buried in the backyard!"

"Yep."

Jeff shook his head in dismay. "Jesus Christ, this is unbelievable."

"Let me carry on. Aaron told you he never owned a blue van. Well, technically, he didn't. But Trend Capital did. At the time of Emily's disappearance, the corporation owned a blue Ford Econoline van. It was sold shortly afterwards.

"But interestingly, prior to her kidnapping, and *after* her kidnapping, numerous vehicles have been owned and sold by that company—all vans."

Dan watched as his friend angrily rubbed his forehead with his knuckles, anguish spreading across his handsome face.

"Geez, Dan, I don't know what to say. I feel like getting on a plane and flying back out to Calgary. Today. With my gun."

Dan held out his hand. "Calm down, one step at a time. We don't want to spook anyone. I need to tell you a bit more. We got a list of all the day care centers and foster homes that Sherry has worked with over the years since she's been a counsellor.

"There were a lot of facilities, spread across four provinces, so for anyone not on the lookout for a common denominator or willing to follow the crumbs, it wouldn't be noticed. But over a period of eighteen years, a dozen children who attended these places have vanished without a trace. That's statistically significant, only because the common denominator in those twelve disappearances was Sherry Dixon."

Jeff was leaning over now, head resting in his hands. "You've uncovered a lot. This is shocking stuff. What the hell have we stumbled onto here?"

Dan shook his head. "All the credit goes to my contacts. Some retired, some still active. It's amazing what can be dug up. And they've only just started. We'll find out more, for sure. These people of mine are from a different world, Jeff. Thank God they're on our side. Hacking is so prevalent these days, and the bad guys are darn good at it. But the good guys, thankfully, are at least as good if not better."

He jumped to his feet. "Come on, let's walk a bit more. I have more to tell you, and something to show you."

They strolled side by side further east along Front Street, to an area where there were some luxurious apartment buildings on the north side.

Dan slid his fingers through his thick blonde hair, attempting to stream away some of the sweat. Another hot humid day in Toronto.

He continued his story.

"It's amazing how many people still use email for sensitive things, thinking it's safe. It's certainly safer than texting or regular post, but not by much.

"We've watched all these government scandals unfold in the news, where national security issues were right out there in the open on email, easily stolen by anyone who knew what they were doing.

"It boggles the mind how freely the medium is used. But that's a good thing when we want to catch bad guys.

"My folks were able to track down an email address for Aaron. And from the same IP address there are several more email addresses, but they're having troubles accessing them. Something about encryption—don't ask, it's all Greek to me. But they're still working on it.

"They recovered several emails that Aaron had sent from that one unencrypted address. Most of it just social stuff—about friends meeting for drinks, or school stuff like class schedules, football practices—stuff like that.

"But there was one strange one that raised a bit of a red flag.

"Aaron sent a brief email to a man here in Toronto. All it said was—'Waiting for orders. Did you get my itinerary?' A reply came back from this man, which simply said—'Wrong mode. Use our agreed method.'

'So, the reply seemed like kind of a reprimand. Basically, he told him not to communicate that way. Which adds credence to the other encrypted email addresses that our hackers are trying to access. And this man who was the recipient also has several locked-up email addresses of his own at his IP address. My guys are digging into those too.

"It seems as if Aaron slipped up and used his regular email address instead of one of the other ones, and sent it to an address he shouldn't have sent it to. The man in Toronto directed him back to the way he should have communicated—via some other address, and *to* some other address."

Jeff suddenly grabbed Dan's arm. "Who the fuck is this guy here in Toronto?"

Dan wrapped his arm around Jeff's shoulders and pulled him along as he walked.

"Just a few more steps."

They walked in silence for another minute. Then Dan stopped, donned his sunglasses, and pointed across the street at an opulent yellow-brick high-rise.

"See that building?"

Jeff shielded his eyes with his hands. Even though he was looking north, the sun reflected brightly back at him from the massive amounts of glass and light brick walls.

"Do you want my opinion? Are you thinking of buying?"

Dan chuckled. "Well, if I had a few million I might consider it."

He raised his hand and pointed his index finger at the top of the building.

"That's where he lives—up there in that twentieth-floor penthouse.

"The man's name is Trevor Kincaid."

Chapter 21

Before even opening her eyes her nostrils picked up the acrid smell of vomit. It was overpowering, and in an enclosed space like she was in, it was enough to make her want to black out again.

It only took her a couple of seconds to realize she was in the trunk of a car, a car that she could tell was moving at a rapid clip. But the ride was smooth—either because the car was relatively new, or they were on a highway. Gaia figured both.

And they'd want to get her out of the city fast, so they'd be heading north. If she hadn't been unconscious for too long they were probably still on the Don Valley Parkway.

She glanced at her luminescent watch. It was only two, she was glad to see. Only unconscious for about fifteen minutes or so.

Her eyes began adjusting to the darkness. The trunk was huge, thankfully, so she could kind of sit up if she kept her head down.

Slid her hands around the side of the trunk and found the button she was looking for. Pushed on it and a lid opened. Gaia felt around inside, bypassing the hydraulic jack and pulled on what she wanted—a thin metal pole thing with a lipped edge. A tire iron. She didn't know what she was going to do with it, but at least it was some kind of weapon.

She'd made a quick move with her head when pulling the tire iron out of the compartment and the sudden bolts of pain reminded her of the hit she'd taken in the parking lot. Didn't know whether they'd used a fist or an object, but the impact had been crushing, whatever the hell it was. Reached her hand around and gently slid her fingers across the back of her head. Yep, a big welt had come up.

The next thing she did was move her hands around the floor of the trunk, searching for her purse. Nowhere to be found. Must still be lying in the parking lot—with her phone inside.

What her fingers did find, though, was a pile of vomit. Gaia shuddered, and rubbed her hand against her sweat shirt only to find more vomit.

She knew she was in serious trouble. Those two guys had targeted her in the parking lot, and she didn't want to think too hard about what they planned to do with her. It was clear to her what their plans were, but she shoved that thought out of her mind.

Gaia rubbed her eyes and rested her head back against the rear wall of the trunk. Stared into the darkness. Suddenly it seemed darker than before, which was strange.

Then she realized her eyes were filled with tears. Pulled at her eyelids and swept the back of her vomit-smeared hand across them. *There, that's better.*

Her mind was working fast now. She couldn't afford to wait until they arrived at their destination. Being a victim in surroundings she had no control over was a death sentence. Her only realistic goal was to do something while they were still near civilization—where she'd be seen, where someone might be able to help, phone the police.

Gaia was certain that this car was fairly new. She didn't get a good look at it in the parking lot, but she knew it was big and shiny, and the carpeting in the trunk was smooth, higher grade, and in pristine shape—except for the vomit.

Suddenly it hit her!

If this was a newer model car, under Canadian law it would be required to have a nice little safety feature!

She felt excitement rushing through her veins. Faint hope excitement.

Gaia stared hard at the spot where she knew the thing would be, right in the middle of the trunk lid. And it would have some luminescence to it, just like her watch.

She focused in the darkness on that one spot.

Sure enough, there it was—hanging down, a little yellowish handle. A trunk safety release latch.

Reached forward and fingered it. Didn't want to pull it just yet. Had to think this through for a few seconds. But only a few, because there were very few seconds to spare.

Gaia knew that the instant she pulled it, the trunk would open wide. Or, she could control it so it only opened partway. That would allow her to stick her feet or hands out and signal for help. But some people driving along might just think it was some kind of prank, or teenagers horsing around trying to harass other drivers.

And no matter how far the trunk opened, she couldn't keep it a secret from the two men in the front anyway. If she only opened it a bit, they might not see in the rear-view mirror that it was open—but the indicator light would come on in the dashboard even if the trunk was open just a wee bit. And if she opened it just a bit, they might just pull over and drag her into the back seat before any other drivers could react.

No, Gaia knew she had to go for broke. Maximum effect. At least other drivers would see that she was a woman being held captive in a trunk, and not some kids horsing around. And she could make motions with her hands, yell out for help.

Yes, the trunk lid had to open all the way, which would serve to also block the view behind. If another car decided to follow them to help, the thugs wouldn't even see them. They'd be blind to the activity behind.

Gaia's heart was pumping fast. The stakes were high. It was do or die, and if she didn't use the element of surprise in her favor now while she was still in the trunk, she knew that in all likelihood she'd never get another chance.

Knowing also that the chances were high that this might be the last day of her life.

Chapter 22

Paul glanced over at Hillary and squeezed her knee. She removed her earphones and smiled.

"No, Paul, I'm not going to give you a blowjob in a moving car. We've been through this before."

"Ha, ha—wasn't on my mind at all. I just felt like squeezing that cute little knee of yours."

He glanced out his side driver's window at the bright red F-150 in the next lane over. Gave the driver and passenger a thumbs-up. "Plus, your brother and Casey are right next to us. They might get suspicious if your head suddenly disappeared from view."

"Okay, dear husband, I believe your sincerity. But I don't think Kurt would raise a fuss anyway. The two of you have become such good friends he'd probably just give you a pass."

Paul laughed and jokingly reached a hand down to his zipper. "Okay, let's get on with this, then."

Hillary slapped his shoulder. "Later! When we have the tent pitched."

"Okay, it's a deal. For that reason alone, I'm glad Kurt and Casey have their own tent."

Hillary sighed. "This is so nice. Every year we do this little camping adventure with them. It's become such a nice tradition. Great that the four of us get along so well, eh? It's not that way with most families we know."

"It is nice. Always so much fun. And this will be the first time we'll have camped up in Muskoka. Should be great. The lakes are so beautiful there."

"So, bore me again with the route we'll be taking?"

"Yes, dear, but your eyes will just glaze over anyway, regardless of how scenic I make it sound. So, I'll keep it simple—once we get off this damn Don Valley Parkway, we'll go west on the 401, then north on 400."

She frowned at him. "We've done that 400 before. You and Kurt aren't going to drag race again, are you?"

Paul chuckled. "We might. Kind of a tradition. He thinks his F-150 can beat my Tundra. He always has to learn the hard way—never edged my truck yet. But if your brother is a glutton for punishment, I'll be pleased to dole it out."

Hillary yawned. "Wake me when we get there."

"Holy fucking Christ!"

In reaction to Paul's outburst, Hillary lurched up in her seat, braced her hands against the glove compartment, and looked over at her husband. "What! What's wrong?"

Paul pointed through the window. "Look!"

The trunk of the big black car in front of them was wide open, bouncing up and down. And kneeling close to the edge was a woman, waving her arms back and forth. Screaming something. From her lips, it looked like she was yelling "Help!"

Hillary brought her hands up to her mouth. "Oh—my—God!"

Paul powered down his window. Casey did the same in the adjacent lane.

He pointed again. "See that?"

She nodded, and leaned her head back while Kurt called out to Paul from the driver's seat. "She's in trouble! What do you want to do?"

Paul's eyes darted back and forth between the road, his friends, and back again, as he yelled over the noise of their trucks. "Unless this is a joke—and she doesn't look like that kind of woman—I think those assholes snatched her. Drive up, and I'll move over into your lane, right behind you. I don't want to be behind that sedan in case she falls out of the trunk. See if you can get beside this prick and motion for him to pull over. We'll stay behind and see if we can talk to her."

Kurt nodded. "Will do."

Paul glanced over at Hillary, just about to tell her to phone the police. But she already had her phone in hand, barking out where they were on the DVP.

Kurt sped up, and pulled parallel to the black sedan. Casey was waving at the driver with her hand and yelling. A bearded face leaned out the window of the black sedan and gestured, his fingers formed in the shape of a cocked pistol. Kurt immediately put on the brakes and eased back from his position.

Suddenly the black car sped up, causing the woman in the trunk to almost tumble out. In response, Paul rammed his foot down on the accelerator and brought his truck up close enough so that Hillary could talk to her.

She yelled. "Don't jump out! You'll be killed at this speed!"

The beautiful lady in the trunk edged closer to the side. Screamed something, but they couldn't hear her.

Paul reached out and grabbed his wife by the shoulder. "She's going to jump out, I know it. Can see the panic in her eyes. I have an idea. We need to give her a cushion."

Hillary's eyes opened wide. "Yes, yes! The inflatable sleeping pads! But they're in the truck bed."

"I have that power rear window in the back. If I roll that down, could you crawl back into the bed, and toss them to her?"

Hillary shook her head. "I could try, Paul, but you know I'm a lousy thrower. I don't have the power."

"Alright, I'll do it. Shift over here onto my lap and I'll slide under you. Take over the wheel, but you'll have to be aggressive. If they speed up, you'll have to speed up. Keep the bed of the truck as close as possible beside the rear of that car. Okay?"

She nodded. "Let's do it. Oh, that poor girl."

They executed their transfer at lightning speed. Hillary was now at the wheel, and Paul crawled into the back portion of the cab. "Push the rear window button, Hillary!"

Down it slid. Paul was glad he was skinny. He knew he was just going to make it through.

Tumbled down onto the floor of the bed and quickly scrambled to his feet. Rummaged through their camping stuff, and dragged out the two bags containing the self-inflatable sleeping mats. He moved over to the side of the truck bed and held one of the bags up above his head to show the girl in the trunk. She was watching his every move, and nodded eagerly. Held her hands out in front of her ready to make the catch.

Suddenly the black car swerved into their lane, smashing into the front side of the Tundra.

Hillary swerved to avoid an all-out collision.

Paul took the brunt.

Lost his balance and fell over the side of the truck bed. Just managed to drop the bag back into the truck while stretching his hands out in desperation for the side.

He grabbed hold of the bed rim with one hand while his body slammed against the outside of the truck frame, both feet dragging along the pavement.

Paul shoved the feeling of panic out of his brain and reached his other hand up to the rim. Then, mustering all of his strength, hoisted himself back into the truck bed.

He fell down on his ass and took a few seconds to catch his

breath. Then, Paul forced himself to his feet once again, silently praying that they would have the luxury of just a few seconds of steadiness. But he knew he would have to be fast. These guys weren't fooling around.

Hillary had managed to pull the truck back up far enough in the lane that he was now within throwing range. It would have to be a three-point basket, but Paul had always been good at basketball. Since he was in the adjacent lane, it would be as challenging as a side court shot.

He raised the bag to chest level and stared into the eyes of the terrified woman in the trunk. She stared right back and nodded her head.

He threw it. She caught it. Not even a bobble.

Paul quickly reached down and grabbed the other bag. Hillary had managed to move the truck closer now, so this time it was only a two-pointer.

Paul took the shot of his life, one that would rival any tie-breaking foul shot.

Threw it with all of his might at the woman who looked like a super-model, kneeling in the trunk of a speeding Chrysler 300.

She caught that one too. Made it look easy. Gave him a triumphant thumbs-up.

Before Paul slithered back in through the rear window, it occurred to him that nothing, in hopefully the many years still ahead of him, could possibly be more surreal than this.

Chapter 23

Gaia moved now as if her life depended on it. And intuition told her it did.

She was amazed at the courage and caring of the couples in the two trucks. They didn't hesitate to help her. She could tell that they were around her age so maybe it was a devil-may-care thing about their common age group.

But her heart sank as the man in the Raptors ball cap fell over the side of his truck. Concerned for him, not for her possible loss of a hero. She thought he was a goner.

But he proved to be as athletic as he looked, and she was close enough to see the fierce determination on his face. He hoisted himself back up and into the truck with what seemed like very little effort. But if he hadn't reached out that one hand to grab the rim of the truck when he was falling, that would have been the end of him.

She looked back at the traffic in the lane behind her. It was apparent that they had been watching the drama unfold, because all of the other cars on the parkway were maintaining a safe distance behind. She had clearance of what looked like at least thirty car lengths. It would have to do.

Her hands moved fast. Pulled both sleeping mats out of their bags and spread them out as best as she could in the confined space of the trunk. Then opened the valves.

She knew how these things worked. No batteries or air pumps needed. The foam inside, when unfolded and released from its compressed state, expanded and sucked in oxygen once the valves were opened. Jeff and Gaia had a couple of these mats at home for the occasional camping trips they took. Great for camping, but she wasn't so sure about sliding on asphalt.

Within seconds the mats were inflated—but at their max, they were only about two inches thick. So, two were definitely better than one.

*****

"What the fuck are we going to do? God, that little lady is not only a fighter, she's a daredevil."

Beard glared at his long-haired partner, while using one of his hands to shift his broken nose back into position. "Hey, you stole this car. You didn't think to check if it had a safety trunk release?"

"Fuck off. You didn't think of it either."

"Now they have those two trucks helping them. What a pain in the ass. And I can't see behind us anymore because of that damn trunk lid, but in the side view mirror I saw that asshole throwing a couple of bags to her. Don't know what's going on there."

Long-hair shook his head and cursed a word that Beard had never heard before.

"We should cut our losses and get the hell away from here as fast as possible. Someone's called the police by now."

Beard turned his head and yelled at him. "No! We're not missing out on this payday."

"She's going to jump out of that trunk! There won't be a payday!"

"Nope, she won't jump. She'll be killed at this speed, and soon I'm going to kick this thing up even faster. She can stay back there with the trunk open for a nice view, but that's all she's gonna get out of her stunt."

"Go faster *now*, then! What the fuck are you waiting for?"

"Once we hit the 401 this thing's gonna race. Those trucks won't be able to keep up to us. The exit's just up ahead. Once we take that, we're home free. We'll put some miles between us and everyone else on the open highway, and then take a couple of sneaky turnoffs until we find a safe quiet spot to pull over. Change cars. And when we do, we'll beat the shit out of that bitch, maybe also have a little fun with her to teach her a lesson, then throw her in the backseat this time."

Long-hair shook his head. "We might not get paid if we don't turn her over in good condition. I don't like what you're saying."

"Okay, okay, maybe I'm just gabbing away because I'm so pissed." Beard then pointed. "Exit's coming up. Our luck will change now."

*****

Gaia tied the two mats together—on top of each other—with the long tie ropes attached to the ends of each. This would give her about four inches of cushion when she hit the pavement.

Then she slid the bottom mat back and forth across the carpet of the trunk, trying to get the large pool of vomit lathered against it to reduce friction. That bottom mat would be the one riding along the road, and she knew that for a few horrible seconds the forward motion of the vehicle she'd be jumping out of would carry her in the same direction at close to the same speed as the car itself. Too much friction would disintegrate the mat in no time.

Gaia carefully slid herself to the edge of the trunk, with the lower half of her legs hanging outside. She then fingered the open ends of the rope through the lock latch on the floor of the trunk. Pulled the mats underneath her and grabbed the tire iron, being careful to hold it sideways with both hands, while her fingers clasped the ends of the rope.

Gaia shoved the mats underneath as far as she could, in an effort to protect the entire length of her body. Then she laid face down, ready to make the final shove backwards.

But she decided to wait just a few moments longer. Waiting for an opportunity that might present itself in the next couple of seconds.

She'd noticed a highway sign announcing the exit to the 401 when she leaned her head around the outside of the trunk. If these creeps intended to make serious distance and serious speed, they would take that exit. Which would mean the car would have to slow down slightly as they rounded the exit. Any reduction in speed, even if small, would augur heavily in Gaia's prospects for survival. It was worth the wait just to see if that was their plan.

*****

Hillary's hands seemed permanently planted against her mouth. They'd switched places again and Paul was once more behind the wheel.

"Oh, Paul, what's she doing? Hanging over the edge on those mats, but not making a move at all. Has she changed her mind?"

Paul glanced over his shoulder to check the traffic in the adjacent lane. He was happy to see that it was clear—all drivers were probably shocked at what they were watching, and were giving the woman in the trunk a clear berth.

He looked over at Kurt and Casey in the next lane. Rolled down his window and yelled over to them.

"We'll just keep pace to help her once she's free, and maybe run those pricks off the road. You guys game?"

Four thumbs up.

He turned his attention back to the lady in the trunk. Suddenly Paul knew why she was hanging there, waiting. It was as clear as day to him now.

The big black car was veering towards the exit ramp for Highway 401, at a noticeable reduction in speed.

"Oh my God, Hillary, that's one cool woman. She was waiting for the exit ramp."

Hillary suddenly pointed and screamed. "Oh, no, there she goes! Holy fuck, Paul!"

Chapter 24

Paul's eyes were fixed on the girl in the trunk. "No, look, she's stopped moving again. Tugging at something."

He glanced over at his pretty wife. "Hillary, when this goes down, are you okay with us chasing these thugs? They're going to make a run for it, and I don't think we can let them get away with this."

Hillary gulped, and went silent for a few seconds.

Then, "Yes, Paul, let's get them. That poor woman, I can't imagine being in her spot. And I would hope that people like us would fight back against this shit."

Paul nodded, then shouted across to the truck next to him.

"Guys, she's going to slide out of there very soon. When she does, we're going to race ahead and stop these fuckers. My truck's heavier than yours, so it'll be a better weapon. When we move up, slide in behind us and once it's safe, pull in to that far right lane and put on the brakes. Stop traffic so she doesn't get run over."

Kurt and Casey both nodded. Casey yelled back. "Go get 'em!"

*****

Beard tapped the brakes as he started veering onto the exit ramp, and the sedan began a gradual slowdown from its breakneck speed.

Long-hair glared at him. "Why are you slowing down? She'll jump!"

"I have to slow down, you fool. This ramp is a semi-circle. We'll flip otherwise. It will only be for a few seconds, then we'll be hitting the open highway at top speed."

"She'll only need a few seconds. This is crazy."

Long-hair glanced into the back seat, then slapped his forehead in exasperation.

"Shit, those back seats have flaps! That means they fold forward! There should be a crawl space I can squeeze through and grab her."

Beard shook his head in dismay.

"Good call. Jesus, it's easy to tell we're not experienced at this snatching stuff. Go get her."

*****

Gaia was almost in position. She started pulling the rope through the lock latch, trying to give herself enough slack that she could gradually let out to ease her down onto the pavement. She'd calculated that a sudden drop to the ground would probably prove fatal.

Suddenly the rope stopped sliding.

A knot!

She quickly pulled it back out again, and frantically worked her fingers on the knot.

Cursed to herself as she felt the car start to slow down. It was entering the exit ramp as she'd predicted it would, and now here she was wasting time undoing a knot.

Finally, the knot gave up its fight. She slid the rope through the latch once again, much faster this time. The car had now slowed down quite noticeably, and the next few seconds would be the optimum time to make her exit.

She stretched her legs back over the edge of the trunk and pushed the mats underneath her once again, to make sure they were down as far as they would go.

Suddenly the seatbacks folded down!

The thug with the long hair was crawling into her space through the narrow access opening, a wicked smile of triumph on his face.

He slithered through the opening, arms outstretched. "C'mon little lady, you don't want to do that. You're gonna kill yourself."

At that moment fear and anger combined together in a complicated cocktail, a mixture designed to confuse Gaia's mind. The fear made her want to freeze, but the anger made her want to lash out.

She fought back against that familiar feeling of nausea in her gut, and in its place summoned up a rage that had been suppressed by the fear.

The anger won.

She snarled in a voice that sounded foreign, one she'd never heard come out of her mouth before.

"You fucker! You're gonna wish you'd never crawled in here!"

She let go of the rope ends with her right hand and slid the tire iron out from between the sleeping mats.

Pulled her arm back and jammed it forward like a spear, directly into the face of the ugly looking creep who was now only inches away from her.

Even though Gaia had no time for slow-motion, that's exactly how it played out in front of her.

The smug look on the man's face, replaced quickly by one of abject horror and shock.

She was surprised by her own strength, but in an instant, she remembered the martial arts training that Dan had drummed into her.

And one particular phrase he'd used when he was encouraging her to find the courage to smash her hand down on top of three stacked pieces of wood.

"Gaia, people don't realize that in martial arts the vast majority of the

strength of impact comes from the abdomen. Discipline of the mind and summoning that strength, is what allows students to break boards and bricks with relative ease."

Once Gaia had managed to chase away that pesky feeling of nausea, she'd automatically summoned the strength from her abdomen. It just happened all by itself.

That training from Dan, recalled in her brain, had accomplished muscle memory, and it worked at this moment exactly the way his training had intended.

The tire iron made impact with the man's forehead, just above his nose.

The force of the impact was so powerful and severe that the tire iron didn't stop there. It went straight through his skull, his brain, and out through the back of his head.

Long-hair's eyes flared wide as he gazed at her for just a second or two—although at that point, probably no longer capable of seeing a damn thing.

The man's hands and arms went limp as his head collapsed down toward the floor of the trunk. Finally coming to a stop—braced upward at a macabre angle by the tire iron.

*****

Hillary thrust her hands over her eyes. "I don't believe this! Did you see that?"

Paul swallowed hard and spoke in a softer voice than he ever thought he'd be capable of.

"Yep, I did. I don't believe it either. This has turned into a horror movie."

One eye on the road and the other on the trunk of the sedan, he watched the super-model wipe the blood splatters and some slimy white stuff onto her sweat shirt.

As the car continued to slow down, turning onto the exit ramp,

163

the man's head, now impaled with some kind of pole, was bouncing up and down in a macabre kind of dance.

The girl didn't seem to care.

She made some last-second adjustments to the rope, then turned her head to the left and seemed to stare right into Paul's eyes. She nodded and gave him a thumbs-up.

For a crazily insane instant, Paul pondered that he might like to have a beer with that girl when all this was over.

He yelled over to his friends. "Okay, she's gonna do it! I'll move up, and you guys move over!"

*****

Gaia ignored the mess in front of her, and concentrated now on what she had to do. The car had slowed down quite a bit as it moved into the stark curve of the exit ramp onto Highway 401.

But she knew that the driver might decide in an instant to become more reckless and kick the speed up again. She didn't know whether or not he'd looked back yet. If not, he wouldn't know what had happened to his friend. But once he did, and he saw the tire iron coming out of the back of the man's head, she figured he'd step on the accelerator.

Had to move fast. She glanced over at the truck next to her, nodded her head and gave them the thumbs-up sign.

Pushing herself back as far as the rope allowed, she let out some of the slack. Gaia slid down a few more inches and let out some more slack. Now the toes of her sneakers were bumping along the pavement and she could hear the dual sleeping mats swishing against the asphalt.

Suddenly the car started to accelerate. He must have seen his dead friend.

No time to waste now. Gaia took a deep breath and held it. Then let it out through her nose. Pushed her hands underneath the top mat and pulled it up around her forehead.

Now or never. Her fingers unclasped, allowing the rope to slip through unhindered. She heard it singing in the air almost like the sound of fishing line being cast.

The mats pounded the surface of the asphalt and bounced a couple of times as they continued sliding forward at the same speed of the vehicle they had just left. Gaia closed her eyes and pulled the mat up tighter around her face.

She couldn't see—didn't want to see. Just wanted to feel herself coming to a stop, and it seemed as if that would never happen.

Started sliding sideways now and Gaia could sense that the lower mat was gone. The ride was rougher and less cushioned. She didn't dare look.

Too much of a sideways slide. She knew there wasn't that much room in the lane for her to slide too far. Allowed herself a quick glance as the guardrail was looming.

No choice. Gaia lurched herself off the mat and let it continue on without her. A second later it slid under the rail, out of sight.

The body refused to obey her will. It went in the same direction as the mat. Forward and sideways motion were forces that couldn't be stopped despite her strong will.

She was tumbling now, and sensed that she was also bouncing. Pulled her arms back over her head and waited for the impact. They were on the bridge of the ramp so the fall beyond the guardrail would probably be at least a few dozen feet. She hoped the guardrail would stop her with bone-breaking force. Because the alternative would be worse.

Airborne now. The top of the guardrail impacted against her back and Gaia could feel herself tumbling over the edge.

In a last desperate move, she flailed both hands out in the hope of catching the top of the sharp metal rail.

*****

Paul slammed his foot down on the accelerator. The sedan was speeding up now, and the driver was taking one hell of a chance in doing that. The ramp was a sharp 180-degree curve. But he figured the guy was desperate to just get away. He'd probably seen what had happened to his friend, and knew also that the girl was out of the trunk. Nothing to lose now.

"Hillary! Get away from that side of the truck! Crawl into the seat behind me and strap in!"

She didn't argue. Hillary knew what he was going to do.

Paul gunned the truck around the curve of the ramp and pulled up flush to the sedan. He honked his horn several times and motioned with his right arm for the man to pull over.

In response, the driver of the sedan gave him the middle finger and swerved his car directly into the truck, the sides of the two vehicles grinding together and producing a sound one would only hear in a foundry.

The Chrysler 300, while being a heavy car, barely made an impact on the gigantic Toyota Tundra. Paul cursed, and muttered to no one in particular, "Okay, I gave you a chance, asshole."

He yelled out. "Are you buckled in, Hillary?"

"Yeah, Paul. Don't worry about me. Just do it."

He clenched his teeth and sped up once again, despite the risk of the ramp curve. Pulled up slightly ahead of the sedan, and then, with all of the anger he could muster, yanked the wheel in the direction of the front of the Chrysler 300.

He was aware of the nose of the car slamming into the guardrail, and then sliding along, sparks flying. It bounced off and seemed to pick up speed again. Paul cursed, slammed his foot down on the accelerator pedal, and rammed the car again with one final thrust of fury.

This time the sedan tipped over onto its two right wheels.

Leaned for what seemed like forever against the guardrail as it slid along, a leaning that was just delaying the inevitable. The violent sideways force that had been exerted against it, combined with the speed the car had been traveling at, caused it to finally, and mercifully, flip.

As Paul applied the brakes to avoid a catastrophe himself, he stole a glance in his right side-view mirror.

Just in time to see the undercarriage of the car as it somersaulted over the guardrail.

Chapter 25

Trevor Kincaid passed through Customs and Immigration easily—just swiped his Global Entry Nexus card and went on his merry way.

Meandered through the concourse of Ronald Reagan International Airport at Arlington, Virginia, and picked up his Lincoln Continental rental car. Same model of vehicle every time he visited—a standing order arranged courtesy of the United States government.

Headed north on the George Washington Memorial Parkway, which skirted the southwest bank of the Potomac River.

He was going to his usual destination—CIA headquarters in Langley, only a 15-minute drive from the airport, and usually traffic was light.

On a nice sunny day like today, Trevor wished the drive was longer—the scenic Potomac was relaxing and even though Trevor handled stress better than the average person, once in a while even he needed to relax.

Oh, well, he'd be able to relax soon once Gaia was back in his hands. He could look forward to that. Didn't know exactly when it would happen, but was confident he'd hear something any day now. Felt a hard-on in his crotch just thinking about it.

Trevor made this trip to Virginia about once a month. Under

contract with the CIA, he spent usually a week at a time conducting interrogation and mind control training sessions, with senior agents and the CIA's own team of psychologists. They were all good people, but not in his league. Plus, the bonus was that Trevor was also a psychiatrist, so as a medical doctor he had inside knowledge of anatomy stuff that the garden-variety psychologist wouldn't have.

In intelligence circles, Trevor Kincaid, aka Brandon Horcroft, had the reputation of being the preeminent expert in his field. He was in demand around the world as a respected consultant, but his first allegiance was to the CIA. They loaned him out once in a while, but essentially he was theirs.

Most people had heard of the MK Ultra mind control experiments that the CIA had conducted during the Cold War. The program began out of sheer paranoia back in 1953 and finally was ordered halted in 1973.

While investigators, including from Congress itself, tried their best to dig into all the salacious aspects of the program, all records were ordered destroyed by the CIA director at that time. So, the footsteps were largely erased. But not the legacy.

Congress was horrified to hear of what the CIA had been doing, but they largely kept their horror to themselves. The public didn't need to know too much.

But like every dirty little secret, aspects of MK Ultra had leaked out over the years when it was in operation, so Congress couldn't pretend they were totally lily white. More to the point, they looked the other way until it become an explosive public issue in the early 70s, at which time the CIA had no choice but to disband the program.

Hell, even Hollywood knew about the program, and dressed it up in a slightly different light in their 1962 film *The Manchurian Candidate.*

Publicized as a fictional movie, but those who ran in the right circles knew otherwise. The public loved the movie and most left the theaters thinking, *Thank God that sort of thing doesn't really go on.*

If only they knew.

The MK Ultra program never really stopped. It just went underground, advanced by experts like Trevor who knew all there was to know about hypnotism, mind control, brain-washing, and the creative use of certain drugs developed right at the CIA laboratories.

History had already seen the flamboyant use of the program with certain assassinations around the globe as well as in the U.S. and the placing of mind-numbed patsies in the right spots at the right times. Those incidents all happened in plain sight, while the truth of those incidents was actually hiding in plain sight as well.

Once the old program disappeared into the ashes in the 70s, a new one was born.

Known as MC Protocol.

This one was truly black ops, off the balance sheet, off the income statement, and totally underground. No Congressional authorization and no budget.

Well, there was a budget, of course, but it was diverted from other sources, particularly the drug trade.

Another thing the public didn't know—that their very own revered CIA was one of the biggest drug cartels in the world.

Every few months Trevor also did double-duty, training FBI psychologists down in Quantico—just an hour's drive south from Langley. The CIA didn't mind lending him out to their colleagues, but of course the FBI had no idea of the extent that Trevor was in the pockets of the CIA.

The two agencies were competitive and resentful of each other. It all went back to their mandates—the FBI did domestic work and the CIA did foreign work—and neither the twain should meet. But once in a while they did meet, and that's when the resentment levels went off the charts.

Trevor turned onto State Route 123 and a couple of minutes later was steering down the private road leading to CIA headquarters.

He rolled down his window once he reached the gate house, smiled at the guard and held out his official CIA credentials. The guard, a guy named Joe, just waived him on without looking at his laminated card.

Security was strict, but certain people were just well known and not to be fucked with.

*****

Jordan Walsh leaned back in his chair and laughed.

"God, I can always count on you. Every time you visit you have a good joke to tell me. I try to remember them afterwards, Trevor, but I never can. Must be age, huh?"

Trevor grinned. "Well, I can fix that. As you know, a little creative hypnosis can go a long way. I can erase memories—or just create them out of thin air. I could download my entire repertoire of jokes into your head if you want."

Jordan laughed again. "No, no … I want to look forward to your visits!"

"What? My scintillating personality isn't enough for you to look forward to?"

"To be honest with you, no. Your intensity is too much even for me. Which brings me to the reason why we flew you in for the day."

Trevor studied his colleague for a few seconds. He could tell Jordan had a few special things on his mind today; noticed it as soon as they shook hands.

He'd known the man for years. He had been instrumental in getting the RCMP to shut down the investigation into him in Canada. And helped him establish new identifications and backgrounds once he'd escaped from the vault.

Jordan had promised the Mounties at the time that the CIA

would spirit Trevor/Brandon out of the country. But his disappearance from the scene due to the unexpected vault incident helped change that agenda. The CIA preferred him to remain in Canada, so arranged to make that happen. But as far as the Mounties were concerned, Brandon Horcroft had simply disappeared into thin air.

Jordan was the deputy director of the CIA's Special Activities Division—where the MC Protocol project resided—as well as every other black ops "off the books" activity that the CIA was engaged in. Jordan was, in effect, Trevor's boss, although in Trevor's mind no one was qualified to ever be his boss.

"Yeah, I was surprised. Usually I'm here for a week. But a one-day fly-in is okay with me. I've got lots going on back in Canada right now."

"I'm sure you do. Okay, there are a couple of things we need you to step in on. Here goes. For about a decade we've had a kiddie porn program going, designed to ensnare influential political leaders around the world. Some right here in the U.S. as well as in Canada. We've used some of our psychologists here to drop the bomb on a few minor characters, with only moderate degrees of success. They weren't as influential as we thought they were."

Trevor raised his hand. "Hold on, you're not actually trafficking in kids, are you?"

Jordan shook his head. "No, not at all. Just photos and videos. And some computer-generated, not the real thing. We set up an authentic-looking porn site and lured men into the trap—targeted of course to a few that we wanted to lure. So, we've got them by the balls, literally, ready to leverage them whenever we feel the need. They have no idea, of course, but they're primed and ready for us to blackmail into granting certain ... favors ... to the U.S."

"You'd be honest with me, wouldn't you, if you were actually doing trafficking?"

"Yes, I would. But hey, spare me the virtuous crap. You do that stuff yourself."

Trevor shook his head. "No, I don't do any trafficking of kids. I facilitate adoptions."

Jordan laughed. "Give me a break. You're in the kidnapping and kiddy sex slave business. You may not be selling them into sex factories, but what you're doing is pretty close."

"It's not trafficking. Let's not argue semantics, though. Carry on."

Jordan took a sip of his coffee. "We have difficult negotiations going on right now with trade issues and arms sales. We need to use our leverage with several leaders we've ensnared. Three in particular: in Riyadh, Brussels, and Paris. The time is right for us to pull the plug. We need someone to lead the charge at a high level with these folks. Someone with your intensity and skill in mind control—as well as boardroom acumen. We need the A-Team for these three men, and we have no one here in Langley up for it. We need you to step in."

Trevor scratched his chin, then folded his arms across his chest. "You need someone who is believable—someone who portrays a ruthlessness that they'll take seriously."

"Exactly, and with all three you already have familiarity. We've loaned you out to them before for special … things they wanted done. So, they know you mean business. And they'll know that if we don't get what we want from them, we'll leak what we have."

"Okay. I can guess the three names you're referring to. They'll be putty in my hands, the snivelling little pedophiles. I'll await the dossiers from you and take it from there."

Jordan sighed with relief. "Glad to hear. Now, for the next project, this is another special one. There's a very troublesome and influential senator on the Intelligence Committee. We have to take him out. He's threatening to go public on some things he's uncovered about our MC Protocol program. Has some sources that we haven't flushed out yet. He's mumbling to some contacts about what he knows, but has expressed fear about exposing it.

"As you know, we undertook to disband MK Ultra back in the 70s, but MC Protocol was never authorized and is totally dark. The CIA can't risk having it exposed. So, the decision has been made to eliminate this senator, while at the same time send a not so subtle message to anyone else."

Trevor nodded. "You need a fall guy. A patsy."

"Yes. We have a couple of candidates in mind—both left-wing radicals who would be perfect and believable. But they'd need to be programmed."

Trevor leaned forward and lowered his voice to a whisper.

"I don't want to know the name of the senator. I'll mind-bend these patsies for you, prime them to be ready for some suggestions. Should be simple. Once I've made them pliable, your resident psychologists can make the suggestions to buy certain weapons, hate certain people, feel invincible, be at a certain place at a certain time, and do the killing. In other words, I'll bake the cake for you, but I won't slice it."

Jordan grimaced. "I understand, and yes, I think that would be best. Compartmentalizing is what we do best here."

"You do. Just tell me when you have these two guys—I assume you'll bring them in for questioning or some pretense like that. Once that happens, I'll fly down and spend whatever time is necessary to condition them for you. I may need your lab to be on call for me. A couple of drugs that I've used before. May not be necessary, but sometimes, you never know. We don't want these guys to be zombies, but we want them to be suggestible at the very least."

Jordan stood and reached out his hand. "Great to see you. Thanks for flying down for the day. Safe flight back to Toronto."

Trevor shook his hand warmly. "I'll line up a new joke for the next time I'm down."

"Ha, ha—you'd better. That's the highlight of every visit."

"What? Not my intensity?"

"No, Brandon … I mean, Trevor. I wouldn't want to be at the business end of that stare. It sends goose-bumps down my back. I pity your victims."

Trevor laughed and left the office.

Down the elevator and into the main concourse where the impressive CIA seal was engrained in the floor. He walked around it, respectful enough not to step on top of that venerable symbol.

His phone rang.

"Kincaid here."

Just three words from the male voice at the other end. "Package delivery failed."

Trevor clicked off.

Felt the familiar burning sensation of acid rushing from his stomach up into his throat.

He coughed to clear his throat—and cursed to clear his anger.

Chapter 26

Sunnybrook Health Sciences Centre was one of Canada's premier hospitals, located on upscale Bayview Avenue in Toronto. And while there were other hospitals that were closer to the scene of the accident, Jeff was relieved that this was the hospital the ambulance had taken her to.

It had been five days now since it happened, and he was still in shock.

They put Gaia in an induced coma due to the concussion she'd suffered. But only for the first two days; then they brought her out. The doctors had been worried about swelling in the brain, but things seemed to have settled down now.

In addition to the concussion, she'd suffered three broken ribs, a sprained left arm, dislocated shoulder, and multiple cuts and abrasions over most of her body. Considering Gaia's ordeal, the doctors considered her a lucky woman.

When Jeff arrived at the hospital after he got the call; she was conscious and talking. But then, quickly started fading, which was when they wisely decided to induce the coma.

He had the pleasure of meeting the two couples who had gone above and beyond to help rescue her. They were at the hospital when he arrived. Jeff was overwhelmed with emotion when he heard their stories about what she'd endured, and what they'd done to help her.

He'd lost count of how many times he hugged each of them.

Detectives were there that first day too, and interviewed the two couples. The lead detective told them he'd be immediately nominating all four for the most prestigious of all Governor General's awards—the Cross of Valour.

The police weren't able to talk to Gaia until she was conscious again. Her account lined up exactly with what the couples had told them.

The officers only briefly mentioned the tire iron through the head thing, but didn't make too much of an issue of it. They had to ask, and just nodded their heads in understanding. Jeff noticed what looked like a subtle smirk of satisfaction on one detective's face.

The Chrysler 300 had landed on its roof, crushing to death the occupants inside. Well, crushed to death one of them anyway—the other had already been killed by that errant tire iron.

Luckily there was no explosion when it landed, so they were able to recover some evidence at the scene. Were able to identify the two thugs. A couple of multiple-time losers; petty thefts, assaults, burglaries, drug convictions.

Kidnapping seemed to be a new adventure for them. This surprised the detectives, since that crime was one hell of a step up from the crap they'd been involved in. It was unusual to see petty criminals jump up to something that serious. And there had been no sexual assaults in the backgrounds of either men. So, it wasn't a certainty that Gaia had been kidnapped for sex.

The car had been stolen, so there was nothing to trace there.

Jeff was sitting in the waiting room of the intensive care unit. Gaia was still in there because of the head injury, but the nurses told him that she would probably be moved in the next day or so. She was recovering fast and showing no signs of any lingering brain trauma.

Right now, before sitting by her side for the rest of the

afternoon, Jeff had agreed to meet the lead detective, Jim Parsons, for an update. He glanced at his watch—the man should be arriving any minute now. He got up, walked over to the water cooler, and guzzled a glass. Then poured another.

"Dr. Kavanaugh?"

Jeff whirled around. "Well, hi, Detective. Good to see you again. Do you want some water, or a cup of coffee?"

"No, thanks. Can't stay long. Call me Jim, by the way. How's your wife doing?"

"Coming along nicely, thanks, Jim. I should be able to take her home in a few days."

The officer motioned to the chairs.

"Let's have a seat and chat for a bit. This is a real rough time for you, so, thanks for giving me a few minutes. We like to keep folks up to date, but I won't keep you long."

Jim nodded his head in the direction of the IC unit. "I know you'd much rather be in there with her."

Jeff shook his head in dismay. "I'm so relieved she got out of that car. Who knows what those pervs would have done to her, or if they would have even let her live."

Jim squeezed Jeff's shoulder. "I don't think they were rapists. Or killers. Doesn't add up. Not in their histories, and believe it or not, bad guys tend to stick with what they know. These guys were petty thugs. No sexual assaults or serious life-threatening assaults in their backgrounds. And they clearly bungled things badly. Didn't think it through all that well.

"They left her in the trunk, but didn't seem to be aware of the safety release handle. And it took a long time for one of them to crawl into the back to stop her from jumping. Which makes me think they weren't aware that the back seats of that car folded forward. Sure, the car was stolen, but you would think they'd make themselves familiar with the features before they snatched someone. They were pretty stupid."

Jeff nodded. "Makes sense. So, why do you think they took her?"

"That's what we're going to have to figure out—if we can. I'll warn you, since both of them are dead, the mystery may have died with them. But there are a couple of other things you should know. Even though she was taken from the parking lot of the supermarket, it doesn't sound like this was random."

"What do you mean?"

"She was stalked for a couple of days—right there on your street. They must have followed her when she finally left the house.

"We interviewed several of your neighbors, and showed them photos of a similar black Chrysler 300. Three of them said they saw that car parked a few doors down from your house. One neighbor saw it only on the day she was taken, and two others said they remembered seeing the car the day before as well.

"While they all thought it was strange, especially with two men sitting in the front, they didn't report it. Didn't think much of it. The passenger was apparently a chain-smoker, constantly tossing cigarettes out the window onto the pavement. That seemed to piss your neighbors off more than the fact they were hanging out there. We checked—there were cigarette butts scattered about in a couple of spots.

"So, it looks like Gaia was targeted, Jeff. This doesn't sound like a random snatch."

Jeff just stared blankly at the detective. He knew his face reflected the shock and horror that he was feeling at that very moment. For a few seconds, he was at a loss for words.

Jim leaned forward and rested his elbows on his knees. "Jeff, do you know of anyone who might have wanted to kidnap Gaia? I suspect these guys were hired to grab her. Which means that someone wants her. Not just any girl off the street—just her. She was the target."

Jeff pondered the question for a moment. What popped into his head was that threatening letter Dan had received from the apparent witness to their murder of Brandon Horcroft. But that seemed remote, and neither was Jeff going to even contemplate opening up that can of worms with the police. That would put all three of them in serious trouble.

He shook his head. "No one comes to mind. As you know, we're partners with Dan Nicholson in an investigative agency, but I can't think of any cases right now that would put Gaia at risk."

"I know Dan Nicholson. We worked together on a few things when he was with the RCMP. One hell of a guy—a real pro. Was sorry to hear that he left the Mounties."

"Yeah, the Mounties' loss was definitely our gain."

"Just a couple more questions for you. Do you know, or have you ever had an encounter—maybe in one of your cases—with a guy named Chuck Walton?"

"Nope. Never heard that name before. What's his connection?"

Jim scratched his forehead. "Well, it may be a connection, or maybe not. But we were able to retrieve data from the satnav in the 300. The location those two guys were driving to was a self-storage unit up in North York.

"We checked—it was rented by this Chuck Walton guy. And on the floor in the back of the 300 was a roll of duct-tape, and a kind of hood thing. We think they were going to restrain her with the tape, cover her head, and leave her in the storage unit. There was also a key to the unit in the pocket of the driver."

"Did you check out the unit?"

"We did. It's full of restaurant and bar equipment—chairs, tables, some commercial kitchen appliances, glassware—that kind of stuff. This Chuck Walton guy owns a club down on Jarvis Street. Called The Rude Rocker. A popular meat market kind of place—live music in the evenings. Frequented by university students—close to

Ryerson—so it draws a lot of that young college crowd. He was obviously using that storage unit for extra supplies for his club."

"Did you talk to this … Walton … guy?"

"Yep. Actually a nice sort. Not what you'd picture a bar owner to be like. He seemed clearly shocked and saddened at what had happened. He said that he'd hired those two guys for moving and renovation work from time to time.

"They did a complete overhaul of the interior of his club when he bought it a year ago. And he said they made several trips back and forth from the storage unit when they were doing the work, retrieving supplies and equipment. Said he hadn't seen them in months. But suggested they must have made a copy of the key to his unit for themselves. We checked—the key the driver had was indeed a copy, not the original."

"Does his story check out?"

"Yes, the club underwent serious and expensive renovations a year ago. And those two guys did the work. One was a carpenter by trade, and the other was a licensed plumber and electrician."

"Sounds like a dead end. Was he aware of them being involved in any criminal stuff?"

"No, which means he didn't do much of a background check on them, because their criminal convictions are public record. He just wanted the work on his club done, and went for the lowest bid."

"What's this Chuck Walton's background? What did he do before being a club owner?"

"Respectable. Has a wife and two kids, about forty years old, give or take. No convictions for anything other than traffic tickets. Was a Bay Street stock broker until he bought the club. Lost his job—fired over some trading irregularities—but never charged with anything. Just given the boot. But owns a nice house up in Willowdale, volunteers with his kids' school, well respected."

Jeff's attention perked up when Jim mentioned that Walton had been a stock broker. It immediately brought back memories of the insider trading crimes and deaths that had taken place at the direction of Brandon Horcroft at his old employer, Price, Spencer, and Williams.

Jeff cracked his knuckles and leaned back in his chair. "He must have left with a big severance. Buying and renovating that bar couldn't have been a cheap undertaking. Just the price of real estate alone in downtown Toronto is a killer."

"Well, we did some checking on that, too. He's lucky that he has a deep-pockets benefactor. An investor backed his nightclub business. So, for Walton himself, it's more just sweat equity. He's the registered owner, but the financing was provided by someone else."

"Who?"

Jim pulled a notebook out of the pocket of his jacket, and flipped through the pages.

"Ah, yeah, here it is. Quite a wealthy guy—a management consultant and venture capitalist to several businesses across the country. Name's Trevor Kincaid."

Jeff's stomach flipped while at the same time his throat went instantly dry. To fight it off, he jumped to his feet and headed for the water cooler again. Frantically sucked back a glass.

Dan's words—the ones he uttered on Front Street, while pointing at the top floor of a luxury condominium tower on the very day Gaia had been taken—flashed through his brain.

Eerily haunting and ridiculously coincidental: *That's where he lives—up there in that twentieth-floor penthouse. The man's name is Trevor Kincaid.*

Jim looked at him curiously, in an observant detective kind of way. "That name seemed to strike a chord with you."

Jeff quickly shook his head, and without hesitation told a bold-faced lie.

He didn't know why, because there was nothing about what they were investigating with Emily's disappearance that needed to be kept from the police. But a nagging intuition, embedded in his psychic sense, told him he had to lie.

"No, not at all. Sorry, but all of a sudden my anxiety over Gaia just kicked me in the gut. She's in there all alone, and I just need to be with her."

The detective stood. "I understand, Jeff. Sorry to have hit you with all this. You have more important things on your mind than a bar owner and two scuzzy blue-collar guys. We'll talk again."

Chapter 27

Riley McCormick was hopping, skipping, and jumping. Singing a song too, but she knew she probably had the words all wrong. But it didn't matter, she just loved the tune. And it sounded nice even with silly made-up words.

She'd just finished summer day camp at the ravine not far from her house. It was great to see a lot of her school friends, but also so many new friends. They came from all over Calgary, some by bus. Riley was lucky—she only lived a few blocks away, so she could skip over there and skip back home again.

She loved summer, but it was coming to an end. Which made her sad. That feeling of freedom, able to run around, laugh, and ride her bike whenever and wherever she wanted to.

And pretending to be a bird. She loved birds, but more than that, even, she just loved the idea of being able to fly. Riley thought that she might like to be an eagle or a hawk. The way they flew was just so different than all the other birds. They didn't just fly, they soared. Somehow able to catch the wind with their big wings, and barely move. They just let the wind do all the work.

She raised her arms out wide and flapped them as she ran. Then she stopped flapping and let them be still; pretending that she was soaring, that the wind was carrying her.

Suddenly Riley stopped and closed her eyes. She concentrated hard and was able to imagine herself up in the air, soaring, looking down. She saw the roof of her school and even the roof of her own house—it always seemed so real whenever she did this. Which was pretty much every day, and even in her bed at night. Able to lift her brain out of her body and have it soar above all the nice pretty things she wanted to see—to be able to experience how things would look if she were a bird.

Or, in an airplane. Or, maybe a rocket ship!

Her parents always chuckled whenever she went into these little trances. Riley's big brother, too. She always had to shush them up so she could concentrate. And her friends at school made fun of her whenever she talked about flying. In a nice way, though—not nasty. They just couldn't understand how she managed to get so much satisfaction out of her imagination instead of a smartphone.

Suddenly she was startled out of her trance by a woman's voice. "Riley!"

She opened her eyes and gazed into the friendly eyes of a lady in a van. A lady she knew very well.

Riley ran over to the open van window, and the lady leaned down and gently kissed her on the forehead.

"How are you, my dear?"

"Oh, Sherry, it's so good to see you! I've missed you!"

"I've missed you too." Sherry reached down and flipped Riley's ponytail into the air. "With that cute ponytail, you never seem to grow up in my eyes."

Riley shook her head from side to side, and it swung back and forth as she did. "See? It's great for when I run, or pretend to fly. Doesn't get in my eyes."

Sherry nodded. "I see that. Hey, Riley, school's starting again soon. Are you excited?"

The little girl nodded her head fast. "Yes, a little sad, but it will be exciting to see my friends again. We can all tell stories about our summers."

"I think you'll be going into Grade 2 in September?"

Riley smiled. "You always made me feel special. Always remembered stuff. You know so many kids, but you still remembered."

Sherry blushed. "Aw, that's nice of you to say. I got to know you so well when you were in day care, then helped out with your teacher once in a while when you were in kindergarten. Missed seeing you once you went into Grade 1."

"But you still came to my graduation thing back in June. You cared enough to do that. That was really nice."

"Yes, I try to do some special things for my favorites even after they don't need me anymore."

Riley could feel herself beaming. "I was one of your favorites?"

"You were probably my favorite of all my favorites!"

Tears started blurring Riley's eyes. Nice tears, though.

"Hey, why don't you hop inside the van and I'll give you a ride home. I was just on my way to the airport to see my friend's new airplane, but I can detour to take you home."

Riley ran around to the side of the van, careful to peek out to look for cars first. Opened the door, hopped inside, and strapped herself in.

But she couldn't stay quiet after what she'd just heard. Her voice was trembling as she asked, "Your friend bought a plane?"

Sherry slapped herself lightly on the side of her forehead. "Yes, but oh, my gosh, I forgot you love birds and airplanes! See, I don't remember everything about my favorites. I'm sorry, Riley."

"That's okay, Sherry. I forgive you. Tell me about your friend's airplane!"

"Well, I haven't seen it yet. It's brand new, very fast, but not a big plane. Only seats four people."

Riley's tummy strained against the seatbelt. "Are you going to fly in it?"

"No, not today. I just want to see it. But hey, I have an idea. Would you like to go with me to see it? It's not far from here—not at the big Calgary airport. He landed at the small Okotoks airport, so just a short drive."

Riley could barely contain her excitement. "Could we? Please? Please?"

"We sure can." Sherry pulled her cellphone out of her pocket. "But first I'm just going to phone your mom. I still have her number. If she's okay with it, then we'll go—I'll have you back in time for dinner."

"Oh, boy, I'm so excited! I've never even been in a plane before!"

"Well, there's a first time for everything. Today's your lucky day. Okay, I'm going to just step out of the van to phone your mom. The signal is better if I'm standing outside. You stay buckled in."

Riley watched through the side window as one of her favorite adults in the whole wide world talked on the phone to her mother. Saw her nodding and laughing. Riley knew it was good news, just by the way Sherry was smiling.

Sherry got back in. "Okay, girl, off we go! Your mom is just fine with it."

*****

Sherry parked the car in a grassy area next to some kind of building—Riley was pretty sure they called these things hangars. She jumped out of her side of the van and followed Sherry along a paved area to an open spot where several planes were parked.

Her eyes felt wide as saucers as she looked at all the airplanes. Riley had never been this close to real airplanes before, only little scale models. These were the real things and it caused her little heart to beat faster than she'd ever felt it beat in her life.

Sherry gestured towards a beautiful silver plane with red stripes.

Three men stood beside it. Riley gasped. The plane was gorgeous, prettier than she imagined it would be. And it looked like it could fly very high and very fast.

"Hi guys! I love the new plane. Hope you don't mind but I brought a little friend along with me. She just loves airplanes, and has never been in one before. This is Riley."

All three men smiled at her.

Sherry introduced only one man. "This is my friend, Rod Milton. Rod's the owner of the plane, and he's also the pilot. The other two are friends of his—psychologists. Do you know what psychologists are, Riley?"

She shook her head.

"Well, they're like doctors. Doctors of the brain. They help people with problems. And Mr. Milton himself owns a big diamond mine."

Riley didn't know what to say. Was overwhelmed. She thought to herself, though, that Mr. Milton didn't look the way she pictured a pilot. He was fat, and had a very odd red face. But it was his head that caused her to want to laugh—kind of an odd shape, with pointy ears. What was gross though, was the stuff coming out of the sides of his mouth—like white drooly stuff.

He took her by the hand. "C'mon, Riley. You can sit in the plane and see what it feels like."

Butterflies in her stomach now. She'd never been more excited in her life.

He led her into the back seat; then went around to the pilot's side, got in, and started up the engine. One of the psychologists got into the front passenger seat, and the other one crawled in beside her in the back.

Riley watched as the three-blade propeller on the nose turned, slow at first, then faster and faster. She couldn't believe how loud it was.

The door was still open and Sherry poked her head in.

"How do you like it?"

Riley jumped up and down in her seat. "It's amazing! I'm in a real plane! I wish we could fly in it!"

Sherry directed her attention to the pilot. "Rod, what do you think? Could you give Riley a short ride in the plane?"

He looked back at her. "Well, sure I could. For such a pretty little girl, that seems like a tiny favor. If she's not too scared, that is."

Riley's voice went up several octaves. "I'm not scared, Mr. Milton! You don't have to worry about me! I'll probably be an astronaut one day! Can we fly? Please? Please?"

He chuckled. "You are adorable. Alright then, strap yourself in, Riley."

Riley looked at Sherry. "Aren't you coming?"

"No, darling, the plane only has four seats. I'll wait right here on the ground for you. You won't be gone long. I won't move an inch."

Riley felt a pout fall across her face. Sherry reached in, gently squeezed her arm, and shut the door.

Before she knew it, the plane had moved out onto the runway and Mr. Milton was saying something over the radio mic.

The plane began to roll—slow at first, then faster … and faster. The butterflies in Riley's stomach had moved up into her chest now, and she was so excited it was getting hard to breathe. She looked back to wave at Sherry, but was sad to see that she'd already left the spot where she'd been standing and was walking away. Walking fast.

Maybe she wanted to wait in the van and was just walking fast to get away from the noise of the propeller. Yes, that was probably it.

Riley turned her excited eyes in the direction of the front windshield at the same moment that she felt the plane leaving the ground. Glanced out the side window and gasped as she watched the ground slipping farther and farther away.

Finally, Riley was a bird; an eagle. It wasn't just her imagination anymore.

She was just about to say something when the man sitting next to her grabbed her left arm, pulled up the sleeve, and inserted a needle in her forearm.

Riley McCormick didn't know whether or not this was what passengers had to have done when they were flying—maybe to stop them from getting sick or something? She just looked at him, too shocked to find the words to form a question. He smiled, withdrew the needle and patted the spot on her arm with a wet piece of cloth.

Riley's mouth tried to speak, but it wouldn't work.

Started feeling drowsy, but she was still able to marvel at the blueness of the sky through the windshield of the pretty plane.

Until that same sky suddenly went completely black.

Chapter 28

Things weren't back to normal yet, but at least Gaia was home. However, she was proving to be a terrible patient.

Jeff tried to fuss and be the surrogate nurse that he was convinced she needed him to be, but most of the time she just got frustrated with him.

When he wrapped her up in a blanket without being asked, she brushed it aside.

"Jeff, it's summer. What the hell do I need a blanket for?"

"Comfort?"

"I'm not going to be in much comfort if I'm sweating!"

And his feeble attempt at providing pillows for support didn't work too well either.

"Why do you think I need four pillows?"

"Well, it just seemed like the right number."

"No, the right number is one."

Making dinner for her was a confounding exercise, too.

"Why did you mash everything up in a blender? I didn't lose my teeth!"

"I thought it might be less effort for you."

"I want real food. This tastes like crap. Make me a hamburger."

She'd been home from the hospital for four days now, and getting stronger with each passing hour.

Gaia was indeed a trooper, evidenced alone by how she'd handled herself with her kidnappers. Jeff couldn't help being overprotective though—he just loved her. And she loved him for it.

But she made it clear to him that she didn't want to be treated like a delicate flower. Her best road to recovery, in her mind—and Jeff couldn't disagree knowing how independent she was—would be to return to normal routines as soon as possible.

She'd already cast aside the sling that the doctors had told her she'd have to wear for a month. Gaia insisted that the sprained arm and dislocated shoulder were almost back to normal, and despite Jeff's not-so-subtle attempts to get her to sling it back up again, she refused.

Even the broken ribs weren't causing her too much discomfort. Except at night. She had to sleep sitting up for probably the next three weeks or so. Breathing was difficult when lying down, and Gaia at least cooperated with allowing Jeff to prop her up every night before going to sleep.

The cuts and bruises were gradually healing. It had been difficult to find one square inch of her body that hadn't been battered by the rolling and bouncing along the roadway.

And the fingers of both hands had been badly sliced from her last-ditch attempt at saving herself from falling over the ramp bridge. She'd managed to grab onto the top of the metal guardrail as she was falling. The impact had left terrible cuts and bruises on the fingers and palms of both hands. She'd just removed the bandages for the last time today. Still raw, but the air would help now.

Jeff jumped up from his seat at the sound of the doorbell. He called to Gaia back in the kitchen. "Dan's here, hon."

He opened the door and Dan came swooping in. Patted Jeff on the back and headed straight to the kitchen.

"Ah, ha—I knew you'd be in here. Jeff told me you're being a bad patient. Now, here you are cooking your own food."

Gaia gave him a gentle hug, careful not to use her left arm.

"Dan, do you blame me? You've tasted his cooking. It's bad enough to send me back to the hospital!"

They all laughed.

"Hey, guys, want to chat for a few minutes?"

Jeff poured three cups of coffee and they sat down together at the kitchen table.

"Okay, my old buddy from the Mounties has agreed to be your protector for a while, Gaia. He'll be here this afternoon.

"With a suitcase. He's going to live with you guys for a while, and if you want to go out anywhere on your own, Gaia, he'll drive you. Until we figure all this shit out, you're not going to be alone. And he'll be armed. Okay?"

She nodded. "Can he cook?"

Dan laughed. "Not really. A meat and potatoes, guy. But he slices a mean carrot."

"What's his name?"

"Allan Cotterhill. A good guy. He'll charge us only a fraction of his usual fee, because we go way back.

"He retired from the Mounties about five years ago and started up his own security company. Could have sent one of his employees to do this, but after I told him all about your ordeal he insisted on doing it himself. A first-class guy—used to be in charge of the protection detail for the Prime Minister. So, you'll be in good hands."

"Thanks Dan. While I don't want to be pampered, this is a good idea. I won't object. Better than those damn blankets Jeff keeps throwing on top of me."

Jeff smiled and rubbed her shoulder. "It's only because I love you, dear."

Gaia flinched. "Jeff! Wrong shoulder!"

"Oops! Sorry! I'm just not good at this, am I?"

She chuckled. "I sure wish that psychic ability of yours would at least remind you of which shoulder I dislocated."

Dan got up and poured himself some more coffee.

"I have some news for you guys. This morning I phoned that detective in Calgary who's handling the Emily Clarkson case. Asked him if he'd had those fingerprints checked yet on the beer bottle. He did. And they're an exact match with the prints on the bicycle. So, your intuition was right on that, Jeff."

"Jesus. So, that tells us something, doesn't it?"

"Well, yes and no. It tells us that Aaron Dixon at one time had his hands on that bike. But he and Sherry were good friends of the Clarksons, so it could have happened anytime. As well, there's not much the police can do because it wasn't a legal seizure of evidence. You guys just wanted to know. So, now you know."

"It does point us in the right direction, particularly with the other stuff you found out."

"Yes, Aaron and Sherry seem to be suspicious as hell. They owned the company that foreclosed on that house before Emily disappeared, so they had full access to the backyard. Your psychic vision saw Emily being taken in a blue van, and we know now that the private equity company they owned was the registered owner of a blue van at the time Emily disappeared.

"As well, both Aaron and Sherry have had access to children for a couple of decades with their occupations.

"And, as you know, my hackers found out that Aaron emailed a man named Trevor Kincaid here in Toronto using unsafe addresses. Mysteriously, that man simply replied telling him to use different addresses. So, there was some secret communication going on, clearly. We don't know what that is yet because everything else is encrypted."

Jeff interrupted. "You showed me where that man lives. A multi-million-dollar apartment. The man's not suffering.

"And now I know, from what the detective told me, that there's another connection with that man. Trevor Kincaid is apparently also the financier of the Chuck Walton guy who owns The Rude Rocker. The guy who rented the self-storage unit that might have been where those thugs were planning to take Gaia."

Dan nodded. "The coincidence is just incredible. We have a connection between Trevor Kincaid and two possible kidnappers in Calgary, and a connection between him and two kidnappers here in Toronto. The only difference is the modus operandi. In Calgary, it's kids we suspect them of taking. But Gaia's an adult. So, it's not totally consistent."

Jeff folded his arms across his chest. "You guys will recall that when I visited my Aunt Louise, she had a vision from that letter you got from someone nicknamed Reper Cussions.

"She described him as a dude, well-dressed, and taking a different fork in the road. She also told me that the reason I got psychic visions of Emily Clarkson still being alive was because I had some kind of connection to her, or to the Clarksons.

"Well, I've never met them before, but maybe the connection is something more obscure. And maybe it's now staring us right in our faces. All of a sudden, we do have a connection. Someone tried to take Gaia, and this Trevor Kincaid is indirectly involved. And Emily Clarkson was taken fifteen years ago, and the couple we suspect of taking her also has a connection to a man named Trevor Kincaid."

Dan cracked his knuckles. "It's the same man, too. My people checked on the guy who financed The Rude Rocker. Same address as the one who emailed Aaron Dixon in Calgary."

Gaia ran her fingers through her hair. "I've been thinking. Is it possible that this attempt to kidnap me was the 'repercussion' that the writer of that mysterious letter referred to? He said he would let you know, Dan, inferred that he'd be in touch again. He never did write again.

"And then, out of the blue, two creeps snatch me out of a

parking lot. Another coincidence? Do you think that whoever ordered my kidnapping was maybe the witness who saw what we did to Brandon Horcroft?"

"I've been wondering the same thing. Gaia. And this rather wealthy man, Trevor Kincaid, seems to fit the profile of the successful man that we put together from the language in that letter.

"And he also fits the profile of the guy Jeff's aunt described in her vision. A successful well-dressed man. Jeff and I saw his penthouse—has to be worth several million. And the Toronto detective who talked to Jeff said this Kincaid guy was a management consultant and venture capitalist. He fits the bill. And the coincidences are really hard to ignore."

Gaia shivered, and gently rubbed her left shoulder. "Are you thinking this may be the man who wrote you that letter?"

Dan grimaced. "Anything's possible, I guess. And maybe the attempt to kidnap you was the revenge he was seeking for Brandon Horcroft. We thought he'd be asking for money, but clearly a guy like that doesn't need money. So, maybe you were the retribution. Which means he knew that Brandon was holding you captive in his vault."

Jeff leaned forward on his elbows. "Aunt Louise asked me a strange question. She asked if I thought that Brandon could still be alive. She didn't have a psychic vision of that, she just wondered if we'd considered that after getting the letter. And, of course, knowing that his house in Forest Hill had been sold and demolished. That is strange, I think we agree on that. Who sold it? And who ordered it demolished? And where did that damn vault end up?"

There was silence around the table for a minute or so.

"Okay, I guess we don't want to talk about that. It's a reach, I know."

Dan pushed his chair back and stretched out his long legs. "After what happened to Gaia, it's only natural we'd let our imaginations run wild. Let's stick to what we know for now, and let the facts unfold."

"Yeah, good advice. Well, I need to fly back out to Calgary. Want to meet with the Clarksons again, and that detective. Tell him what we know about the Dixons and see what he has to say. When you talked to him over the phone, Dan, did he ask whose fingerprints were on that beer bottle?"

"He did. I didn't tell him. Best face to face. I'm going with you to Calgary. Gaia, you're not fit for travel yet. Allan will be here this afternoon. Best you hang out here and let us handle this part."

Nodding agreement, she added, "Yes, I was told not to fly for a few weeks due to the concussion. So, I'll wait here. Allan can cook me some meat and potatoes."

Jeff gently squeezed her knee and leaned in to kiss her on the cheek. "See, this time I stayed away from your shoulder."

He opened his laptop and fired it up. Scrolled through some news headlines until he found the one he wanted. He spun the computer around so that Dan and Gaia could see it.

"Here's an Amber Alert that went out in Calgary a few days ago. A little girl went missing on her way home from day camp—her name's Riley McCormick. Seven years old. Take a look at her."

Gaia put her hands up to her mouth, and whispered, "Oh, my God. She's blonde, with a ponytail."

Jeff spun the computer back and clicked on an article that he'd favorited.

Then turned the machine around again. "This is Emily Clarkson fifteen years ago."

Dan gasped. "Jesus Christ! They could be twins!"

Chapter 29

The big house seemed a wee bit smaller now. Not that there was any less space with just one extra person in the family, but it still seemed as if her world had shrunk. The change of atmosphere was noticeable—nice in one way, but unsettling in another.

For as long as Rachel could remember since Angie had been taken away, it had just been her and Dad. Now there was someone else. Her new sister, Olivia.

Olivia Milton—had a nice ring to it. Rachel Milton and Olivia Milton. Sisters.

But it wasn't the same as when Angie had been there with her. They were both the same age. They'd played together and talked about things. And consoled each other when they were feeling down.

It was different now with Olivia here. Dad said she was Rachel's new sister, but Rachel was twenty-three and Olivia was only seven. To Rachel, it felt more like motherhood than sisterhood.

Olivia was a pretty little girl, and Rachel could tell that her dad was excited to have adopted her. Said her parents had died in a car accident and a private adoption had been arranged to get her out of foster homes. Apparently, most couples looking to adopt children wanted only infants, not seven year olds. That gave her dad an edge because there was very little competition.

This was the first day that Rachel had had the chance to actually get to know Olivia a bit. She'd been isolated for the first week, spending almost all of her time in a separate wing of the mansion. That wing had been reserved for servants at one time, but since Rachel had done all the cooking and cleaning since her early teens, there were no servants anymore.

She remembered the day Olivia arrived. Dad had flown her to Yellowknife in his own plane, along with two skinny bespectacled men. They were psychologists that Dad said he'd hired to help Olivia with the trauma of losing her parents a year ago, and to assist with getting her assimilated into her new environment.

They'd had to carry Olivia in from the car. She seemed unconscious, but Dad said not to worry. That they'd had to sedate her due to the anxiety of flying and about starting a new life. The two psychologists were trained and qualified to do sedation, so there was no reason for concern. She was in good hands.

That day, Rachel had retreated to her computer; wanted to read up on anxiety and adoption stress. To be able to help in some way if she could.

But for the first time she could ever remember, the internet was down. Her dad said he was upgrading to a new wireless connection, but that it would probably be a couple of weeks before things were back up and working again. It felt strange to be disconnected—the internet was the only real link Rachel had with the outside world.

That first day, once Olivia was tucked away in the separate wing of the house with the two psychologists, Dad had sat her down for a chat.

"Well, finally you have a sister again. How do you feel about that?"

"I don't know. It's a weird feeling. It's been just you and me for so long. When Angie was here, I was real happy to have a sister. But then when you sent her away, it broke my heart. Now, there's someone new and I'm much older now. Olivia's around the same age we were when you adopted me and Angie. It feels more like I should be her mother instead of her sister."

Her dad leaned forward in his chair, bits of white drool oozing out of the corners of his mouth. "I think you could be both. She'll look up to you since you're older. It would help me a lot of you could act as kind of a mother to her. And it would help her too."

He pulled a handkerchief out of his pocket, wiped his mouth, and stuffed the hanky back in his pocket again. "I'm not here most days, so you'd be in charge of our little family. Cleaning the house and cooking as you always do, but also keeping Olivia company until I get home. And I would trust you to make sure that when she goes outside she only stays around the lot—no further. The same rules would apply to her as apply to you."

Rachel shook her head. "I don't understand. I'm a grown woman now and you promised me I'd have more freedom. Why do those same rules still apply to me?"

His pointy ears twitched—something Rachel noticed every time Dad was annoyed.

"I've kept you sheltered from things, Rachel. To protect you. I'm a very rich man, and members of my family could be the targets of kidnapping. I fear that you and Olivia could be targets. We have to be careful."

"But no one's ever attempted anything. We have an alarm system here and there's never been any trouble."

He clasped his fingers together and squeezed tightly until they turned white.

"You think that way because I haven't told you everything. There have been threatening letters sent to me at my office, suggesting things that could be done to you—sexual things, violent things. There are people who know I have a daughter and think that they can use that threat to extort money from me."

"Do you know who they are?"

He shook his head. "No."

"Have you ever paid anyone off?"

"No. I've ignored them. Once you start paying, the paying never stops. I increased security patrols around our house—maybe you've noticed them. They're not out there all the time, just occasionally. They try to be discreet."

This was news to Rachel. She'd never seen any cars patrolling outside. In fact, they were in such a remote area it was rare to see any cars at all, except for her grocery delivery guys. And she found herself disbelieving his story about threatening letters. If men wanted to kidnap her for ransom, why would they send letters? That seemed like kind of a stupid thing to do. Why wouldn't they just take her instead of giving advance warning?

"I promise that you'll start to get some freedoms. We'll start slow. But for now, I'll need you to concentrate on looking after Olivia when I'm not here. And when I get home, I'll take over."

A little voice in Rachel's head told her what that last sentence meant.

"I know you've changed. You're mature now, and have certain … needs … that are different from what I can give you. I was shocked to find you with that delivery guy, but I understand it now. It doesn't upset me anymore, particularly since I've now adopted your new sister."

A little voice in Rachel's head told her what that meant also.

"So, you'll let me go out on dates with boys?"

He shook his head.

"Let's not get ahead of ourselves. Not yet. Maybe later. Let's see how Olivia comes along, and how much progress you make with her—you know, making her feel safe and comfortable and happy to be here. I'm counting on your help with those things.

"And your reward will be more freedoms like perhaps dating men. Once I feel that Olivia has warmed up to me as her new father, we can talk again. Okay? And by the way, no one from outside our little family and my trusted friends is to know anything about Olivia. No one can see her. If someone comes to the door, like your delivery friends, you're to lock her in her room and tell her to keep quiet. For at least the first year, no one is to see her."

"Why? Those delivery guys won't try to kidnap her."

"No, but they might tip off someone else that there's a little girl living here. Someone of my wealth and position has to be extra careful, Rachel. You've lived a sheltered life—that's my fault, not yours. But someone like me has to be extra careful, and that makes me perhaps overly protective sometimes. You'll have to forgive me for that, but I do demand that you abide my wishes."

Rachel could tell that her dad was much more relaxed and happy since Olivia had arrived. He wasn't so easy to lose his temper anymore, and the fact that he was even considering letting her date other men was something she never would have expected.

Clearly, just the mere thought of Olivia had put new zest in his life. He was still as firm as he always had been with rules, but at least he was explaining things to her now rather than just yelling at her.

But it was strange. With Olivia locked up in another wing of the house for a week now, it seemed as if she was being housetrained like a pet. And with Rachel's new role as one of making Olivia feel safe and comfortable, it almost felt like they had a new puppy in the family instead of a new little person.

Rachel was expected to watch over her, train her, comfort her, and prime her to be ready and chirpy by the time Dad got home from work. It just seemed—weird. Rachel had never had a puppy before, but she'd read about them over the internet. The feeling she had right now was similar to the stories she'd read about the special challenges pet owners faced.

Rachel and her father had had a few more conversations about Olivia since that first day. He'd warned her that once she was allowed out of the far wing of the house, she might seem off—subdued, confused, and not very alert. He said those were just the effects of having the two psychologists counseling her for hours at a time. As well, the medications they'd been giving her would have some lingering side effects.

Today was the day the two nerdy men were leaving, and today was the day Olivia would be living full-time in the regular wing of the house.

The men shook hands with her father and told him to call them if he had any concerns. They said they'd be back again in a couple of weeks for another few days of sessions with Olivia. Until then, she should gradually start coming into her own and begin acting like a normal seven-year-old.

He closed the door behind them at the same time as Olivia came skipping down the hall from the far wing of the house. She was barefooted, as was Rachel, and wearing a blue dress. Her blonde hair in a ponytail bounced behind her as she skipped.

Rachel stood and greeted her. "Hi there, Olivia. I talked to you for a bit on the second day you were here. Do you remember?"

The little girl shook her head.

Rachel lifted one of her own feet up in the air. "Look! I'm just like you. We both like to be barefoot."

Olivia spoke softly. "I don't remember if I've ever walked barefoot before. It feels nice, though, especially because I was skipping, I think."

Their dad tugged on Olivia's ponytail, then headed off towards his office. He called back. "I'll let you girls hang out for a bit. Call me when dinner's ready, Rachel. Maybe you can start teaching Olivia how to cook."

She smiled at the little girl. "Would you like that?"

"I don't know."

"Well, there's one way to find out. I'm a gourmet chef, so I'll be a good teacher for you."

Olivia scrunched up her face. "Are you my new mommy?"

"No, I'm your sister. My name's Rachel. Did you remember my name?"

She shook her head. "How can you be my sister? You're too old."

"Well, we have the same father. He adopted me fifteen years ago, and now he's adopted you. So, that makes us sisters."

"Do we have a brother?"

"No, no brother."

"That's strange. I thought I had a brother, a little older than me."

"Maybe that was just a nice dream you had. Or, did you have a brother in your other family or at the foster home?"

Olivia leaned her head against the armrest of the couch. "I don't know. I can't remember any other family. I should, shouldn't I? I get little pictures in my head, but they don't last long. And my name is Olivia, but it feels as if I've never heard anyone call me that before. Until you and … him."

"Well, maybe some things hurt too much to remember. Those doctors probably helped you think nice things instead over the last few days. What was it like talking to them?"

"They were nice, I guess. They weren't mean or anything. They talked a lot, but I don't remember what they said. But it seemed like they were saying the same things over and over again. Maybe they thought I wouldn't be able to remember what they said, so they had to keep repeating stuff."

Rachel had a flash of memory. Olivia was describing the same feeling she'd had after she spent time with two men when she arrived fifteen years ago.

"What else did they do?"

"Played lots of music. Soft music, and sounds of waves and wind. And shone lots of lights at me—made me very tired. I know I fell asleep a few times, but they kept waking me up. Wouldn't let me sleep even though I couldn't keep my eyes open anymore. I feel like I need to go to sleep right now, Rachel."

Another flash of memory. Rachel remembered the music, the sounds of waves and wind, bright lights. And she remembered the desperate need to sleep, but not being allowed to.

"They told me my parents died in a car accident a year ago. But I don't remember that and I don't remember them. Why is that?"

Another flash of memory for Rachel. The same kind of confusion and memory blank that she'd had, and still had.

"That's a nice blue dress you have on, Olivia. Is that your favorite?"

Olivia giggled and played with the fringes. "It is nice, but I don't remember if it was my favorite. The closet in that room had lots of clothes. They all fit so they must be mine. But I don't remember wearing them. They're all really pretty, though."

Rachel squeezed her hand gently. "I think it would be a good idea if I showed you to your new room in this wing of the house. I can go get all those clothes for you, and move them into your new closet."

Olivia smiled. "That sounds nice, Rachel."

She looked around the large room and off towards the kitchen and the dining room. Olivia closed her eyes and took a deep breath. Then giggled again.

"What's so funny?"

Olivia kept her eyes closed. "Oh, this is great fun! I'm floating around the room looking down at everything. I can see you from above. I'm looking down at you with your legs crossed and you look so mature; like such a lady—just like how I'd want to look when I'm older. Try it, Rachel!"

Rachel laughed. "Okay, I'll try." She closed her eyes and concentrated. But nothing happened.

She opened them again and tugged on Olivia's ponytail. "You must have a great imagination. I tried—I can't do it."

Olivia opened her eyes too. "It's so neat. I can't believe it. It's magical! Maybe we can try again tomorrow, and I can teach you how to do it. You can teach me to cook, and I'll teach you to float. I must be a magician or something."

Rachel stood. "Yes, you can teach me tomorrow. But first, let's get you to your new room and you can have a little nap before I wake you for your first cooking lesson."

Olivia jumped to her feet and threw her arms around Rachel's waist. "I'm going to like being your sister, Rachel. You're so nice, and so pretty."

Rachel bent down and kissed the top of the little girl's head. At that exact moment, there was a strange tingling warmth in her bosom that she'd never felt before.

She held Olivia's hand and started guiding her toward the hallway that led to the first-floor bedrooms.

Suddenly the little girl pulled away and spun around in a circle, almost like a ballerina. Then, she closed her eyes once again and raised her arms high in the air. Began flapping them up and down, accompanied by the biggest smile Rachel had ever seen in her life.

"You're such a little sweetheart. But why are you flapping your arms up and down?"

"I'm an eagle, Rachel! Trying to fly like an eagle! You know what? I think I'd like to be an astronaut someday. I just thought of that now!"

Chapter 30

Trevor took the subway north from Union Station and got off at Dundas. Then made the short walk to Jarvis Street.

He liked downtown Toronto on Sundays. Much quieter than any other day, and the subway wasn't as crowded either. He hardly ever took the subway, but he figured that tonight it was probably a better idea than having his distinctive Mercedes spotted parked near where he was going. Just in case Murphy's Law intervened. A parking ticket, or license plate picked up by street cams.

With the kidnapping of Gaia that had gone so wrong, and the story of it being splashed all over the front pages, it was better that he stayed under the radar. The connection of the kidnappers and Chuck Walton had already been reported and covered by the press, and the fact that the apparent destination of the kidnappers was a storage unit rented by Walton.

So far, Trevor's connection to Walton hadn't been reported, and neither did Trevor expect it would be. He was just the financier of The Rude Rocker, and it was only one of twenty businesses that Trevor financed across the country. So, any connection of Trevor to the kidnapping would be a stretch in the very least.

He'd had Walton by the balls of course. Agreed to finance his bar when no bank would take a chance on him. His checkered background as a stock broker went against him. And trying to line up financing while unemployed was a pipe dream.

So, Trevor stepped in to help out. Financed the purchase of the building on Jarvis Street, as well as providing the operating capital that Chuck needed to make a go of it. As well, the extensive renovations that were needed just to get the thing up and running.

And so far, the club had been a big success. The university crowds loved it, and Chuck was managing to attract some good local rock acts to perform in the evenings.

Trevor'd had a relationship with Chuck even before that, though. Back in his previous life when Trevor Kincaid was Brandon Horcroft, and an executive with Price, Spencer and Williams.

For the insider trading that Brandon had been engineering from secret information gleaned from his hypnotized clients, Chuck was his front man on the trading floors. Placed the buy/sell orders, took handsome under the table payoffs from Brandon, and kept things on the low-down.

A lucrative partnership.

Until Chuck got fired for doing a few illicit trades on the side with others.

So, after he got fired, he came crawling to the newly-named Trevor Kincaid for help, desperate for a bail-out. He had a big mortgage on his house, two young kids and a stay-at-home wife. He was in trouble.

Trevor was glad to help. But he wanted some things in return.

First of all, Chuck was told in no uncertain terms that he was never to tell anyone that Trevor Kincaid was the former Brandon Horcroft. As well, Trevor made it clear that he was not interested in being in the nightclub business, so the only reason for helping him out was because of their history together. Ergo, one day Trevor would come asking for a favor and Chuck would be expected to deliver.

Trevor had one final condition attached to advancing the funds.

Because they would basically be in partnership together, Chuck had to agree to let Trevor hypnotize him. He balked at first, but Trevor insisted. And he told him that it was common practice back when he was at Price, Spencer and Williams—all the top executives had to agree to be hypnotized, as did most of their executive clients.

Chuck already knew about the clients being hypnotized. They came to the Price firm for executive counseling and coaching—and part of that coaching was to provide them with techniques to handle the normal stress and anxiety that went along with the typical executive life. But what those clients didn't know was that when they were under the deep hypnosis that Trevor was famous for, they gave up corporate secrets. And those corporate secrets were then used to buy and sell stocks, with Chuck as the favored trader.

So, Chuck knew full well how powerful Trevor's hypnotic talents were, because he'd benefited directly from them himself.

But he couldn't understand why Trevor wanted him to go under deep hypnosis just because he was advancing money for his club. Trevor insisted, and told him that it was his way of helping Chuck be the very best nightclub operator he could possibly be. Give him skills he wouldn't have otherwise.

And eventually, Chuck did admit to Trevor that he felt different—more confident and more relaxed. Grudgingly, he had no choice but to accept that the hypnosis had worked wonders.

Trevor walked from the subway station to Jarvis Street and turned left. He could see the darkened club just up ahead. He and Chuck had agreed to meet there tonight, rather than talking on the phone. It was a Sunday, so the club was closed. But Chuck used Sundays to deal with the paperwork that always piled up during the days when the club was open.

Trevor put his face up to the window and saw that there was a light on in the back office. He rapped loudly on the window.

Chuck came running out from the office and opened the door for him.

"Hey, Brandon. Glad you could make it tonight. C'mon in."

"Chuck, you make that mistake all the time. My name is Trevor, not Brandon."

He led the way to the back office. "Sorry, old habits are hard to break."

"Well, you'd better break that one. It could be dangerous for me if you don't."

"Gotcha. You're right. Can I pour you a coffee?"

"No. I can't stay long. Let's chat about what happened and get the story straight."

"Okay, fair enough." Chuck sat in the leather chair behind his desk, and Trevor sat opposite him in the guest chair. "Hey, business here in the club is great, by the way. You'll be glad to hear that we're packed almost every night."

Trevor smiled, with a cruelness in his lips that he loved to use to keep people on their toes. The contrast between the smile and the lip curl always left people perplexed.

"That's good. But I really don't give a shit. You're just one of many businesses I've financed. All I care about is that you make your monthly payments."

"Yeah, yeah sure—I get it."

Trevor got right down to business. "The first favor I asked you for since I bailed out your ass and you dropped the ball. What the hell was that all about?"

Chuck looked sheepish. "Well, I thought those guys could pull it off. I'm sorry."

"Sorry doesn't cut it. You chose a couple of clowns by the sound of it. And it was pretty stupid to give them the address of a storage unit rented under your own name. Christ, what the hell were you thinking?"

"I thought it would be easy. It was just a girl. Didn't expect any trouble."

"Well, you got trouble, didn't you? And lots of press coverage. It was a pretty sensational event. It didn't take long for the police to track down your connection to that storage unit. I want to know what they said to you."

"They asked me some questions, my background, and my connection to those two guys. They seemed to be okay with my answers."

"Did you give them my name?"

"No! Of course not! They asked about financing of the club and I told them I'd arranged private capital. I'm sure they've checked that out by now, but I haven't heard back from them again."

"What will you say if you do hear from them again?"

Chuck started fidgeting with his hands. "Well, I don't know. I'm not going to go to prison for kidnapping, Brandon."

"My name's Trevor, you idiot!"

"Yes, yes, sorry. Well, I'm worried about what to do if the police do come back again. That's why I wanted to meet with you tonight—to see if we can work out something fast."

Trevor frowned. "What are you talking about?"

"Costa Rica has a nice lifestyle—and no extradition treaty with Canada. I'd like to get out of the country while I still can. Kidnapping carries a long sentence. And I like you Trevor, but I'm not going to go to prison for you. I don't even know why you wanted that girl—don't want to know. That's your business. But I did it for you."

"What are you asking?"

Chuck's brow was covered in sweat. Slouched over in his chair, his eyes squinted into tiny little beads as he stuttered his reply.

"I think … three million should do it. Wired … to a Costa Rican bank … in my name. I could bundle up my family and leave, say, tomorrow. Sooner the better."

"So, tonight's meeting is a shakedown. What are you not telling me? Why are you so worried? All you did was rent a storage unit.

That doesn't tie you in as the kidnapper."

Chuck nervously cracked his knuckles, the sound reverberating around the walls of the tiny office.

"I sent those guys a couple of emails. The girl's name, her address. And the address of the storage unit. I deleted all of the emails, but these things can still be tracked down in servers and hard drives if detectives know where to look. At least, that's what I hear."

Trevor stared at him for a few painful seconds—watched him squirm and fidget.

"Your Costa Rican idea is a good one. I can live with that. And the three million is an easy matter for me to transfer down there in your name. Until you open an account there, it can just sit in suspense. My bank will arrange it."

Chuck let out a deep sigh. "Oh, thank you, Brandon. I'm so relieved. I didn't know how you'd react, but you're smart enough to know that if they come back here to arrest me, I'd have to tell them the truth. I'd hate to have to mention your name, but … I have a family."

"Trevor."

"What?"

"You called me Brandon again. The name's Trevor. You're a slow learner, aren't you?"

"Sorry."

Trevor leaned forward in his chair and rested his elbows on his knees.

"Now that I've agreed to finance your escape from the long arms of Canadian law, I want the absolute truth from you. And don't lie to me. The Canadian courts may not be able to reach you in Costa Rica, but I certainly can. And I will. You won't live long enough to enjoy the beach life. So, tell me right now—did you use my name in any of your emails, or in any other forms of communication related to this kidnapping?"

Chuck shook his head. "No, absolutely not."

"Did you use my other name, the one you keep blurting out?"

"No. I only use that name with you because, I guess, your face reminds me of the good old days."

"So, are you telling me the truth that there is nothing in this office, in emails, at your home, or anywhere else, that can connect me to the kidnapping?"

Chuck held up his right hand. "I swear. Scout's honor."

"Okay, then, I guess we have a deal."

Trevor reached into his pocket, pulled out two ultra-thin painting gloves, and slipped them over both hands.

"What … are those for?"

Trevor smiled. "You'll see."

He reached under his jacket and pulled a long razor-sharp gutting knife out of a sheath on his belt. A knife that had never been touched by his fingers without gloves.

Trevor calmly laid the knife on the desk in front of Chuck.

His voice now dropped to a deep monotone. "You're going to pick this knife up in your right hand and slit the wrist of your left hand."

Chuck started trembling. He tried to talk, but couldn't find the words.

Trevor leaned his elbows on the desk and stared deep into Chuck's eyes; into his very soul. He said four words and only four words, spoken in a tone that he only used for special occasions like this.

"Thou shalt go forth."

At the mention of those words, Chuck Walton's body stiffened. His eyes glazed over and Trevor thought that he actually looked like one of those cyborgs portrayed so often on the silver screen. He found it amusing.

Chuck's right hand reached out for the gutting knife and

clenched it tightly by the handle. Pulled up the sleeve on his left arm and with one swift movement he swiped the sharp knife hard across his wrist, so deep that his hand was flopping. The blood immediately began spurting, and Trevor had to back up his chair to avoid getting sprayed.

There were no sounds coming out of Chuck's mouth—no crying, no whimpering, no signs of feeling any pain whatsoever. Trevor knew that he wouldn't feel any pain. The suicide command was designed to block any sensations. Not out of any sense of humanity, but out of a concern that if pain was felt, the spell would wear off and help could be sought by the target.

No, Chuck just sat there in his chair and watched the blood spurt out of his left wrist, a curious look of detachment on his face. A face that was very quickly turning as pale as a vampire's.

Trevor waited until the end—which didn't take too long.

When he sensed it was over he walked around the desk, careful to avoid stepping in any of the blood. Placed his gloved fingers against the man's neck, and nodded approval of the diagnosis.

Satisfied, he turned and strode through the club towards the exit. He passed all of the tables with the chairs turned upside down, the bottles of booze in the bar all filled and ready for Monday's reopening, the iconic juke box which for now was silent and eagerly awaiting commands.

He carefully peeked outside before opening the door.

As Trevor walked down Jarvis Street in the direction of the Dundas subway station, he turned around and took one final glance at the darkened neon sign for The Rude Rocker.

An appropriate name, he thought. And for Toronto bar-crawlers, a name that would now live forever in infamy, and in morbid curiosity.

Chapter 31

"It's a cold case. A very cold case. I feel for the parents, but the trail went cold a long time ago."

Jeff and Dan were having coffee with Inspector Bill Rogers in his office at the 47th Street N.E. headquarters of the Calgary Police Service. They'd flown in the evening before and spent the night at one of the airport hotels.

Dan opened his briefcase and pulled out a note pad. Flipped a few pages until he reached the one he wanted.

"I see you're in the Major Crimes Division, Bill."

"Yep. My speciality unit in that division is homicide."

"So, this was assigned to you because it's assumed Emily Clarkson is dead?"

He nodded. "That's right. And after all this time, we have to assume that. That wouldn't be news to you, Mr. Nicholson, seeing as you were RCMP."

"Call me Dan. And yes, I can see why you'd conclude that. But it's never a certainty. What if the crime was kidnapping? Would that fall under you?"

"Within the first year after a child or adult disappears, we have missing persons detectives who handle those. After a year, they refer the cases over to me because, once again, we assume the end result was probably a tragic one."

Jeff had been studying Bill as he and Dan interacted. Seemed like a decent sort, but for a homicide detective he didn't appear to be all that on the ball. Jeff had expected more energy and intensity—instead, what he saw was a man who was just kind of laid back.

And not slick and articulate the way Dan was. Jeff found it interesting to contrast the two law enforcement veterans. But maybe he was being unfair—Dan had been a Mountie, which was Canada's federal police force, equivalent to the FBI in the states.

While municipal police forces like Calgary's were first-class, Jeff figured that a lot of the people who qualified for municipal policing probably wouldn't qualify for the federal force. As well, Dan had a master's degree in criminology, and Jeff hadn't noticed any framed degrees hanging on Bill's wall.

Dan paused, so Jeff jumped into the conversation.

"Bill, do you have a team that specializes in cold cases like Emily's?"

He shrugged. "Well, not really in an official way. We just bring specialists from the different units together to investigate when something comes up on old cases."

"Have you done that for Emily?"

He shook his head. "No, because all we have is a bicycle. That doesn't really lead us anywhere. But we did test those prints that Ken Clarkson asked us to do. From that beer bottle. They do match with one set of prints on the bike. Dan told me on the phone that you know whose prints they are."

"Yes. That beer bottle was handled by the owner of the house where the bike was found. Aaron Dixon."

"How did you get the bottle?"

"I took it."

"I see. Well, you know that's not a legal capture of evidence, don't you?"

"Of course. But my intuition told me there was something

wrong with Aaron and his wife, Sherry. So, I had to know if my intuition was right."

Bill laughed. "What are you, psychic or something?"

As he continued chuckling, Jeff replied, "Yes, as a matter of fact, I am."

Bill stopped laughing and just stared at Jeff for a few seconds.

"You're fucking with me, right?"

Jeff shook his head. "No, this is too serious a matter to fuck with. I have a history of psychic incidents, and several times Dan and I have used my intuition to solve cases in our agency."

"Well, okay, be that as it may, I'm not a believer in stuff like that. Here on the police force we deal with evidence and facts."

"You have no choice in the matter, but a lot of police forces have used psychics to solve crimes, especially cold cases. You've probably used them, too, on the Calgary force."

"Can't say that we have—at least not that I know of."

"Well, you have to admit that my psychic intuition proved right. Aaron's fingerprints were on the bike and the beer bottle."

"I already told you we can't use that evidence."

"But doesn't it raise a question in your mind?"

Bill shook his head. "Not really. The Dixons were close friends of the Clarksons, so it's reasonable to expect Aaron may have touched the bike at one time or another. It's very thin circumstantial evidence, and we could never arrest someone on something that thin."

Dan had been looking through his notes as Jeff and Bill were bantering. He looked up.

"Jeff and I both agree with you on that, Bill. At the very least though, the fingerprints send us in a possible direction for a closer look. Did you check into the private equity firm that had foreclosed on that house when Emily disappeared?"

Bill flipped through a few papers in his file. "Yeah, here it is. A firm named Trend Capital. They owned the property then, and for fourteen years after Emily disappeared. Sold it to the Dixons a year ago. Looks like they've liquidated now—not in business anymore."

"Are you aware that Aaron and Sherry Dixon were the owners of Trend Capital?"

Bill sat with his mouth slightly open for a few seconds. Then, a stern look came over his face. "Is this some kind of gotcha moment, Dan? Trying to trip me up?"

"No, not at all. For me, it's more of an ah-ha moment. And it should be for you too. This isn't a competition here."

Bill laughed—a sarcastic kind of laugh. "For you feds, it's always a competition."

"Um, you know I'm a private citizen now. Not with the RCMP any longer."

Looking more and more uncomfortable, Bill leaned his elbows on the desk and propped up his chin with his fists.

"As they say, once a Mountie, always a Mountie. But, you private dicks also love to get in our way just like the Mounties always did. Cut corners and try to make us local cops look bad."

Dan sighed. "Let's get back to the subject at hand here. I've just told you some startling information, and your reaction to that is to try to bust my balls. Park your ego for a second and tell me what you intend to do about this. Aaron and Sherry Dixon owned that property at the time Emily went missing. They hid their ownership through a private equity firm.

"They had full access to that vacant property at the time the bike was buried there fifteen years ago. And then a year ago they bought that house from themselves.

"I guess they never figured that one day a storm would come along and uproot a tree and that bike from the ground. So, they never had to worry about their ownership of the house under Trend Capital. Because it was irrelevant. No one knew the bike had been buried in that yard until the storm came along.

"And then even after that, they haven't volunteered to the police or the Clarksons that they owned the house when the bike was buried there. That sounds to me like two people who were trying to hide something."

The detective had completely lost his friendly demeanor. There was the hint of a scowl on his face now. He glanced at his watch.

"I only have a few more minutes. Is there anything else you wanted to bring up?"

"Why don't you answer Dan's question? What are you going to do about this information we've just given you?"

"Well, again, it's circumstantial."

"It may be, but it's damn suspicious, is it not? Doesn't that give you probable cause to legally obtain Aaron's fingerprints?"

Bill shook his head. "It's still weak. Lots of people have investment companies that are separate from their private lives."

Jeff shook his head and got up from his chair. "Clearly, we're wasting our time with you. Do you intend to spend any time investigating this? We'd like to know."

Bill spread his hands, gesturing to the files piled high on his desk. "Look at this mess. I have enough current cases to spend the department's time on. I can't be running down rabbit holes.

"Feel free to continue on your own, and if anything more concrete comes up, we can talk again. As far as I'm concerned, the case is cold and old. In all likelihood the girl is dead, sad as that is to accept. And to waste time on a fifteen-year-old case when I have trails that are fresh on new cases would be a terrible use of the limited resources we have."

He chuckled. "Maybe you'll get some voodoo visions that'll solve the case."

Inspector Bill Rogers was still chuckling as they left his office. Dan flashed Jeff a stern look that basically said, "Punching him in the face won't make things better."

*****

"The prints match—and they're not going to do anything about it?"

Dan shook his head. "No, but please understand this—Jeff and Gaia stole the beer bottle, so they wouldn't be able to use that in court anyway. All it does is give us some inside knowledge and an inside track."

They were sitting on the backyard deck at Ken and Cathy Clarkson's house. Cathy had brought out a pitcher of lemonade, which was a welcome treat. It was another hot day in Calgary.

Cathy's face said it all. And her frustration came out in her voice. "What's wrong with the police? Those prints should raise all sorts of alarm bells."

Jeff nodded in agreement. "We're with you on that. But you haven't heard the worst of it yet, and that's the main reason Dan and I wanted to drop in on you guys before we fly back to Toronto tomorrow."

He told the Clarksons what Dan's investigation of Trend Capital had turned up.

After he finished, they were speechless for a few minutes. Dan filled the silence with a few more details.

Finally, Ken spoke. "They bought that house from themselves. And they owned it at the time Emily disappeared and her bike was buried there. They kept those things secret. Now we know, and I just want to go right over there and rip their heads off with my bare hands."

Dan squeezed Ken's shoulder. "We understand. I'd want to do the same thing myself if I were you."

"Emily needs revenge."

Jeff held up his hand. "Well, let's keep the faith. I'm still

220

convinced Emily's alive, and that's what we have to focus on."

Dan took a long sip of his lemonade. "When Jeff and Gaia were here last time, they told you about his visions. And that he'd seen a man that Emily seemed to know lead her into a blue van. When Jeff asked Aaron if he'd ever owned a van, he said that he hadn't. But I checked. Trend Capital indeed owned a blue van at the time Emily disappeared.

"And my hackers were able to track down one suspicious email from Aaron to a very wealthy man in Toronto. A man who just happens to be connected to another case we're involved in right now. Totally unrelated, but the same man in both cases."

Jeff turned on his laptop and showed them the Amber Alert photo that had gone out across Alberta a couple of weeks before for the still missing Riley McCormick.

Cathy gasped, and put her hands to her mouth. "My gosh, I never saw that. But it looks so much like Emily at that age. It's spooky to see this."

Dan leaned forward and lowered his voice. "As you know, Sherry is a specialist in early childhood education. Works on contract with day care centers, kindergartens, and foster homes. A lot of children have disappeared over the years who attended facilities she counseled.

"Emily didn't attend any that she handled, but the Dixons knew Emily personally, so they already had a trusting connection with her. It's likely that Emily wouldn't have been fearful at all about getting into a van if invited by either Aaron or Sherry.

"But I did some checking on this latest disappearance, Riley McCormick. She did indeed attend a day care center that Sherry helped establish. There might still have been a connection as well when Riley moved on to kindergarten."

Ken frowned. "So, you think they're still at it?"

"Again, I'll caution that right now we have no proof of anything.

But if this is how they've been making all of their big money all these years, chances are they're still doing it. Particularly if they don't think there's much chance of being caught, or tied to anything."

Chapter 32

Cathy had laid out a big breakfast for all of them the next morning. They were sitting around the kitchen table enjoying bacon and eggs, but not much conversation. Jeff figured the couple were still in shock over what they'd told them the day before.

Finally, Cathy spoke. "I'm just stunned. They've been our friends for so long. To think that they might have taken our daughter is just a kick in the gut. What did they do with her? Did they kill her? Send her away? I shudder to think about it."

Ken put his fork down hard on the plate. "I still want to just go rip their heads off. If you guys weren't here to calm me down, I probably would have done it already."

Cathy turned to Jeff. "The last time you were here, you looked at that old photo of Emily and saw a diamond necklace. Yet, she wasn't wearing one. And you picked up the yellow cutting knife, and immediately blurted out that you thought she was in Yellowknife. Do you still feel that?"

He shook his head. "Nothing else has come to me along those lines. But that doesn't mean those visions weren't real. I just haven't had any more stimulation. So, for now, we'll just have to hang on to that as a possible link, or clue. Do you folks have any connections up there? Or, do the Dixons?"

Ken folded his arms across his chest. "Not that we know of.

We've been puzzling over that. And you got two visions that relate to the same city. But maybe we're linking the two as meaning the same thing. Sure, Yellowknife is the home of some of the richest diamond mines on the continent—and I don't understand this psychic stuff—but wouldn't the sensation you got from the yellow cutting knife be enough to identify the city? Why would your psychic nature give you diamonds as a clue for the city also? Could that be a separate clue entirely, for something else?"

Jeff scratched his chin. "That's a really good point, Ken. You're right—there would be no need for two different vision things for the same subject. Although this psychic stuff isn't rational at all, I've never had two different sensations identifying the same thing before."

Cathy jumped in. "Maybe it means she's been living a life of privilege? She's wealthy now perhaps?"

Dan nodded. "Yes, and I doubt there are a lot of wealthy people living in Yellowknife. It only has a population of about 40,000, so there can't be a lot of millionaires."

He snapped his fingers. "But what millionaires they do have up there are probably involved in diamond mining!"

Jeff grimaced. "Suddenly, the diamond necklace is making more sense."

Dan got up and poured himself some more coffee.

"Okay, this was productive. Anyway, before Jeff and I head back, we wanted to toss out an idea to you guys. If you don't like it, we won't do it.

"We were thinking of swinging by the Dixon's house, and if one or both of them are at home, see if we can shake them up a bit—maybe force them to make a mistake. At the very least, maybe they'll lay low and not kidnap any more little girls."

Ken stared off into space, and spoke slowly. "So, you want to tell them what you know, provoke them a bit, force them to let down their guard maybe? I like it. How about you, Cathy?"

She nodded. "I think it's worth a try. As you said, Dan, it might force them to stop any other plans they might have had. But will this put us in any danger?"

Dan sat back down. "Well, that's impossible to know. But I seriously doubt it. They have nothing to gain by hurting you guys, and it would only draw attention to themselves.

"And they already know you have private detectives working on this for you. So, it's only natural that we would talk to them since the bike was found on their property.

"But there are no guarantees that they won't snap. That's why I wanted to ask you first before we did something like this."

Dan dropped a piece of bacon onto the floor for Max to eat, then reached down and patted his head. "And you have Max here to protect you anyway."

Ken stood up and walked to the window.

"I don't care about any danger. If they took our daughter, then we have to get them. And if it puts us in danger, that's a small price for losing our daughter.

"Life hasn't been the same for fifteen years anyway—it feels like danger has been with me constantly since then. The anxiety, the loss, the ache in the pit of my stomach. It's the same feeling as being afraid. I've lived with it. And you know what? I'd like them to give me an excuse to just kill them anyway."

Cathy walked up behind Ken and wrapped her arms around his waist. "Shh … it's okay. Good to vent. We'll weather this storm together. Our friends here will do what they do best, and the chips will fall where they may."

Dan dropped one last piece of bacon into Max's open and eager mouth.

"Okay, guys, we're going to head over there now. We'll report back to you as to how it went. Stay calm—and stay positive."

*****

"Your fingerprints were on the bicycle, Aaron."

Aaron stared at Dan, speechless.

They were standing in the front foyer of the Dixon home. Neither Aaron nor Sherry had invited them in any further than that. No friendly glasses of lemonade offered.

Sherry waved her hand in the air, dismissing the comment. "So what? We were friends. I probably handled her bike myself a few times. Did you come here just to tell us that?"

Jeff shuffled his feet. "No, actually we came to remind you that you bought this house from yourselves. And that your company, Trend Capital, owned this house at the time Emily disappeared. Which means you two owned this house then, and had full access to the backyard."

Both of their faces went as white as sheets.

"Your company also owned a blue Ford Econoline van at the time she went missing. And Aaron, we know that you stopped the van on this very street, put Emily's bike in the back, and took her for a ride. Where did you take her, Aaron? Does Yellowknife ring a bell?"

Still silence.

Dan took over. "A little girl named Riley McCormick was kidnapped a couple of weeks ago, a girl that you, Sherry, had a relationship with back in day care. Funny, she looked a lot like Emily did fifteen years ago. Why would that be? Did you take her, Sherry?"

The couple stood tongue-tied in the foyer, glaring at them with contempt.

"Did you send her to Yellowknife too? Or, somewhere else? And why do we think diamonds are involved with Emily's disappearance?"

Suddenly, Aaron lunged.

The muscles that were on full display under his tight T-shirt flexed with rage, as he clenched his big hands around Dan's throat. He threw him backward against the wall, and then backed up a couple of steps, positioning himself in a boxer's stance.

"C'mon, big man! Show me what you got!"

Dan laughed. His next move was a blur. Right arm flashing out, picking an open spot right between the man's two clenched hands. Dan's fist smashed into Aaron's mouth, and Jeff heard, before he saw, the tinkling of teeth bouncing off the hardwood floor.

Aaron and Sherry gasped in unison, and Aaron brought his hands up to nurture his bleeding mouth.

But he didn't have much time for nurturing.

The heel of Dan's foot crushed into the man's gut. He doubled over and went down. Curled up in a fetal position and started sobbing—one hand over his mouth, the other one rubbing his abdomen.

Dan rushed forward and easily dispatched Sherry to the floor with a quick thrust of his right hand. He then grabbed Aaron by the hair and twisted his head around so he could look into his eyes.

Knelt down on the floor and spoke through gritted teeth.

"You fucking pervert. If the police don't get you for all this, we certainly will.

"In fact, we'll probably just kill you. And your twisted wife as well. We won't discriminate.

"In the meantime, though, we'll just leave you with one question: Will Trevor Kincaid protect you?"

Chapter 33

Trevor turned off the projector and switched off the spotlights. Closed his laptop, packed his briefcase, and headed for the door. He was done. He'd been hard at it for four days straight, creating these human robots, and he was confident they were primed and ready.

Oops—forgot the drugs.

Headed back to the table and picked up the two vials and the leather case which contained all the essential needles. He stuffed them in his jacket pocket.

Before leaving the room, he took one final glance at the two dazed men sitting at the far end of the table. Two Iranian Americans. Good looking sorts, he thought. Dress them up and they should blend in just fine in the senator's neighborhood, wherever he lived. For Iranian heritage, they looked more on the white side, too, so that would make it even easier to avoid standing out.

He still didn't know the name of the senator, and didn't want to know either. But all of these senators lived in the best neighborhoods in Washington.

Senators certainly didn't get rich on their $200,000 salaries. Most of them were already wealthy before they even ran for office—from their careers in the private sector before they finally felt the urge to serve their country.

But there was also a substantial under-the-table gravy train that greeted them once they arrived in D.C. From lobby groups, campaign donors—there were so many avenues that money found its way around all the corners and into the pockets of legislators. Being a senator was lucrative business indeed.

They didn't glance up at him as he was leaving. Just stared straight ahead at the screen where for the last four hours images had appeared—swirling images, surreal images—the same ones over and over again.

Those images had been complemented by the constant sound of Trevor's voice, planting command phrases over and over again. From each side of the long table spotlights pointed towards the peripheral vision of the two men. This prevented them from looking away from the screen. They had no choice but to look straight ahead.

Trevor closed the door behind him and headed off to the small office at the front of the building. This was a smallish warehouse-looking building not far from the CIA's Langley headquarters. No signage on the front—totally innocuous. A building no one would give a second glance at.

But in actual fact it was an interrogation center, complete with interview rooms and dormitories. Quite comfortable for the inhabitants—not what one would think of when they considered the word "interrogation." And it wasn't intended to be a torture chamber—not physically, at least.

It was an interrogation center that specialized in torture of the mind. Just one of many facilities used in the secretive MC Protocol program.

Jordan Walsh was waiting for him in the office.

"Are you done?"

"I sure am. And glad to be done. Looking forward to flying back to Toronto. It's been a long few days."

"I'll do a money transfer to your bank today. We agreed on one million, didn't we?"

Trevor winced. "Excuse me? It was three mill."

Jordan laughed. "I was just fucking with you. Of course it will be three million."

Trevor reached into his pocket and pulled out the two vials and the leather case.

"Okay, just a quick refresher. These vials are clearly marked. One is secobarbital, which is a barbiturate derivative. It enhances deep hypnosis—makes the state linger. The other vial is mescaline, which produces a psychotic paranoid state. Similar to LSD, but much more manageable and doesn't stay in the system as long.

"Used together in small quantities, they'll create the ideal conditions for erasing memories or creating new ones—with the proper suggestions. These two drugs used together will cause those two guys to be ultra-suggestible.

"And with the deep hypnosis I've used on them, they're now perfectly conditioned to be suggestible. All your psychologists have to do is plant the suggestion of who it is that must be killed, make sure they're equipped to do it, and plant them at the right time and location to carry it off. They won't fail, I can guarantee you that."

"Are there instructions in the case?"

"Yes, on how to administer the drugs. But you can't let up on the state they're in. No rest for the weary. They've been sleep-deprived for the last few days. Only a couple of hours of shut-eye each day. So, you need to move fast on this. They're in the best state now that they'll ever be. They need to keep getting the drugs every day until they do the deed. But if you drag this out too long, the drug effects will immobilize them. So, I'd say two days from now, no later, would be your opportune time to act."

Jordan nodded. "Understood. We will act fast. The tips we've been getting from our sources indicate that this senator is going to get up in the chamber very soon now and deliver a speech disclosing all that he's found out about MC Protocol. Once he's done that, the gig is up. We can't let him get to that point.

"The advantage to us on this hit is that most senators are totally unprotected when they're not in the Capitol region. At home, at restaurants, they're completely vulnerable—which would surprise a lot of Americans if they knew. Some hire private security, but the vast majority don't. This particular senator doesn't—a lucky stroke for us."

Trevor nodded his head in the direction of the interrogation room. "Where did you find those two guys? I thought you were going to go with white liberals, not Middle Eastern."

"We decided these guys would be ideal. They're American born Iranians who run a left-leaning radical news rag in Virginia. They're actually brothers, and everyone loves brother acts with terrorist attacks. They write articles expressing their anger about American immigration laws, and the prejudice being shown towards Iranians. They're also staunchly against Israel's occupation of Arab lands, and they write about that all the time too.

"The senator they're going to kill is Jewish, and a strong advocate for Israel, so it will fit within their radical writings. It will be believable to the media and the public. And—for us, it kills two birds with one stone. This assassination will enrage the public in favor of the Republicans—the senator will be a martyr. Our case for continuing military escalation in the Middle East will be helped immensely."

"Makes sense. Good strategy."

Trevor glanced at his watch, and then sat down in the guest chair. "I still have a few more minutes before I have to head to the airport."

He paused for a couple of seconds, glanced back through the open office door, then spoke softly.

"Jordan, we talked about this part before. They have to die after the senator is dead. The effects of the drugs and the few days of hypnosis will wear off. They haven't been subjected to this mind control long enough. So, some memories may come back to them if they're in captivity and not subjected to any more of this stimulation. You can't allow the police to capture these guys."

Jordan nodded. "Yes, I understand. We'll have a Washington police officer in the neighborhood—one of the city's finest who's also on the CIA payroll. He'll be the hero of the day, someone who just happened to be driving by at the time this terrible murder takes place.

"But I wanted to ask you to reconsider again giving them a suicide command. That would make it easier for us."

Trevor shook his head. "I could do that, but I can't guarantee it would work. You'll be giving them the command to kill that I wrote out for you. I've already planted it in their heads to react once they hear it again.

"But a second command of suicide might confuse their minds. Remember, they'll be in a semi-hallucinogenic state with all that they've had to endure, and of course, all the drugs. Two commands might get mixed up and actually nullify each other. You're better off to just take them out."

"Okay, we'll stick with our plan of using a 'hero cop' then. We don't want to take any chances that they could escape and then get picked up by the Washington police. Things will be out of our control then."

Trevor checked his watch again. "Gotta run."

He held out his hand and they shook. "Pleasure doing biz. Let me know when you want me to move on that 'honey pot' extortion stuff."

Chapter 34

Senator Joseph Farber skimmed through his newspapers. Each and every morning several were delivered to his house. He never had time to read them all, but he enjoyed getting the different perspectives from both the right and left leaning media. The same stories could be twisted in so many different ways. Wasn't one for spending much time on a computer, so he didn't get his news that way. Preferred old-fashioned newsprint.

Two soft arms wrapped around his neck from behind. Turned his head and kissed his pretty wife on the cheek.

"Eva, I love how you do that every morning. You never fail. Although, if you ever stop I think I'd better start worrying."

She moved in front and sat down on his lap. "That is quite the record, isn't it? We've been married thirty years and I haven't missed a day. Well, that's not right—when our darling sons were born I think I might have slacked off a bit."

He kissed her again, and slipped his hand under her nightgown. "You're forgiven."

"Don't pretend to be horny, Joe. I know you hate morning sex."

He chuckled. "Yeah, I do. I don't know why, but I just do. Somehow I don't associate sun streaming through the window with sex. I must need the stars and the moon. Now, doesn't that sound romantic?"

Eve nestled her cheek against his. "Yes, hon, it does sound romantic. And lucky for me, you've always been a big romantic. Hell, you even love chick flics. Not many wives can brag about that."

Joe brought his index finger up to his lips. "Shh—don't tell anyone. Can't ruin my image."

She gave him a warm hug, then slid off his lap. "Can I make you some breakfast? Do you have time?"

"Thanks. But not today. I had some coffee, and I'll grab something in the Senate. We're voting on a couple of things today, and I'm going to also try to get some access time to make a speech in the chamber. So, if you need me, don't bother phoning my office number. I'll have my cell with me, though, and I'll try to answer if I can."

"Oh, let me make you a little something. Some eggs maybe? You're only four miles from the Capitol building, so a real quick drive. You need to take care of yourself. Your days are long."

Joe shook his head. "No, dear, gotta run." He drained the rest of his coffee, pushed his chair back, and got to his feet.

Eva helped him on with his suit jacket. Then she adjusted his tie and tightened the knot.

"Have you thought about where you'd like to live after you retire from the Senate?"

"Hey, I'm not ready to retire yet! And I thought you loved it here in Woodley Park. Would you really want to move from here?"

She pouted. "Maybe out in the country, away from all this politics buzz. If we don't move, it will continue to suck you back in. You know that. And don't think I haven't noticed how stressed you've been over the last few weeks. A wife knows these things."

"I have been, you're right. I've learned some things that are very disturbing. If I get permission to speak on the floor today, or tomorrow, I intend to blow it all wide open. You'll be able to watch on TV—floor speeches are always covered. And it'll be all over the news afterwards anyway, so you'll find out soon enough what it's all about."

Eva's face said it all. Joe could tell she was worried.

"Can't you tell me what this is about? You usually share notes with me when you make speeches."

Joe shook his head. "I have no notes at all on this—what I've learned has been verbal only, and I haven't written anything down. It's deep throat stuff. This isn't the kind of subject you want to write notes about before blowing it open. Once I make my speech it'll be recorded, and then I'll feel a lot better. All I'll tell you is that it pertains to my work on the Intelligence Committee, and it involves the CIA."

"Joe, you've got me worried now. Do you know what you're getting into?"

"I have to do this, hon. And if I've been off in space for the last few weeks, I'm sorry about that. I thought I'd hidden it from you. Not a good hider, am I?"

"Have you told any other senators about this—whatever it is?"

"No. Best not to drag others into it. My sources told me in confidence. It's up to me to deal with it. But don't worry—all will be fine. One thing about going public on things—while it creates a firestorm, it does tend to make things safer."

Eva wrapped her arms around her husband's strong neck, and gave him a long lingering kiss on the lips.

"You've always been a brave man. And I trust your judgement. We can talk about it more tonight. If you get to make your speech today, you'll probably be quite the celebrity. You'll also feel better. I'll have my husband back."

Joe kissed her one last time. He loved her lips—always so luscious, even in the morning.

He grabbed his briefcase and opened the front door. Then he looked back at her and smiled. "And yes dear, when I leave this bullshit behind, we'll move out to the country."

She giggled, folded her arms across her chest, and stood in the front doorway as he walked out to his car. Not only did she always hug and kiss him from behind every morning, she also never missed watching him drive off.

Joe walked around to the driver's side of his Lexus.

At that point, he entered a different world. A slow-motion world.

He noticed a brown sedan parked on the street two doors down. Why he paid any attention to that, he didn't know, but it was rare to see cars parked on the road in Woodley Park. As well, a police cruiser had been parked way down at the end of the block and it just started pulling out as he rounded the side of his car. It was rare to see police cars parked on his street too.

The police car moved slowly up the street as Joe raised his hand in a final wave to his wife. She waved back.

The slow-motion reel suddenly brought two men into the screen, jumping out from behind the bushes along the side of the driveway. Joe was aware that they were each holding pistols, extended in his direction.

He looked over at Eva standing in the doorway and yelled something. Couldn't remember what. He waved again at her—this time a backward wave motioning her to get inside. Heard a scream and was pretty sure it came from her pretty mouth. In panic, Joe looked for the police car, but it was still too far away to react.

Glanced back at Eva, who now had her hands covering her mouth, a look of abject terror in her glistening eyes. They stared at each other—silent words exchanged, but Joe couldn't decipher what they were.

He looked back at the two men. Slightly dark-skinned, well dressed. Guns still extended.

Instinctively, he pulled his briefcase up in front of his chest. Just in time. He felt the first impact right at chest level, through the briefcase and into his rib cage. Enough to knock him to the ground.

He pulled the briefcase farther up now, to cover his face. He heard the next shot, and it felt as if his stomach had exploded. He didn't dare look.

Despite the crippling pain in his ribs and in his gut, Joe managed to muster enough strength in both hands to throw his briefcase up and into the face of one of the shooters. He heard the man curse and sensed that he fell backwards.

Joe turned his head in the direction of the street, hoping against hope that the policeman had finally arrived.

He had!

Even though Joe's eyesight was fading fast, he could make out a uniformed officer down on one knee at the end of the driveway. His gun was drawn and aimed in the direction of the shooters. The gun was in his right hand, supported by his left. He looked ready to pull the trigger.

What was he waiting for?

Joe felt something against his forehead. Cold steel. He looked up into the dark orbs of the man who was about to kill him and saw absolutely nothing. No rage, and no regret. He'd never encountered killers before, but expected to see something at least.

Senator Joseph Farber turned his eyes away from his executioner, and directed them up into the clear blue sky.

Just before his head blew apart, Joe began reciting in Hebrew—a language he hadn't used in years—prayer words of the Shema Yisrael.

Chapter 35

He was pacing the floor, anger practically oozing out of his pores. Finally, he leaned his head back and yelled at the top of his lungs. "Fuck!"

Trevor marched over to a cabinet, opened the glass doors and pulled out his Fergie Jenkins autographed baseball. Then he spun around and pitched a fastball at a Ming vase standing majestically in a corner. It smashed into a million pieces, but he still wasn't satisfied. Dashed over to one of his four televisions and thrust his foot through the screen.

Stood back and surveyed the mess.

Then he picked up his satellite phone and rang him one more time. He counted this as the tenth message he'd left Jordan Walsh in the last five days. They still hadn't connected, and Trevor knew the man was avoiding him. That really pissed him off.

Sat down at his dining room table and checked the latest news headlines. A breaking news item flashed across the top of his screen in a red banner.

Manhunt Over. Second Assassin Captured.

Washington police have just announced the capture of the second alleged assassin of a prominent senator. He has been identified as Armeen Darhandi, brother of the deceased

Farhad Darhandi.

Police responded to an anonymous tip from a homeowner in the Washington area. He was spotted entering a garage on the property.

Darhandi was apprehended without incident. However, he was overheard by the homeowner screaming that he wanted a lawyer as he was hauled away in handcuffs.

Senator Joseph Farber, who was in his fourth term in Congress, was brutally assassinated last week by two men, allegedly the two Darhandi brothers, in his own driveway.

Farhad Darhandi was killed at the scene by Washington police officer Ian Henderson, who bravely confronted the shooters. Sadly, Officer Henderson was allegedly shot and killed in the Farber driveway by Armeen Darhandi before he fled the scene.

The entire nation is in shock at the death of the prominent senator, who was also a member of the Senate Intelligence Committee. Senator Farber was loved and admired on both sides of the aisle. He was a Republican his entire political life, but was respected as being one of those few senators who could work productively with member of both parties.

The alleged assassins were residents of Alexandria, Virginia, and were American citizens, although their heritage was Iranian. Together, the brothers published a small politically-oriented newspaper called *Persian Watch*. Columns in the paper focused on Middle Eastern issues, as well as harsh opinions on U.S. immigration and foreign policies. The newspaper was particularly critical of Israel and its treatment of Palestinians in the occupied territories.

Senator Farber was Jewish, and although no motives for the assassination have been established by police as yet, there is speculation that possibly his heritage could have been a reason for the attack.

Neither of the brothers had criminal records.

Eva Farber, the senator's wife, is reported to have witnessed the shooting. She was unhurt in the incident. The Farber family lawyer announced that Ms. Farber will make a short statement later today, however the statement will be issued through the lawyer. Ms. Farber has refused to make any comments to the press at this time.

More details to follow.

Trevor scrolled through a few more headlines and read several other versions of the story. They all basically told the same tale.

Suddenly his satellite phone rang. *Finally!*

"Kincaid, here."

"Hi Trevor. It's Jordan."

"Christ, it's taken you long enough! What the fuck is going on?"

"All hell has broken loose in this town. Sorry, but I've been busy. We had our own teams out looking for the brother, hoping to find him before the police did. But they beat us to it."

"That's unfortunate. You'll have to come up with a way to take him out."

"Difficult. He's under a tight shield right now."

"Well, it won't be the first time you guys pulled off something like this. Don't you have some kind of Jack Ruby guy you can enlist into action?"

"That was before I was born. Different town, different time. Dallas was a far more pliable city than Washington. We had several ranking members of that force on the take back then, from what I hear, and they cleared the way for Ruby to take out Oswald."

"Well, you had a Washington police officer on the take—that Ian Henderson clown. Pretty inept, for God's sake. They were sitting ducks, and he only got one of them? And then got himself killed? Jesus, what a fuck-up."

"Trevor, I have to run. We'll talk again in a couple of days or so. Just hang tight."

Trevor started pacing the room again after clicking off his phone. Then, went back to his computer.

He was obsessed with this now.

It was so high profile that news would be coming out by the hour, as it always did with incidents like this one.

He cursed himself that he hadn't at least tried to give those Iranian guys a suicide command. Something that would tie in with the killing of the senator—the vision of the senator dead on the ground could have been the trigger.

But he hadn't even tried. He was being honorable with his CIA bosses. Didn't want a command like that to confuse the murder command. Didn't want to jeopardize the mission.

Fuck these missions! Have to start looking out for myself first!

An alert popped up on his newsfeed. A live statement from the lawyer of Eva Farber. The man was poised behind a microphone stand in front of what looked like a courthouse.

"Good morning, ladies and gentlemen of the press. This will be a brief statement on behalf of Ms. Farber, and I won't be taking any questions. First, I'd like to pass along her request for the privacy that she and her family need right now. Please respect that request and refrain from staking out her home as some of the media have been doing over the last few days.

"Media reports are accurate so far, in that Ms. Farber did witness her husband's assassination. She was standing on her front porch bidding him goodbye as he was getting ready to get into his car. Ms.

Farber saw two men rush out from behind bushes and shoot the senator several times. He tried to use his briefcase as a shield, but to no avail.

"Ms. Farber wanted me to say that her husband was quite nervous that morning, and had been suffering from some anxiety over the last few weeks. He was hoping to make a speech on the Senate floor the very day of his death.

"Ms. Farber said that her husband told her there was a disturbing subject that certain sources had told him about, and he was intending to expose it during his speech in the Senate. The senator did not give her any details, but said that it had to do with his work on the Senate Intelligence Committee and that it involved something to do with the CIA.

"Thank you for your attention, and that's all we wish to say at this time."

Trevor whistled as he clicked off the live feed.

What a fucking boondoggle!

Suddenly there was a knock. Trevor walked to the door and looked through the peephole. A uniformed man was standing in the hall. Trevor knew him—building security.

He opened the door and smiled.

"Hi Albert. How can I help you?"

The man made a respectful bow.

"Mr. Kincaid, sir, I'm sorry to disturb you. But I wanted to check if everything was okay. We've had a couple of reports of loud noises coming from your suite."

Trevor reached out and rubbed his shoulder. "Oh, thanks for checking, Albert. No, nothing's wrong. I broke a couple of expensive things—clumsy as I am. That's probably the noise they heard."

"There was also some yelling, apparently. Is there someone else here, sir?"

Trevor spread his arms. "Nope. Just little ole me. I had the TV on too loud for a few minutes. That was probably what they heard."

"So, just to be certain, sir, there's no one in your suite who needs medical attention?"

"Absolutely not. You're welcome to check it out for yourself if you wish. I don't mind. I know you're just doing your job, and domestic violence is always a worry these days."

Albert bowed again. "No, sir, I believe you. Sorry again for disturbing you."

"You can disturb me anytime you want, Albert. How are the kids?"

Albert smiled. "Growing up way too fast, sir. Thank you for asking."

"Goodbye, Albert."

Trevor closed the door and walked back to his dining room table. Couldn't resist checking his news feed once again.

A few minutes later, he wished he hadn't.

A taped press conference was highlighted on the screen, being held by the lawyer for Armeen Darhandi.

Trevor cursed.

For fuck's sake, it's a media frenzy! The man was just arrested today, and already his lawyer is holding a press conference? What a fucked-up world!

He clicked on the video.

"Thanks for being here for this announcement. My client, Armeen Darhandi, has been arraigned for the killings of Senator Joseph Farber and Officer Ian Henderson.

"There is an abundance of speculation in the media over possible motives and other matters. So, on behalf of my client, I wanted to get out in front of this.

"My client, and his deceased brother, have been law-abiding Americans. There is no criminal background for either of them, and neither is there any connection to terrorist organizations.

"They were in the media, just like you folks, and while some of you may not have agreed with their positions on controversial matters, that is, as you all would agree, freedom of the press.

"There is a strange aspect to this story that we will be investigating further. The brothers were taken from their place of business approximately a week before the killings. They were being held against their will in a location that we have not been able to pinpoint.

"They were interrogated and subjected to various methods of—I'll just say—mental stimulation, for lack of a better description.

"My client has been examined by doctors at my request, and there is clear evidence of needle marks on his right forearm.

"The medical examiner has advised me that similar needle marks were discovered on the right forearm of his dead brother.

"Toxicology tests have been ordered on both my client and his deceased brother.

"Mr. Darhandi has fully admitted to shooting to death Officer Henderson. But that was in response to the officer's shooting of his brother, Farhad.

"While he was on the run and hiding out, certain things started becoming real to him. He didn't recall shooting Senator Farber at the time, but he does now.

"This may sound to most of you in the media as a weak defense, but at the time of shooting the officer, he only remembered the shock of seeing his brother shot to death, and he responded to that. He has described it to me as being in almost a state of trance up until that point.

"Now that his memory is completely clear, he admits to being involved in both deaths. He is remorseful, and has no idea whatsoever what would cause him and his brother to want to kill the senator. Again, the shooting of the officer was only in response to seeing his brother shot.

"Due to the strange nature of this case, I have asked for

protection for my client while he is in custody. That request has been granted, and we thank the Washington authorities for their consideration.

"No questions today. Thanks for being here."

Trevor felt a headache coming on. He got those once in a while, usually when he was angry, or felt the walls closing in on him. The angry part happened often, but the walls thing was rare. But today, he felt as if his apartment just wasn't big enough for him.

The ring of his landline. He cursed and picked it up.

"Kincaid, here."

It was Albert again.

"Sir, sorry to bother you once again. But I just got a call from someone who has asked me to pass along a message to you. He'd like you to meet him in front of the building, out on the sidewalk. I'm sorry, sir, maybe it's just some kind of crank call. Be careful."

"Did he give a name?"

Trevor heard a rustling of papers.

"Yes, sir, someone named Aaron Dixon."

Trevor sighed. "Okay, Albert, I'll be right down."

After he clicked off, Trevor yelled again at the top of his lungs. "Fuck!"

Could this day get any worse?

Aaron should know better. Flew here from Calgary? What the fuck was he thinking?

Trevor donned his shoes and headed out the door. He could feel the angry adrenaline rushing through his veins.

*****

Jeff put down the disposable phone and waited.

He was sitting in his car on Front Street, just across from The Gainsboro Residences. The security officer had taken his call and promised to pass the message along to Trevor Kincaid. Now, all Jeff had to do was wait and see if the man took the bait.

With his connection to Aaron Dixon, Jeff had no doubt that he would appear.

Finally, Jeff would see who this mysterious millionaire was, the man mixed up in the Aaron Dixon mess, as well as the kidnapping of his own wife.

Jeff pulled his regular phone out of his pocket, and got ready to take a photo. Shouldn't be long now.

A tall bald man suddenly dashed through the front doors. He seemed impatient. Walked back and forth along the street, clearly looking for someone. He had a distinctive beard, and was dressed to the nines.

Jeff felt like someone had kicked him in the gut.

He caught his breath and managed to regain his composure enough to raise his phone up to the window and snap a good full-on photo.

The baldness threw him off for a second, as did the beard.

But those aspects didn't change the build, or the gait.

The way the man swaggered was painfully familiar. His shoulders were painfully familiar.

The way he swung his arms up in the air in frustration once he realized there was no one on the street to meet with him, was also painfully familiar.

A man who had always felt that the world owed him something.

Unmistakably, the man on the street was Brandon Horcroft.

Chapter 36

Rachel was so glad the internet was back up again. She'd felt isolated from the world for the last two weeks, and it was a terrible feeling. Her world was isolated enough, but being disconnected from the news, online magazines, and especially the latest stats on her beloved Blue Jays made her feel even lonelier than she already felt.

But it sure was nice having Olivia in the house as her new sister.

They'd been doing lots of things together—playing outside, cooking lessons, Olivia doing little fashion shows with all of the clothes in her closet.

She'd seemed more alert over the last few days. Those two psychologists were scheduled to come back again for more sessions with her, but had to postpone due to a trip to the East Coast. Rachel was glad about that—it meant Olivia could stay in the main wing of the house and not be isolated again like when she'd first arrived.

It was weird. Rachel was her new big sister, but she felt more like her mother. And Olivia treated her like a mother; at least the way Rachel thought a mother would be treated.

She looked up to her, confided in her about how she felt. Told her about how weird it was to have so many blank spots in her memory.

And she knew she'd arrived in Yellowknife by airplane, but was heartbroken that she wasn't able to remember anything about the flight. She clearly had an obsession about birds, and flying, airplanes and rocket ships.

Rachel found that endearing.

She reminded Olivia that she'd apparently been sedated during that flight due to the psychologists feeling that she was suffering from anxiety. But there would be other flights. Rachel promised her that. Told her that she sort of knew how to fly a plane herself. That Dad had taught her some things, although she didn't have her license.

Olivia was so excited when she heard that. She looked at Rachel with a new kind of awe in her eyes. Wondered if Dad would take her up in the plane someday, and maybe teach her to fly too. Rachel assured her that he would, but she'd have to wait to learn how to fly until she was a bit older. Surely, though, Dad would take her up for at least a ride sometime soon. Rachel promised she'd tell him how excited Olivia was over that idea.

She was scrolling through the news headlines, trying to catch up after being two weeks in the dark.

Suddenly she heard a girlish squeal from the living room.

Ran out of the office and saw little Olivia looking out the window, resting her tiny hands against the glass.

She motioned excitedly. "Come here, Rachel! Look!"

Rachel rested her hand on Olivia's shoulder and followed her gaze.

Out on the main road, two people were horseback riding. Looked like Palominos with brown and white spots, and beautiful long black manes.

"Oh, Olivia, aren't they beautiful?"

Olivia started jumping up and down. "I have to do that! I have to! That's my new dream, Rachel!"

Rachel tugged on her ponytail.

"You have lots of dreams. I love that about you. Hey, want to see some horses on my computer? That city of Calgary has the Stampede every year and it just ended a few weeks ago. They have videos of some of the races and riding horses on the internet. It would be fun!"

Olivia jumped up and down again. "Oh, yes, let's do that! Can I get a glass of chocolate milk first?"

"Sure. Bring me one too."

While Olivia was getting their milk from the kitchen, Rachel went to the Stampede website. Looked at all the video highlights that were available to view, and quickly ruled out bronc riding and the chuck wagon races. Too violent. She didn't want Olivia to see horses being used that way. So, she chose the barrel racing event—she knew Olivia would love that one.

Her little sister came scampering back into the study, spilling some milk along the way. Rachel pulled up a chair for her and they sat side by side in front of the computer.

Olivia was transfixed and speechless for almost fifteen minutes. They watched one heat after another, right to the final championship event.

When it was over, Olivia was gushing.

"Oh, Rachel, I have to do that! Those horses are so beautiful. So fast. And they seem to know what to do, turning those sharp corners around the barrels. And those ladies are beautiful too. Their cowboy hats and their hair blowing behind them under the hats. They wear the cutest tops and jeans. I think I wanna be a cowgirl, Rachel!"

Rachel hugged her.

"You're so sweet. You have so many dreams—to be an eagle, an astronaut, a pilot, and now a horseback rider. I think I love you, Olivia."

She kissed her on the forehead.

Olivia hugged her back. "I love you too, Rachel. Do you think I'd look good as a cowgirl?"

Rachel entered a few words into the search bar of her browser.

"Well, let's look at some cowboy and cowgirl clothes stores, shall we? Maybe Dad will let us order some clothes to be delivered here."

Olivia squealed with delight. "Oh, wouldn't that be great? Do you think he would?"

"We'll see. First, let's take a look and see what clothes you like best."

Up popped a list of western wear stores in Calgary. Rachel clicked on the first one on the list: Lammle's Wear.

She chose children's clothes.

Suddenly there was a display of vests, shirts, jeans, boots and best of all, cowboy hats.

Olivia squealed again, and started tapping her little index finger on the screen.

"Oh, I want that hat—that pink one. It's so pretty. And a pink shirt to match. Maybe that brown vest with the sparkles on it, too. Do you like them, Rachel?"

"I do. Good choices. You'd look like a real cowgirl in those clothes."

Olivia was jumping up and down in her chair. "I'm so excited! Can we order?"

Rachel shook her head. "I can't. But when Dad gets home, we'll ask him, okay?"

"Okay. Is that the only store?"

Rachel shook her head. "Oh, no, there's lots more. Let's visit another one."

She went back to the listing of the stores and clicked the next one on the page.

The home page popped up for Riley and McCormick Western Wear.

Again, she clicked on children's clothes and the catalogue choices appeared.

"This store is called Riley and McCormick. It looks like it has even more choices than Lammle's. We might be better ordering from here."

Silence from Olivia. Rachel had expected to hear another squeal.

She turned her head to look at her. Olivia was staring blankly at the screen—her lips trying to form words, but no sound.

"What's wrong, Olivia?"

The little girl shook her head, and Rachel could see that her eyes had clouded over with tears.

Then she said softly. "Say … the name … of the store again."

"Riley and McCormick."

Suddenly Olivia started to shake—her head first, then her arms and chest, moving quickly down to her legs. She toppled off her chair and onto the floor.

Rachel panicked, thinking she was having some kind of a seizure.

She bent down and swept Olivia up in her arms. Carried her over to the couch and laid her down, propping up her head with a pillow. The shaking had stopped now and Olivia's eyes were wide open, staring into Rachel's eyes. She was crying, tears streaming down her cheeks.

"What's wrong, darling? Are you feeling sick? Tell me so I can help you."

Olivia shook her head. "Say that name again."

"What name?"

"The store."

"Riley and McCormick."

"Say it without the 'and' word."

"Riley McCormick."

Suddenly Olivia repeated the name herself several times. "Riley McCormick, Riley McCormick, Riley McCormick—"

"What is it about the store name that's upsetting you, Olivia?"

She rubbed her eyes with her tiny fists. "I think that's my name,

Rachel. I don't think Olivia is my real name."

Rachel felt like she'd been hit by a lightning bolt.

She stiffened, and then felt like she was going to throw up.

She put her hands over her mouth and gasped.

It was as if all of her confusion and feelings of being lost all these years were brought to the forefront from those simple heartfelt words out of the mouth of the sweet little girl lying on the couch.

This wasn't just about Olivia; it was about Rachel too.

She stroked her fingers against Olivia's cheek, and then leaned over and kissed her.

"I want you to stay here and relax for a few minutes. I'll be over at the computer. I have to check something. Okay?"

The little girl nodded. "Okay, Rachel. Do I sound crazy? I don't want you to think I'm crazy."

"No, you don't sound crazy at all."

Rachel dashed over to the computer and entered the name Riley McCormick in the search bar.

Then sat in shock for a few seconds when she saw all of the articles that popped up for that name. She clicked on the first one—something called an Amber Alert.

Rachel stiffened again, and this time she did throw up. Managed to pull the garbage can out from under the desk just in time.

"Rachel, are you okay?"

"Yes, dear, don't worry."

She wiped her mouth with the back of her hand and stared at the screen. Hypnotized for a few seconds by the image staring back at her.

It was, without a doubt, Olivia.

She scrolled down the page, and stopped at the family photo of a mom and dad, standing proudly beside their two children—a boy and a girl.

Rachel rushed over to the couch and picked Olivia up, cradling her like a baby. Took her back to the computer and sat her on her lap, facing towards her.

"Before you look at this, are you okay? Can you handle a big shock?"

Olivia nodded.

Rachel turned her around and let her look at the Amber Alert on the screen.

"That's you. You are Riley McCormick."

She scrolled down the page again. "Do you recognize these people?"

Olivia just stared with her mouth open. Began to sob. "My mommy, my daddy … and Tommy. Are they dead?"

Rachel spun the laptop around so she couldn't look at it anymore.

"No, I don't think they're dead."

She kissed her on the cheek, and whispered softly in her ear. "Riley—that's what I'm going to call you from now on—I want you to go to your room for a few minutes while I do something. Okay? Do you trust me?"

Riley nodded. "I trust you, Rachel. But … what happened? Why am I here? And why did I forget them? And my own name?"

"I don't know—I can guess, but let's not talk about this anymore for now. Keep this just between you and me. I have something to do, though, so I want you to just lie down in bed, close your eyes, and have a lovely nap. You know that I'll protect you, don't you?"

Another weary nod.

Rachel carefully lifted the little girl up and marched down to her bedroom. Tucked her in and closed the door.

Then glanced at her watch and rushed back to the computer.

He'll be home soon.

Her fingers weren't moving as fast as she wanted them to. She went to the main screen and clicked on the Gmail thingy that her favorite delivery man, Gerry, had put on there for her.

It opened and it looked like it was ready for her to send a message. *But—to who?*

She panicked, clicked off and went back to the search bar again.

That Amber Alert said that Riley had been taken off a street in Calgary. She entered Calgary Police in the search bar. Quickly scrolled through their website until she saw several email addresses. She memorized the first one, and then saw a phone number.

Ran over to the landline phone and dialed the number. Some recorded voice came on and told her that she hadn't done it right. Tried again. Same recording. She was doing something wrong—had never dialed long-distance before. The message said she had to enter the number '1' first. She tried again—didn't work. It didn't seem to recognize her entry of the number. Was the phone blocked for long-distance calls, she wondered?

Rachel gave up on the phone and went back to the computer. Back to Gmail, and then entered the police email address that she'd memorized.

In the subject column she inserted the name: Riley McCormick.

Then down to the message section. Began to type.

Her fingers were working just fine until a big hand swept the laptop off the desk and onto the floor. Then a foot smashed it so hard it began to smoke.

That big hand went for another target now—her face. Her dad slapped her so hard she fell out of her chair.

"What the fuck are you doing, bitch?"

She glared at him from down on the floor. "You kidnapped her, you bastard! Her name is Riley, not Olivia!"

"So, you were going to tattle on me to the police? Your own father?"

She seethed. "You're not my father. You probably stole me, too, you sick little man."

"I have adoption papers. You're mine—and so is she."

Rachel struggled to her feet.

"Let us go. We'll catch a bus to Calgary, and I promise I won't tell anyone anything. Just let us go. She has real parents to go back to, and I can only wonder who my real parents are. It was the same with Angie too, wasn't it? You kidnapped her too, and then shipped her off to someone else. Maybe she didn't suck your ugly dick hard enough? Was that it? Was that why she had to go?"

Rod grabbed her by the throat and began to squeeze. Rachel could feel herself starting to choke.

"You ungrateful bitch! I've given you everything—and this is the thanks you give me?"

He squeezed harder. Rachel feebly beat her fists against his face. He brushed them away with simple turns of his head.

Suddenly there was someone else in the room.

Tiny fists pounded him on the lower back.

A high-pitched voice tempered by sobs. "Leave Rachel alone! Leave her alone! Don't hurt her!"

Rod took one hand off Rachel's throat, reached behind his back, and grabbed Riley by the ponytail. Swung her around in a semi-circle and tossed her into a corner of the room with as much ease as the flip of a baseball.

With one hand still clutching her throat, he thrust Rachel backwards. She hit her head on the side of the desk and collapsed to the ground, gasping for breath.

In a daze, she was only vaguely aware of him turning away from her.

Rod sauntered over to the corner of the room where he'd thrown Riley.

"Get up! I've been patient and gentle with you long enough. It's about time we got to know each other a bit better. You'll like me more after that, I'm sure. And you are my daughter, so you know that obedience is demanded. Go to your room, Olivia. I'll be right behind you."

"No! And my name's Riley!"

He reached down and grabbed her slender shoulders with both hands. Flung her down the hall along the slippery hardwood floor as if she were a bowling ball.

Before marching after her, he made a detour over to Rachel and struck her hard across the back of the head with his fist.

She sensed him staring at her for a few seconds, presumably to make sure she was out cold.

Rachel felt as if unconsciousness would be only moments away anyway, but whether or not that really happened she figured her best option was to pretend that it had.

She allowed a long sigh to escape from her lips—and then faked the rest.

Chapter 37

Jeff was at the helm.

It was a hot and sunny day, perfect for being out on Lake Scugog. He steered the sleek thirty-one-foot Bayliner out towards the middle of the lake.

After about ten minutes of cruising, Louise motioned that they'd gone far enough.

She moved into the cockpit as Jeff turned off the ignition. Louise pushed the electronic anchor button and within mere seconds they were stabilized in place while the waves lapped lazily against the hull.

Jeff loved being out on her cabin cruiser. It had a spacious cabin down below, as well as full kitchen and bathroom facilities.

But the best place was up on top where the four of them were right now. Luxuriating on plush white leather couches in the upper lounge area.

Louise flipped open the lid on a cooler, and they each helped themselves to their choice of canned beverages.

Dan raised his beer in a toast. "Louise, it's been years since I've seen you. You're looking younger than when you were on the force."

Jeff had forgotten that Dan and Louise actually knew each other—not well, but they'd bumped into each other at a few law enforcement conferences back when he was with the RCMP and Louise was deputy police chief of the Toronto force.

"Thanks, Dan. You're looking great too. I think there's something about leaving police work—it's made both of us young again."

"Isn't that the truth? Now I have the pleasure of trying to keep your nephew and his lovely wife out of trouble. Jeff's been a good boy so far, but Gaia just seems to step from one mess into another."

Gaia playfully slapped him on the shoulder. "Hey, that's not fair! I've protected you from Jeff's cooking, haven't I? That's a mess no one should have to deal with."

Dan laughed. "Yes, you have—maybe that's what's been keeping me young."

"Very funny, guys. I'm gonna take some cooking lessons and surprise all of you."

Louise smiled. "I think my nephew takes after me that way. His mother was a great cook, but I don't have those gourmet genes. My dear sister got them all."

Dan grinned. "Yeah, but you had other genes—and your nephew did inherit those."

Louise took a sip of her beer.

"He sure did. And now they're starting to show some fruit with this case you're working on.

"I told Jeff that there was a reason he had such a psychic reaction to the photo of Emily and her bike. He had a connection to her. And it turns out that connection was Brandon Horcroft.

"It was obscure until you guys uncovered the connection. The emails between him and that guy, Aaron, in Calgary—and then the attempted kidnapping of Gaia, which was totally unrelated to the Calgary case.

"But since Brandon's still alive, it was inevitable that he would attempt revenge against the three of you for trying to kill him. So, he wrote you that cryptic letter, Dan. And then he decided his repercussion was to take Gaia once again. In fact, he might have already planned that at the time he wrote you the letter—he was just toying with you, having some sadistic fun.

"By taking Gaia, Brandon was going to make history repeat itself. And I think when Jeff saw that story in the news about Emily, his psychic sense picked up not only the connection of Horcroft to her, but it also perceived that the man was still alive and that danger was imminent.

"That connection between Horcroft and the kidnappers in Calgary was why Jeff had such a strong reaction, but also, there was a little voice telling him that the man was still alive."

Louise pointed her finger at Jeff. "In fact, after you discovered that the man's Forest Hill house had been sold, and then demolished, I think you knew he was alive. You were just in denial.

"As you always did when you were a little boy, you refused to embrace your intuition. And you didn't tell Gaia because that little voice told you she'd be worried. And you weren't confident enough that Brandon was dead to assure her that all was okay. So, you retreated instead—just ignored your intuition."

"God, now I feel guilty. Thanks Auntie."

They all laughed. Gaia wrapped her arms around Jeff's neck and kissed him on the cheek. "I know you were just trying to protect my feelings. You knew it would upset me."

She wagged her finger at him. "But don't ever do it again!"

Gaia grabbed a couple of beers from the cooler, and tossed a fresh one to Dan who'd just drained his.

She sucked back half the can and then sighed. "So, now our worst nightmare has come to life. Brandon Horcroft is still alive. And he's continuing to create hell on earth."

"Well, it's better than not knowing. At least we know who we're dealing with."

Jeff reached into his briefcase and took out four printed copies of the photo he'd taken of Brandon out on Front Street. He passed them around.

"I enlarged the photo. It's a pretty good shot of the guy. He went to some lengths to disguise himself. The beard, the bald head—but it's clearly Brandon."

They all stared at the photo for a couple of minutes. Then Gaia shivered and folded her arms tightly across her chest.

"It's hot as hell out on this boat, but the man still gives me the shivers. Brings back some terrible memories of being trapped as a slave in his vault." She pounded her finger on the photo. "This is one sick man, let me tell you."

Jeff rubbed her shoulder. "I have some other news for us. That Toronto detective, Jim Parsons, brought me up to date this morning on the latest about your ordeal, Gaia. That Chuck Walton guy, the man who rented the storage unit, who owned The Rude Rocker, and who Brandon financed? Well, he was found dead in his club. Suicide. Slit his wrist."

Dan shook his head and whistled in astonishment.

"Sounds like a standard Brandon Horcroft modus operandi. Loose end. Commanded suicide. He must have hypnotized that prick once upon a time and embedded his favorite command for some rainy day when he might have to use it. Gotta admit, he does attend to details."

Dan opened his briefcase and pulled out four copies of a sketch.

"I printed this sketch off. It appeared in all the major American newspapers yesterday. You probably all read about the assassination of that famous senator, Joseph Farber?

"Well, one assassin was killed, but one survived. His defense attorney has held a couple of press conferences, asserting that the two brothers had been held against their will and were subjected to mind control and hypnotism for several days until they were released.

"Then they immediately went out to the Washington suburbs and killed the senator. The surviving assassin admits he did it, but doesn't know why.

"His lawyer is suggesting that he was possibly programmed to do it. Well, yesterday, he published this drawing that a sketch artist did. It was based on a description the assassin gave of the man who conducted the mind control."

Dan passed around copies of the sketch.

The three of them gasped.

Jeff held his photo of Brandon—and the sketch—up in front of his face, side by side.

He whispered. "Jesus Christ. Couldn't be more bang on. Brandon basically killed the senator."

Louise jumped in. "Did you guys ever see that movie, *The Manchurian Candidate?*"

Nods all around.

"Well, that's what this sounds like to me."

Jeff stood up and stretched his arms.

"Dan, you'll remember all that stuff I photocopied out of Brandon's office vault years ago. We discovered he was doing all sorts of nefarious stuff for the CIA, and then when you tried to have him charged with insider trading and murder, your bosses shut the thing down. The CIA pressured them to drop it, because he was their guy.

"If this sketch is accurate, it looks like Brandon's still active as a CIA operative—just under the Trevor Kincaid name now."

Dan took off his sandals and stretched his long legs out over the side rails of the lounge. "While we're out here, might as well get some color on my pale legs."

"Changing the subject, are you?"

"Kind of. I'm still disturbed about that. It's pretty sad when justice becomes political. But the fact remains, he's a dangerous man and still on the loose.

"I have a good mind to fly down to visit the CIA and tell them that we know he's still alive, and that we know he killed the senator.

"But the rational side of me tells me that would be stupid. The CIA would just drive him underground and give him another new identity.

"It's better that we know where he is, and that he doesn't realize we've discovered his real identity.

"Which reminds me, Gaia, I've asked Allan to stay on as your live-in bodyguard for a few more weeks. He's agreed, and was thankful we gave him the day off today.

"Brandon, despite all these other things he has going on the side, is still obsessed with you. He may try again. If he does, Allan will put a bullet between his eyes."

Louise got up and went down to the cabin below. Came back with a hamper of sandwiches. "Here, guys, dig in."

They ate in silence for a few minutes until Louise broke it.

"Jeff, did you bring along copies of those photos of Emily Clarkson and that recent girl that went missing, Riley McCormick?"

"I did." Jeff reached down into the side compartment of his briefcase and pulled out the two photos. He handed them to her.

"I'm going to look at these for a few minutes. Please chew quietly for a bit."

The three of them stopped eating and stared at her, transfixed.

Louise focused intently on the two photos, then closed her eyes and kept them closed for a good five minutes.

Finally, she sighed and opened them again. Handed the photos back to Jeff.

She began to speak—very slowly, and very softly.

"Jeff, when you first came to me and showed me the photo of Emily and her bicycle, I didn't see anything. But now I do.

"I see three females. Two older, one young. All three are blonde and have their hair in ponytails.

"But this part is interesting. It's like a video playing in my mind.

"One of the females—one of the older ones—is standing off to the side. She isn't together with the other two. And I see her reaching up and taking the clip off her ponytail and allowing her hair to fall to her shoulders.

"The other two females are holding hands—one young, one older. Both of them have their hair in ponytails while the third one, as I said, is getting rid of the ponytail.

"All three females are blonde, blue-eyed, but one of the older ones—and I can't tell which—isn't really blonde. I see dark roots. She must have dyed her hair blonde. It was a separate image flashing at me—showing me a close-up of the top of one of the blonde heads. There were dark roots.

"The two holding hands have diamond necklaces around their necks.

"The other older one, the one off to the side, doesn't have a necklace. But there's an image of the Eiffel Tower standing behind her. And she's bending over, picking up what looks like wheat— letting it sift through her fingers. Then she bends over and picks up some more. This is the female who took her hair out of the ponytail."

Silence all around.

Then Jeff spoke.

"The diamonds are consistent with what I saw in the photo of Emily that her parents showed me. And I got the feeling she was in Yellowknife, the land of the diamond mines. But that third girl is puzzling. So, there were three?"

Louise nodded.

"That's what it's showing me. But only two are together. The other one is away from them—possibly in Paris? The Eiffel Tower is the hint there, but I'm confused about the wheat sifting through her fingers."

Jeff leaned forward in his chair, focusing intently on his intuitive aunt.

"And one is no longer wearing her hair in a ponytail, and one is not a natural blonde."

Louise rubbed some sunscreen on her bare arms.

"Yes, and two are together; one young, one older—and when I say older, the two older ones are young women, early twenties."

"So, there's a possibility that Riley McCormick is the young girl you saw, and one of the two older ones could be Emily."

"Yes, that's possible—but my visions don't identify them to me."

Gaia was playing around on her phone.

Suddenly she gasped.

"Oh, my God!"

Jeff leaned towards her to see what she was looking at.

"Jeff, when you were first telling me about the research you did on sex trafficking, I remembered you mentioned that it was rare to have children be taken out of the country due to the risks involved."

"Yep, that's true."

"I've just googled here about which cities in Canada are compared to Paris. There's one city that has the nickname, The Paris of the Prairies.

"Well, that city is Saskatoon, because of all of its beautiful bridges. And one of its prime economic commodities is wheat! Those prairie lands around Saskatoon are Canada's prime producers and exporters of wheat."

Chapter 38

Trevor was on his satellite phone, parked on a downtown side street.

"I've been trying to reach you for days. Where the hell have you been, and why haven't you returned my calls?"

"Had to get some serious dental work done. Then, Sherry and I decided to get away for a few days. Things are getting hot, here, Trevor."

"Aaron, did you fly here to Calgary a few days ago?"

"Of course not—and I would have let you know if I was planning something like that."

"Well, someone used your name and phoned in a message to the security guard at my building. Said he wanted to meet me out on the street. I went out and no one was there."

"It must be those damn private detectives. You and I haven't talked in a while, but two of them were here again—one of the bastards knocked out a few of my teeth. Before he left he mentioned your name—he asked, "Will Trevor Kincaid protect you?" They know about my private equity company owning my house back at the time we took Emily. They also know my fingerprints were on the bike, and that our company owned a blue van at the time we took her. As I said, things are getting hot."

Trevor took a deep breath before replying. Could feel his heart beating faster and his mouth going dry.

"Did he say how he knew my name?"

"No. But this guy is apparently a former Mountie, so he must have connections."

"I didn't pay much attention before when you said detectives were working with the Clarksons. It's such an old case that there's not much to investigate. But now you have my attention. What's that Mountie's name?"

Trevor heard a drawer open and close. "Yeah, I've got his card. A Dan Nicholson of Nicholson Investigations. The other guy's name was Jeff Kavanaugh. There was a women here once, too, but I don't recall her name."

"I see."

"Do you know these people?"

"No, not at all. I wouldn't worry too much—they're just digging around. But I think I can guess how they got my name. You emailed me that one time to my regular address. They've obviously been doing some snooping on your online activity. That's why I insisted you only use the encrypted addresses. Don't ever do that again, Aaron."

"You're right. I screwed up. Well, hopefully they don't know too much else."

"Just calm down, Aaron, and tell Sherry to take it easy as well. They're trying to flush you out. Blowing smoke up your ass to cause you to make a mistake. Don't fall for it. They have nothing or you would have been arrested by now. In the meantime, though, we'll cool activity a bit. No more adoptions for a while."

"Okay—makes sense. But Trevor, you didn't comment on that question the detective asked me. So, I gotta know. You will protect me and Sherry, won't you?"

Trevor laughed. "That's a stupid question, Aaron. You've known me a long time, and we've done business together for a couple of decades now—way back when I was known by my alter ego, Brandon Horcroft. Friends stick together. I have your back; don't worry."

Trevor clicked off, drove to the end of the side street, and pulled out into Queen Street traffic. As he drove aimlessly along, he replayed the conversation in his head. He hadn't admitted to Aaron that he knew the detectives. Didn't want to alarm him into thinking that they were getting too close for comfort—which, of course, they were.

He shook his head, thinking about what a ridiculous coincidence it was that they were the ones investigating the Clarkson girl's kidnapping.

Why would they get involved in a case way out in Calgary? Maybe Jeff, Dan or Gaia knew the Clarksons and were drawn in to help them when that bike was found buried in Aaron's yard?

He shook his head again, and cursed.

Sometimes the world was just too fucking small a place.

He had no doubt it was one of them who had phoned his building security pretending to be Aaron, tricking him into coming outside. And since no one approached him, that told Trevor that they must have wanted to get a look at him, maybe take a photo. He was well disguised now with the bald head and beard, but maybe not disguised enough. Jeff or Gaia would no doubt recognize him for sure. Which meant they now knew that Brandon Horcroft was still alive. Trevor's radar was now on full alert.

Chapter 39

"Jeff and Gaia—this is Jason Watkins. I told you about him. Was probably the RCMP's most brilliant hacker. Now, he's making real money out on his own."

They shook hands, then Jason put his hands on his hips and glared at Dan.

"Dan, I resent being referred to as a hacker. I prefer the more respectable title of Cryptic Systems Analyst."

Dan laughed and patted Jason on the back. "Okay, we'll go with that, Jay."

Jason chuckled and said, "Okay, now that we have that settled and I have some semblance of respectability again, where shall we sit?"

Jeff motioned to the stairs leading to his basement. "I have a larger office downstairs, and lots of room for us to stretch out. The living room's too formal for an afternoon beer meeting."

Once they were seated downstairs, and Jeff had passed around beers, Jason opened his briefcase and pulled out a large notepad.

Gaia giggled. "Jason, I thought you were a cryptic systems analyst. What are you doing with a notepad?"

He smiled at her. "Screw that tech shit. I still prefer pen and paper!"

They all had a good laugh at that.

Before Jason began, Dan gave a bit of a longer intro to Jeff and Gaia. "Jay was one of the Mounties on my organized crime team. So, while this tech stuff is his speciality, he also carried a gun and a badge just like the rest of us. As well, he's a tenth-degree black belt in Taekwando. So, I would suggest that if he asks you for another beer, you jump to it!"

Jeff studied the man sitting across from him. Tall, well over six feet, with a lanky build. Athletic looking, so the martial arts part was believable. But it was his wrists that Jeff noticed the most—not thick, but sinewy. Very powerful looking. He guessed that Jason was around fifty years old, a good-looking man who was still blessed with a thick head of hair.

He had to know. "Jason, before you start into your report, I have a question for you. Did you ever play baseball?"

"Yeah, how'd you guess that?"

"Your wrists. An infielder, right?"

"You're sharp—but I hear you're a psychic. Maybe you saw me in an Expos uniform?"

"Expos? Really? That's fabulous."

Jason shook his head. "Not so fabulous. I was a short-stop, came up from Triple A in the early 90s. Then, after two seasons tore my ACL. So, that was the end of that."

"You must have been just shattered."

"No, not really. I already had my degree, so at least I had that to fall back on. It's just life, though, isn't it? Hey, if I hadn't injured myself, I never would have met your partner Danny boy here, and be in the position of having to save his life a couple of times."

Dan laughed. "More like the other way around, bud."

Jason opened his notepad. "I must admit, though—I looked a hell of a lot better in my red tunic than Dan did. Okay, now that we have the frivolous stuff out of the way, let's get down to business."

He pointed at Jeff. "That detective, Jim Parsons, told you about

Trevor Kincaid being the financier of The Rude Rocker. Owned by that Chuck Walton guy, who's now dead. And of course, Walton had the connection to those two creeps who tried to take Gaia, with the storage unit they were probably taking her to."

Jeff nodded. "That's all correct, Jason. And of course, we now know that Trevor Kincaid is actually Brandon Horcroft."

"Call me Jay. Everyone does. Yeah, on the Brandon thing, Dan brought me up to date. We'll leave that for now, though.

"I hacked into—oops, I meant to say 'cryptically analysed'—the CRA site." He put a finger up to his lips and chuckled. "Shh—don't tell anyone." They all laughed.

"Anyway, the CRA is kind of a snap. You can get in and out without being seen—the security really sucks. If any of you would like me to go back in and change your income tax slips, you know how to reach me.

"I did some flitting around with the Kincaid name. The company he set up for things like the financing of that Walton guy is called Centrus Capital Management. It's a legitimate company with genuine activity. Pays taxes every year, looks like a good corporate citizen. Kincaid is the sole owner. Has clients right across the country. Capital investments in all sorts of ventures, and seems to get good returns on all of them. Generally smaller companies that probably wouldn't be able to land conventional loans from banks. That's where venture capitalists like Kincaid step in—advance the funds and charge higher than market interest rates. Most of his investments seem to be in the Toronto area, but he has a couple in Vancouver and Montreal as well. So, that part all looks legit."

Jeff was trying to take it all in. So far, nothing seemed out of the ordinary. "You didn't see any money transfers to Aaron Dixon out in Calgary?"

"Nope. There's nothing in this company's financials that shows expenses or income to or from private individuals."

"Okay, well I guess that's a dead end."

Jason shook his head. "Not so quick. I'm not finished yet. There is also income coming in from various companies across the country for management consulting services. They look to be long-term agreements, usually ten years, but paid one hundred percent up front. The financials realize the entire income during the first year, even though the agreements are for ten years. Kind of stupid to do it that way from a tax standpoint, but that's the way he does it. Most management contract payments seem to be for ten million, but there are some for smaller amounts. He also has income coming into the company from the United States, on a pretty steady basis. A few million each month. The man does very well indeed."

Dan nodded. "Yeah, I told you about his connections with the CIA, Jay. That must be what that American income is."

Jeff leaned back in his chair and rested his feet up on the coffee table.

"Jay, these management agreements he has—could you tell what kind of services he offers? And are the companies he does consulting for similar?"

Jason shook his head. "No similarity at all; they cover the whole spectrum. From developers, to retail establishments, factories, and even a diamond mine."

Jeff suddenly perked up. "What did you say? A diamond mine?"

Jason looked at his notes. "Yeah, Great White North Diamonds Inc., owned by a guy named Rod Milton."

"Where is it?"

"Based in Yellowknife."

"Holy shit!"

Jason chuckled. "Sounds like I struck a nerve. Okay, I'll carry on. This Rod Milton guy owns the mine, which is a couple of hundred miles north of Yellowknife. But his company's office headquarters are in the city itself. He has a personal net worth of about half a billion, so he does well for himself.

"But this one's a bit strange. There's reference in the materials we hacked into that Centrus had a previous contract with this diamond mine fifteen years ago, but it expired five years ago. There was an initial payment of ten million, but then three years into the contract term, five million was refunded by Centrus back to Milton. Doesn't explain why. But suddenly there was new activity back on the same account again just a few weeks ago. Another payment of ten million was deposited into Centrus' corporate bank account from Great White North Diamonds, for a new term of ten years."

Gaia's hands were over her mouth now. Dan stared at Jeff. "Starting to make sense, isn't it Jeffy?"

"God, is it ever. Emily disappeared fifteen years ago. That's when the first contract was signed for ten million. Then, a refund of five million three years later, but we can only guess what that was about. But a new contract a few weeks ago, for another ten million payment—that's when Riley McCormick disappeared.

"And I can't help but remember what Louise said—*two of them are together with one being older.* And they both had diamond necklaces in her vision—meaning, to us, that the two of them were in Yellowknife. But there was a third girl, in her early twenties Louise said. She wasn't with the other two."

Jeff turned his attention back to Jason. "I'm bracing myself for your answer here, Jay. Does Centrus have a contract with any companies in Saskatoon?"

Jason looked at his notes again. "Yep. A company by the name of Hunt Development Corp., a large property developer. Owned by a guy named Foster Hunt. Net worth about two hundred million. The contract with him came into effect twelve years ago, so it's expired now."

Dan cracked his knuckles. "Jesus! So, that contract came into force right around the same time as that partial refund was given to the diamond company on their first contract. Coincidence?"

Chapter 40

The ruse had been worked out in advance. The Clarksons were nervous about it, but agreed that they would summon up the courage and just do it.

Dan convinced them to invite the Dixons over for afternoon tea—purportedly to make nice and apologize for the behavior of their detective, Dan Nicholson, during his last visit when he'd caused Aaron to lose four of his teeth.

So, the Clarksons sucked up their hate for their former best friends and invited them over. They told Dan that Aaron and Sherry seemed surprised, but also sounded a bit relieved. Dan knew that's how they'd react. Their assumption would be that if the Clarksons were inviting them over, seemingly to toss them an olive branch, that maybe, just maybe, the investigation into them was dying off.

So, Dan was in Calgary once again. He'd just picked up one of Canada's most prominent defense attorneys Abe Mendelson from his office in Bankers Hall. Dan knew him from his days back on the force, when they'd both been involved in cases together, always from opposite sides of course. But Abe was one of the best—and he had serious clout with prosecutors.

Dan steered down the Clarksons' street and pulled into their driveway. He glanced over at Abe. "Are you ready, bud?"

"Sure am. This should be interesting. With most of the evidence so far being circumstantial, this couple is probably the only way you'll be able to blow this thing open. Let's see if we can scare the shit out of them. A little bit of bullshit usually goes a long way."

They walked up to the front door and didn't bother to knock. Dan and Abe marched into the living room where the two couples were enjoying their tea and cookies.

Aaron lurched to his feet. "You!" Then he looked over at Ken and Cathy. "What the fuck is this? A set-up?"

Ken glared at him. "You're damn fucking right it is, asshole! Sit the fuck down and listen to what these two men have to say. Otherwise, I'm sure Dan won't hesitate to knock out those replacement implants the dentist gave you."

Sherry grabbed Aaron by the hand and pulled him back down to the couch. "Doesn't hurt to hear what they have to say, dear."

Dan couldn't wipe the angry frown off his face. Just looking at Bonnie and Clyde sitting there smugly on the couch, made him want to just smash their heads together.

"Good choice. This is Abe Mendelson, a criminal defence attorney based in downtown Calgary. He's one of the most prominent in his field, and he's not cheap. But from what we've been able to determine, you can afford him. Abe has agreed to represent you, if you so choose. I'll let Abe take it from here."

Abe cleared his throat. "Everyone deserves a defense. I won't share my opinions on the things you've allegedly done. However, anyone involved up to their necks the way you two are, needs to make decisions before all hell breaks loose."

Aaron pulled his hand away from Sherry and leaned forward on the couch.

"What do you mean? We haven't been charged with anything."

"Trust me, you will be. And then it will be too late to strike a deal. The evidence is mounting—I won't share with you all that we know. You know some of it, but not all of it. And soon officers will be arriving with handcuffs. Kidnapping carries a possible life sentence. And please, don't deny that that's what you've been doing. Don't insult me."

Sherry spread her arms out wide, palms up. "You have sweet dick-all nothing. You're bluffing."

"I charge two thousand dollars an hour. I wouldn't waste my time being here if I was bluffing."

Aaron jumped back in. "The cops haven't even talked to us since the bike was found. Clearly, they don't see a crime."

"Police investigate in silence most of the time—until that inevitable knock comes on your door. But let me continue. I'm here to help you, not convict you. There's a man behind all of this, so you two are just the small fry.

"A man by the name of Trevor Kincaid. We know he's been raking in millions for certain services, and we are fairly certain those services were the kidnapping of young girls. And delivering those girls to certain buyers, for whatever purposes.

"You two, and probably many more just like you across the country, were the actual kidnappers. He paid you for those activities, and since there's not a hell of a lot in your bank accounts, you've probably stashed it offshore. That can be traced, don't worry. Just takes a little more time.

"We think that Emily Clarkson was sent by you to Yellowknife. And we think you were also involved in the recent kidnapping of Riley McCormick, and we suspect she is also in Yellowknife.

"Online investigations disclose payments from the same man in Yellowknife back when Emily disappeared, and again recently when Riley disappeared. We know that you, Sherry, had a relationship with Riley when she was in day care and kindergarten. And of course, you both had a neighbor relationship with Emily.

"We suspect there's another girl in Saskatoon that you were both involved with taking as well. Someone who was first in Yellowknife, then transferred to Saskatoon. Online records point to this. Considering how wealthy the two of you are with only modest jobs, we suspect that over a couple of decades there are many more children who you've kidnapped.

"You two are going to prison for the rest of your lives. Unless you come clean and give evidence against the ringleader and the people who commissioned his services. Trevor Kincaid is the ringleader, Rod Milton in Yellowknife is a buyer, and one other buyer who we know of right now is a man named Foster Hunt in Saskatoon.

"You would need to provide evidence against all three of those men, including documents and emails. Those emails right now seem to be encrypted, so you'd have to unlock them. And you would have to be totally open and honest about everything—not just the three who I've mentioned, but everyone over the years who you've provided your services for, and all of the children you've kidnapped."

Aaron raised his arms in the air in exasperation. "Why the hell would we want to do that, assuming we even have anything to tell?"

"Oh, I'm certain you have a story to tell. A story that would probably make most of us sick to our stomachs. But you two are just in the middle. You're guilty as hell, but you're not the instigators. Trevor Kincaid is the instigator, and that's who the courts would want. And the buyers are also who they'd want.

"But if not you, then someone's going to talk. It all depends on who points the finger at who first. We could approach any of those three men and offer a similar deal to them. They might decide to implicate you in a bigger way to cut themselves a deal. Which means, you'd take the biggest fall.

"You should know that I've already discussed your situation hypothetically with the courts here. I didn't share any names or specifics; just gave them a 'what if' scenario. Their best guess for your cooperation would be ten to fifteen years for each of you. No guarantee that a judge would agree, but judges usually do when significant help is given. And I stress, your help would have to be significant—like, everything, no holding back. That's the only way I'd be able to cut the best deal for you both."

Aaron stood, grabbed Sherry's hand and yanked her to her feet. "We're going to leave now."

Abe pulled a couple of business cards out of his pocket. "Here, take these. Call me anytime, but don't wait too long. This investigation is moving at warp speed."

Chapter 41

It was as if there was a fog in the room. A dense shroud of mistiness that filtered everything she looked at. She was sure that her eyes were open, but nothing looked the way it was supposed to look.

Even the floor Rachel was lying prone on seemed to have waves in it—waves that were moving, cresting, making her feel dizzy.

She rolled onto her back and stared at the ceiling. It was moving too, towards her, seemingly coming down to crush her.

Moved over onto her side and supported herself with one elbow. Shook her head back and forth several times, then rubbed her eyes with her free hand. That made things a bit clearer, but the sudden movements of her head summoned terrible waves of pain.

She remembered now.

The images were coming back to her. He'd had his hands around her throat and then shoved her backwards—her head had hit the desk and she'd gone down. Then he came back and hit her in the head one more time.

Rachel recalled that she'd pretended to be unconscious so he'd leave her alone, but now was sure that she really had passed out. For how long, she had no idea.

She shifted up onto her knees and the waves of pain came back instantly. Every sudden move brought the cascades of aching, starting from the back of her head, into her forehead, and settling behind her eyeballs.

Rachel figured that must be why her vision was so blurry.

She reached up, grabbed the edge of the desk and pulled herself to her feet—but still held onto the desk for dear life. She knew that it wouldn't take much for her to simply topple over again.

The dizziness was unbearable. She felt like she was drunk, even though Rachel didn't really know what that feeling was like.

Took a deep breath and started concentrating on what had happened. She knew she was at the computer when he came home, and then he smashed it.

Why?

Rachel looked down at the floor—sure enough, the machine was lying there, destroyed. Then he'd put his hands on her throat and begun to squeeze so hard that she found it hard to breathe.

Rachel brushed her fingers across her neck—it was wet. Her fingers were now covered in blood. He must have squeezed so hard that his fingernails had drawn blood.

Who was I trying to email? What was it that got him so angry?

Suddenly it came back to her in an instant. Maybe it was the latest wave of pain in her head that awakened her.

She'd been trying to email the Calgary police. About Olivia.

No, not Olivia—her name was Riley. Riley McCormick!

She recalled the Amber Alert, the solo photo of Riley, and the other photo of Riley with her parents and brother Tommy.

Riley had reacted to the photos right away. Whatever drugs they'd given her since her arrival in Yellowknife, and despite the long sessions of repetitive words and images, it hadn't been enough. All it took was the name of that western wear shop, Riley and McCormick, to trigger the memories that they'd tried their best to suppress.

And when Riley was convinced that was her real name, Rachel had googled it. And the truth was disclosed in the Amber Alert.

She concentrated again. What happened when he had his fingers around her throat?

Riley had come out of her room and started pounding their dad on the back. Begging him to stop.

Then the bastard grabbed her by the ponytail and threw her into a corner of the room. But he wasn't finished. He ordered her to her room and announced that he was going to go there with her. She refused. He grabbed her by the shoulders and slid her on her back all the way down the long slippery hallway.

Her room. Him with her. Sweet little Riley. Memories were coming back.

Ever since Rachel had read that article about the discovery of the bicycle that had been buried in a yard in Calgary, and seen the photo of Emily Clarkson—who had disappeared without a trace fifteen years ago—she'd noticed a change in herself.

More desire for independence, questioning things more, demanding answers from him. Had sex in the kitchen with her favorite delivery man, Gerry. That song she'd started singing about swinging on a star, and moonbeams in a jar.

Then she'd asked her father questions about Angie, and why she'd been sent away twelve years ago.

After he'd spanked her bare ass with his belt for daring to ask questions he didn't want to answer, Rachel remembered that Angie had written her a letter when she left—something she'd blocked out all these years and didn't know why.

Was there something wrong in her brain? She wondered sometimes. She'd removed the letter that had been taped to the underside of her dresser, and read it. Almost as if for the first time.

And discovered that Angie's new last name was going to be Hunt instead of Milton. And that she'd be living in Saskatoon. That 'swinging on a star' song was mentioned in the letter as well—she and Angie must have sung it together when they were sisters.

Suddenly Rachel heard sounds from down the hall.

She steadied herself against the desk, then shoved her body towards the couch, and from there to the armchair. Lurched towards the hallway and leaned against the wall to catch her breath.

Her eyes were clearer now and so was her brain.

Their dad was a kidnapper. He'd taken Riley from her family. And with the reaction Rachel had had the instant she saw the photo of Emily Clarkson and her little pink bicycle with the white handlebars, Rachel was wondering now. If he'd taken Riley, had he kidnapped her too? Was Rachel actually Emily Clarkson?

Which meant that Angie had probably been kidnapped as well. Then sent away for whatever reason. Emily had disappeared fifteen years ago, and her father had adopted Rachel and Angie fifteen years ago. The coincidence was too much. Rachel knew that while her brain might have been damaged in some way, she also knew that she was smart, and capable of connecting the dots.

Rachel focused her eyes on the door at the very end of the hall.

Riley's room.

She pushed herself off the wall and into the middle of the hall. Wavering on her feet, she reached both hands outward against the walls. Began moving down the hallway using the walls on both sides to help keep her balance.

The door was getting closer with each shaky step, and the sounds from the room were becoming less muffled.

She heard Riley's voice clearly now.

"No, I don't want to!"

Then his voice—angry and desperate.

"Lie down on the bed! Now!"

The sound of little footsteps, then the sound of heavy ones.

"Goddamnit, I'm your father. You'll do as you're told!"

"Let me go! Stop it!"

Then the sound of bedsprings, as if someone was jumping on the mattress. But Rachel knew that he'd thrown her.

"Now, stay there. Get under the sheets if that makes you feel better."

Riley was crying now. Sobbing. Begging him to leave her alone.

"Olivia, stop that!"

"I'm not Olivia! I'm Riley! I want my mommy! Take me back!"

"Your name is Olivia. And your parents are dead. Rachel was just playing games with your mind."

"She was not!"

Rachel was in front of the door now. She took one hand off the wall and tried the door handle. It was locked.

Then she heard a scream. "Get off me! I can't breathe!"

Rachel felt panic in her heart, and an ache her bosom. She used her hands to steady herself against the two walls again and raised her right foot into the air.

Who am I kidding? I can't kick in this door.

Her brain was working fast now. The horror of the moment had returned it to total alertness.

What can I use?

Suddenly she knew. Rachel spun around and rushed down to the living room. No longer needing the walls to steady herself. She was as steady as a maple tree now.

Skidded into the living room and grabbed the heavy mahogany bar cart. It had rubber wheels—he wouldn't even hear it coming. She took the bottles of booze and glasses out of the cubbyholes, to enhance the cart's silence, and tossed them to the carpeted floor.

Grabbed the handle at the back of the cart and made a quick detour into the kitchen. Reached into the cutlery drawer and took out her favorite cutting knife. It was the longest and sharpest, and if there was anyone who knew of such things it was a gourmet chef like Rachel.

Stuck the knife into the back pocket of her jeans and wheeled the bar cart back out to the hallway again.

Stood at the apex of the long expanse and glared down the fifty feet of hall. Towards her target—the door to Riley's room. She focused on it, and summoned the anger that was surging through her veins.

The sobbing from Riley was continuous now.

Suddenly her anguished voice yelled out. "Ow! That hurts! Stop it, stop it!"

Rachel couldn't contain herself now. She'd wanted her approach to the room to be silent, but her emotions got the better of her. That plan of stealth and silence suddenly flew out the window.

She knew instinctively what was driving her. Even though she'd never experienced it before she met Riley, she knew what it was.

Motherly instinct.

Rachel reared her head back and screamed at the top of her lungs. Then she gripped both hands tightly onto the handle of the cart and raced the entire length of the hall—Riley's bedroom door being the target in her mind's eye.

The rage in her heart caused her to scream one last time, at the very instant that the heavy cart splintered the door into pieces.

Chapter 42

Aaron Dixon was down in his basement hammering nails into a board. Not to accomplish anything in particular, because he wasn't trying to build anything. He just wanted to hammer some nails, and he did this whenever he felt helpless or frustrated. It was a good stress reliever.

But he was too lazy to use a real hammer. He always used a pneumatic nail gun. Loved the sound and power of it. Even loved the recoil. It helped distract him from the crap.

Sherry came down the stairs quietly, not wishing to disturb his concentration. She knew what he could be like.

She sat down in a chair opposite his workbench and watched him shoot.

Aaron ignored her for a few minutes while he shot in ten more nails. Finally, he tossed the nail gun onto the workbench and hoisted himself up onto the rough unfinished wood, feet dangling a couple of feet off the ground.

"So, what are we going to do, Aaron?"

"We're up shit's creek is where we are. Boxed into a corner."

"I asked what we're going to do, not where we are. I know where we are. You dragged me into this shit years ago, convincing me that it was foolproof. Now, I guess, we're the fools, aren't we?"

He glared at her. "Hey, you didn't need too much convincing.

Don't pin this shit on me. We got paid handsomely for all the girls we took. I can't even count how many there were now, we've been doing this for so long. And you were involved with every single one of them. You were a willing goddamn participant."

"Okay, Einstein, what are we going to do? It was your brilliant plan when you hooked up with that Brandon prick. Now, cleverly transformed into this new Trevor prick. He does know how to take care of himself, doesn't he? And now here we are, the fall guys."

"We're not going to be fall guys for anyone."

"So, you have no ideas? Hammering all those nails didn't trigger any brain cells? Well, I'll tell you what we should do, then. Get the fuck out of this country now, while we still can. We have millions stashed away in Bermuda, so it's time we grabbed our own money and escaped. The walls are closing in."

Aaron shook his head. "No, not possible unless Trevor releases the funds."

"What? That's our money! He's been depositing it in a numbered account in Bermuda for us for a couple of decades. Why do we need him to release them?"

Aaron sighed. "Because those accounts are also in his name. He insisted that the accounts be joint—our names and his."

Sherry stood and planted her hands on her hips. "I never knew that! Why did you agree to this?"

"I dunno. I guess I just didn't understand that stuff. He said that for him to deposit money in that account, under Bermuda laws he'd have to be signatory, and that we would have to make each other joint beneficiaries. If he dies, it reverts to us—if we die, it reverts to him."

"That's bullshit! Jesus, why did I trust you with this? You're clearly just the typical dumb football coach, aren't you? That's the extent of you."

Aaron jumped off the workbench and took a threatening step

towards her. "Fuck off! I don't need your shit!"

Sherry stood her ground.

"The only shit we need to deal with right now is getting our money so we can get the fuck out of here. Aside from that Bermuda account, all of our money is locked up in this house. It will take forever to sell this place, especially now after all the bad publicity from that bicycle being dug up.

"We have no substantial funds otherwise. It's either the Bermuda accounts or it's nothing."

"Well, we could take that lawyer's offer and just testify against Trevor and all the buyers. That option is still one we could take."

"What? And spend ten to fifteen years in prison? Are you nuts?"

"Well, it's better than life in prison. We are kidnappers after all. They'd throw away the key."

"I'm not fucking going to prison, Aaron. I want our money. It's ours. We're entitled to it. Let's phone Trevor and get this done. Get him to release our funds, and let him know that if he doesn't do that, we're going to tell all. That threat will get his ass in gear."

Aaron reached over to the corner of the workbench and picked up his satellite phone.

"Alright. We'll do that right now. Time's a-wastin."

*****

Dan was relaxing in his executive class window seat. He was happy that the woman sitting next to him wasn't one of those who wanted to tell her entire life story in a four-hour flight. They'd said hi to each other and that was the extent of it.

They were one hour into the Air Canada flight from Calgary to Toronto, and he was looking forward to getting home. These quick back and forths were exhausting.

But he thought the trip had been worthwhile.

They were pushing the envelope now in a serious direction, and he thought Abe Mendelson had handled things with the Dixons like the true pro that he was.

Aaron and Sherry now had a choice to make, and he was confident they'd realize that there was no way out.

To avoid a life sentence, they'd have to throw Trevor Kincaid, or Brandon Horcroft, or whoever the fuck he really was, under the bus. And the buyers who he'd sent the girls to as well. This was the breaking point in the case, and the Dixons were now in a box.

And Dan had to reluctantly admit that without their testimony, everything was circumstantial. They needed those two, the actual kidnappers, to bring justice to bear. Without them, the authorities probably wouldn't act. Because, the whole thing was so compartmentalized—Trevor Kincaid, the buyers in Yellowknife and Saskatoon and elsewhere—with the Dixons smack in the middle.

Dan smiled as he gazed out the window at the vast prairies below.

His mind wandered a bit, but something suddenly started nagging at him.

One of those things that pops into your mind at idle moments. Sometimes, useless stuff. But oftentimes, something that the subconscious was straining to remind you of.

The suicide of Chuck Walton, the owner of The Rude Rocker, popped into his head. The loose end.

Then it came to him.

He blurted out loud, "Shit!"

His seatmate looked at him, alarm written all over her face. In a voice that was an octave or too higher than when she'd said hello, she asked, "What is it? Is something wrong with the plane?" She strained her neck to take a peek out his window.

Dan patted her arm. "No, nothing's wrong. No engine fire or anything. I apologize—I forgot about something and my frustration poured out. Sorry to alarm you."

She stared at him with a look that said, *"Are you daft?"*

Dan turned his gaze back to the prairies below.

And silently admonished himself.

How could I have been so stupid? Could Trevor have hypnotized the Dixons too? The instant we land I have to phone and warn them not to talk to him.

*****

Aaron was on the phone, with Sherry's ear pressed up against his cheek.

"So, Trevor, as I said, the best option is for us to just get the hell out of here. We don't want to testify against you, but we're not going to spend the rest of our lives in prison.

"If that's what we'd be facing, I can tell you right now that we're going to tell them everything. And pass along documents that will incriminate you and all of your clients. This has turned into a shit-storm.

"That lawyer laid everything out for us. I like you, Trevor, I really do, but I'm not going to prison for you."

Aaron heard a frustrated sigh at the other end of the phone.

"I understand. You could, of course, just call their bluff. They really don't have anything at all. As I told you before, if they had anything, you both would be under arrest by now."

Aaron raised his voice to a level just shy of yelling.

"Fuck, they know about Yellowknife, they know about Saskatoon! That's getting pretty fucking specific! They know about you, they know the names of those two buyers. Geez, Trevor, wake up! The gig is up. Just give authorization to the bank in Bermuda for us to be able to access our funds and we'll be on our way. It's that simple."

Aaron was feeling a tinge of worry. Trevor wasn't exactly jumping at the idea of releasing their funds. Why was he so reluctant? It was their money—hard earned.

After about a minute's silence, he heard another sigh; this one Aaron was glad to recognize was a sigh of resignation.

"Okay, Aaron, you've made your case. I'll get on it right away. But I need to give you guys some instructions on how to access the funds. Put the phone on speaker so I can talk to both you and Sherry at the same time."

Aaron punched the speaker phone button.

"Okay, we're both on, Trevor."

All they heard were four words, spoken in a deep monotone voice.

"Thou shalt go forth."

Sherry immediately walked over to the workbench and picked up the heavy pneumatic nail gun. Checked to make sure that the cylinder was full, and then pressed it up against her forehead.

Pulled the trigger.

She collapsed to the ground. A massive nail through her brain.

Aaron didn't rush over to her in panic or anguish.

Nor to give her a hug, kiss, or even check for a pulse.

He simply pried the nail gun out of her limp hand and pressed it against his own forehead.

Nothing of any substance was registering in his mind at that moment.

All he knew was that he had to squeeze the trigger. He had no choice in the matter. Squeezing the trigger seemed like the only thing that mattered at that moment.

So, that's what he did.

Chapter 43

She was amazed at her own strength; wondered where it came from. The door buckled and splintered, and the bar cart just kept going. It cleared a path for her.

Rachel shoved the cart off to the side and, for just a moment, stood in shock as her eyes took in the spectacle before her.

Riley was hiding under the sheets, one of them pulled up over her face. Her little hands were clasped to the edges of the sheet desperately trying to keep it in place, while he was trying to pull it away from her. His other hand was under the sheets, and Riley was squirming.

The little girl cried out, pleading with him. "Stop, please stop. You're hurting me."

Rod was lying on his side and naked from the waist down. Half of his body was on top of her, moving back and forth, accompanied by groaning and moaning.

She cried out, "You're too heavy! I can't breathe!"

Despite the noise and chaos of the door being smashed in, he seemed oblivious. If he was worried about having his sanctuary invaded, he didn't show it. He was obsessed with what he was trying to do, and nothing was going to interfere with that. Rachel felt like she was just an observer; like watching a movie, seeing something unfold that she wasn't a participant in.

She screamed. "Get off of her! Now!"

Finally, he looked over.

Sneered at her. Little bits of white drool dripped from the sides of his mouth. His face was redder than it usually was and his pointy little ears were twitching the way they usually did whenever he was annoyed.

Suddenly Riley pulled the sheet from her face. "Rachel! Help me!"

"Dad, I won't ask again. Get off Riley. Now."

He pulled his hand out from the under the sheet and dismissed Rachel with a backward wave. Then he slid it down to his crotch, and for the first time since she'd crashed into the room Rachel noticed his erection. He was pulling on it now, sneering at her, mocking her.

With his other hand, he yanked hard on the sheet, pulling it away from Riley.

Rachel was relieved to see that she was still fully clothed, but her relief was short-lived. Rod took his massive hand off his erect penis and wrapped it around Riley's tiny throat.

Her innocent eyes said it all. They magnified in fear and seemed to speak to Rachel. Begging her.

He started to squeeze her throat, and as he did, his erection seemed to get bigger.

Rod snarled at Rachel. "Get out of here, or I'll kill her. She's mine, not yours."

Riley gagged as his grip got tighter.

Suddenly the rage Rachel had felt out in the hallway seeped into her being once again. She felt it in every muscle and bone in her body—a tingling feeling that got stronger as the seconds wore on. Adrenaline was making its presence felt in a way that Rachel sensed she had no control over.

Her beating heart threatened to pound itself right out of her chest.

She reached behind and pulled the knife out of the pocket of her jeans.

Then she lunged for the bed. He saw her coming and raised his leg. His foot made contact with her stomach, stopping her forward motion in its tracks.

But it didn't stop her knife hand.

Rachel screamed in a pitch even she didn't recognize—the rage in her heart filled the room with the sound of a banshee.

Being the expert chef that she was, the knife in her hand was like a pen to a writer.

She raised it above her head and sliced it downward on her target in a single violent strike.

Her target was his erect penis.

Rod screamed. Yanked his hand from around Riley's throat, and thrust it down to his crotch.

All that was left now was a stump. The quivering and quickly shriveling penis was lying on the sheets.

Desperate to stop the bleeding, he rolled off the bed, pulling one of the sheets with him. Squeezed it up into a tight bundle and pressed it against his crotch. But the blood was spurting far too fast and within seconds the sheet and his hands were painted red.

Rachel stood in silence—just stared at him, waiting for him to drop dead. The kitchen knife dripping with blood was still in her hand.

But Rod wasn't ready to die. He glared at her; the shock painted on his face made him unrecognizable.

Suddenly he growled—a deep-throated sound that chilled Rachel to the bone. He lunged for her, one hand extended, the other one still pressing the blood-soaked sheet against his stump.

Rachel extended her knife hand out in front. "Don't come any closer. I swear, I'll cut you again."

He had no fear. Probably knew his life was slipping away.

Rod continued his charge, and grabbed her knife hand before Rachel could react. Brought his knee up and banged her wrist hard against it. The knife popped loose and slid across the floor.

Out of the corner of her eye, Rachel saw Riley pull the remaining sheet back up over her face.

She raised her hands to defend herself, but it was too late. His fist made contact against her cheekbone and she fell back against the wall. He grabbed the bar cart that Rachel had used just minutes before to crash into the room. With his one free hand, he spun it around and rushed at her. She was just starting to recover from the fist to her face, when the cart smashed into her hip.

The cart was heavy and it hit her hard. She fell back against the wall again, and he thrust it forward once more, pinning her to the wall. It knocked the air out of her and she gasped, desperately searching for a precious breath.

Rod yanked the cart back and inserted himself in its place. He grabbed Rachel by her ponytail, spun her around, and flung her across the room.

She fell to the floor.

And then he was on her. The sheet was gone now, and his lower body was a fountain of red. His ugly face mere inches from hers, blood spurting from his crotch onto her legs.

No longer trying to stop the flow of blood from his stump, both hands were free. He brought them up to Rachel's throat and began to squeeze.

His sneer seemed now to be a permanent feature of his face. He struggled with his words—the life blood was oozing out of him quickly, and he probably knew it.

"This … time … I'm going to … finish you."

His beady little eyes bore into her, and the white drool from the corners of his mouth was like an avalanche now.

Rod used his elbows to pin her upper arms to the floor. She had no leverage to lift her hands and fight back.

His squeeze was like a vice grip—she started to gag. He laughed, and squeezed even tighter.

Rachel closed her eyes and waited for the inevitable. Her only hope was that he'd bleed to death before he finished squeezing the life out of her.

Suddenly, the pressure in his hands let up. She opened her eyes just as his neck stiffened, forcing his head upward. His eyeballs rolled out of sight.

It was then that she noticed a sharp metal tip poking through the front of his throat, just above his Adam's apple.

A last gasp escaped from Rod's lips as his head collapsed onto Rachel's chest.

It was only then that she was able to see her.

Little Riley, sitting on his back, both hands still on the hilt of the kitchen knife. She'd rammed it through the base of his neck—so hard that it came out the front.

Her pretty little tear-stained face just stared down blankly at what she'd done. No words, no sounds, just a sad little face, and hands frozen to the hilt of the knife.

Rachel reached up and gently removed the child's hands from the weapon. Then, shifted her off Rod's back and onto the floor beside her. She rolled his heavy body off, and slid over to where Riley was squatting. Wrapped her arms around her, and kissed her gently on the cheek.

Rachel whispered, "You saved my life. Thank you, Riley."

Suddenly a torrent of tears. The little girl started shaking, which made Rachel only hug her tighter. "It's okay. It's over now. We're safe."

Riley was sobbing so hard that the words came out muffled. "I … killed … him."

Rachel rubbed her back and kissed her wet lips. "No, Riley, you didn't. I killed him. All you did was stop him from killing me. The place where I … cut … him is what would have killed him. It was only a matter of minutes before he would have died. You have to believe that, sweetie. I killed him, not you."

Riley encircled her arms around Rachel, and nestled her cheek against her neck. "What are we going to do, Rachel?"

Rachel leaned back and stared into Riley's eyes; into her very soul.

"We're going to leave here—and we have to do it quickly. Even though we were defending ourselves, the police will take us anyway. We have to go very far and very fast. Our mission is to get you back to your mommy and daddy … and Tommy. To Calgary—that's your home. But first, we're going to get out of these bloody clothes and take a really quick shower."

Riley looked up at her, puzzlement in her eyes. "We can't walk to Calgary, Rachel. It must be far away."

Rachel shook her head and gave Riley another hug.

"No, we can't walk. And we're not gonna drive—we could get stopped.

"We're gonna fly."

Chapter 44

Rachel chose the Audi. It was the least flashy of Rod's four cars. She didn't want to draw attention to themselves on the way to the airport. Getting stopped wasn't an option. She didn't have a driver's license.

She didn't have a pilot's license either, but at least once they were up in the air they couldn't be stopped by the police like down on the highway.

They were traveling light. No bags or extra clothes. After their warp speed showers, they quickly got dressed in jeans and T-shirts, and left the house without looking back.

And without setting foot in Riley's bedroom again.

Neither of them wanted to take a last look at the mess they'd left behind.

Rachel had her purse, car keys, ignition key for the Cessna—and that was basically it. Before leaving, though, she did remember to grab that letter from Angie that was taped underneath her dresser. She didn't want to leave that behind; the letter that was so precious to her and the only connection she had to her first sister.

Rachel drove slowly for two reasons—she'd never driven before, and didn't want any unwanted attention. She'd only watched Rod drive, but had never been behind the wheel.

Riley hadn't said much since their ordeal in her bedroom.

Usually vivacious and full of life, Rachel could tell that what had happened was weighing heavily on her mind.

She took one hand off the wheel and rubbed Riley's knee.

"Are you okay, Riley?"

She nodded. "Yes, Rachel. I'll be better when we get on a big airplane and fly away."

Rachel glanced over at her. "We're not flying on a big plane, darling. We'll be in that plane that brought you here—his plane. It's just a little one."

She could feel Riley's eyes boring into her. "But you're not a pilot. How can we fly in that plane?"

"We have no choice. I can't buy a ticket on a big plane—I have no money, no credit card, and no picture identification. So, his plane is our only escape from here."

"You're so brave."

She rubbed Riley's knee once again to reassure her. "I've flown his plane several times—but only when he was with me. I'm pretty sure I can do it on my own. You'll be my co-pilot."

"Where is the plane?"

"At the Yellowknife airport—same as where all the big planes are. It's parked off the ramp at an aviation service at the far end of the airport. We'll just get in, start it up, and get on the runway."

"Do we need permission to fly?"

Rachel nodded. "Yes, we're supposed to get permission from the tower. But we're not going to, because I don't even know how to do that, and I'd also have to identify myself. Riley, we're just going to sneak away. This late in the day there won't be many planes coming or going, so we should be okay."

Riley went silent for a couple of minutes. Then, "Rachel, are they going to put us in jail if they catch us?"

"Not you, honey. You're just a child. But they'll put me in jail until we convince them that we were just defending ourselves. He was a kidnapper, Riley. He kidnapped both of us, and also my other sister a long time ago."

"Why did he do that?"

Rachel shook her head. "I don't know. I know the things he did were wrong, but I don't have much experience in the real world. I've been so sheltered for the entire life that I can remember.

"I can't remember anything prior to being around your age. I hope there are nice people out there, and that they're not all like him. I think there are. I've met a few who visited the house, and they weren't like him.

"It was like he had some kind of sickness. The way he expected us to live our lives with him doesn't seem natural—my brain tells me none of it was natural."

Riley rubbed her tummy. "It's given me a sick stomach, Rachel. I threw up back at the house before I got dressed. I didn't want to tell you."

Rachel grabbed hold of her hand.

"That's okay sweetie. It's normal to be sick in the stomach once in a while, especially when we're scared or nervous. I threw up earlier in the day when I saw your photo on the computer and read about who you really were."

Riley opened her mouth to reply, then closed it again. After a couple of minutes, she whispered, "Do you think it hurt when I did that thing with the knife to him?"

Rachel shook her head. "No, I don't think it hurt at all. It was too quick; he died almost right away. Try not to think about it."

"Okay, I'll try."

She started to sob, and rubbed her little hands across her eyes. Rachel reached into the glove compartment and took out a box of tissues.

"Here, Riley, use these. And cry all you want—best to get it out. You'll feel better."

"Will … someone … find him?"

"Yes, they will. When we get to Calgary we'll report all that happened to the police, so they'll contact people up here to go to the house."

"Then they'll lock you up?"

She nodded. "Maybe. Probably. But I'm not afraid. We did the right thing. We're alive, and that's all that matters."

Rachel steered the Audi onto the Yellowknife Highway which she knew led right to the airport.

Suddenly she saw flashing lights behind her. A police car!

She slowed down and pulled off to the side of the road.

"Riley, there's a police officer behind us. He's going to come and talk to us. Don't say anything, okay?"

Riley nodded nervously.

Rachel struggled for a couple of seconds with the power window buttons. Rolled the back window down by mistake. Then found the right button, and watched in the side mirror as the officer approached.

He was just a young guy, she could tell, and was walking casually—which was a good sign, she thought.

He tipped his hat. "Good afternoon, ma'am. Everything okay?"

She smiled at him and turned on the charm that she knew she had.

"Just fine, Officer. How are you today?"

"Doin' good. Sorry to pull you over. I noticed you were driving kinda slow, so I wanted to make sure you weren't having car trouble or something."

He leaned his head down and peered into the car. "Hello there, little girl."

Riley smiled back at him, and said hi.

"No, no trouble with the car. We were just driving slow hoping to see some planes. I know we're close to the airport and we wanted to watch a few take-offs and landings.”

The officer gazed over in the direction of the airport. “Well, nice day to fly, that’s for sure. But kinda quiet today, especially this late. You probably picked the wrong time.”

“Maybe. If we don’t have any luck, we’ll just drive by again tomorrow—earlier.”

“Well, worth a try anyway. You might get lucky. There’s a nice pull-out up ahead when you get closer to the terminal buildings. Just park, and get out. A nice day to just be out in the sunshine even if no planes.”

“Thanks for the tip. We’ll do that.”

“Oh, before I let you head on your way, I’m pulling cars over today along this stretch of road because of some aggressive moose that have been reported further along. Just be careful. They’re usually nothing to worry about, but this week they seem to be hanging around and charging some vehicles. So … just a warning for you.”

Rachel smiled, relieved. “Oh, that’s so nice of you to do that. Thank you for the warning. While we’d love to see some moose, it’s kinda scary to think of them charging us.”

He chuckled. “Especially with the car you’re driving. An Audi just wouldn’t look the same with an antler dent in it. Bye ma’am. Bye little girl.”

Rachel sighed with relief as he walked back to his vehicle. She waited until he drove off before starting the car again.

She looked over at Riley. “It’s our lucky day, dear. If he’d asked for my identification, that would have been the end of our escape.”

Rachel pulled back out onto the highway and drove slowly in the direction of the airport.

“Do you know the way, Rachel?”

“Yep, no problem. In fact, we’re turning in right now.”

She steered the Audi onto Archibald Street and drove towards the northwest section of the airport. Up ahead were some hangar buildings and the sign advertising the aviation company that looked after Rod's plane and kept it fueled.

"We're here!" She pointed through the windshield. "There's the plane that brought you here, Riley, and the one that will now be our getaway."

Riley put her hands up to her mouth when she saw it.

"I remember it now. Silver with red stripes. I remember my friend Sherry taking me to it and letting me get in. We took off and it was so exciting. But then, I must have gone to sleep because I don't remember anything after that."

"They drugged you, Riley. That's why you don't remember. This time you'll remember the whole flight."

Riley shivered and wrapped her arms across her chest. "I'm so nervous. Scared. But I'm glad I'm with you, Rachel."

Rachel tugged on the little girl's ponytail. "I'm a bit scared too. But don't worry, we'll be fine. I have the best co-pilot in the whole wide world."

Riley beamed. "Do you have a name for this plane?"

Rachel laughed. "No, but this type of plane is called a Cessna 182. It's a single engine—you can see the three blades on the nose. The engine makes that propeller turn. That's what gives it power. It's supposed to be one of the safest planes ever made."

Riley smiled. "Can we call it Runaway?"

Rachel wrapped her arms around the sweet little girl and kissed her gently on the cheek. And she whispered, "We sure can. From now on, that's its name."

Chapter 45

Rachel stopped the Audi on the grass near the hangar building.

"Okay, Riley, this is the sneaky part. The doors of the plane will be open. Go around to the right side of the plane and get into the front seat. We have to be fast. I'll get in on the left. The pilot's seat is always on the left, and the co-pilot—you—sits on the right.

"I'll need you to be real quiet once we're in the plane. Just until I look over all the gauges and remind myself what I'm supposed to do. I'll need to concentrate.

"Then, I'll start the plane up and we'll ride out to the runway. After that, we'll take off. We're not going to talk to, or stop for, anyone. Okay, Riley?"

She nodded eagerly. "I understand, Rachel."

Rachel turned off the Audi, grabbed her purse, and shouted, "Okay, let's run!"

The doors of the Cessna were unlocked as they usually were. They hopped inside.

"Put on your seatbelt, Riley!"

She reached under the seats and pulled out two headsets and plugged them into the console. She adjusted one of them to fit Riley's tiny head and slipped it on her.

"We'll need these. It gets noisy in here with the engine, but I'll have it on intercom so we can still talk to each other."

She flipped up the intercom button. Reached into her purse, pulled out the ignition key, and slipped it into the key slot. Checked the throttle and pushed it in halfway. She shoved the trim button in all the way to get the proper fuel/air mixture for starting the engine. Then set the rpm button.

Rachel took a deep breath, said a silent prayer, and turned the ignition key.

The propeller started to turn. She sighed with relief. Then remembered at the last second to apply her feet to the brakes.

There were two pedals on the floor—the upper half were the brakes, the lower half were the rudders. The rudders were used for steering the plane along the runway, while the yoke that she had both hands on were used for steering the plane once in the air, or for climbing or descending.

She applied the brakes and waited for the engine to warm up and for the rpms to reach an optimum level.

Rachel's stomach was in her throat. Every time she'd done this before, she was with him and they'd always done it slowly. Lots of time to think. This time there was no time to think. And she didn't have a qualified pilot sitting beside her to bail her out if she made a mistake.

Riley's life was in her hands right now and she felt the weight of the ominous responsibility. The sweet little girl trusted her, and Rachel hoped she could live up to that trust.

She scanned the gauges. From what she could remember, everything looked okay.

Oil pressure was fine, the fuel gauges for both tanks showed full. She knew that Rod had purchased the plane with extended fuel tanks, so in her calculation Calgary, was thirteen hundred kilometers away, which meant they would just make it without refueling.

Flying at about two hundred kilometers an hour, which was the max this plane could do, they'd be above Calgary in just over six hours.

And she knew that the higher she flew, the better fuel mileage she'd get. The air was so much thinner the higher up she was able to go. But with a plane like this, she'd learned that twelve thousand feet was pretty much the limit. And if she went that high, she'd be burning too much fuel in the climb. So, Rachel figured eight thousand feet would be just about perfect.

The rpms looked to be within range, so Rachel started letting off on the brakes and moved her feet to the lower half of the pedals— the rudders.

All of a sudden there was a rap on her side window. She took off her headset and stared out at someone she'd seen several times before. Couldn't recall his name. A big burly guy who worked in the aviation service company.

He yelled through the closed window. She knew she could unlatch it and swing it upwards to hear him better, but didn't want to.

"Ms. Milton. Where's your father?"

She shook her head.

"You can't take off! You don't have a license!"

She shook her head again.

He grabbed the door handle and began to open the door.

In a fit of frustration, Rachel rammed the door outwards with her left arm and knee, smashing it into his chest and face. He went down.

No one was going to stop them now. Riley had nicknamed the plane Runaway and that's exactly how it was going to perform.

She closed the door again and put her headset back on.

"Okay, here we go, Riley!"

Rachel released the brakes completely and the plane began to roll down the ramp. Within seconds they were on the runway.

She pushed the throttle all the way in, adjusted the trim button, checked to make sure the flaps were retracted, and held on for dear life to the yoke.

The plane raced along the runway almost as if it wanted to escape too.

Rachel glanced down at the speed dial. She knew that as soon as the plane hit 120 kilometers an hour it would be ripe for take-off. Aside from the speed, another trick she'd learned from Rod was that once the plane itself felt light in her hands, it was ready to lift off.

She waited, glancing up and down at the speed gauge.

It was time. She pulled back on the yoke and the nose of the plane lifted into the air.

Riley yelled out something that Rachel couldn't make out, but it was a happy yell so that's all Rachel needed to know.

At full throttle and max rpms Rachel remembered that the plane would climb at five hundred feet per minute. She was aiming for around eight thousand feet so in about fifteen minutes they would reach the altitude she felt safe at.

She called out to Riley through the intercom.

"Reach under your seat and you'll find a map and some charts. Pull them out and you can help me find our way."

She looked at the compass and realized they were heading in the wrong direction. They needed to head south.

Rachel slowly turned the yoke to the left to make the plane gradually correct its direction.

Suddenly there was a shudder and the plane bounced in the air. She lost her firm grip on the yoke and it shifted forward.

The plane went into a dive.

Long Lake, which was adjacent to the northeast side of the airport, suddenly loomed ominously in her vision.

Chapter 46

It was now well into September, but still hot in Toronto.

Jeff was glad that the end of August had also signalled the end of the insufferable humidity that the city was famous for.

He and Gaia were having breakfast out on the back deck. September was always such a nice time of the year. Fall was right around the corner.

Toronto and areas north of the city were renowned for their autumn colors and they were discussing when might be the best weekend to drive up to the Haliburton Highlands for a romantic, and colorful, getaway. But with the tension of the Emily investigation forefront in their minds, both of them knew that their light-hearted banter was just a distraction from reality. There would be no weekend getaway, not until this case was closed.

"We'll take the Vette. It hugs those country roads perfectly."

"But it has such a small trunk area. I do need to bring clothes with me, Jeff."

He dismissed her with a hand wave. "Oh, Gaia, it's just for two days. Throw some stuff in a knapsack and you'll be fine."

She pouted.

"We women need our things, Jeff. You guys just don't seem to understand that. Sometimes, you really are such a *boy*."

"Well after that criticism, I'll have to agree to the Jeep, then.

Can't have you spreading some rumor about me being a boy."

Gaia laughed. "I love that you're such a pushover with me. My pouting always seems to work."

He leaned across the table and kissed her.

"Yes, that pout is one of your cutest features, and you look so sad and vulnerable when you do it. Who can resist?"

Suddenly the phone rang. Jeff dashed into the house, then came right back out and put it on speaker. He whispered to Gaia, "It's Ken Clarkson."

"Okay, Ken, I've got it on speaker so Gaia can hear you too. I was going to phone you myself today to see if you'd heard from Abe Mendelson. Hoping that the Dixons got back to him. I have some other information to tell you guys about, too."

"You must not have read the news yet—well, it's Calgary news, so you probably wouldn't have seen it anyway."

"No, we've just been lazing around this morning. What's happened?"

"The Dixons are dead. Double suicide."

Jeff felt like he'd just been kicked in the gut.

"Oh, for fuck's sake! Dan was afraid of this happening. He mentioned his concern to me when he got back from Calgary. Said he'd phoned and talked to you guys?"

"Yeah, he phoned us as soon as his plane landed back in Toronto. Said he forgot all about that suicide danger and asked us to call and warn them."

"So, Dan filled you in on what this Trevor Kincaid guy is known for?"

"He didn't tell us very much. Just said that some person that Kincaid did business with in Toronto died of suicide recently, and that you guys suspect he's involved in hypnotising people into receiving commands—or something like that.

"I didn't really understand it. He said it was just a theory you folks had, and that we should only talk to the Dixons—not to leave a message or send an email or text."

Jeff breathed a sigh of relief. Dan had told them only the bare minimum and nothing about their previous encounters with the alter ego of Brandon Horcroft.

"So, did you phone them?"

"Tried to. Even went and knocked on their door once. They never phoned back. Were probably already dead. Aaron's high school called the police to check on him after he'd missed classes and football practice."

Gaia jumped into the conversation. "Ken, how did they do it?"

"Nail gun—into their heads."

Gaia winced and said softly, "Oh, my God. Was it murder/suicide?"

"Nope. The police don't think so. Both sets of fingerprints were found on the nail gun and the trigger. Sherry's were also found on the ammo compartment. Their bodies were found in the basement. Sherry got it first, because it sounds like Aaron's body fell on top of hers."

Jeff muttered, "This is an unfortunate setback for us."

Cathy came on the line. "Jeff and Gaia, what does this do now for our search? That couple was key to the evidence we needed."

Jeff paused for a couple of seconds before replying. "Cathy, it is a setback, and the Dixons could have blown everything wide open for us. Their testimony would have guaranteed that the police would get involved. But remember that we've found out a few things. We know about Rod Milton in Yellowknife and we know about Foster Hunt in Saskatoon. So, we're not in the dark here."

"But what can we do? We can't prove anything now."

"No, now we can't, not with the Dixons dead.

"But I mentioned to Ken that I was going to phone you guys today—to find out if Abe had heard from the Dixons, but also about another important discovery. In fact, it's pretty astounding. We have a computer expert working on the case with us, a former RCMP officer, Jason Watkins. He's the one who tracked down Milton and Hunt for us.

"He's managed to do some more digging into the personal lives of both of those men. He hacked into government records. Brace yourselves. Milton has two adopted daughters: Rachel and Olivia. Rachel is twenty-three years old, and Olivia is seven. Rachel was adopted fifteen years ago, and Olivia just a few weeks ago."

Jeff heard gasps at the other end of the phone.

"He also hacked into records for this Hunt guy in Saskatoon. He has an adopted daughter named Angie. She's also twenty-three. We told you that we suspected this girl was first adopted by Milton, but then for some reason she ended up with Hunt in Saskatoon after only three years in Yellowknife. We deduced that after seeing the financial transactions both of these guys had with Kincaid."

Ken was speaking now. "This is incredible, Jeff. One of those two older girls has to be Emily."

"We think so. And the younger one, Olivia, is probably Riley McCormick.

"But I'm not finished yet. Jason tested this theory about the transfer of Angie to this Hunt guy in Saskatoon. There was indeed a registered adoption of a girl named Angie fifteen years ago by Rod Milton.

"Her name on record showed as Angie Milton. But then, three years later there was a registered adoption by Foster Hunt of an Angie. Her name is Angie Hunt. Has to be the same girl. And that's the other one who's twenty-three now."

Cathy was practically gushing now. "So Emily could be either Rachel or Angie!"

"Yes, and this is an important point that you'll both want to hear. Both of those young women are still alive, because Jason couldn't find any death records for either of them."

Cathy was crying now, and Jeff could hear Ken soothing her. Then he spoke again.

"Okay, Jeff and Gaia. What do you want us to do? Where do we go from here?"

"Just sit tight for a bit. As soon as you told me about the Dixons' deaths, a plan started formulating in my mind.

"Might work. Leave it with me. We're not giving up, that's for sure. Before we hang up, though, I wanted to ask how you feel about the deaths of your friends. Mixed feelings?"

Ken answered. "Nothing mixed about it, Jeff. We hope they rot in hell."

*****

Jeff, Dan, and Jason were sitting in the Rosewood Lounge on King Street. In a quiet booth at the back of the bar. The waitress brought over three beers and they toasted.

Dan took a long sip, then lamented, "I'm so sorry, Jeff. I really screwed up. I must be getting old. This is what Horcroft does—he kills people who are loose ends.

"Don't beat yourself up, Dan. The man's evil, and I guess neither of us are evil enough to think like him or anticipate his next steps. And as you know, I did the same thing myself a couple of years ago. Gaia almost died because it didn't occur to me that he could have hypnotized her, too. I repeated that phrase to her like an idiot, and I was just damn lucky I didn't lose her. I wonder how many zombies are walking around out there who he's done this to."

"I suspect more than we can count, Jeff. Here in Canada, down in the U.S. with his CIA work, and possibly around the world. When you took photos of those documents he had in his vault way back when, there were references to him having caused the poisoning of a politician in Ukraine, and then the suicide death of the perpetrator afterwards.

"And some shootings down in the states committed by people he'd hypnotized. Now, this latest assassination of the senator. The man is the devil incarnate. I think we've only seen the tip of the iceberg."

Jason clasped his hands behind his head. "You guys are close on this one. Not enough yet to get the police to do anything, but you're closer than you realize. However, the legwork will still have to be done by you folks for a while still."

Jeff raised his beer in Jason's direction. "No small thanks to what you've done for us, Jason."

Jason lifted his beer in a return salute. "I've found out a couple more things. Rod Milton's office is in Yellowknife, and his diamond mine is quite a way north of the city. His estate is just outside the city boundaries, a large spread. He's the sole owner of his company—I think I told you guys that already. I wanted to find out if his adopted daughter, Rachel, was an officer of the company—but she's not. No record of any employment for her, no driver's license, no credit cards, and no passport. She's quite sheltered.

"As for this Foster Hunt guy in Saskatoon, he's also the sole owner of his company but the records show that his daughter, Angie, is an officer of the company. Listed as a vice president.

"Now, this guy is a large developer with a net worth of around two hundred million, but he has virtually no other employees except his daughter. This is typical of a lot of developers—they hire contractors, tradespeople, landscapers, architects, and engineers as each project gets going. But no permanent employees.

"Of course, developers have lawyers and accountants on retainer, but no real employees. In this case, the only real employee is Angie. And Hunt doesn't have an actual office—works out of his home. A massive house, a mansion, really, on a large plot of land outside the city limits of Saskatoon.

"Angie is different from Rachel. She does earn a salary and pays taxes—has a driver's license, credit cards, and a passport. She doesn't at all seem to be living a sheltered life, not like Rachel. Interesting, huh?"

Jeff motioned to the waitress to bring over another round.

"That is interesting. Which brings me to why I wanted us to meet today. I was thinking that Dan and I could bust in on both these guys. I haven't even talked to Dan about this yet, so he can tell me to go to hell if he thinks it's a bad idea. But is it possible for you to create fake profiles for us online?"

Jason laughed. "That's child's play. I could fabricate something pretty convincing for each of you. What were you thinking?"

"Well, both of these creeps are rich businessmen. So, it's conceivable that they would agree to meet with other business folks who have attractive ventures to offer. If we had that kind of background—and no doubt they'd each check us out online before agreeing to meet—we might be able to get in the front door."

Jeff looked at Dan. "What do you think, Dan?"

"I like it. I'm game."

Jeff nodded. "Okay, good. I was thinking that for this Milton guy, who owns a diamond mine, what if Dan and I were executives with a large diamond wholesale firm in Toronto. Into import/export. We could propose that we'd like to meet with him to conclude a very large purchase of diamonds that we'd intend to then farm out to manufacturers and retailers.

"And for this Hunt character, he's a developer, so what if we were architects who had a unique plan for a large resort development, say, in British Columbia, on a large tract of land that we own options on. Something we could farm out to the right developer to make our vision become reality."

Jason smiled. "I like it. And I think both of them would go for it."

"We'd need different names of course, for each of these ruses, and impressive looking business cards. And as I said, believable profiles on the internet—maybe websites as well—the full monty."

Jason drained his second beer, and stood. "I'm gonna hit the road, guys. You've given me some work to do. Leave it with me. Trust me, I'll make you relevant!"

Chapter 47

Panic took over. Rachel tried to fight it, but seeing the lake looming larger than life in her windscreen was a sight that overwhelmed her.

Riley screamed. "Rachel! We're going to crash!"

Out of the corner of her eye she saw Riley cover her eyes with her hands.

She gripped the yoke and pulled back hard. But it resisted her strength. They were diving too fast. It moved back, but only slightly.

"Riley! Grab the yoke in front of you and help me! Pull back with me!"

Riley dropped her hands away from her eyes and squeezed the co-pilot yoke.

She screamed, "What do I do?"

"Pull back with me! Just pull!"

Together they yanked back on the dual yokes. At first the movement was so slight as to not be noticeable. The lake was getting closer and closer. Rachel feared they were only a few dozen feet above the water now, although she knew that height over water was always deceiving. But, there was no doubt in her mind that if they didn't level out fast, they would nosedive.

The nose started to move up, ever so slightly. Suddenly, she remembered the throttle. They were going too fast! Rachel took one hand off the yoke and pulled the throttle knob out as far as it would go.

Right away she noticed the difference.

The rate of dive declined as the nose moved upward at a higher pitch.

Her eyes were transfixed on the water below, which now seemed close enough that she could practically reach out the window and touch it. In an insane moment of analysing options, she figured that at the worst, they'd do a belly landing instead of a nose dive.

But that was a bad option. She wasn't going to let that happen.

"Pull, Riley! Pull!"

Riley was huffing and puffing as she yanked back with her tiny hands on the resistant yoke. They pulled together, and to Rachel's relief the view through the windscreen changed. They were level now, and she no longer saw water. They started to climb again.

"Keep the yoke back as far as it will go!"

Rachel needed to get the plane away from the water as fast as possible. If they stayed level too long there was the risk that one or all of the three fixed wheels would catch the lake. Which meant that they would somersault.

In this model of Cessna, the wheels didn't retract. Which, she remembered Rod saying was both an advantage and a disadvantage. With retractable wheels, there was always the danger that they wouldn't extend. But with fixed wheels, they created drag, which slowed down the speed of the plane, as well as challenging its ability to climb.

She knew that at this moment of peril, the fixed wheels were a problem. They could not only catch the water, but would also slow down their climb—at a time when they needed to climb desperately.

The climb was slow and sure, but they needed to get higher, fast. The plane had now cleared the shores of the lake and was aiming for the terminal buildings.

She reached forward and turned off the intercom so Riley wouldn't hear her.

Then she yelled out to herself, "I'm a strong woman! I'm a strong woman! I will not be beaten! I can do this! I can do this!"

Rachel flipped the intercom back on again.

She reached across the cockpit and shifted Riley's hands to a position higher up on the yoke. "That should help you. Now, let's do it together—all the way back." They pulled, and the nose moved noticeably upwards.

"Hold the yoke in that position, Riley! Use all of your strength to keep it there!"

She glanced over at the child. Riley's lips were pursed together and her eyes were locked on the view through the windshield. A view that wasn't comforting.

Rachel focused her own eyes once again on the windscreen. The terminal buildings were only seconds away and her altimeter showed the plane at only sixty feet above the ground. They were climbing, but ever so slowly.

The heat in the cockpit was overwhelming—either from the temperature outside, or just the mere stress. Sweat was making it hard to see.

These little planes didn't have air conditioning, so windows that opened were essential. She was starting to feel light-headed from the extreme heat. Afraid that she was going to pass out, Rachel used her elbow to flip up the catch on her side window, then used the same elbow to shove it outwards.

"Riley! We need some air in here. Take one hand off the yoke and flip open your window!"

The little girl did as she was told, and then quickly put her hand back on the yoke, squeezing it for dear life.

As the terminal buildings loomed closer and closer, Rachel saw several people out on the tarmac waving their arms back and forth at her. Then, the sight of two emergency vehicles pulling out of a hangar and racing onto the runway. With the windows now open, she also heard the sirens.

She glanced at the altimeter—still hovering around sixty feet.

Then her eyes scanned over to the airspeed indicator. Only 140 kph. That was only slightly higher than her take-off speed.

Then it hit her. The throttle!

She'd pulled it out when they were diving, to reduce their speed, and had forgotten to shove it back in again.

Rachel took one hand off the yoke and rammed the throttle knob back into its full position. Suddenly the engine roared.

"Keep pulling, Riley!"

The plane's rate of climb increased instantly. They cleared the terminal buildings with only feet to spare.

She glanced at the air speed indicator—they were already back up to 160.

Riley squealed. "Rachel, we did it!"

"Yes, we did! We did it together, co-pilot!"

She giggled. "What do you want me to do now, Captain?"

"Just keep that yoke pulled back, Riley. We still need to climb— a lot."

"Okay!"

The wind whistled through the open windows. Normally this bothered Rachel. But not today.

It was a refreshing respite from the sweaty experience they'd just gone through.

She drank in the breeze and thought back to how close they'd come to disaster.

Rachel knew that if they'd hit the water at the speed they were flying, that would have been the end for both of them. And if they'd hit the terminal buildings, it would also have been the end—a fiery end. They came so close on both counts.

Now that things had calmed down a bit, she allowed her eyes to skim over the indicators.

Oil pressure still looked good and the gas tanks were full. The altimeter displayed that they'd reached one thousand feet—seven thousand to go. In about fifteen minutes they'd be able to level off. The airspeed indicator read one-eighty, so they were almost at their maximum speed of two hundred.

She reached down and pulled out the trim lever, which she'd set at high during takeoff to get the maximum amount of oxygen into the engine during ignition.

Then her eyes focused on the horizon indicator. It showed the plane in a steep climb, which didn't surprise her. She'd been so frightened of the height they were flying at during the close calls, that she'd allowed them to climb faster than she had ever experienced before.

This was a new thing for her—to see the plane's attitude aiming with the nose so high on the horizon indicator. Always, when she'd flown before, the climb was more gradual. She considered suggesting to Riley that they both push forward on their yokes to slow down the climb.

But she never got the chance. What her intuition had been warning her about happened in the blink of an eye.

Suddenly there was absolute silence.

The engine stopped roaring and the three-pronged prop began to slow down. While it still continued to turn, Rachel knew that was merely the effect of the wind. The engine was dead, no mistake about it.

The plane began to slide, tail down.

Rachel's brain was in overdrive now. They'd stalled. The climb had been too fast.

She whipped off her headset, and reached over and pulled Riley's off. Then she unplugged the headsets from the console, and shut off the navigation and beacon lights. She knew that she'd now have to re-start the plane in mid-air, and any drain on the battery would hinder that effort.

"Rachel, we're falling!"

"Yes, the engine shut off, Riley. I'll have to re-start it. Push forward on the yoke. Not too much. Copy me!"

They pushed their yokes forward in unison, and the plane began to level off. Without power, the plane was now no better than a mere glider.

Rachel glanced at the horizon indicator. The plane was now completely level, but the altitude indicator gave a stark warning. They were at a precarious twelve hundred, and their airspeed had fallen to one-forty.

Not enough height, or speed, for error.

"Okay, hold that yoke level, Riley. I'm going to re-start."

But fate had other plans. A sudden burst of wind turbulence turned the plane onto its side.

And then, upside down.

Chapter 48

Rachel wanted to scream, and if she'd been the only one in the plane she probably would have.

But she had to worry about Riley—the little girl was counting on Rachel to be in charge and have all the answers. Rachel didn't have many answers but there was no need for Riley to know that. The sweet little girl had already been scared out of her mind several times in one day, and that broke Rachel's heart.

The plane was upside down, but leaning slightly to one side because of the wind. If that turbulence hadn't hit, she might have already succeeded in starting the engine again. Now, they were upside down, and unless the wind did them a favor and flipped them right side up again, she'd have to try to start it in the position they were in.

The proper thing to do before taking off in a plane was to go through the check list—she hadn't had time to do that. As well, most pilots took a couple of minutes to re-read the procedures for mid-flight ignition, just as a refresher, even though it was rare for engines to fail while in the air.

Rachel felt sudden pangs of guilt—the life of a precious little girl who she loved was in her hands, yet she'd done everything wrong.

And she knew why the engine had died. They'd been climbing too fast and stalled out. She should have known better.

The blood was rushing to her head now. She looked over at Riley—the girl looked petrified, almost as if in shock.

Rachel knew that both of them would start feeling lightheaded soon if she didn't get this plane righted again. And in order to get it righted she first had to get it started. If not, since they were losing altitude dangerously fast, they would crash in a minute or so, maybe even less.

Everything seemed distorted upside down. The view through the windscreen was confusing—at times it even looked like they were level and right-side up. She'd heard of illusions like this confounding pilots, and even read about the crash of John Kennedy Jr.'s plane into the Atlantic when he reportedly lost all sense of reality and points of reference.

Rachel was determined not to let that happen to her.

She yelled out. "Hold on, Riley, I'm going to start us back up!"

Still nothing but silence from the co-pilot's seat.

The plane continued to fall, and Rachel didn't dare look at the altimeter. She didn't want to know how far they'd fallen.

She turned the ignition key to the left. Then, held her breath and turned it all the way to the right again.

Nothing.

Her stomach was doing flips, and it was getting hard to see. The blood rushing into her head was taking its toll.

She took a deep breath and went through the ignition routine again.

Still nothing. Her mind was racing now—it had no choice; time was running out.

What haven't I done?

Then she saw it. The trim button was full out. She immediately shoved it all the way in again in order to get the richest mixture of oxygen and fuel for ignition. Then she noticed that the throttle button was halfway out—she was sure that she'd pushed it in to achieve the climb away from the lake. But maybe she'd pulled it out again once they reached a safe height? Couldn't remember. But didn't matter—she shoved it back in again, all the way.

Held her breath and turned the ignition key once more, knowing that this might be the last chance she'd have.

Suddenly the comforting sound of an engine roaring to life! And the sight of the propeller starting to turn—slowly at first, then faster and faster.

"Riley, we have power!"

Rachel pulled the trim button back out again—didn't want to risk another stall with a mixture that was too high on oxygen. Kept the throttle knob all the way in.

Then she looked out at the upside-down horizon and gauged which way the wind had turned them. The right wing was on an angle downward, which meant the wind was coming from the west. She decided to use the wind turbulence to their advantage to help right the plane.

Rachel pushed the yoke forward and then turned it to the east, allowing the wind to do the rest of the work.

The plane shuddered, then started its excruciatingly slow flip. Now she had to be concerned with it going all the way around once they were right side up. The wind was strong and if she had the plane flipping around in a certain direction no doubt the wind would continue pushing it that way.

She stared at the horizon indicator, then glanced up at the windscreen to double-check what she was seeing on the indicator.

The very instant they seemed level, and before the plane started its inevitable roll again, Rachel made an aggressive pull on the yoke and then gently turned it in the opposite direction; towards the wind this time.

The plane stopped its flipping motion, leveled off with the horizon, and began to climb.

Rachel screamed in triumph. "Riley! We're okay!"

She glanced over. The little girl was still staring straight ahead, no emotion on her face at all. Rachel feared that she might really be in shock, or, maybe this was a side effect of all of the hypnotism and medication she'd endured with those psychologists. They'd screwed with her brain just like they'd screwed with Rachel's and Angie's so many years ago.

She decided to just give her some time. Her first concern was the plane right now.

Started glancing around to get her bearings again. The compass showed they were going in an easterly direction so she made a slight correction by turning the yoke to the west. The plane banked and as soon as she saw the compass indicating south, she leveled off the yoke.

They were still climbing nicely—the altimeter showed twelve hundred feet again, the level they were at before the engine quit. She suddenly remembered what had probably caused the flame-out— they'd been climbing far too fast. To prevent that happening again, she pushed the yoke slightly forward to make the climb more gradual.

Pulled out the throttle to ease up on the power a tiny bit. Didn't know if that was the right thing to do or not, but at least it would save fuel. She could tell that they now had tailwinds, so their airspeed could be maintained without wasting too much fuel.

She glanced longingly at the avionics screen and auto-pilot button. But she had no idea how they worked and didn't want to take a chance on screwing something else up.

Rod used to say that the plane could basically fly and navigate itself, but when they were up together he never used those toys or showed her how they worked. They'd always flown on visuals and manual only. He'd even synced the plane with his phone, but Rachel didn't have a phone.

So, their trip today to Calgary would have to be visuals only, with the help of some maps and charts. A scary thought, especially knowing there were other planes in the air too and the avionics could help prevent a mid-air accident.

Rachel crossed her fingers and said a silent prayer.

Considering the close calls since they'd taken off, Rachel began to question her wisdom of deciding to make a run for it.

She knew she was panicked and hadn't been thinking rationally after they'd killed Rod. And the realization that she'd actually taken someone's life was something she hadn't wrestled with in her mind yet. But it was something she knew she'd have to deal with in the days, weeks, months, and even years ahead. As would little Riley.

She'd spent fifteen years of her life with Rod, and there weren't very many fond memories. Being up in the plane with him had always been a thrill, and cooking meals that he occasionally raved over gave her satisfaction.

Other than that, her life had been empty and unfulfilling. Especially after Angie was sent away. Then, finally, a new purpose in life presented itself when little Riley came to live with them.

But suddenly she'd started feeling more like a mother than a sister. The need to protect Riley in a way that she'd never even protected herself.

So, when he was dead, she just wanted them to get away fast. Leave it all behind.

What went through her mind when she made that decision back at the house was her knowledge of how rich and powerful he was.

And from what she'd read on the internet over the years, rich and powerful people always got what they wanted. And people covered for them. Rod had powerful friends and rich family members.

And she remembered how he'd pummeled her delivery man, Gerry, after he caught them having sex in the kitchen. He seemed to know everything about Gerry, and told him that he also "owned" the police. That he could have him charged with rape.

Rachel had worried that it might not be safe to turn themselves in to the police in Yellowknife. Who could she trust? And who would take her side when she'd just killed the richest man in town? And poor Riley—they'd probably send her away to some place where Rachel would never find her again, or force her to live with Rod's relatives. She'd have no say, and Riley would never have the chance to be back with her real parents again.

She pulled back on the yoke to give the plane a bit more climb. The tailwinds seemed to have died off, so she shoved the throttle all the way in again. The engine roared.

Rachel started pondering the entire concept of the kidnappings.

How could Rod have pulled those off? He was a busy man, and while she knew that he'd flown Riley north to Yellowknife from Calgary in his own plane, had he actually grabbed her off the street, too?

She didn't think so. He wouldn't have taken the chance on getting his hands that dirty.

There had to be other people involved, particularly since this was the third child he'd adopted.

And Rachel knew that there were at least those two psychologists, but she also remembered other men from back when she was very young. Particularly one man—tall, thick blondish hair, blue eyes, deep voice. A handsome man. He told her he was a psychiatrist. She never forgot him. He was one of those people who was hard to forget. But who did the actual kidnappings?

She and Angie must have been kidnapped too, and at this point Rachel was pretty certain that her own real name was Emily Clarkson. There was a reason why the photo of Emily and her little bicycle had awakened Rachel's brain from its slumber.

Memories had been suppressed in her, Angie, and now Riley—

but those memories were always still there, she was certain of that. Riley was proof positive of that—she only remembered her real name once Rachel read out the name of that clothing store. And then she recognized her parents and brother in the Amber Alert photos. And of course, the photo of Riley was definitely her. Riley was Riley, not Olivia.

The big difference between Rachel and Riley was that many years had gone by for Rachel, and she had undergone more treatments from those psychologists than Riley had. They'd only really just gotten started with Riley. Not long enough to completely erase loving memories.

But Rachel had no memories at all. She had no idea what her parents looked like, or if she had any brothers or sisters—and even the name Emily Clarkson didn't ring a bell with her. Whatever memories she had were now buried so deep she wondered if they could ever be revived.

Suddenly she felt a soft hand on her bare arm.

"Are we close to Calgary yet, Rachel?"

"No, darling. We have about five more hours to go. But we're doing really well. We've already climbed to seven thousand feet and once we're at eight thousand I'll level us off."

She glanced at the compass. "And we're still heading south, so we're going the right way."

"Do you need me to pull this thing again?"

Rachel laughed. "No, not right now. But I'll call on you if I need you. You did a great job! What you can do is grab those charts and maps from underneath your seat now. You can be my navigator."

Riley pulled them out and started unfolding. "This is fun! I'm a really good reader, so I'll be a good help to you!"

Rachel studied her face. It was full of life and excitement. Not at all like the almost catatonic little girl of half an hour ago. Rachel's newfound parental intuition told her that she needed to be careful now about what she said and how she said it.

"Did you have a nice nap, Riley?"

She nodded eagerly. "Oh, yes. I think the motion of the plane put me to sleep. I feel much better now."

"You were a big help to me with that yoke thing. Thanks so much."

Riley bobbed her head up and down. "It was stiff. We really had to pull hard."

"Do you remember what happened after that?"

"Yep. The engine stopped. But I must have fallen asleep. Because it looks like it's working just fine now. You fixed it."

"That's all you remember?"

Riley looked at her, puzzled. "Well, I remember what … happened … back at the house, but I don't want to talk about that. And I remember we decided to name this plane Runaway. And we almost crashed into the lake. Did I miss something else when I was asleep?"

Riley had completely forgotten that they'd been flying upside down. Or, more likely, had completely blocked that horrifying few minutes out of her brain.

Her brain had been conditioned by evil experts to do just that, not just for loving moments, but also horrifying moments. Any moments at all, probably, without discretion.

Nefarious hypnosis and mind-altering drugs had power, and Rachel had seen them at work many times in the movies she'd watched. Those were supposed to be just fantasy. *But were they?*

Rachel caressed Riley's soft cheek.

"No, honey, you didn't miss anything at all. I'm so happy that you had a nice nap. When we get you back to your parents and Tommy, just think how nice it will be to have your old bed again. You'll be able to nap in it any time you want."

A warm smile came over Riley's face. So warm that Rachel's

heart skipped a beat.

"I just remembered. I have dollies in my room, Rachel! My favorite is named Alice. I can hardly wait for you to meet her."

Chapter 49

It was time to move again—at least for a little while.

His instincts had told him that he needed to get out of his safe sanctuary, which didn't feel so safe anymore. Too much had happened. The failed kidnapping of Gaia, and the connection of that fiasco to Chuck Walton. The now very dead Chuck Walton, who had been connected to Trevor—and they knew he was connected.

Then, whoever it was who had impersonated Aaron Dixon just to lure Trevor out in front of his own building. He knew that person wanted to get a look at him, and perhaps even get a photo. To go to that trouble meant they knew he had a connection to Aaron Dixon as well. The now very dead Aaron Dixon—and his lovely wife, Sherry, also very dead.

Trevor now knew that Nicholson Investigations had been looking into the disappearance of Emily Clarkson, and had taken the investigation so far along that they'd even offered Aaron and Sherry a deal. Went so far as to employ a defense lawyer to act on their behalf. And Aaron had admitted that they told him they knew he had a connection to Trevor Kincaid.

And Nicholson Investigations was Dan Nicholson, as well as Jeff and Gaia Kavanaugh. Trevor deduced that one of them must have been parked in front of his building after luring him out. If a photo had been taken, by now the three of them knew that Trevor

Kincaid was actually Brandon Horcroft. Surely they would have recognized him, despite his disguise. They weren't stupid.

Which meant that they knew Brandon Horcroft was still alive.

Even though Trevor had eliminated the loose ends of Walton and the Dixons, he felt vulnerable. They knew where he lived. He needed to disappear for a while, under a new name and a new address.

Trevor packed up a couple of suitcases with his favorite clothes, stuffed his laptop into its case, and then filled another case with his two cellphones, satellite phone, and Glock pistol with silencer. That would be all he'd need for a while. The place he'd be renting was furnished, and while not up to his usual high standard, it would have to do for now.

It was a two-bedroom apartment on the thirtieth floor of a rental apartment building located on Sherbourne Street, close to Richmond.

Only a few minutes' drive north from Trevor's condo. Being that his new residence was just a rental building, it didn't have the same air of class. In fact, it was kind of crappy. In kind of a crappy area too, although some considered the Sherbourne/Richmond area trendy. But those who thought so hadn't lived in the places Trevor had lived in.

Parking was underground, which was good, and the apartment was spacious enough. The furniture sucked, but again, it would have to do for a little while. Hopefully he'd be back in his Front Street condo in short order.

He just needed things to cool down a bit.

He liked that the apartment had a balcony, because he'd gotten used to that amenity. Actually, the balcony at the Sherbourne apartment was slightly bigger than the one he had at the condo, and it had bars with a concrete pad on top. His balcony on Front Street didn't have bars—it was all concrete, which was kind of claustrophobic. The only way he could see down to the street was if he was standing up.

He looked forward to being able to sit down and relax, and snoop on what was going on down below.

So, while there were mainly negatives with his new place, there were a few pluses. It would do for the short term, and at least he would feel safer.

He could have easily moved into a higher-class building, but if someone was looking for him that's the kind of place they'd expect to find him. So, Trevor decided that going against type would be a better way to hide. And while he had to give a name and show identification at the new place, he paid a year's rent in advance to avoid any bank transactions or credit checks. The fewer traces left, the better.

He'd be going under a new name now, with identification to match. Actually, this was an identity that the CIA had set up for him long ago, and he'd only used it a couple of times. Just for CIA business. It was handy to have now.

And he certainly didn't want to revert back to his Brandon Horcroft identity. That would probably have to stay buried forever now, even though he still had all those documents, too.

He walked over to the full-length mirror and examined himself. Blue jeans, T-shirt, sneakers. Yep, he looked like he'd fit in at the new building.

Well, maybe one extra touch needed.

Went to the kitchen and pulled a pair of scissors out of the drawer. Cut a slit in the right knee of his jeans and pulled it apart slightly to make it look more tattered. Then went back to the mirror and took another look.

Yeah, that was better.

Grabbed a Blue Jays ball cap out of the top shelf of his closet and pulled it down over his bald head. Took another look.

Yep, he'd blend in nicely now in his new six-pack neighborhood.

He made a mental note to walk down to Yonge Street later and shop for some more crappy clothes. Couldn't be seen wearing his pressed slacks and expensive suits. Would raise too many eyebrows amongst his new neighbors. Some might get too curious. He wanted to just blend in and hopefully just be invisible.

He took one last look in the mirror at the new William Balderson. He was struck by how handsome he was even though he was dressed in crap. Some things one just couldn't hide.

He loaded his bags onto a luggage cart provided by the building. Opened the door, took one last look at his opulent suite, sighed, and closed the door behind him.

I'll be back.

Once in the lobby, he pushed his cart over to Albert at the security desk. Trevor was going to miss this convenience. There was no security at his new building—just a primitive buzzer system. But, he was going to let Albert in on where he was going, and drop a few dollars on him at the same time. Albert had always idolized him, so he was sure he could be trusted. As well, he wanted to hear from the security man if there were any enquiries about him while he was away.

Albert glanced up from his newspaper.

"Are you going on vacation, Mr. Kincaid?"

"No, Albert. I have to move to a different building for a while. Some business troubles I'm being pestered about, and I need to live somewhere else for a little while. I'll be back."

"Oh, I'm sorry to hear about that. I'll miss you. Does it have something to do with that man who phoned me asking for you to meet him in front of the building?"

"That's just one of the little games they're playing with me. I hope you understand, Albert, that a man of my wealth sometimes has to be careful."

"Oh, I do, sir. You're not the only one in this building who's had to do things for privacy. I'm used to it."

Trevor smiled. "Glad to hear."

He pulled a sheet of paper out of his back pocket.

"I trust you, so I've written down my temporary new address here, and my temporary name. You have my three phone numbers so you can reach me if there's any funny business. Also, while I don't get much mail, you can forward it to me at this address."

Albert frowned as he read. "Oh, this address doesn't really suit you, sir. Do you think you'll be happy there?"

Trevor shook his head. "No, I'm not going to like it at all. But— it's just temporary, so I'll be okay."

"I like your new name, though, sir. William Balderson. It fits you."

Trevor laughed, and pulled a wad of bills out of his side pocket.

"This is for you, Albert. There's a thousand dollars here. And if you keep my new address and name secret, there'll be another thousand when I move back."

Albert gave a slight bow. "Oh, thank you, sir. That's so generous."

"You're welcome, Albert. See you again soon."

Trevor pushed his cart over to the garage elevator and pushed the button. Albert called after him.

"Oh, sir, once you've loaded your luggage into your car, you can just leave that cart down in the garage. I'll deal with it."

Trevor Kincaid gave him a two-finger salute as he entered the elevator.

Primed and ready to emerge at his new residence as William Balderson.

Chapter 50

"Rachel, do you think my mommy and daddy will be glad to see me?"

"Oh, my gosh, Riley—they've probably been worried sick about you. They'll be over the moon. And Tommy too!"

Riley blushed. "Well, Tommy's always liked my room better than his. I'll bet he moved into it after I left."

"What color is your room, Riley?"

"Pink, with white flowers painted on top."

"Well, I don't think Tommy moved in there—unless he repainted it."

Riley shook her head. "He doesn't know how to paint."

"Did you and Tommy get along well?"

"Well, he used to tease me a lot. But we never fought or anything."

Rachel laughed. "Well, from what I've read, when people tease each other it means they love them very much."

"Really?"

"Yep, really. It's going to be such a happy moment when you and your family are together again. It won't be long now, Riley. We're making good time."

Riley bounced up and down in her seat with excitement, and ran her finger down the map. "I can see where we've been so far. That big lake you said was called Great Slave Lake. That was such a long one."

Rachel remembered the butterflies in her stomach as they were flying over that massive body of water. After the close call they had with Long Lake, she really didn't relish flying over water again. But it would have been a drain on fuel if she flew around it, so she decided to brave it.

It had been a clear evening for flying—so far—but she could see thunderheads building up ahead. As well, the further south they flew, the darker it was getting. She reached towards the dashboard and flipped on the navigation and beacon lights. She'd forgotten all about them after she shut them off to preserve battery power when trying to re-start the plane.

Riley looked out the side window, and strained her neck to see the ground below.

"We flew over a town a little while ago." She glanced at her map. "I think it was called High Level. And now I see another lake below us—on the map it's called Slave Lake. So, it must be a sister to that other lake, Great Slave Lake."

Rachel rubbed Riley's back. "Or, could be a brother?"

Riley shook her head defiantly. "No, no—lakes are girls. They're so peaceful and gentle. Men aren't gentle."

Rachel knew what had caused her to say that. "Well, some men are gentle, Riley. I'll bet your daddy and Tommy are gentle."

"Yes, I wasn't talking about them."

"Okay, I understand, honey."

She glanced at her watch. They'd been flying for about five hours. Not far now—maybe another hour or so. But she couldn't ignore the stomach cramps as the thunderheads got closer and closer.

The two fuel tanks were showing less than a quarter full. It would be tight.

Suddenly the little plane bounced and shuddered, causing both of them to gasp.

Riley ignored the sudden movement, and shouted, "We should be over Edmonton really soon, Rachel! It's a big city so we should see the lights."

Rachel pointed through the windscreen. "I think I already see them. Look at that glow ahead of us in the distance."

"You're right, you're right! So, Calgary isn't far after that!"

"Nope, should be only an hour of flying after that."

Suddenly the plane shook again, at the same time as a massive lightning bolt shot down from the clouds above.

Rachel glanced at the altimeter. They were hovering around seventy-five hundred feet, and the airspeed was looking good at two hundred kilometers an hour.

But there was a storm in their path and she couldn't risk flying through it. They needed to climb now, before it was too late. Which, while it was the only real option, she knew would drain precious fuel.

Rachel kept her voice calm. Didn't want Riley to blank out again like back when they were upside down.

"Riley, we're going to climb above this storm. It's starting to get kinda bumpy, and I think we should avoid that. What do you think, co-pilot?"

Riley bobbed her head up and down. "I don't like storms, Rachel. Yes, let's do that."

"Okay, grab onto your yoke and we'll pull back together. I'm going to need your help. When we go through those clouds it's going to get rough."

Riley grasped the yoke and nodded her head. "I'm ready, Rachel!"

"Okay, then, here we go."

They both pulled back at the same time and the plane began to climb. The higher they got, the bumpier it got. Rachel wasn't sure, but she thought if they got to the ten thousand-foot level they should be okay.

More lightning bolts in their vision, a vision that quickly went blind to everything else.

They were now in the midst of the thunderheads, and their view of the ground below had completely disappeared. Rain began pelting the windscreen.

Rachel flipped on the wipers.

They were climbing fast, and while that was what she really wanted to do, she remembered back to what had caused them to stall out before.

"Ease forward on the yoke a bit, Riley."

Riley glanced over at her. "Am I doing good, Rachel?"

"You're doing perfect, darling. I couldn't do this without you."

Suddenly, a gust of wind slammed into them from the right, and the plane slid sideways and slightly downward. Rachel struggled with the force of the wind—the yoke seemed to resist.

"Riley, pull back again, and turn to the right—into the wind!"

Within seconds she felt like they had control again. But the compass indicated they were going in an easterly direction now.

"We'll turn together, Riley—slightly to the right. To get us back heading south again. The wind is strong so we'll have to turn hard."

"Okay, Rachel."

She was glad to see that Riley was staying calm so far. It was unsettling even for her to be flying blind through a thunderstorm, but she was glad she'd made the decision to climb before they were into the worst of it. If she'd waited, climbing safely might have proved impossible.

Suddenly they burst through and the air became calm.

Riley yelled out. "Rachel, I can see the stars! Look!"

A wave of relief swept over Rachel's entire being. She took a deep breath, and silently complimented herself for making the decision to climb as early as she had. She noticed two other small planes off in the distance, their beacon lights flashing. They'd had the same idea.

"Oh, those stars are beautiful, Riley. Much better than seeing them from the ground."

In a pouty voice, Riley replied, "But I really wanted to see Edmonton. We've missed it now."

"Yeah, that's too bad. But the most important thing is, we missed the storm."

"And we did it together!"

Rachel reached over and tugged on her ponytail. "We sure did. We'll remember this adventure forever."

Riley turned her head and smiled at her. "I love you, Rachel. Will you come and live with us?"

"I love you too, Riley. But I have to try to find my own family. I was kidnapped fifteen years ago, and my parents don't know if I'm alive or not. I don't even know who my parents are, but I have to try to find them."

Riley nodded. "I understand. But if you don't find them, will you live with me?"

"That would be up to your parents—but we'll see, sweetie. The main thing right now is to get you back to them."

She glanced out the side window at the storm below. Thick dark clouds, and lightning bolts traversing between them. She was so glad they weren't in the midst of that chaos.

The altimeter showed ten thousand feet and their airspeed was holding at two hundred. But the fuel tanks were a concern now. Less than five percent full, and a light was flashing a warning to her on the dashboard.

"What's that light mean, Rachel?"

She didn't want to lie to the child. "It means we're running out of gas, Riley."

They'd burned a lot of fuel climbing and were now paying the price.

"Okay, we're past the storm now, so I'm going to take us back down. Let go of the yoke, hon, I'll take care of it."

She pushed the yoke forward, while at the same time pulled out the throttle. No need for power they didn't require, and gravity would handle the descent speed that she needed.

They were well past the storm now, and the view to the ground was clear.

"Look Rachel! The lights! Is that Calgary?"

"I don't think so. It's too soon. What does it say on the map?"

Riley ran her finger down the sheet. "Oh, I think it must be Red Deer."

Rachel gazed ahead through the clear sky as they descended down to five thousand feet. "But I think I can see Calgary, Riley. Look at that mist of lights way ahead of us."

"I see them, I see them! I'm almost home!"

The warning light was flashing faster now as Rachel brought the plane down to twenty-five hundred feet.

Suddenly the engine sputtered.

Once again—a repeat of a few hours ago—there was silence in the cabin. The engine had stopped, fuel-starved. The propeller became impotent.

Rachel fought against the knot in her stomach and forced herself to look at the gauges. The fuel tanks showed empty—it seemed as if the gauges had dropped off suddenly in just the last few minutes. They must not have been showing an accurate display before.

"Rachel, what's wrong?"

"It's happened again, Riley. The engine's stopped."

"Can you start it up again like before?"

"Not this time, Riley. We have no gas left."

Riley thrust her hands up over her eyes. "Oh, no!"

The altimeter showed one thousand feet now. Rachel had no idea where the Red Deer airport was, and scanning the horizon, she couldn't see runways anywhere. She didn't even know if they had an airport, but if they did, it would just be a small one anyway.

"Riley, we're gonna do this! Don't cover your eyes. I may need you!"

The airspeed was still high—showing one-fifty. Without fuel, the plane was now just a glider, but she still had electrical power and hydraulics. So, there were still things Rachel could do.

Suddenly she remembered the flaps, which were crucial in slowing the plane down when coming in for a landing. They were a three-stage contraption, so she flipped the switch down to the first stage. She heard the whir and glanced out both side windows to make sure that they'd executed.

Satisfied, she turned back to the yoke and her view of the ground.

They were down to five hundred feet now. Rachel frantically scanned her eyes back and forth across the windscreen.

Suddenly she saw it.

A highway, illuminated in the darkness by cars heading north and south. It was wide enough. It could handle a plane.

A frantic high-pitched voice from the co-pilot's seat.

"Are we going to land Rachel?"

"We have to, Riley. No choice." She pointed off to the right. "Down there, on that highway."

Rachel turned the yoke gently to the west and the plane banked. She continued the turn until they were lined up with the highway. Then she lowered the flaps to the second level. That familiar and comforting whir sound once again. She felt the decrease in speed instantly.

She lined the plane up with the southbound lane of the highway, and thanked God that there seemed to be no crosswinds.

Glanced at the altimeter. Down to one hundred feet now.

Pushed the flaps lever down to the third and final notch and felt another drag on the speed. The indicator read seventy kilometers an hour. She remembered that at that speed they should be primed to land. She eased the nose up a little to help slow the plane down a tiny bit more. The slower the better if they had a rough landing.

"Rachel, isn't there a horn we can honk to warn those cars?"

"No horns in these planes, Riley. We'll have to just pick a good clear spot."

She pulled the yoke back slightly again to avoid a cluster of vehicles, then set her sights on a large open expanse of the highway dead ahead.

She concentrated hard, as she pushed forward on the yoke.

The plane was level and the speed was good. They were now just a couple of dozen feet off the ground.

Rachel gritted her teeth, then yelled, "Riley, tuck your head between your knees and clasp your hands over the back of your head!"

Chapter 51

The plane hit the highway with a jolt that reverberated all the way up through Rachel's backbone right into her forehead. The aircraft bounced and sent itself into the air again, only to come back down quickly, careening off to the left, narrowly avoiding one of the many cars that had already pulled over to the side.

She tapped the right rudder with her foot and the plane instantly corrected itself.

They were racing down the highway now. It seemed to Rachel as if they'd actually picked up speed since hitting the asphalt. She alternated her feet across the two rudders to make sure that the aircraft would stay as straight as possible. Wanted to remain in the middle of the road, away from the cars that had pulled off onto the shoulder.

But they were gaining quickly on a grouping of cars in front that didn't seem to be aware that an airplane was looming in their rear-view mirrors.

Riley cried out. "Can I lift my head now?"

Rachel yelled, "Yes, but extend your arms out in front and push forward on the yoke! That will help keep you from banging forward if we hit something!"

Rachel was pushing hard on her own yoke, even though now that they were on the ground it was a totally useless instrument. The only things that would control the plane now were the brakes and the rudders. But the yokes were at least something to brace against to slow down forward motion if they collided with anything.

The cars in front were making no effort to get out of the way. Rachel was certain that within mere seconds they'd run up on top of the low-lying convertible sports car that was in the back of the group. The plane would, without a doubt, crush the car and the people inside.

"Hold tight, Riley!"

She positioned her right foot and pushed hard on the rudder, while pumping the left brake with her other foot. The plane veered to the side, missing the sports car by inches.

Then it kept going—off the highway, bouncing in and out of a narrow ditch and up into what was a brightly lit congested area with gas stations and restaurants.

The plane careened towards a parking lot.

Looming ominously in Rachel's vision now was a light standard.

She slammed her foot down on the left rudder but there wasn't enough distance for the plane to adjust. They hit the pole and the right wing and its strut were cruelly ripped away from the fuselage. And since, with this model of plane, the wings attached to each other across the top of the airframe, the left wing gave up, sagged, and fell away as well, dragging alongside the plane by its strut.

The collision with the pole caused the Cessna to spin in an almost perfect three-sixty, and then carry on in the direction it had been heading. The parking lot was still their apparent destination.

The wingless aircraft they were riding in now resembled nothing more elaborate than a large metal buggy.

A picnic bench was next in line along their route. A happy family quickly erased their cheerful expressions and leaped from the table. Left their hamburgers and fries behind and ran for their lives.

Rachel and Riley braced hard against their yokes as the aircraft rammed into the picnic table, smashing it to pieces.

A particular restaurant would be the last destination for the out of control plane.

Rachel stared in abject horror through a massive plate glass window at a full table of people sitting just inside.

Even though she knew they couldn't hear her, she yelled, "Move! Move!"

But somehow they seemed to hear her anyway. All six of them jumped up from the table and dove off to the side just as the fuselage slammed through the glass, and into the table they'd been sitting at only milliseconds before.

Finally, mercifully, the plane came to a rocking rest, its back wheels lodged against the outside steel window frame.

*****

It was a hive of activity. Two ambulances, three RCMP police cruisers, a fire truck, curious onlookers outside in the parking lot, and a few dozen more crowded over into a corner of the restaurant.

Luckily, the ambulances and fire truck weren't needed. Remarkably, despite the carnage, not a single person was hurt. And there was no fire or explosion because the plane had been riding on empty.

Rachel and Riley were huddled together at a table—tea for Rachel, hot chocolate for Riley.

The staff were so nice, which surprised Rachel since they'd destroyed their front window only an hour before. They brought out hamburgers and French fries for them; a welcome respite considering that they hadn't eaten for hours.

Paramedics examined both of them and declared—aside from the non-stop shaking from the experience—that they were perfectly fit.

Within the first fifteen minutes a Mountie was already

interviewing them. He was a constable, but once Rachel started telling her story he said he needed to call someone with a higher rank.

Now, that someone was approaching their table.

Sergeant Roland Metcalfe's first reaction when he saw them was one of surprise. They weren't at all what he'd expected.

Reports of a plane landing on the highway, debris of two wings lying outside in the parking lot, the crippled fuselage rocking up and down halfway through the window of the restaurant. And yet, the people who caused the carnage were as sweet and innocent-looking as could be.

The little girl was clinging to the young woman. Both of them were crying, shivering, and whispering to each other.

Just as a quick observation, Roland surmised that they were two people who loved each other very much—or, were just so scared about what they'd gone through that the stress made them co-dependent.

He wondered if they were mother and daughter, although the woman didn't appear old enough to be the little girl's mother.

He pulled up a chair across from them and took off his cap.

"Hi, ladies. I'm Sergeant Roland Metcalfe of the RCMP. I just want to have a little chat with you, if you don't mind."

The woman held out her hand. "Hello, Sergeant, I'm Rachel Milton. And this is my sister, Olivia Milton—but that's not her real name, and I don't think my name is real either."

He shook her hand and then held up his other hand in a stop sign gesture. "Okay, maybe we're getting ahead of ourselves here. Just relax—you can tell me everything. And call my Rolly, by the way. Everyone does."

"Thanks, Rolly."

"And you, little girl, this is your big sister?"

She nodded enthusiastically. "She saved my life!"

Rolly pulled out a pad and started jotting down some notes. He looked up at Rachel again. "You have quite the story to tell, I expect. Do you want to start?"

She nodded.

"Where did you come from?"

"Yellowknife."

"There was no fuel left in the wings. You flew all that way today, without refueling?"

"Yes."

"Are you a pilot?"

She shook her head. "Not licensed."

"Where did you get the plane from?"

"I stole it. It was my father's."

"Was?"

Without expression, she replied, "Yes, I killed him earlier today."

Rolly felt his stomach jump into his throat. He tried not to show any expression, but probably didn't succeed. This wasn't something even a Mountie heard every day.

He held up his hand again. "Ms. Milton. You don't have to continue talking to me. We can get a lawyer over here for you."

She shook her head. "I know my rights under the Charter. I've done a lot of reading. But I don't care. I want to tell our story."

Suddenly the little girl started crying. The woman wrapped her arms around her and squeezed her tight.

"Is Olivia okay?"

The girl spoke for only the second time since Rolly had arrived.

"My name's Riley. Riley McCormick. I'm not Olivia."

He smiled at her. Thought she was kidding, like little girls tended to do with their imaginations. "Just like the cowboy clothing store, huh?"

"It's true. That's my name. And Rachel didn't kill our dad. I killed him. She's trying to protect me. He was killing her and I had to stop him."

Rolly pulled a handkerchief out of the top pocket of his blazer and wiped his forehead. Even though it was cool in the restaurant, all of a sudden, he felt the sweats. So far, this was one of the strangest stories he'd ever heard.

Rachel brushed her fingers across Riley's cheek, and then stared at Rolly. "You have an iPad there. Search for the Amber Alert that went out on Riley McCormick in Calgary a few weeks ago."

He shrugged, and obliged. Tapped in the words and then stared transfixed at the screen. He looked up at Riley, then back down at the screen again.

Rolly couldn't hide his shock, and as a trained RCMP officer he was surprised by his sudden lack of restraint. He whispered, "Holy Mother of God."

"She was kidnapped, Rolly. And so was I fifteen years ago, along with another girl named Angie, but I doubt that's her real name and I doubt my name is Rachel. I think my name is Emily Clarkson."

He looked up from his iPad, knowing once again that he wasn't doing a good job of managing his shock. "I know about that case. It made the headlines after Emily's bicycle turned up in someone's backyard. You think that's you?"

Rachel nodded. "Yes, and that girl Angie that I mentioned was sent to Saskatoon twelve years ago. I wonder where she came from originally."

Rolly wiped his brow again.

"I'm going to pull up what I have on that Clarkson case."

He tapped on his iPad.

"Well, isn't this interesting? That cold case is being investigated by a firm owned by an old Mountie colleague of mine, Dan Nicholson. I'll call Dan tomorrow and let him know about this latest development."

He turned his attention back to what Rachel and Riley had just told him.

"Both of you say that you killed him. What's his name and address? We'll have to go there."

Rachel leaned her elbows on the table and rested her chin in her hands.

"His name is Rod Milton, and I don't know the actual address. Everyone knew the house—it's a big estate outside Yellowknife, off the Yellowknife Highway. He owns Great White North Diamond Mines."

"Okay, it sounds like his house will be easy to find. We'll send Mounties out there."

Rolly paused for a second. Then, in a soft voice, he asked, "How did he die?"

Rachel rubbed her eyes. "He was attacking Riley. I broke into the bedroom and used a knife to cut off his …"

Rolly looked away, suddenly feeling uncomfortable. "Okay, say no more. I understand."

Riley jumped in. "Officer, Rachel was only trying to protect me. Then he started choking her to death. I had to save her. I stabbed him in the neck. I'm the one who killed him."

The little girl started to cry, and her raw emotion was making Rolly's own eyes tear up. He thought of his own young daughters and it made him want to just go home and hug them.

"I understand, Riley. And I believe your story—both of your stories. And I believe that you are the Riley McCormick everyone's been looking for. But it's not up to me. A court has to decide. You're just a child, but Rachel has to face a different system."

Rachel wiped a tear away from her cheek. "Rolly, what happens now?"

"I'll drive you down to the Remand Centre in Calgary, Rachel. You'll have to stay there until a prosecutor decides whether or not they want to proceed with a case against you. I would recommend that you get a good lawyer.

"As for Riley, for tonight at least, I'll have to hand her over to Social Services, who will then proceed to contact who you both think—and I agree—are her parents."

Riley was crying again.

"Please, Officer, don't lock Rachel up. She saved me, and flew me all the way here so I can be with my mommy, daddy, and Tommy. Rachel shouldn't be punished for that, should she?"

Rolly suddenly did something a properly impartial RCMP officer should never ever do. He got up from his chair and walked around to Riley. Bent over and gave her a warm hug and kiss on the cheek; the exact type of hug and kiss he would give his own girls.

"Riley, I'll do what I can to make sure that she's not. You have my promise as a father."

Chapter 52

Trevor stretched his neck muscles after completing his morning routine.

He always made sure to take care of his body immediately after waking up, before doing anything else.

Otherwise, if he got distracted, he knew he would forego the workout. He possessed that kind of brain—it was always working and always focused. If something else caught his interest, that thing would consume him to the detriment of other things.

His wake-up routine consisted of one hundred double-handed push-ups, followed by twenty one-handed versions for each arm, then one hundred and fifty crunches, and finishing off with fifty squats.

The finale of his exercise regimen always consisted of a pose in front of a full-length mirror. But in his new apartment he didn't have one of those, so he made do with the bathroom mirror.

Puffed out his chest, flexed his muscles, and smiled at what he saw.

He was proud of the fact that at his age he was quite the physical specimen. But then he quickly corrected himself—at *any* age he was quite the physical specimen.

He walked barefoot and naked into the living room from the guest bedroom, which functioned as his new gym. Switched on the small-screen TV; a screen that took some getting used to. He sure missed his condo and all of its luxuries. Trevor hoped he wouldn't have to stay at this place too long.

Flipped through various channels, then paused the remote at a news report flashing a scene that caught his eye. The rolling chyron at the bottom of the screen read: "Airplane drops from the sky outside Red Deer."

He clicked Play and managed to catch the tail end of the report before the reporter switched to a different story.

The last words he heard were, "This looks like a happy ending to the search for little Riley McCormick who went missing from Calgary during the summer."

Trevor flipped off the TV and turned on his laptop.

That Riley name rang a bell.

He went into his encrypted files and clicked on Rod Milton in Yellowknife.

Sure enough, Riley McCormick was the last girl he'd delivered to him—Trevor had arranged for adoption papers for her under the name of Olivia Milton.

He cursed, exited his encrypted files and went to his news feed. Located the Breaking News article and began to read:

Highway Drama in Alberta

Motorists were treated to some unexpected excitement last night, when a single-engine Cessna landed on Highway 2 just outside of Red Deer. It narrowly missed several vehicles, then careened into a rest stop area known locally as Gasoline Alley. The plane hit a light standard, which tore off its wings, and then crashed through the front window of a popular restaurant.

No one was injured in the incident, and the woman pilot and

her seven-year-old passenger escaped the aircraft unharmed.

The RCMP were on the scene quickly, and haven't yet provided much information to the media. However, they do promise that later today or tomorrow there will be a press conference. Anonymous sources within the department, however, have indicated that the young passenger in the plane is reportedly Riley McCormick, who was the subject of an Amber Alert in August. Riley went missing from her Calgary neighborhood in broad daylight and searches have been conducted across Canada since she disappeared.

The Cessna was apparently being flown by an adult woman identified as Rachel Milton, who was not a licensed pilot. The plane was reportedly owned by a Rod Milton of Yellowknife, North West Territories. The RCMP have confirmed that a search of the home of Rod Milton was carried out this morning, and he was found deceased.

More to follow as further details are released by authorities.

Trevor turned off his computer and leaned back in his chair. Sat quietly and thought for a few minutes.

Then, he got up and went into the kitchen. Even though it was only 11:00 a.m., he felt like he needed a drink. Poured himself a Scotch, neat, and sucked it back in one gulp.

Then he yanked a throw off the couch, wrapped it around his naked mid-section, and walked out onto the balcony.

Looked up, down, and sideways.

Shuffled over to the far right edge of the space, leaned out, and peeked around the corner of the four or so feet of masonry that separated his balcony from the next one. There was no furniture on that balcony—no drapes on the windows either. No signs of life. He then grabbed hold of the farthest metal railing spindle and pulled hard on it.

Leaned out and looked down the thirty floors to the street.

Lots of activity down there today. He gazed off in the direction of Yonge Street a couple of blocks or so to the west.

Trevor sighed and accepted that at this moment in his life he was vulnerable, and for good reason.

He'd already tied up some loose ends, but others just kept appearing. Just to complicate his life.

Rod Milton had been a loose end, but at least he was now dead.

The only thing that could trace Trevor to Rod was their business transactions, and Trevor had been smart enough to make sure those appeared as legitimate consultancy contracts.

Riley McCormick was a loose end—but not really. There wasn't much she could tell about anything.

Rachel Milton was definitely a loose end, though—he'd spent time with her during her early days of deprogramming fifteen years ago. He'd forgotten what her real name was. It was in his computer somewhere—but it really didn't matter. Trevor just didn't care.

Could Rachel identify him now? Trevor doubted it. As well, he was not only older but he looked a lot different. His analytical brain dismissed her as a concern.

Regardless, he still felt vulnerable. The three human irritants at Nicholson Investigations were clearly relentless.

He was glad that he'd moved residence.

And relieved as well that he'd had the presence of mind to change his name to William Balderson. For now, he was insulated from any danger, provided he kept himself under the radar.

And provided he was cautious enough to keep one or two steps ahead. Which, Trevor always did. He was brilliant that way.

He shielded his eyes and looked up at the sun.

It was a nice day for a walk. He gazed around again and marvelled at what a nice view his new balcony gave him. Not as nice as his Front Street condo, but considering this was just a rental, it was darn special.

Trevor decided to get dressed and stroll over to Yonge Street. There were some things he needed. And after reading the news, he was desperate for a walk to help clear his head.

*****

He had a bag full of crappy jeans bought from a denim shop.

Picked up some flip-flops and T-shirts as well; a couple of them were Blue Jays adorned, and one had the Raptors logo. Trevor loved basketball—used to play it back in university. His main sport then was football though, so he couldn't resist buying a New England Patriots jersey.

He was well-equipped now, he figured, to be able to blend in nicely with his new casual neighborhood.

But the main store he wanted to visit was a sporting goods shop. It was a large emporium, one that carried equipment for virtually every sport imaginable.

Trevor walked two blocks further north along Yonge Street until he found the place he wanted. Entered the store and was immediately greeted by an eager athletic-looking guy who identified himself as Jim.

"Welcome, sir. How can I help you?"

"Mountain climbing stuff."

"No problem. We have lots to choose from. Follow me."

Jim led Trevor to the back of the store, where all of the alpine equipment was on display.

He held out his hand. "What's your name, sir?"

Trevor shook his hand. "William."

"Nice to meet you, William." Jim flourished with his hand. "We have a good supply of high-quality climbing equipment here, as you can see. What are you looking for today?"

"Rope."

"Do you plan to use it outside, or in a climbing gym?"

"Outside."

"Okay, well that narrows down the choices. We have a good selection of weather resistant polyester ropes. Have you climbed before?"

Trevor nodded. "Yes, quite a bit, mainly down in Peru. But the ropes I have are old and frayed. Need a fresh one. Want to tackle some of the mountains out in the Banff area."

"Do you want Dynamic or Static?"

"Not Static. No give to those ropes. Dynamic gives a nice stretch to absorb impact, so I feel it's safer to always go with Dynamic. Do you agree, Jim?"

"Absolutely. What length do you want, William? They come in sizes from thirty meters to eighty."

"Thirty meters will be just fine. And I'll want about four centimeters thick."

"The minimum is just shy of that. So, we can set you up just fine."

Trevor glanced around at the different selections hanging from the wall.

"I don't want any bright colors. Pick an earth version for me."

Jim frowned. "We have those. But as an experienced climber you know that brighter colors are safer. Easier to see if you're falling and suddenly have to reach out and grab on."

"You're right. But I prefer a more sedate color—brown or beige."

"Okay." Jim pulled a rolled-up sample from the wall and handed it to Trevor. "Would this work for you? It has the thickness and the length you want. On sale right now, too."

Trevor examined it. "I want a rope with a loop at one end, for slipping into a locking position."

"Don't you plan to use clamps and anchors?"

"I've got those. But I want the flexibility of having the rope self-locking if I choose to use it that way."

Jim nodded his understanding, and reached for a long pole. He raised it to the top of the wall, hooked on, and brought down another sample.

"This is exactly what you're looking for. Has a strong loop at one end, and is especially suited to bare-hand climbing as well. The polyester fibres are forgiving on the hands."

"That's exactly what I'm looking for. I don't like to use climbing gloves, so this one will be perfect."

Jim smiled. "Most experienced climbers don't like to use gloves. Something about the purity of bare-hand climbing, and of course, the grip is so much better with bare hands. The fear of blisters can be overcome with knowing that it's safer without gloves."

"I agree, Jim."

"Is there anything else you need, William? Helmet, clamps, pitons, hammer?"

"No, I'm good. I'll buy this for now, but if I ever need anything else I'll make sure to pop in again and ask for you."

Jim beamed. "I appreciate that. But before I check this item through, I should tell you that this is the most expensive rope we have. No sale price on this."

Trevor laughed. "Oh, that's okay, don't worry about it. Can't put a price on safety, can we?"

Chapter 53

The conference room was as bare-bones as could be, but Jeff didn't really expect anything more elaborate in a remand centre. He waited patiently for the other guests to arrive. All important people in this incredible saga.

His flight from Toronto arrived around eleven in the morning. He'd picked up his rental car and immediately made his way over to the northwest section of the city where the remand centre was located.

It had been four days since Rachel and Riley had escaped from the madness of Yellowknife, and Riley was reunited with her family the very next day. Rachel, however, had been held over at the remand centre pending a decision by the Crown Prosecutor. That decision was expected today, as were the results of a DNA test.

Ken and Cathy Clarkson had already visited Rachel in the jail, and then chatted with Jeff on the phone afterwards. They didn't think Rachel was Emily, but the DNA test would determine that for sure. They were disappointed—were hoping that it was her, but Cathy in particular just didn't get the right feeling. One thing Jeff always trusted was that mysterious thing called "motherly instinct." Mothers just knew.

But the Clarksons wanted to be there when the DNA test came back, and the RCMP promised that today would be the day.

Jeff and Dan had spent some time on the phone over the last few days with the office of the Crown Prosecution—on behalf of Rachel. What they told the lawyers about all that they'd discovered since starting the investigation gave them a clearer picture of everything. They'd also done extensive interviews with both Rachel and Riley, and of course their stories matched.

Jeff understood the position of the prosecutors—after all, a man had been gruesomely murdered in his own home, and then his two adopted daughters escaped in his airplane. It didn't look good. But the case for self-defence was a strong one, and Jeff prayed that the prosecutors would show some humanity.

The other important people coming today were Riley herself, along with her parents, Doug and Lisa McCormick. Riley hadn't seen Rachel since they'd been separated, and her parents were anxious to meet the woman who had rescued their precious daughter.

The door opened and in they walked, all three of them beaming. Little Riley was holding her mother's hand, pulling her along, no doubt excited to introduce her to Rachel.

Suddenly her pixy face went downcast once she noticed that Rachel wasn't in the room.

Jeff got up and squatted to be at eye level with her. "You must be Riley. I'm Jeff, the detective who's been searching for Emily."

"Hi Jeff. Where's Rachel?"

He stood up. "They'll bring her in soon, don't worry."

Jeff and the McCormicks made their introductions, and they all took seats around the big conference table.

"I can't imagine what it must feel like to have Riley back home again."

Lisa dabbed at her eyes. "Oh, Jeff, we thought we'd never see her again. This is just so incredible. It's a miracle. And we owe a world of thanks to Rachel. My gosh, the story of the two of them and what they went through is heart-wrenching. The bravery is just hard to imagine."

"It is a miracle, Lisa. Rachel and Riley were troopers, and they stuck together, saved each other's lives, and made it home. Well, at least Riley made it home—we don't really know yet whether Rachel's home or not. We'll have some answers today."

Doug lifted his little girl up out of her chair, plopped her on his lap and gave her a warm embrace.

"Jeff, it sounds like you've been embroiled in this for a while now. It's so nice what your firm is doing for the Clarksons. I hope they get good news today."

Jeff looked down at the floor. "So do I, Doug. But if not, we won't stop looking."

The door opened again and in walked the Clarksons. Jeff introduced them to the McCormicks.

Cathy Clarkson took Riley's hand and gently squeezed it. "I've heard the whole story, Riley. You're such a brave little girl. And you're famous now too!"

Riley shook her head. "I shouldn't be famous. Rachel should. She did everything."

"I hear that you helped her fly the plane."

Riley's little face beamed and her head bobbed up and down. "Yes! Rachel told me what to do and I did it! She called me her co-pilot, and I also helped with the maps and stuff!"

Cathy looked up at Lisa. "Your daughter reminds me so much of Emily. She looks a lot like Emily did at that age, right down to the blonde hair, blue eyes and ponytail."

Ken nodded in agreement. "It's uncanny. And kind of eerie to think these girls were targeted."

Riley started squirming on her dad's lap, so he shifted her down onto her feet. She turned around and looked at him. "Daddy, no one's going to make me talk about what happened, are they?"

Doug brushed her cheek with his hand. "You've already been

talking about how brave you were in the plane, sweetie."

She shook her head. "No, I meant back at that house. What we did. To that … man."

He wrapped his arms around his little girl and hugged her again. Held her close to his chest, and whispered soothingly, "No, Riley, no one's going to make you talk about that. We're here today to meet your friend, Rachel, and thank her. That's the only reason we're here."

Riley pulled back and looked at her dad. "Can I call her my sister, Daddy? We were sisters when we lived together, so why can't we still be?"

"Yes, of course you can still call her your sister."

The locked door at the other end of the room opened, and a uniformed female guard appeared.

"May I bring her in now, Mr. Kavanaugh?"

"Absolutely. We're all here."

The guard disappeared for a couple of minutes, then the door opened again. She escorted Rachel in and removed her handcuffs. She then left the room, closing the door behind her.

Rachel was dressed in a pink pantsuit—nothing fancy; standard jail issue, Jeff guessed. She was also wearing a yellow wrist band, similar to the ones they attached to you at an all-inclusive resort.

Rachel stood still for a few seconds rubbing her wrists. It was if she didn't know what to say, until her eyes fell on Riley.

She knelt down on the floor and held out her arms. "Come here, co-pilot!"

Riley squealed and ran over to her. They embraced each other for a good couple of minutes, rocking back and forth. Jeff lost count of how many kisses they shared. It was clear they loved each other very much.

Both of Riley's parents were crying. Even her father, and he made no attempt to hide it.

Rachel stood and lifted Riley up into her arms. "Are you going to introduce me to your mommy and daddy?"

"I sure am! Mom and Dad, meet Rachel. My big sister!"

Rachel walked over to them, with Riley still in her arms, and they exchanged kisses.

She then gently sat Riley down in a chair and walked over to Jeff. "You must be Jeff."

"Yes, Rachel, and it's such an honor to meet you. The story of your escape left me breathless. I don't think I've ever met a braver person in my life."

She blushed and looked down at the floor. Jeff was taken aback at how attractive she was. A stunner. Blonde, blue-eyed, with the figure of a supermodel. And a radiant warm smile that would light up any room she walked into.

Rachel sat down in a chair between Jeff and the Clarksons. "And it's so nice to see both of you again. Thanks so much for coming back today. I guess we'll know for sure in a few minutes."

Cathy rubbed Rachel's shoulder. "My dear, Ken and I both hope that you're our daughter. We couldn't be more proud if that's the news we get today."

The door opened once again, and the same guard walked in with an envelope in her hand.

"Mr. and Mrs. Clarkson?"

Ken raised his hand. "That's us."

She walked over to him and placed the envelope in his hand. "This is the test you've been waiting for." The guard disappeared.

Ken stared at the envelope, and then gazed into his wife's eyes. He glanced over at Rachel and asked a silent question. She nodded.

Riley suddenly ran over to Rachel and jumped up onto her lap. Wrapped her arms around her neck and whispered, "My fingers are all crossed for you."

Ken opened the envelope and pulled out a single sheet of paper.

He stared at it, then passed it over to his wife. After a few seconds, Cathy looked at Rachel and slowly shook her head. "I'm sorry, Rachel."

Jeff noticed that they all had tears in their eyes. Rachel rubbed her fingers across her cheeks, and then Riley reached up herself and brushed away one of Rachel's tears. They hugged each other tighter.

"It's okay, Cathy. I was hoping—but it just wasn't to be. I hope you find Emily. And I hope I find my family too."

She reached into her pocket and pulled out an envelope. "They took away my purse when they put me in this place, but they let me keep a couple of little things. This is a letter that my sister Angie left for me under my pillow before … he … sent her away. That was twelve years ago."

She handed it to Cathy. "Please, read it."

Cathy pulled the letter out of the envelope and read it slowly. Tears were rolling down her cheeks by the time she finished. She passed it over to her husband.

Between sobs, she said, "That sounds … so much … like Emily. Maybe I just want it to be, but I have … a feeling. Particularly when she writes about swinging on a star and collecting moonbeams in a jar. That was Emily's favorite song. She just loved it, and always sang it around the house or when she was riding her bike."

Ken finished reading the letter and passed it over to Jeff. Tears were running down his cheeks now, too.

Jeff quickly scanned the letter, then looked up at the Clarksons.

"Our investigation also indicated that Angie ended up in Saskatoon, just like she says in the letter. And the last name Hunt is what the records also show for the adoption there. I don't want to get your hopes up, but in showing you this letter Rachel must suspect that Angie may be Emily. And I suspect that too."

Suddenly the door opened again. This time a bespectacled man came into the room and introduced himself to the group as one of the Crown Prosecutors—a Simon Farrow. Jeff remembered that name as one of the attorneys he'd talked to over the phone from Toronto.

Farrow took a seat at the head of the table and began to talk. Simon seemed to be one of those people who had a personality equivalent to a stone. No charisma or warmth, and a voice and expression that were both deadpan.

"As you know, Rachel has been here for four days now. There are several possible criminal charges that could be brought against her, including murder or manslaughter, and theft of an airplane. Also, apparently a worker at the Yellowknife airport was injured when Rachel slammed the door of the plane into him. So, a possible assault charge there. Violations also of federal air traffic rules and regulations.

"The body of Mr. Milton was discovered at the house, as you all know, and an autopsy has been concluded on the body."

Suddenly Simon's lecture was disturbed by Riley. She covered her ears with her little hands and shook her head back and forth, muttering over and over again, "No, no, no …"

Jeff gestured with his hand. "Stop it right now, Simon. What's the point of this? There's a little girl in this room, and both Rachel and Riley have been through hell and back. Just cut to the chase. Are you going to charge Rachel, or not? That's all she needs to know."

The man took off his glasses and rubbed them against his shirt.

"In consideration of all of the evidence and the investigation, which has covered all aspects, and the autopsy results which show—"

Jeff cut him off again. "Just answer the damn question!"

Simon swallowed hard, and then stood. "No, we won't be charging Rachel Milton with any crimes. She's free to go."

He turned on his heel and left the room.

Rachel put her hands up to her mouth and gasped. Riley, who was still sitting on her lap, squealed with delight and kissed her over and over again on the cheek.

Smiles all around, and a collective sigh of relief.

Rachel giggled for a few seconds, and then went suddenly silent.

Lisa seemed to know. Motherly instinct at work again, even though at Rachel's age she probably didn't need too much mothering. Or, maybe she did, since she hadn't had any since she was eight years old.

Lisa whispered in Doug's ear. He smiled and nodded.

She then rubbed Rachel's shoulder. "Alright then, let's get you home. We have a lovely room waiting for you. But if you want to change the color, you can. That's up to you. And Riley tells me you're a gourmet chef, so you can give all of us lessons."

With a stunned look on her face, Rachel's entire body began to shake as a torrent of tears rolled down her cheeks.

"Really? You want me to … live with you?"

Lisa nodded. "Yes, and you're not allowed to say no. But not just to live with us—to be part of our family. After all, you are Riley's big sister, aren't you? So, where else should you be except with her … and us?"

*****

Jeff's flight back to Toronto wasn't due to leave for about three hours, so he asked Ken and Cathy to meet him at a coffee shop near the airport.

They went to the back of the café and squeezed into a nice private booth. They each ordered coffee.

"I wanted to chat with you guys alone before flying back. I have a plan that I'd like your participation in."

Ken leaned forward across the table. "We're all ears, Jeff."

"Dan and I have arranged for fake identifications and a web site, pretending to be architects who have options on a large parcel of land in B.C.

"This man, Foster Hunt, in Saskatoon, is a large developer. We've already approached him by phone for a meeting in Saskatoon next week. Under the pretext that we want to hire a developer to transform that land in B.C. into a high-end resort.

"His daughter, Angie, is an officer of the company. She seems to have full freedom, unlike the way the Rachel had been living. So, that's a bit unexpected, if she was indeed kidnapped. Hunt doesn't seem to restrict her in any way.

"We think that Angie is Emily. It all adds up—the timelines and the money transactions. She was adopted by Rod Milton at the same time as Rachel was, but then sent away and re-adopted by this Foster Hunt guy three years later. By that time, because of the three years she lived with Milton, her mind had probably been programmed and manipulated to erase any prior memories. Hypnotism, mind control, drugs.

"Now, this Angie seems to be functioning as a rather independent young lady, active in her dad's business. As well, we just discovered the other day by our computer expert's digging, that Foster Hunt is actually married.

"This information didn't show up the first time our expert started searching. Hunt got married two years after he adopted Angie. And he was married before that as well. His wife and daughter were killed in a car accident three years before he adopted Angie.

"So, this is a totally different situation from the conditions that Rachel and Riley were living under. Anyway, we need to check it out, and we'd like you both to come with us. We'll just introduce you as employees who are part of our firm. It would be important for you to see Angie up close and personal. And any probing questions we ask may unlock some things that you two might clue into.

"So, are you game? This could turn out to be the golden goose."

Ken and Cathy glanced at each other, and then nodded in unison.

Ken clenched his teeth, and muttered, "Just tell us what day next week, and we'll meet you in Saskatoon."

"Good. We'll coordinate our flight plans. I'll be in touch."

Jeff reached into his briefcase and pulled out a sheet of paper.

"Here's a sketch of what Emily would probably look like today. An RCMP sketch artist, one of the best around, prepared this for us based on photos you gave us of Emily when she was young. He's accurate ninety percent of the time in his aging forecasts."

Chapter 54

Jeff stuffed the last few items into his duffle bag and walked out into the hallway.

Gaia was waiting for him at the front door. "What time is your flight?"

"It leaves in a couple of hours. Dan's meeting me at the airport. When we get to Saskatoon we only have an hour's wait there for the Clarksons' flight to get in from Calgary."

She wrapped her arms around his neck and kissed him.

"I wish I could come with you, Jeff."

Gaia had been suffering from dizziness ever since her concussion from jumping out of the kidnappers' trunk—an event that seemed so long ago now.

The doctors recommended that she not fly, or do anything strenuous, until all of the symptoms of the concussion had disappeared completely.

Alan Cotterhill, the bodyguard Dan had assigned to Gaia, was still living with them in the meantime until Jeff and Dan were convinced that the risk to Gaia's safety was reduced dramatically, and/or her health was back to normal.

"You've been through enough, Gaia. That bastard, Brandon, put you at risk once again, just like he did two years ago. Let me carry the load right now. You've earned the right to relax."

She smiled at him. "Okay, Jeff."

Gaia tickled him under the chin. "Is it okay if I carry a little load of my own, though?"

"No! Not until you're back to normal."

"I won't be back to normal for about seven months."

Jeff frowned. "The doctor never said that. He said it would just be a matter of weeks."

"That was a different doctor. There's another doctor I saw who says that anything less than seven months from now would be very risky."

Jeff put his hands to his forehead. "Christ, why didn't you tell me? This is more serious than we thought."

"It's serious, darling, but nothing to worry about. More like something to be excited about."

Suddenly it hit him. She'd been playing with him.

"We're having a baby?"

"Yes, Jeff. Boy, for a smart guy, and a psychic, it sure took you long enough!"

Jeff grabbed Gaia's hands and swung her around in a tight circle.

"Oh, my gosh, I'm so happy for us! Gaia, it wasn't fair teasing me like that."

She laughed. "Oh, it was fun. How many chances does a woman get to do that? And apparently, all this dizziness had nothing to do with the concussion."

Jeff hugged her, kissed her hard on the lips, and then glanced at his watch.

"I have to run. We'll celebrate tomorrow night when I get back. Right now, I'm the happiest man on earth."

Gaia giggled. "I'm happy too. And now we can have fun picking out names. Do you want a boy or a girl?"

Jeff grimaced. "You know, everyone always says they don't care. But I never believe that. I'd rather just be honest. So, that's what I'll be—I'd really like us to have a girl, especially after the heartbreak of what we've been investigating.

"It would be like some kind of redemption, for me at least, for us to raise a happy, and healthy little girl. And be the ones responsible for keeping her safe. What about you?"

Gaia laughed. "I'm one of those who really doesn't care. Either would be perfect for me knowing you'll be the father."

*****

Jeff and Dan met the Clarksons at the Saskatoon airport, rented a van, and made their way to the Hunt residence which was a few dozen kilometers outside the city limits.

They talked about strategy during the ride.

Jeff volunteered to be the lead on the discussion and questions.

They all agreed that, with him being a psychologist, he'd be more inclined to ask the right questions without raising alarm bells.

Jeff's approach was going to be one of trying to draw the Hunts into conversation rather than an interrogation.

Try to uncover as much as possible—to help each of them in deciphering the body language and mannerisms.

Such as, were there any visible signs of coercion, stress, or robotic-type behavior?

And were there characteristics of the grown-up Angie that reminded the Clarksons of their little girl, Emily?

Was there any hint of recognition?

And most importantly, considering how fast Cathy had determined with her motherly instinct that Rachel was not her daughter, what did her motherly instinct tell her about Angie?

Jeff followed the directions on the satnav and after a scenic drive he turned into the long private roadway of the ranch-style home.

It was large and sprawling, but not pretentious like he'd expected it would be. It had a homey feel to it, surrounded by acres of rolling

369

hills and forests.

Isolated, for sure, but it didn't feel lonely like most large spreads did.

Off to the east side of the house was a large stable adjoined by a fenced-in riding ring. Several horses were being put through their paces by what looked like a skilled team of trainers.

Before they got out of the car, Jeff turned and addressed the three of them.

"We need an 'escape phrase.' Something we all agree that if uttered will bring an end to the meeting."

Ken leaned forward from the back seat and rested his arms against Jeff's headrest.

"What do you mean, Jeff?"

"Well, Dan and I can continue the conversation for as long as you want. But we're here because of you and Cathy. We may have finally found Emily. But if you're not convinced it is Emily, then we can cut the meeting short.

"Or, if you think you want to take a break and the four of us talk things over, that would be another reason to use the escape phrase.

"Consider it like being on a blind date, and you ask a friend to phone you in an hour just in case you want to make up an excuse to bring the encounter to an end."

Cathy whispered, "Jeff, this makes me so nervous. Excited too—but mainly nervous. I can't believe that after all this time we may finally be face to face with Emily in just a few minutes."

Dan reached back and gently squeezed Cathy's shoulder.

"Just take it in stride, Cathy. And try not to show your nervousness. We don't want to set off any alarm bells.

"But as Jeff said, let him handle it. You don't have to speak at all—just be an observer. Your observations, and Ken's, are the most important reasons why we're taking this bold step."

Ken wrapped his fingers around the back-door handle.

"Dan's right, Cathy. Don't worry. We have the professionals here handling this."

Ken then turned his attention to Jeff.

"Good idea about the escape phrase, Jeff. What would you like it to be?"

"I would suggest something conversational. Like, make some observation about how nice the city of Saskatoon is, and say that you read that it's known as the Paris of the Prairies.

"Which it is—for all the bridges alone, of which there are seven. And the arts and culture reputation the city has. If Dan and I hear that phrase, Paris of the Prairies, from either you or Cathy, we'll make an excuse to wrap things up. Okay?"

They all nodded.

With an undeniable degree of anticipation, the four of them exited the car and approached the front door of the massive bungalow.

The end of a long ordeal was possibly only minutes away.

*****

Foster Hunt himself answered the door.

He greeted them with one of the friendliest smiles Jeff had ever seen.

A tall man with bushy gray hair. Jeff guessed he was around sixty years of age, but in great shape.

What struck him most, though, was just the engaging way he welcomed them. One of those people who had that knack of making a great first impression. Jovial, happy, gregarious, and warm.

He ushered them into a large living room where a pretty woman was laying out some snacks and a large pot of tea.

Foster wrapped his arm around her, and they all made their introductions.

"Natalie, my long-suffering wife, takes care of everything around here. Well, her and Angie. I really do nothing at all—which is the way they both like it."

Natalie slapped him playfully on the shoulder. "Foster is far too modest. He's the genius here; he just lets us girls pretend that we control things."

They sat down, and Jeff started things off.

"Thanks for meeting with us today. We wanted to have a preliminary meeting to see if there might be some commonality between us regarding the vision we have."

Foster smiled. "Well, we're honored that you're considering us as your developer. I did some checking on you folks, and you seem to have quite the reputation as creative architects."

Dan jumped in.

"Thanks, Foster. We checked on you too. You've done some pretty impressive developments right across the country.

"It was your personal approach to landscape amenities that we were most impressed with. Our proposed development is all about the great outdoors and nature, and virtually all of your projects have those elements."

Foster laughed. "Well, I have my daughter to thank for that— particularly the projects we've completed in the last three years. She was clever enough to be able to graduate from university at a very young age as a landscape architect. Needless to say, I'm very proud of her. So, I've been blessed with Angie's wisdom and creativity.

"So, tell me, are all four of you architects in your firm?"

Dan shook his head. "No. Jeff and I are the lead architects. Ken and Cathy run our procurement division, scouting out possible development sites and then acquiring options on them. They both have a good eye for the awe-inspiring."

Foster laughed again, in his jovial Burl Ives way. He pointed at Ken and Cathy. "You two are my kind of people, then. Anyone with an eye for beauty and the wonder of nature is someone I like to work with."

Jeff was starting to feel conflicted.

He really wanted to hate this man, but just couldn't.

Foster had a special way about him that was modest, but also confident.

Endearing, but also comfortable in his own skin.

There didn't seem to be an ounce of indecency about him.

And as a psychologist, Jeff was an astute observer of body language.

The way he hugged his wife, the way he looked at her, and the way she looked at him. There was just something about this encounter that didn't fit with the expectations he'd had before flying to Saskatoon.

All of a sudden a vision of loveliness entered the room.

Not just entered the room, but stole the room.

Adorned in a flowery summer dress, long blonde hair flowing over her shoulders, and sparkling blue eyes that seemed to be backlit. And an uncanny resemblance to the drawing that the sketch artist had done.

"Hello, everyone. I'm Angie."

Foster jumped to his feet and gave her a hug. She hugged him back.

"Sweetheart, these are our new friends: Jeff, Dan, Ken and Cathy."

She shook hands with each of them, making slight bows as she did.

"So, are Dad and Mom taking good care of you all? I see you have proper tea and cookies, but would you like something stronger, something more improper?"

They all laughed.

Foster gazed lovingly at her, unmistakable pride written across his face.

"I'm so glad Angie is here today for you to meet her. She's the one who really runs the business now. I'm too old to pay attention to all of the details. I step in once in a while, but only when she needs me."

Angie waved her hand dismissively in the air. "As you can tell, my dad is very modest. He's been a creative genius his entire life. I just add that little bit extra."

Jeff knew that she was right. From what he'd read about Foster Hunt's accomplishments, he had indeed been a creative genius—one of the most respected high-end developers in the country.

Foster took a sip of his tea, then took over the conversation again.

"Just to give you some background, I adopted Angie about twelve years ago. It was a private adoption, so luckily there wasn't as much red tape as there would have been through normal channels for a single man adopting a young girl.

"She was only eleven when she blessed my life. I was widowed a few years before that, and lost my daughter at the same time."

He paused, and wiped a tear from his eye.

"Both in the car, hit by a train at a level crossing. Mary must not have been paying attention. She and Heidi were killed instantly—or so they told me. I've always hoped that was true.

"So, a few years later I decided I wanted my daughter back— Angie knows that was my motivation. But she knows now that she didn't replace Heidi. Angie is her own person and I love her for who she is.

"And a couple of years after I adopted Angie, I married Natalie. One can never replace what one loses—the only solution is to treasure the memories, and then move on with life. Mary and Heidi would have wanted that for me."

Natalie and Angie plopped down on the couch on either side of Foster and wrapped their arms around him.

He kissed them, then gently pushed them away.

"I apologize, folks. I get sentimental at times, and I'm just so proud of these two. I hope I haven't made you feel uncomfortable."

Cathy brushed her fingers across her eyes, and whispered, "Not at all. It's refreshing to see such uninhibited love. The world needs more of that. You seem like a lovely family."

Angie jumped to her feet, and broke the mood of the tender moment.

Picked up a remote control that was resting on the coffee table. Pushed a button and a screen rolled down from the ceiling. Pushed another button and a rear projector started whirring.

"I wanted to show you a little presentation. Dad has told me all about the parcel of land you've optioned in B.C., and it sounds similar in aesthetics to some of the other developments we've done. So, sit back, relax, and enjoy."

The presentation took about fifteen minutes, and it consisted of a beautiful travelogue, showcasing all of the major developments that Hunt Development had created over the years. The video was narrated by Angie herself.

Jeff was stunned at how beautiful the projects were, and for a second he caught himself wishing that he really wasn't pretending at this; that he really did have a project to discuss with these wonderful people.

When the video was finished, Angie proclaimed, "As you can see, we're not content with mediocrity. Some developers say they like to 'swing for the fences.' Well, at Hunt Development, we 'swing for the stars.'"

Cathy choked up, but managed to ask, "What did you say?"

"Sorry, Cathy, I speak too fast sometimes. We like to swing for the stars. A little thing with just me, I guess, more than dad.

"My favorite song since I was a little girl was *Swinging on a Star*. I think that song is now just a wonderful business motto."

She continued to stare at Cathy for a few seconds after

answering her.

"Have we met before, Cathy? You look sort of familiar to me."

Cathy shook her head. "No, Angie, I don't think so. Although, I wish we had."

Cathy glanced at Jeff for just a brief moment, then continued, "You're lucky to live in such a special area. Saskatoon is a pretty city. I read somewhere that it's nicknamed, The Paris of the Prairies. So many bridges, and the arts culture is apparently magnificent."

"Oh, it is, Cathy. You'd love it here. You'll have to make sure to come back for pleasure sometime rather than just this boring business stuff—I'll take you on a tour."

Jeff pulled his phone out of his pocket and clicked on.

While pretending to study his screen, he said, "Oh, I'm so sorry, folks. We have a bit of a crisis to deal with. We'll have to cut this meeting short. Do you mind if we schedule a second meeting for some time in the next couple of weeks or so?"

Foster chuckled and threw his hands up in the air. "Tell me about it! Those things happen to us all the time. No problem, Jeff. You just let us know and we'll schedule some time."

The Fosters walked them to the door.

Hugs all around.

Jeff noticed that Angie hugged Cathy the longest.

Then she leaned back and said, "Cathy, you're so familiar to me. I hope we'll be doing business together so we can see each other, and maybe take that tour of Saskatoon?"

Cathy couldn't help herself. She started crying. "I hope … so too … dear."

*****

Halfway back to the airport Jeff pulled the van over into a rest stop, and they all got out to stretch their legs.

There hadn't been any conversation at all since they'd left the

Hunts. Jeff and Dan had been respectful enough not to probe.

Dan lit a cigarette, and Jeff decided he needed one too.

They both smoked away, waiting for Ken or Cathy to say something.

Ken finally broke the silence. "Well, that was interesting."

Jeff gestured with his cigarette in Cathy's direction.

"You said the escape phrase, Cathy. You must have had a reason."

She nodded, and started crying again.

"I did. That was Emily, no doubt about it. And I think Ken agrees."

She glanced at him. He nodded slowly, all the while staring off aimlessly into space.

Dan shuffled his feet. "So, how would you guys like to proceed? We could confront them, tell them what we suspect. Or, try to file a civil court order demanding a DNA test.

"We could also try to involve the police now, although that may be difficult. Legitimately, Foster Hunt performed a private adoption. There's no evidence pointing to him as a kidnapper, or knowingly supporting a kidnapper."

Cathy wiped the tears away from her eyes.

"I think I can speak for both of us. We want to do nothing. Absolutely nothing at all."

She looked at Ken, a question in her eyes. He nodded agreement.

Cathy continued. "I may be crying, but I'm happy. We've found our baby. She's alive. And she's just fine.

"That lovely man did nothing to her. He loves her as a daughter, and she loves him back. He truly thought he was conducting a private adoption, and he did it for all the right reasons.

"He gave her a home, and lots of love. I don't know if Ken and I could have done any better than Foster has done. To me, this is not a possession thing. This is closure, and we've had the best closure imaginable. Our daughter is alive, happy, and with wonderful people.

"That little pink bicycle was meant to be uprooted—it was meant to lead us to this happy conclusion. It was fate. We've been rewarded in a magical way.

"The Hunts are special people, happy and in love with each other. I wouldn't dream of disturbing that. Dan, we can't thank you, Jeff, and Gaia enough for giving us this gift. You have to believe that. Our lives will no longer be empty."

Chapter 55

He gently rubbed her tummy, hoping to feel something, anything. It was such a mysterious thing, knowing a life was growing inside of her, a life that he and Gaia had created together.

Gaia laughed. "Impatient, aren't you? It's far too early to feel any movement or kicking, dear. You'll have to wait a little bit longer for that."

"I can't help it. It's just so darn exciting."

Jeff had flown in late the night before from Saskatoon. This morning he'd allowed himself the guilty luxury of sleeping in. And it had been a restful sleep—he hadn't had one of those for several weeks.

Gaia had slept in late with him, wrapped up in his arms. One thing led to another, and morning sex was the end result.

Now, both spent, they were enjoying a breakfast of bacon and eggs.

He rubbed the back of her hand. "That was nice this morning. But is it safe for us to have sex while you're pregnant?"

"Yes, dear one. That's just an old wives' tale. As long as we don't hang from the chandelier or something like that, we can have sex for the entire time I'm carrying. Although, a couple of months from now I won't look myself. You may not want to."

"Sure I will. I'll always want to have sex with you, even when you're old and wrinkled."

She kissed his hand. "Oh, that's sweet. I'll hold you to that. You know, the doctor said he was surprised I didn't miscarry when those creeps tried to kidnap me. We haven't had sex since that day, so I was already slightly pregnant and didn't know it."

"It is surprising. We got lucky. Such an unbelievable ordeal for you. I think our little girl is maybe going to turn out to be one tough little cookie, just like her mom."

"Or, little boy?"

"Yes, or little boy. Maybe tonight after dinner we can start coming up with some names. And we have to start planning out the nursery, buy some things that you're going to need."

Gaia shook her head. "We won't buy anything yet—I'm a bit superstitious about that. Don't want to jinx us."

Alan Cotterhill came into the kitchen.

"There's the lovely couple. Welcome back, Jeff. I was just talking to Dan on the phone and he brought me up to date. Sounds like it was a successful trip."

"It was, Alan. Bittersweet, though. The Clarksons found their daughter, but that's where they want the trail to end. There will be no family reunion for them."

Alan sat down at the table and poured himself a cup of coffee from the thermos.

"The main thing is, Emily is alive—and happy. She has a wonderful family by the sounds of it. I haven't had the pleasure of meeting the Clarksons, but it sounds like they are the most unselfish couple on the planet. They did the right thing for their daughter by just leaving that final stone unturned."

Jeff sat back and crossed his legs. "Alan, I was blown away by their decision. And so proud to have gotten to know them. Those are two special people. And Emily is indeed a charmer. Foster Hunt raised her with love and respect; it's so obvious. And, she's so well adjusted, it seems clear that Emily probably has no recollection at all of the time she spent with Rod Milton and Rachel before she was sent off to Saskatoon. Brandon must have arranged for new sessions of hypnosis and reprogramming after he transferred her to Hunt."

Alan stood. "You guys did it. You had a vision that Emily was still alive after all these years and you tracked her down. And inadvertently, you got to learn that two other girls caught up in this insidious affair are now happy and safe—and together."

Jeff couldn't hide the smile of satisfaction on his face.

"Oh, Alan, the scene I got to witness at that remand centre was something I'll remember for the rest of my life. The love between Rachel and Riley was so heartwarming. And what they went through together in defending themselves and then bravely escaping in that plane. Unbelievable. The icing on the cake was when the McCormicks invited Rachel to join their family. You should have seen her face—it lit up like a Christmas tree. And little Riley was just over the moon."

Alan patted Jeff on the back. "Well done. A lot of work that paid off in spades."

Jeff laughed. "And not even a cash payday to go along with it! But it feels as if this case has paid me the largest fee that I've ever earned. I'll never forget this one, and I think all three of us are a lot richer because of it. You know what I mean, I think."

"I sure do. Enjoy the feeling. Hey, guys, I have to head out today to tend to a few details on a security assignment for one of my employees. He's struggling with a difficult client of ours, so I need to mediate. Will you be hanging around the house today, Jeff? If not, and Gaia will be left alone, I can assign someone else to come over to replace me for today."

Jeff waved his hand. "No, feel free to go, Alan. I'm taking the day off to hang out with my wife. I know she told you our news while I was in Saskatoon. I only found out myself just before getting on that flight. We're going to start picking baby names later."

Alan laughed. "That should be fun. Just don't pick any of those modern flaky names, okay? Stick with nice normal names, like … Alan!"

He grabbed his car keys off the counter and headed for the door. "Okay, I'm off, guys. Be back tonight."

*****

Jeff was stretched out on the recliner in his basement study. Gaia was napping up in the bedroom, having dealt with another bout of nausea. She was never content to put up with the nagging threat of morning sickness—instead, she just got rid of it by sticking her fingers down her throat, gagging, and getting it over with.

Her lovely breakfast of bacon and eggs had a short shelf life. Hopefully, only a couple more weeks of this and she'd be past the sicky phase.

He checked his phone for messages, and then scrolled through some of the photos he'd taken while in Calgary and Saskatoon. Happy pictures of the Clarksons, the McCormicks, Rachel and Riley. Nice memories to hang onto. He smiled when he saw the family picture he'd taken of Foster and Natalie Hunt, with their beautiful daughter, Angie. In reality, Emily, but forever to now be contentedly known by the Clarksons as Angie.

As he scrolled along he stopped at the photo he'd taken outside the condominium tower on Front Street. Brandon Horcroft, now known as Trevor Kincaid. Bald head, beard, piercing blue eyes.

Jeff enlarged it and stared at the bastard. The cause of the uprooting of who knows how many little girls. The ringleader, the puppeteer; yet he was still roaming free.

The loose end in this tragic story. The one that the CIA had protected two years ago when Dan had tried to have him arrested. The madman they thought they'd killed when they entombed him in his own vault. The Teflon Man, who always managed to weasel out of every predicament, despite ruining so many lives and fully deserving of the full weight of the law.

But there would be no weight of the law. He'd be bailed out and protected once again—just like the last time—by his powerful employer in America.

Jeff glared at the photo now, his anger simmering to a boil. The man who had kidnapped Gaia two years ago and imprisoned her as his sex slave. Dangerously obsessed with her to the point of putting her life in danger. Obsessed with her because he couldn't have her.

And he'd been so brazen that he'd tried it again just a few weeks ago. An ordeal that almost killed her, and at the very least, could have caused her to lose the baby she had no idea she was carrying.

Jeff's eyes were starting to blur. He rubbed them, thought there might be tears—but there weren't.

Suddenly the photo of Brandon began morphing in front of his eyes. He blinked and rubbed his eyes again. When he looked back at it, it had transformed into a video. Brandon's blue eyes seemed to be flashing slivers of light at him. And then he smiled—in that arrogant evil way that Jeff was more than familiar with.

Suddenly, the video changed. He was watching Brandon from behind now, walking down an alleyway. Carrying a lifeless woman over his shoulder like a sack of potatoes. Jeff could see that her abdomen was distended. He couldn't see her face, but he knew who it was.

Jeff would recognize his own wife from any angle.

The video changed back to Brandon's face. He smiled once again, and mouthed the words, *"Catch me if you can."*

Jeff jumped up from the recliner, but then suddenly lost his balance and collapsed to the floor as if he'd been shoved. His phone fell onto the carpet a few feet away.

He crawled over to it and flipped it up so he could see the screen.

A new video was playing. Brandon, once again from behind, walking down the street. Recognizing the buildings, Jeff could tell that it was Front Street.

Brandon was pushing a cart along the sidewalk, a cart that held several pieces of luggage.

Jeff's eyes were clear now, and the videos disappeared from the screen. He shook his head, clicked on the phone button, and punched a speed dial number.

"Hey, Jeff, how you doing, bud? I was just going to phone you myself. You are psychic, aren't you! I have some important news for you."

"Dan, I'm having a tough time. Get over here now and we'll talk."

"On my way. Hang in there."

*****

"Christ, I had some disturbing visions, Dan. I guess the stress of all of this has just bottled up, and all it took was for me see his face on my phone. It all gushed out at me."

Dan walked over to the bar in Jeff's basement office, and poured a couple of glasses of scotch.

"Here, take a good long sip and tell me what you saw. Remember, you're probably excited and nervous about the baby coming. When you told me the news in Saskatoon, I was so happy for you guys. But, you're psychic, so I worried that visions might start working overtime."

"That's possible, I guess. I'm more worried about Gaia now, because she'll be more vulnerable over the next few months. But, as I told you before, I've learned to trust my visions more now. What I saw was a scene in an alley—Brandon was carrying Gaia over his shoulder. She looked unconscious, and she also looked to be about six months pregnant. He's going to try again, Dan. He still wants

384

her—or he just wants vengeance—I don't know which.

"Then the vision switched to something else. He was walking down the street pushing a cart loaded with luggage. Like he was going away somewhere.

"Then another view of the prick's face—he smiled and mouthed the words, "Catch me if you can." He's daring me to come and get him. At least that's what my visions are warning me about."

Dan downed his drink, got up, and poured himself another.

"I've learned to trust your visions, Jeff. You don't get them that often, but when you do they're always bang on. Which brings me to the news that I wanted to tell you about. Brandon has moved out of his Front Street condo."

"What? Well, that explains my vision of him walking along with suitcases in a cart."

Dan nodded. "Yes. I never told you, but I've had him under surveillance. I wasn't comfortable with just having Alan here protecting Gaia. I wanted us to have eyes on him, too. So, an operative I use from time to time—a lovely lady named Laura—has kept watch. Laura's a former Mountie, a surveillance specialist. Brandon drives a very distinctive Mercedes, with a personalized license plate, so it's easy to follow him when he leaves the building. She's been watching him for quite a while now.

"A couple of weeks ago his pattern changed. It became apparent to her that he'd moved out of the Gainsboro Residences and into a tower on Sherbourne Street called The Summit. Laura then got Jason to hack into the tenant list for The Summit. Only one person, a man, moved into the building around that time. A man by the name of William Balderson.

"It's apparent that Brandon got spooked, moved, and changed his name again. So, he's gone from Brandon, to Trevor, and now to William. Jason also obtained his apartment number from the records he hacked. He's on the thirtieth floor, apartment 3009."

Jeff got up and started pacing back and forth across the room.

"Dan, we can't pursue this madman through the courts. He'll be protected, as he was before. He's laughing at us—because he knows we can't touch him.

"He's arranged the kidnapping of countless young girls across this country, primarily for the sexual gratification of despicable old pedophiles. Emily was the exception, thankfully, because she was transferred from that Milton lunatic to a legitimate adopter. Foster Hunt was probably the only decent man Brandon has ever placed a girl with.

"He kidnapped Gaia two years ago, and attempted it again just a couple of months ago. She almost lost her life on both occasions.

"The man has performed mind control, producing assassins around the globe, including the most recent ones against that senator. He's also hypnotized people he's dealt with and commanded them to commit suicide. The man's a fucking monster."

Dan got up and paced the room beside his friend. He put his arm around his shoulder and gave him a hug. "I know what you want to do. I'll go with you."

Jeff stopped pacing and shook his head. "No, I'm not dragging you into this. It's personal with me now, and I have no right to put you at the scene."

"Okay, I understand. But I'll help you. Laura checked out the security of The Summit. Basically, there is none. Brandon's slumming it right now, probably because he thinks that will keep him under the radar. There's no security guard, no receptionist, no video cameras. And the locks are shit. She used a little Mountie tool to get her in the lobby door, and then tried the tool on one of the apartment doors. Child's play. I'll give you that tool."

Jeff nodded. "And I have my own gun."

Dan shook his head. "That gun is licensed to you under the Firearms Act. As a private investigator involved in occasional bodyguard work, you were granted an ATC certificate to carry. You can't use that gun. Far too traceable. I have a throw-down I can give you."

"What the hell is that?"

Dan chuckled. "All of us old cops have throw-downs. Guns confiscated in raids. Untraceable. I have a good one for you—a Beretta, complete with silencer."

Jeff sat down on the couch, feeling weary all of a sudden.

"He's going to try to take her again, Dan. And if he fails, he might go after our child. I have to bring an end to this."

"I understand. But if you change your mind and want some company, just ask."

Jeff gave an emphatic shake of his head. "This is for me to do, Dan. I'm going to kill this bastard for the second time. And this time, the fucker's gonna stay dead."

Chapter 56

Jeff made sure to don his jacket while he was up in the bedroom, so Gaia wouldn't see that he was wearing a shoulder holster stuffed with a Beretta. She'd seen him carry a gun before, as on many assignments he'd needed one. But his own gun was a Smith and Wesson carried in a hip holster.

He shoved the silencer into his jacket pocket, along with the little key instrument Dan had given him. It was a slick little thing, pretty much guaranteed to bypass any lock. Made in Israel, of course, a country famous for high-tech nefarious gadgetry.

Jeff reached into the closet and grabbed his squash racquet. Then pulled a Blue Jays cap down low over his forehead.

He was ready.

Ran down the stairs, pulled open the cabinet drawer in the foyer and chose the Jeep keys. The Corvette would draw too much attention—a Jeep would stay under the radar.

"Are you going now?"

"Yep, be back in a couple of hours."

"Come and give me a kiss!"

Jeff zipped the jacket all the way up to his neck, and walked down to the kitchen. Gaia was chopping up something at the counter. He grabbed her from behind and kissed the back of her neck, making sure not to press himself so close that she would feel the bulge of the Beretta.

"Oh, that's nice. I love it when you kiss my neck. Who are you playing tonight?"

"Meeting up with Chris. He demolished me the last time we played, so he's graciously agreed to give me a rematch. I'll kick his ass."

Gaia giggled. "You're pretty competitive—I'm sure he's going to regret giving you a chance at redemption."

Jeff turned on his heel and headed down the front hall. "Gotta run. See you later. Alan's downstairs in the office, so you're in good hands."

As Jeff closed the door behind him, he heard her yell out, "Have fun!"

*****

Jeff parked his Jeep on a side street off Richmond, and walked west towards Sherbourne.

Stopped to listen to a busker. A long-haired guy in ratty clothes, his guitar case open on the sidewalk. He was expertly strumming his instrument and singing the Sting song, *Every Breath You Take*. Jeff couldn't pull himself away. One of his favorite songs of all time, but considering the lyrics, also ironic that he was listening to it at this moment.

When the man finished, Jeff walked up and tossed a ten-dollar bill in his case. The busker looked up at him and smiled.

"Hey, thanks a lot, bud." Then he cocked his head. "Are you okay? You look troubled."

"No, I'm fine. I was just astonished at how good you sounded. That's one of my favorite tunes, and you pulled it off perfectly."

"Thanks. I could sing another one for you, if you want. That ten dollars should cover about three songs, I would think."

"No thanks. I have to get going."

"You look like you have the weight of the world on your shoulders. Music can fix that."

Jeff smiled. "It usually can, you're right. But tonight, something else will."

The busker waved. "Well good luck with whatever it is. I'll be here all night if you change your mind. Godspeed, and thanks again."

Jeff continued on his way, and found that the farther he walked the slower his steps became.

While he'd tried to kill Brandon before, that was a spur of the moment decision made by him, Dan, and Gaia, after he'd rescued Gaia from the vault in Brandon's house. The three of them had conspired together, and in just a matter of seconds agreed on what they were going to do with the monster. And they did it, without much thought.

But now, two years later, they discovered that it hadn't worked. He'd escaped from the vault. Somehow. As usual, he'd been one step ahead of them.

Now, here Jeff was actually planning his murder. Doing in advance the things necessary to pull it off. Dan had given him the key instrument and the throw-down gun. And Jeff had lied to Gaia. She had no idea of what he was planning to do.

It was weird to be fully aware that this murder he was about to commit was premeditated. He was about to become a murderer, and that thought was unsettling.

He turned onto Sherbourne Street and saw his target building just up ahead. A tower with a cheap sign out front that declared itself The Summit.

Jeff stopped and leaned up against the wall of a vacant building. Took a deep breath through his nose, held it for twenty seconds, and then exhaled through his mouth. Repeated this several times until he felt that his heartbeat had settled down a bit.

Started walking, but then decided he needed to stop again. It was already dark, and most of the stores were closed. He sat down in the alcove entrance of one store and rested his head in his hands.

Started focusing on what he had to do, and why. Regret had entered his mind—not the regret of killing a monster, but the regret of just taking a life. And the regret of what this had all come down to.

He wondered if planning something like this was a slippery slope. If it was this easy to do, how easy would it be the next time? Hopefully there would never be a next time, but what if there was?

As Jeff continued to ponder what he was about to do, the famous quote from Friedrich Nietzshe popped into his head. *"Beware that, when fighting monsters, you yourself do not become a monster. For when you look long into the abyss, the abyss also gazes into you."*

Jeff shook his head, and pushed that unsettling quote out of his mind. What did Friedrich Nietzshe know about this? Easy to lecture, but not so easy to live with what this particular monster had done to not only the lives of Jeff and Gaia, but so many others.

He focused his powerful brain on the motivations he needed to propel him just the few remaining steps down the street.

Gaia's smiling face flashed across his brain—then he allowed her face to transform to how it looked when she was lying in a hospital bed, bruised and broken from Brandon's attempt at taking her.

Then he allowed his mind to travel two years back, when he was frantically searching for her in Brandon's mansion. Pulling her frail body out of the vault, which had already begun starving her of oxygen due to a mechanical failure. Reviving her, wondering if she was going to survive.

The only sin she'd committed was being desirable to a lunatic, a man who felt he was entitled to have whatever the hell he wanted.

Then Jeff almost lost her when he'd discovered by accident that Brandon had hypnotized Gaia while he had possession of her, and planted the suicide command. Those four insidious words: *Thou shalt go forth.*

And now they'd be welcoming a new life into this world in just seven months' time. After their investigation had uncovered how Brandon had financed the kidnapping of probably countless children, would their own child be Brandon's next target? A man who was still obsessed with Gaia, obsessed with control and revenge, and a man who had learned at some point early in his miserable life that he could just take whatever the fuck he wanted.

Jeff jumped to his feet. Could feel the adrenaline rushing through his veins and his heart was keeping a steady beat. His breathing was fine now, and his mind was in the right zone.

He was ready. Ready to do the world a favor.

Walking at a brisk pace now, he reached the lobby door of The Summit in just a few short seconds.

He looked behind him, and up and down the street. All clear. The cheaply-adorned lobby was also empty. Jeff pulled Dan's contraption out of his pocket and inserted the narrow end into the lock. Then pushed the electronic button on the handle, heard a click, and pushed the door open. Easy peasy.

Walked into the lobby and surveyed the interior. Walked to the end of the corridor and saw that there was a back fire door exit. He decided that would be his way out.

Walked back to the bank of elevators, pushed the button, and waited patiently.

Fell off into a bit of a daydream until the ding of the elevator shocked him back to reality. A woman got off and smiled at him, politely holding her hand against the door frame until he got in.

Punched the button for the thirtieth floor, and the elevator began its ascent. Jeff looked at himself in the mirror. He didn't think he looked any different, but after tonight he knew that he would be. He might never look at himself the same way again. He hoped that at least Gaia would be able to.

He shook the negative thoughts out of his head as the elevator came to a stop.

The door opened and he walked out into the dimly lit hallway, turning left towards apartment #3009.

His heart was beating fast again, and he took a few more deep breaths to settle it down.

There was a chance that Brandon might not even be there. If that was the case, Jeff intended to simply remain in the apartment until the bastard returned; as long as it took.

He stopped in front of the suite and put his ear up against the door.

The muffled sound of a TV.

Now or never.

As a final check, he glanced up and down the corridor. All clear.

Jeff pulled the Beretta out of his shoulder holster and held it poised forward in his right hand. With his left hand he pulled out the contraption and silently inserted it into the lock. Pushed the button, heard the click, and then quickly shoved the thing back into his pocket.

Turned the door handle and pushed it forward.

It opened about an inch and then stopped. He could see one of those security latches keeping it from opening all the way.

Shit!

Jeff stood back, raised his right foot and slammed it against the door. The latch broke off and the door crashed open.

He rushed in and slammed the door behind him.

A blur of movement—a figure was rushing over to a cabinet in the foyer.

Jeff raised his gun and shouted, "Stop, asshole!"

Brandon Horcroft, in the flesh, turned slowly and faced him, hands in the air.

"I knew we'd meet up again."

Jeff motioned with the Beretta. "Get away from that cabinet."

Brandon shuffled over into the living room, hands still in the air. "How did you find me?"

"I don't want to have a conversation with you Brandon—or Trevor—or William, or whoever the fuck you really are."

"You've come here to kill me, then."

"Yes."

"I can make it worth your while not to do that. Bank transfers are fast these days. We can go on my computer and do it right now. Name your price."

"I don't have a price."

"You won't fire that gun, Jeff. The sound will be heard by everyone on this floor."

Jeff reached into his jacket pocket and pulled out the silencer. Screwed it onto the barrel. "Oops, looks like I almost forgot one little detail, huh?"

All of a sudden, Brandon looked defeated. He grimaced, and said, "Can I lower my hands? My arms are getting tired. I'm not a young man anymore."

"Go ahead."

Brandon lowered his hands. "You don't have to do this, Jeff. You're not a killer. You're not like me. I deserve whatever you're going to dish out to me, but it should be someone else doing this, not you."

"It has to be me."

Brandon's face suddenly transformed in front of his eyes. Tears started rolling down his cheeks, and his mouth began opening and closing. Trying to find words that just wouldn't come.

Then they finally came, in a whisper. "I need to die. You're doing the right thing. I've caused nothing but misery to so many. This is the end, and if it didn't end this way, it would end some other way. I'm at the end of my rope."

Jeff felt something come over him. He didn't know how to

define it. Pity? Sadness? Watching someone at the end of his life trying desperately to capture some redemption?

"How do you want it, Brandon?"

"You're in control here, Jeff. Can we end my life my way? Can you agree to that? As the final request of a dead man?"

Jeff shrugged. "Sounds fair. As long as you're dead, I don't care. What did you have in mind?"

"I'll commit suicide. Like how I've caused so many other deaths. Only fitting that I go the same way. We're thirty floors up. I'll jump. As I said, I'm at the end of my rope, and it's time. I can live with that decision. And being the control freak that I am, if you could grant me that wish, it would be fitting—and appreciated."

Jeff thought about it for a couple of seconds, and then gestured towards the balcony with his Beretta.

"Go for it."

Brandon allowed a tiny smile to cross his face. "Thank you. You're a good man, Jeff, you always were. You deserved better than me."

Jeff gestured again. "Move. Let's get this over with, otherwise I'll just put a bullet in your fucking brain."

Brandon walked backwards towards his open balcony door and stepped outside. Jeff didn't follow. He didn't want to take the chance on being compromised out there. For all he knew, Brandon could have a gun hidden.

"If you make any funny moves at all, I'll shoot. And I'm a good shot. Your forehead is firmly in my sights."

Brandon shuffled over to the far right corner of the balcony, and stood on top of a chair that was positioned there. He then eased himself up onto the concrete ledge that was attached to the metal spindles of the railing.

Then he bowed his head and began reciting:

"Hail Mary, full of grace, Our Lord is with thee. Blessed art thou among women, and blessed is the fruit of thy womb, Jesus. Holy Mary, Mother of God, pray for us sinners, now and at the hour of our death."

Jeff had to fight off the feeling of regret, watching someone basically reciting his last confession. And a plea for forgiveness. Raised as a Catholic, he found it hard to be cynical. These were the last seconds of this man's life, and he was pleading for forgiveness.

Jeff didn't know how the heavens would respond, but he found it a surprisingly sad spectacle to watch. Part of him wanted to yell out, *"Fuck off! Jump, for God's sake!"* But the other part of him wanted to give Brandon whatever time he needed for redemption.

A paradox, for sure.

Brandon continued to recite the prayer as he eased himself down off the ledge and clung to the metal spindles of the railing.

He was now just hanging on by the power of his arms. Their eyes met. Brandon recited once again the last verse of the prayer: "Holy Mary, Mother of God, pray for us sinners, now and at the hour of our death."

Jeff couldn't resist reciting a prayer of his own—or more correctly, a prayer of Brandon's that he'd used over and over again: "Thou shalt go forth."

Brandon released his hands from the bars and he was gone.

Jeff lowered his head and muttered, "God, forgive me."

He waited a couple of minutes before mustering up enough courage to go out onto the balcony.

Tentatively, he leaned his head over the railing and looked down at the street below.

Nothing.

He'd expected to see the monster's body splayed out on the pavement thirty floors below, but—nothing.

All he saw was a rope looped around a spindle at the farthest edge of the railing, hanging down about four floors, swinging lazily back and forth.

Outsmarted once again, Jeff couldn't help but reflect on one of the last phrases the evil, but brilliant bastard, had uttered.

"I'm at the end of my rope."

About the Author

Peter Parkin makes his home in Alberta, Canada, on the outskirts of the city of Calgary and on the threshold of the beautiful Rocky Mountains. He's blessed with two sons and two grandsons.

Prior to writing novels Mr. Parkin was an executive, his career culminating with the role of Chief Operating Officer with a large national company. He retired from the business world in 2007, but still keeps his fingers in by serving as a director on corporate boards.

Mr. Parkin's novels tend to have common threads: abuse of power and how the average person finds the courage to rise up against all odds. The wonders and dangers of the natural world are also areas of interest to Parkin, as are the machinations of government.

The protagonists in Parkin's books tend to be people unafraid to challenge, who are not prepared to just accept the status quo.

Uprooted is Parkin's ninth novel. Previous works are Mule, Metro*Cafe*, Serpentine, Majestic, Headhunter, Skeleton, Letters from a Killer, and The Ascendant.